# THE
# DARLING DAHLIAS
## AND THE
# ELEVEN O'CLOCK
# LADY

# THE
# DARLING DAHLIAS
## AND THE
# ELEVEN O'CLOCK LADY

*Susan Wittig Albert*

BERKLEY PRIME CRIME, NEW YORK

# BERKLEY PRIME CRIME

**An imprint of Penguin Random House LLC**
**375 Hudson Street, New York, New York 10014**

This book is an original publication of the Berkley Publishing Group.

Library of Congress Cataloging-in-Publication Data

Albert, Susan Wittig.
The Darling Dahlias and the Eleven O'Clock Lady / Susan Wittig
Albert.—First edition.
pages ; cm
ISBN 978-0-425-26062-3
1.   Women gardeners—Fiction. 2.   Nineteen thirties—Fiction.
3.   Alabama—Fiction. I.   Title.
PS3551.L2637D38 2015
813'.54—dc23
2015012221

FIRST EDITION: September 2015

PRINTED IN THE UNITED STATES OF AMERICA

10   9   8   7   6   5   4   3   2   1

Cover illustration and logo © by Brandon Dorman.
Cover design by Judith Lagerman.
Interior text design by Tiffany Estreicher.

Penguin
Random
House

*For readers and friends whose*
*fathers and grandfathers served in*
*FDR's Tree Army and whose mothers and grandmothers*
*made the best of things in the worst of times.*

*The Darling Dahlias Clubhouse and Gardens*
*302 Camellia Street*
*Darling, Alabama*

*Dear Reader,*

*We've all been pretty much up in the air with all the recent happenings in town, most of them connected, one way or another, with Camp Briarwood, the new Civilian Conservation Corps camp out beyond Briar's Swamp. In fact, there's been so much going on lately—so many threats to the peace and welfare of our dear little Darling—that some of us Dahlias are beginning to worry. And after what happened to Rona Jean Hancock, we are even more concerned.*

*So when Mrs. Albert dropped in at the clubhouse the other afternoon to tell us that she had decided to write another book about our town, we weren't sure what to think. We've always imagined Darling as a beautiful place where mostly good things happen. After all, the people who live here are mostly very good, or at least above average. There are exceptions, of course. But when our Darling citizens do something bad, it's usually a mistake or an accident or (at worst) a case of bad judgment.*

*Lately, though, it seems that the outside world has been pushing awfully hard to get into our dear little town, like that proverbial camel who keeps pushing his nose under the tent, and the threat has begun to worry some. Of course, when the camel brings jobs and boosts business (like Camp Briarwood, our local CCC camp), folks don't complain too much. But there are those who would just as soon that the camel went back where he came from and left us alone, while others argue that if Darling is going to have any future, our town is going to have to wake up and join the modern world. It's a puzzle— or a conundrum, as Miss Rogers says. (She's a librarian and very fond of big words.)*

*Well, enough of that. When Mrs. Albert asked us to recommend a title for her book, it was our club president, Miss Elizabeth Lacy, who came up with the winning suggestion:* The Eleven O'clock Lady. *This is the name of Liz's favorite spring wildflower, so called because the starry white blossoms don't open until the sun shines directly on them and wakes them up. Miss Rogers wanted to insist that this little plant be called by its nine-syllable botanical name:* Ornithogalum umbellatum. *But Mrs. Albert pointed out that if the book were called* The Darling Dahlias and the Ornithogalum Umbellatum, *probably nobody would read it. When she put it that way, even Miss Rogers (who, as a librarian, always encourages everyone to read) had to agree. As to how* The Eleven O'clock Lady *fits what happened here in Darling—well, you'll just have to read it and see. We hope you will.*

*And we also hope you will remember our club motto, which Aunt Hetty Little has embroidered with a beautiful vase of sunflowers for our club wall:* We keep our faces to the sun so we can't see the shadows. *It's how we manage to stay (mostly) cheerful during these depressing times. We recommend the practice. Maybe it will work for you, too.*

*Sincerely yours,*
*The Darling Dahlias*

# The Darling Dahlias Club Roster, Summer 1934

CLUB OFFICERS

**Elizabeth Lacy**, club president. Secretary to Mr. Benton Moseley, attorney-at-law, and garden columnist for the Darling *Dispatch*.

**Ophelia Snow**, club vice president and secretary. Holds two jobs: at the Darling *Dispatch* and as liaison officer in the quartermaster's office at Camp Briarwood, the new CCC camp. Wife of Darling's mayor, Jed Snow.

**Verna Tidwell**, club treasurer. Cypress County treasurer and probate clerk. A widow, Verna lives with her beloved Scottie, Clyde.

**Myra May Mosswell**, club communications secretary. Co-owner of the Darling Telephone Exchange and the Darling Diner. Lives with Violet Sims and Violet's little girl, Cupcake, in the flat over the diner.

CLUB MEMBERS

**Earlynne Biddle**. A rose fancier. Married to Henry Biddle, the manager at the Coca-Cola bottling plant, and works part-time in the office there. Teaches reading at Camp Briarwood.

**Bessie Bloodworth**. Proprietor of Magnolia Manor, a boardinghouse for genteel elderly ladies next door to the Dahlias' clubhouse. Grows vegetables and herbs in the Manor's backyard and manages the vegetable garden at Camp Briarwood.

**Fannie Champaign Dickens**. Proprietor of Champaign's Darling Chapeaux and noted designer of women's hats. Newly (and happily) married to Charlie Dickens, the editor of the Darling *Dispatch*.

**Mrs. George E. Pickett (Voleen) Johnson**. Widow of the former bank president and notable town matron, specializes in pure white flowers. Part owner (with Miss Tallulah LaBelle) of the Darling Savings and Trust Bank.

**Mildred Kilgore**. Owner and manager of Kilgore Motors. She and her husband, Roger, have a big house near the ninth green of the Cypress Country Club, where Mildred grows camellias.

**Aunt Hetty Little**. Gladiola lover, town matriarch, and senior member of the club. A "regular Miss Marple" who knows all the Darling secrets.

**Lucy Murphy**. Grows vegetables and fruit on a small market farm on the Jericho Road and supervises the kitchen at Camp Briarwood. Married to Ralph Murphy, who works on the railroad.

**Raylene Riggs**. Myra May Mosswell's mother and the newest Dahlia. Cooks at the Darling Diner and lives at the Marigold Motor Court with Pauline DuBerry.

**Miss Dorothy Rogers**. Librarian for Darling and for Camp Briarwood. Knows the Latin name of every plant and insists that everyone else should, too. Resident of Magnolia Manor, where she plants her small flower-and-vegetable garden in very straight rows.

**Beulah Trivette**. Owns Beulah's Beauty Bower, where all the Dahlias go to get beautiful and catch up on the latest news. Artistically talented, Beulah loves cabbage roses and other exuberant flowers.

**Alice Ann Walker.** Grows irises and daylilies, which don't take a lot of time or attention—important for Alice Ann, who works full-time as a cashier at the Darling Savings and Trust Bank. Her disabled husband, Arnold, tends the family vegetable garden.

# THE
# DARLING DAHLIAS
## AND THE
# ELEVEN O'CLOCK
# LADY

# "I've Got the World on a String"

In less than an hour, Violet Sims' well-ordered life was going to change. But right now, she was enjoying what in her opinion was the very best hour of a summer's day—the earliest hour. That was the time when she went out to work in the vegetable garden behind the Darling Diner, which she owned and managed with her friend, Myra May Mosswell. And *this* hour, on *this* Saturday, seemed especially perfect. It had been hot and sultry all week, and the day ahead was likely to be another hot one, with the prospect of a storm in the afternoon. But the morning air was still cool and fresh, the dew was a silvery sheen on the ripe and flawless tomatoes, and the sun had just begun to peer over the rooftops of the little town of Darling to see if something of interest might be happening there on this very last day of June 1934.

And yes, things were already happening, interesting or not, depending on your point of view. Next door to the diner on the east, J.D. Henderson, who helped Mr. Musgrove in the hardware store, was burning trash in an old metal barrel behind the store. Across the alley and two doors to the north on Robert E. Lee, Mrs. Vader's rooster was letting Mr. Vader know that it was high time he jumped out of bed and started for his foreman's job at the Pine Mill Creek, where another big lumber order from the new CCC camp down by Briar's Swamp was waiting to be filled. In fact, Camp Briarwood had placed so many orders recently (construction materials for officers' quarters, a headquarters building, and a mess hall) that Mr. Vader had to get up extra early to supervise the three new men he'd just hired. But he didn't complain. Everybody was happy that the sawmill was hiring again.

On the other side of Robert E. Lee, Bill Board, the milkman, was whistling as he delivered two quarts of Board's Best milk and a pint of Board's Best cream to Mr. and Mrs. Hart and the three little Hart grandchildren, who lived next door to Hart's Peerless Laundry. Bill Board was whistling because the Harts had not only doubled their dairy order but paid their bill, to boot. The laundry business was flourishing, so much so that the Harts had had to hire two colored girls from Maysville to help with the extra washing. More jobs!

And from the diner's kitchen window came the not-so-melodic sound of Myra May Mosswell singing along with Bing Crosby's rendition of "I've Got the World on a String." The song made Violet smile as she bent over and began filling her lard bucket with fresh green beans for the noon lunch. Actually, she thought, she'd better fill two buckets while she was at it. Now that the CCC camp was shifting into high gear, business was picking up nicely. In fact, it had gotten so good that she and Myra May were finally able to pay themselves a halfway decent salary. Under her breath,

Violet hummed along with the radio. She had the world on a string and the morning was off to a glorious start.

Which was exactly how she felt for the next, oh, ten minutes or so. After that, the storm clouds began to gather (metaphorically speaking) and the day went downhill in a hurry.

In the sunshine-filled kitchen, Myra May glanced up at the clock over the sink. It was six thirty, and the diner would be open for business in a half hour. Violet's sourdough bread was baking in the oven, and it was time to get the breakfast items started. She opened the refrigerator and took out eggs and milk, in preparation for stirring up pancake batter. On the menu, the pancakes were paired with her mother Raylene's Southern fried apples and bacon or ham. Raylene's fried apples had become a big hit with the Darling Diner's breakfast customers.

Over in the corner, three-year-old Cupcake was dressing her Patsy doll and warbling gleefully with the radio. "Sittin' on a rainbow, gonna make the rain go!" she crowed, and danced the Patsy doll up and down in time to the music. Seeing the morning sun glint off her soft strawberry curls, Myra May thought that Cupcake was much cuter than little Shirley Temple, the child movie star. She was an even bigger hit with the customers than her grandmother's fried apples. In fact, she was such a popular little girl that she had been selected as Little Miss Darling for the town's Fourth of July celebration coming up next week.

On the other side of the kitchen partition, behind the diner's long counter, Cupcake's grandmother, Raylene Riggs, had just finished making a pot of coffee, and the aroma of fresh coffee filled the air. Myra May could hear Raylene singing along, too, in her odd little tuneless way: *Life's a wonderful thing as long as I've got that string.*

The song had it right, Myra May thought as she began breaking eggs into the heavy yellow pottery bowl. Life was a wonderful thing these days—well, it was going in that direction, anyway. She was her own boss, serving good, wholesome food to customers and friends in her very own place of business. Around her were gathered the three people she loved most in the world: her dear friend Violet, their little Cupcake, and her mother, from whom she had been separated for most of her life. Best of all, the gray skies of the Depression were finally beginning to lighten, at least here in Darling, where people seemed to have more money than they'd had in the past three or four years.

And the credit for this improved state of affairs, in Myra May's opinion, was almost entirely due to the Civilian Conservation Corps camp, a half-dozen miles south of town. Some of the local people were working at the camp in various capacities, so they had a little extra money to spend. The camp quartermaster bought supplies, equipment, and services from local merchants, like the Pine Creek Sawmill and Mann's Mercantile and Hart's Peerless Laundry. The camp advertised its needs in the *Dispatch* and bought milk, butter, eggs, and produce for the camp kitchen from the local farmers. And when the CCC boys came to town on weekends, they spent their money at the Palace Theater, the dime store, the new roller rink, the pool hall, and (of course!) the diner. A couple of months ago, Myra May had started staying open late on Friday and Saturday nights just so the boys could stop in for a hamburger or a milk shake after the last picture show.

All of these new customers added up to a *lot* more money flowing into Darling. Why, according to Mayor Jed Snow, the camp had pumped some forty-five hundred dollars into

Darling's economy in just the last month alone! Which in turn meant that Darlingians who had been flat broke and despairing could now afford to pay thirty-five cents for a meal at the diner or a dollar fifty for a new pair of shoes at the Mercantile or a quarter for a kite or an O-Boy Yo-Yo for the kids at the Five and Dime.

*Sitting on a rainbow.* Myra May was smiling as she beat the eggs and milk together. Yes, it was actually beginning to seem that they had put the worst of the dark clouds and hard times behind them. Life was good and getting better and better every day.

At least, that's how Myra May felt at that instant. She would be feeling very differently a few moments from now.

On the other side of the partition, behind the lunch counter, Raylene finished with the coffee percolator and began wrapping the silverware in paper napkins, so they would be ready to set the tables as the customers came in. She was making extra wraps this morning, because she had the feeling that today was going to be a busy day—and something of a strange day, she thought, wrinkling her nose and frowning just a little.

Raylene had learned long ago to trust her feelings, for she was psychic. "Not very much, actually," she told people when they noticed. She liked to downplay her ability so folks wouldn't pester her to read their palms or tell their fortunes. "And mostly just about little things."

Like what things people wanted to eat. At today's lunch, for instance, Raylene already knew that Sheriff Buddy Norris was going to change his mind and order liver and onions instead of the usual meat loaf, while Mayor Jed Snow would go with the meat loaf instead of fried chicken, and the county commissioner,

Amos Tombull, would top off his stewed chicken and dumplings with peach pie and ice cream. It was a good thing to be psychic about, as she told her daughter, Myra May. It meant having a pretty good idea of how much of everything to cook.

But occasionally there was something else. Like right now, she had a disquieting feeling that she couldn't quite shake when she thought of the day ahead. She frowned again, catching a fleeting glimpse, in her mind's eye, of men traipsing through the diner's backyard and strangers coming into the place and asking questions about—

"Miz Raylene," came an uncertain voice. "Miz Raylene, you busy?"

Raylene looked up. It was Lenore Looper, a slight, brown-haired young woman who worked the eleven-to-seven shift on the switchboard three times a week. The Darling Telephone Exchange was located in the back room of the diner. When the Exchange first opened, with only a couple of dozen customers, it had operated from seven in the morning until seven at night. Now, practically everybody in town had a phone and the Exchange had to be staffed around the clock. The girl who worked the night shift was allowed to nap on the narrow cot along one wall, as long as she kept an ear cocked for emergency calls. It looked to Raylene as if Lenore had been doing just that, for the bobby pins were falling out of her hair, her print dress was twisted, and she was rubbing the sleep out of her eyes.

Raylene reached up and turned down the volume of the Philco radio that sat on a shelf behind the counter. "What is it, Lenore?"

Lenore pulled at the bodice of her dress to straighten it. "It's Bettina Higgens, who works over at the Beauty Bower. She just called the switchboard, askin' about Rona Jean."

"Rona Jean?" Raylene asked, frowning. The room seemed

suddenly darker, as though a couple of the light bulbs over the counter had just burned out. "She worked the three-to-eleven shift yesterday, didn't she?"

"Yes, ma'am. But it seems she didn't come home last night." Lenore yawned, covering it with a dainty hand. "Bettina is Roma Jean's roommate. She's asking if anybody here knows where Rona Jean might've went. If they do, she says would they please call her."

Feeling a flutter of apprehension, Raylene went to the pass-through and leaned across the shelf into the kitchen. "Myra May, Bettina Higgens is calling about Rona Jean, her roommate. Seems she didn't get home last night."

"She didn't?" Frowning, Myra May dropped the big whisk into the crockery bowl. "Where did she go?"

"That's what Bettina wants to know. Any ideas?"

"Afraid not." Myra May wiped her hands on the cotton apron she wore over her slacks and plaid blouse. "I checked her out at eleven last night, when she finished her shift. I didn't ask where she was headed—I just figured she was going home." She quirked an eyebrow. "But you know Rona Jean."

As a matter of fact, Raylene did know Rona Jean, who—while she was an excellent switchboard operator when she paid attention—was a little on the wild side. She'd be late to work or ask to get off early. Or she'd be talking to one of her friends when she was supposed to be on duty and let the calls get ahead of her on the switchboard. Worst yet, she had listened in at least once on a private telephone call, which was against the Exchange's hard-and-fast rule. Myra May had cautioned her that if she was caught listening one more time, she'd be looking for another job.

By now feeling distinctly uneasy, Raylene turned back to Lenore. "Myra May says that Rona Jean finished up here at eleven last night, and that's the last we've seen of her. If Bettina is worried, she should let Sheriff Norris know, so he can keep an eye out for—"

At that moment, the back door banged open and Raylene turned to see Violet, ashen faced and trembling, in the doorway. "Come quick!" she cried breathlessly, clinging to the doorjamb for support. "It's awful! Oh, please, please, come!"

"Awful?" Myra May was peering through the pass-through. "Come where? What's going on, Violet?"

"It's . . . it's Rona Jean," Violet gasped. "In the garage. She's . . . she's . . ."

But whatever Violet was going to say was lost in a long sigh. She slumped to the floor in a dead faint.

Myra May left Raylene to tend to Violet and dashed out to the ramshackle garage where she parked Big Bertha, her large green 1920 Chevrolet touring car. With 29,012 miles on her odometer, Bertha was cruising on her third carburetor and sixth set of tires, and she occasionally suffered from the hiccups. But the red-painted spokes in her wheels were bright, her green canvas top was sound, and her chrome-plated headlights twinkled. When Myra May climbed behind the wheel and revved Bertha up to her top speed of thirty-five miles an hour, she always imagined that the car was smiling.

But Bertha wasn't smiling now, and it wasn't Myra May behind her wheel. It was Rona Jean Hancock. She was sprawled across the front seat, the top buttons of her red dress undone, her legs splayed in an unladylike way, her head bent back at an awkward angle. On her left leg, she was wearing a silk stocking, held up by an elastic roll garter just above her knee. The right leg was bare, and her other silk stocking was wound tightly around her neck.

# TWO

# Sheriff Norris Investigates

"Thanks for being willing to talk to me, Violet," Buddy Norris said, as he sat down on a straight chair next to the sofa where Violet lay.

Buddy was a lean, gangly man with brown hair and blue eyes, a look-alike (many said) for Lucky Lindy, who had flown his *Spirit of St. Louis* all the way to Paris, only to lose his first-born son to a kidnapper and murderer just two years ago. The mildness of Buddy's expression—he rarely frowned—was somewhat contradicted by the pale thread of a scar across his cheek, a souvenir of a knife fight at the Red Dog juke joint over in Maysville. He was wearing the khaki shirt and pants that passed for the Cypress County sheriff's uniform, with the nickel-plated star pinned to his pocket flap.

He flipped to a clean page in his notebook, checking his wristwatch for the current time, seven thirty a.m., and jotting it down with the date. "So you saw that the garage doors were open and went to see why," he said. "Is that how it happened, Violet?"

He was feeling a little awkward. A couple of years ago, Buddy had been sweet on Violet Sims, who once was one of the two young ladies he most wanted to get to know. (The other one was the girl who was out there in the front seat of Myra May's car with her stocking wrapped around her neck, waiting for Lionel Noonan to drive up in his funeral parlor hearse and take her to Monroeville for an autopsy.) But Buddy had given up on Violet when she made it clear that she wasn't interested in going out with him, although she said it in such a sweet way that he couldn't feel hurt by the rejection. She simply preferred to spend her free evenings with Myra May and Cupcake in their flat over the diner.

So he had turned his attentions to Rona Jean, who maybe wasn't as pretty as Violet but had seemed sweet and eager to please him (at least in the beginning), which was always a compliment to a fellow. He and Rona Jean had gotten along just fine, for a while. He felt a fist of hot anger tighten in his belly when he thought of what somebody had done to her, and then a quick, warm wash of sadness that was accentuated by the strains of "Goodnight, Sweetheart"—Rona Jean's favorite song—from the radio downstairs. But this wasn't the time or the place to dwell on that. He had to put his mind to his investigation and let nothing interfere. He poised his stub of a pencil over the page and waited.

Violet's "Yes, that's how it happened" was almost inaudible. Pale and wan, her soft brown hair in a mass of curls around her face, she was lying on the sofa in the apartment over the diner, where she lived with Myra May. Raylene Riggs had spread a crocheted granny afghan over her and was kneeling beside the sofa, holding her limp hand.

"Maybe just one or two questions, Buddy?" Raylene asked

in a low voice. She'd said that Violet had fainted again after she and Myra May had gotten her upstairs. "This is so difficult for her. She and Rona Jean both worked in the Telephone Exchange, and they sometimes went to the movies together. They were close friends."

Buddy hadn't known that, actually. He scribbled the words *close friends with Violet—movies* in his notebook, then wondered briefly how Myra May felt about that and wrote *Myra May??* with a heavy underline. When he'd been trying to get Violet to go out with him, before he'd understood about her situation, he had felt that Myra May was acting kind of jealous. Or maybe "protective" was a better word, like a mama hen ruffling her feathers and snapping her beak, hovering over her chick and not wanting anybody to get too close. He wasn't quite sure why it was, but after Violet had made it clear that he was wasting his time, Myra May had eased up. Then he wondered who else (besides Violet, that is) Rona Jean might have counted as her close friend, and added *other friends?* He guessed that was something he had better find out. He bit his lip and focused on his next question.

This was Buddy Norris' first investigation as the sheriff of Cypress County, and the fact that he was investigating a murder—and Rona Jean Hancock's murder, on top of that—made it a lot more important than the usual humdrum routine of minor thefts, car wrecks, gambling, and moonshining that the sheriff's office dealt with every week. Rona Jean's murder had struck Buddy like a bolt from the blue, and investigating it was not at all what he wanted to be doing on a bright and pretty June morning.

But the sadly ironic truth was that whoever had strangled Rona Jean had handed Buddy his first big case, the opportunity he needed to show the citizens of Darling that they had been right to elect him as their sheriff. It was a test of what he had learned so far, a measure of his abilities as an investigator. He couldn't afford to fail.

Until several weeks ago, Buddy had been Darling's deputy sheriff, and not an altogether popular one, at that. Some folks criticized him for his youth (he was in his late twenties but looked younger) and others for his "swagger and derring-do," especially when he arrested Reverend Craig, the traveling revival preacher, who was driving his 1926 Studebaker sixty miles an hour out on the Jericho Road. On the front seat was a bottle of what the reverend claimed was communion fruit of the vine. When Buddy tasted it, however, the bottle proved to contain something a sight more potent than grape juice. It was Bodeen Pyle's Panther Juice, and as illegal as sin. Nevertheless, some folks said that Buddy didn't show good judgment when he arrested a man of God. If he was going to be sheriff, he had a lot to prove.

But Buddy was good enough to be a deputy, almost everybody agreed. He had taught himself how to take crime scene photographs and dust for fingerprints out of a book on scientific detective work that he had mail-ordered from *True Crime* magazine. He was especially interested in fingerprint evidence, which had been used as forensic evidence in the United States since 1911, when Thomas Jennings was convicted of murder after he broke into a Chicago home and killed the owner during an attempted burglary. Jennings left his prints on a freshly painted railing, was convicted, and hanged. Buddy didn't have much confidence that fingerprints would ever solve a case in Darling, but he wanted to know how to use them if the opportunity ever presented itself.

All things considered, Buddy had proved himself to be a good deputy. He wasn't afraid to wade in with his fists when that was necessary, as it sometimes was. He was strong and athletic and (having been a sprinter in high school and a regular winner of the hundred-yard dash) he got around much faster than the sheriff, who had forty years and fifty-plus pounds on him. What's more, he rode his red Indian Ace motorcycle when he was on patrol duty, which guaranteed Sheriff Burns some serious bragging rights: Buddy was the only mounted deputy sheriff in all of southern Alabama.

In fact, everybody said that the sheriff and his deputy functioned as a pretty good team—until the sheriff was struck down dead by a rattlesnake. He was fishing all by himself below the waterfall at the very bottom of Horsetail Gorge when it happened, which was a very bad place to have a rattlesnake tuck into you. Roy Burns weighed well over two hundred pounds, and with his arthritis, he couldn't move too fast on a good day. On a bad day, when the rattler had bitten him hard on the wrist, he didn't make it back up to the camp. He sat down and died beside the waterfall. It took three men, a mule, and a block and tackle to hoist him out of the rocky gorge.

The county commissioners met the next week, as Amos Tombull announced somberly, "to plan for a special election to fill Sheriff Burns' empty size twelves." There were two candidates on the ballot, Buddy Norris and Jake Pritchard, who owned the Standard Oil station on the Monroeville highway. But although many had misgivings about Buddy, the endorsement of the Darling *Dispatch* helped him eke out a win. He was also helped by the fact that Jake had recently raised the price of his gasoline from ten cents a gallon to fifteen, which made some of the voters a tad bit unenthusiastic about him. Jake had the only gas station in town. Some folks may have thought that making him sheriff was giving him too much of a monopoly.

With all this in mind, Buddy knew better than anybody that, in Darling's eyes, the investigation into Rona Jean's murder would be a test case. His reputation, his career, and quite possibly his entire future were on the line here. Which meant that he had to take full charge of the investigation and do most of the legwork himself, rather than rely on his new deputy, Wayne Springer. Wayne, who had learned his policing over in Montgomery, already knew how to dust for fingerprints. He was working on the car right now, and doing a good job. That's the kind of deputy he was. But everything else connected with this murder, all the interviews, all the people stuff, Buddy knew he would have to do himself.

He straightened his shoulders, suddenly aware of the burden on them. "Just a couple more questions and I'll be finished." He leaned forward. "When you went into the garage, Violet, did you hear anything or see anybody? Or maybe when you were out in the garden, picking beans?"

"No," Violet whispered. "I didn't hear a thing when I was in the garden—except for the rooster up the street and Bill Board delivering the milk and Myra May singing along with the radio. And then I saw the double garage doors open and thought I'd better close them. When I went in, at first, I couldn't believe what I was seeing. It was just too awful. The way Rona Jean was . . . all spread out, I mean. Like she'd been—" Her voice trembled and she bit down hard on her lip. "And then I saw that stocking around her neck. I just ran." After a moment she looked up at Raylene. "I'm so sorry, dear. I spilled the bucket of beans I was picking for lunch."

"Don't worry about it, Violet," Raylene said in a comforting tone. "Eva Pearl came in early to give us a hand at the counter. After the breakfast rush, I'll send her out to pick up the beans. Or I could just open a couple of jars of that sweet corn the Dahlias canned for us last summer and make corn pudding instead. Most folks like that just as well as green beans."

Buddy felt that the interview was getting away from him.

"One more question," he said. "Were you here when Rona Jean . . . when Miss Hancock finished her shift and left last night?"

He felt Raylene's curious eyes on him and shifted uncomfortably. Both she and Violet and just about everybody else in town would recall that he and Rona Jean had gone around together fairly recently. He hadn't called her "Miss Hancock" then. In fact, on their second date she had called him "sweetheart," in that slow, sweet, suggestive Southern voice of hers. They were trading moonlight kisses on the back porch of the house she shared with Bettina Higgens, and the Victrola was playing in the parlor. *Goodnight sweetheart, 'til we meet tomorrow. Goodnight sweetheart, parting is such sorrow.* And then the third time they were together, when—

But that was when Rona Jean had proved to be too . . . "dangerous" was the word that came to mind. Not the kind of woman Buddy wanted, or could afford, at this point in his life. Still, Rona Jean was dead now, and it was his job to find out who had killed her. It didn't seem quite respectful to use her personal name when he was asking questions about the last hours of her life.

"I was, yes," Violet said slowly. "But I didn't see her when she left. I was upstairs here, reading. Cupcake was asleep in her crib. Myra May had gone down to check on the shift change and do a last-minute check on the kitchen, the way she usually does. Rona Jean went off at eleven, and Lenore—that's Lenore Looper, she's Alva Looper's middle daughter—was scheduled to come on. Myra May always likes to see that the next girl is ready to take her shift on the switchboard before the other girl leaves. Otherwise, there could be a gap, which wouldn't be good."

Buddy looked down at the words *close friends with Violet.* "Myra May came right back upstairs after the shift change?"

Raylene slid Buddy a puzzled glance, as if she was wondering what that had to do with anything. He was glad she didn't put the question into words, for he couldn't have answered if she had. He was remembering once when Myra May saw him talking to Violet and had gotten kind of bent out of shape about it, to the point where she put his cup down hard on the counter and splashed hot coffee on his hand.

There was a moment's silence. Violet looked away, her lower lip caught between her teeth, and Buddy could tell she was thinking about his question. She frowned a little.

"Right back upstairs? Well, I guess maybe not. There's always stuff to do in the kitchen. Sometimes one or the other of us is down there until midnight." She looked up and managed a small smile. "Breakfast for twenty-five or thirty doesn't get cooked by wishing it would, you know, Buddy. There's plenty of night-before work that goes into it."

"I reckon," Buddy said, and wrote *midnite* in his notebook, after *Myra May.* "Well, I guess that does it for me, for now anyway. I'll maybe think of something else later." He pocketed the notebook and pencil. "You get some rest, now, Violet. Y'hear?"

"Thank you," Violet said, but she didn't immediately take his advice. She raised herself up on one elbow and put out her hand, catching at his sleeve. In a low, fierce voice, she said, "You go out there and get whoever did this, you hear, Buddy? Rona Jean might've been a little wild, but she was a good girl at heart. I was hoping—" She fell back, closing her eyes. "She . . . she didn't deserve to die like that. Nobody does."

Buddy stood looking down at Violet, wondering what Violet had been hoping. But Raylene took his arm and walked him to the door. "If there's any way Myra May and I can help," she said in a low voice, "please let us know."

Buddy nodded. "Thanks. Deputy Springer will come in

later this morning and take everybody's fingerprints. And maybe—"

"Fingerprints?" Raylene asked blankly. "What do you want *our* fingerprints for? We didn't—" She stopped, frowning.

"I understand," Buddy said. "But we've already found prints in the car, and Wayne—Deputy Springer, that is— will likely find more. We need to get the prints of everybody who has ridden in that car in the last few months so we can eliminate them. Any prints that are left might belong to the killer." That was how it was *supposed* to work. Buddy had yet to see it work that way in practice. There were always unmatched, unidentified prints left over, which pretty much rendered the process useless, practically speaking.

"Oh," Raylene said. "I see."

"It would also help if you and Myra May and Violet could come up with a list of the people Rona Jean knew—who maybe had some kind of connection with her. People she worked with, especially." Usually, he'd ask about family, but in this case, he already knew the answer. Rona Jean had been an orphan. She had told him once that she had nobody on this earth. "I'll ask Bettina Higgens for a list, too," he added.

"Poor Bettina," Raylene said with a sigh. "This is going to be so difficult for her. She and Rona Jean were as thick as thieves." When Buddy frowned, Raylene took a breath and added, "I didn't intend anything special by that remark, Buddy. It was just a way of speaking. If you come in for lunch, we'll have the information for you then."

"Yes, ma'am," Buddy said. But before he went back to the garage, he took a moment to jot down Bettina's name and the phrase *thick as theives*. (Buddy had not been at the top of his class in spelling, and the i-before-e rule always confused him.) He was well aware that Raylene hadn't consciously intended anything special. But everybody knew that she had the "gift," as Aunt Hetty Little put it. She saw things other people didn't see. Buddy couldn't help wondering whether she might know something she didn't know she knew.

Back at the garage, Lionel Noonan had pulled his black 1930 Packard into the alley, and he and Wayne were waiting for Buddy to tell them it was okay to put Rona Jean into the hearse for her last ride.

Buddy took one more look. Her bright red lipstick was a streak of garish neon in a face that was pale as death, and her scarlet nail polish made her fingers look as if they had been dipped in blood. "All right, boys," he said with a sigh. "Load 'er up."

# THREE

# The Dahlias Bloom in Beulah's Beauty Bower

"I just can't believe something like this would happen in Darling." Earlynne Biddle lowered herself into Beulah's haircutting chair and smoothed the pink shampoo cape tied around her neck. "Rona Jean was a hardworking girl and polite to her elders—well, mostly, anyway. She didn't have a mother to keep her on the straight and narrow, but she wasn't any wilder than other girls her age, far as I could see. I cannot *imagine* who would want to up and strangle the poor thing."

"I always feel so sorry for girls who don't have a mother," Beulah Trivette said sadly, combing through Earlynne's wet brown hair. "Seems like they get off on the wrong foot in life."

Beulah thought of her own daughter when she said that—dear little Spoonie, who always said she wanted to grow up and be a beautician, "just like Mommy." Spoonie's ambition delighted Beulah, for she believed there was no higher calling than making women beautiful. She considered herself an artist and had an abiding pride in what she'd accomplished, especially considering that she'd had to cross over from the wrong side of the Louisville and Nashville Railroad tracks to do it, and then take the Greyhound bus to Montgomery and get a job as a waitress to put herself through the College of Cosmetology, where she learned every single thing she needed to know "to make the ordinary woman pretty and the pretty woman beautiful."

Now, she owned her very own Beauty Bower, which occupied what had once been a screened porch across the back of the house that she and Hank bought on Dauphin Street. Hank had enclosed it, put in electricity and a new hot water heater, and installed twin shampoo sinks and haircutting chairs and mirrors. Beulah added the finishing touches, painting the wainscoting her favorite peppermint pink, wallpapering the walls with fat pink roses, and spatter-painting the pink floor with blue, gray, and yellow.

A couple of months after she opened, business was so good that Beulah advertised for a beauty associate, and Bettina Higgens had applied. Bettina wasn't the prettiest blossom in the garden. Her brown hair was stringy, she was thin as a rail, and she had never been to beauty school. But Beulah saw the hidden talent in Bettina's nimble fingers and the desire in her heart, and knew that she had what it took to make women beautiful. What's more, she was reliable, very reliable. Within a couple of weeks, the two were working elbow-to-elbow at the shampoo sinks, eight to five, six days a week.

Except this morning. The reliable Bettina wasn't there.

"*Strangled*? Rona Jean Hancock?" Leona Ruth Adcock had just come into the Beauty Bower and was hearing the news for the first time. Her eyes were large in her narrow face. She looked around for a moment, then demanded shrilly, "Well, don't everybody talk at once."

"Yes, strangled," Bessie Bloodworth confirmed, looking up from the *Ladies' Home Journal* she was reading. "With her own stocking. Silk chiffon, I heard. Havana heel."

"Havana heel," Leona Ruth muttered under her breath.

Beulah glanced up at the clock and saw that it was just after nine. "I'm running a little behind this morning," she told Leona Ruth. "I'll do you as soon as I finish Earlynne and Bessie, Leona. I hope you don't mind waiting." She reached over and turned up the radio, which was broadcasting a weather report—something about a storm out in the Gulf. But whatever it was, she'd missed it. What came up next was her favorite Irving Berlin ballad, "Say It Isn't So."

Saturday mornings were always busy at the Beauty Bower, with ladies getting beautiful for Sunday church. But the Bower was one of the best places in town to find out what was going on (right up there with the diner and the party line, depending on which branch of it you were on), so Beulah figured that this Saturday was going to be even busier than usual. And since Bettina wasn't there to help out, she would be doing all the shampoos and sets herself. It was going to be a long day, and another hot one, in a weeklong string of hot, steamy days. Beulah was glad for the big fan in the ceiling and the other two fans strategically placed on the counter and the floor.

"Take your time, Beulah. I'm not in a tearing hurry." Leona Ruth took off her purple straw hat and white summer gloves and went back to the subject. "Who found her? Where?"

"Violet Sims," Aunt Hetty said from under the hair dryer. "In the backseat of Myra May's old Chevy." She frowned. "Although what that girl was doing in Myra May's garage after eleven o'clock at night is a mystery."

"It was the front seat," Beulah corrected, "and she'd just come off her shift at the Exchange." She knew it didn't matter, though. Leona Ruth never met a fact she couldn't ignore. She would rummage up the family secrets of every sausage she ate and pass them along to everybody at her table, and if a fact or two didn't fit her story, she changed them or just left them out. Beulah picked up her scissors. "Earlynne, how short do you want to go today?"

"About here, please." Earlynne held a finger up to her ear. "I'm working at the plant this summer, and it's like a blast furnace out there." Earlynne's husband, Henry Biddle, was the manager at the Coca-Cola plant, and she worked in the office. She glanced at Beulah in the mirror. "Poor Bettina must just be beside herself, Rona Jean being her roommate and all."

"That's the good Lord's truth." Beulah began to snip. "Bettina said she was up all night, worrying. Rona Jean gets off the switchboard at eleven, and it's no more than six blocks' walk. But she never got home."

Bettina had telephoned just as Beulah was sitting down to breakfast, to say she couldn't make it in to work that morning. Myra May had just called Bettina to tell her the tragic news about Rona Jean. She was sobbing when she relayed the story.

Beulah had been shocked almost speechless. "Oh, Bettina, honey," she gasped. "What a horrible thing to happen! I am *so* sorry!"

She was, too, very sorry—but at the same time, maybe just the teensiest bit not surprised. Of course, it went without saying that murder, right here in Darling, was utterly unthinkable. But Beulah had felt from the very beginning that Bettina was making a serious mistake to ask Rona Jean to move in with her, even if it did cut the rent in half. The two girls were both in their early twenties, but they were badly mismatched, personality-wise. Bettina was shy and didn't make friends easily (at least with people her own age—she was fine with the ladies at the Bower), while Rona Jean was just the opposite. She wasn't any prettier than Bettina—her face was plain as a tin pie plate and her brown hair wouldn't any more hold a curl than a horse's tail. But she had . . . well, what Beulah would call a buxom figure, which made her popular with a certain kind of boy. As a result, Rona Jean always had more dates than she could shake a stick at, while poor Bettina didn't go out with a boy more than once in a blue moon. Beulah had felt that there was bound to be some friction and unhappiness over this disparity, sooner or later. Now wasn't the time to say so, though. Now was the time to stand by Bettina, in her hour of greatest need.

"I want you to go right back to bed, Bettina," Beulah instructed. "You've had a terrible shock. We'll miss you, but the Bower will survive without you for a day or two—or however long you have to be gone."

Of course, it was a terrible time for Bettina to be away from her comb and scissors. With the new CCC camp going great guns outside of Darling, people had more money to spend, there were more doings to attend, and the beauty business had picked up. For instance, there was a dance every Saturday night at the camp, so the younger girls were coming in this afternoon to get their hair done. And coming up on Wednesday was the Fourth of July, always an exciting event in Darling, with a parade around the square and speeches on the courthouse steps and fireworks at the fairgrounds. Beulah knew that Monday and Tuesday would be a madhouse, with all the ladies wanting to look their best for the Fourth.

"Oh, I won't be out *that* long," Bettina said quickly. "Just a couple of hours, I hope. The only reason I can't be there this morning is that Buddy Norris is coming over to ask me some questions."

"Buddy Norris?" Beulah asked blankly. Then she remembered that Buddy had recently been elected sheriff. It was a little hard to think of him with that much responsibility, though. He'd always been kind of a big kid, zooming around on that red motorcycle and not very serious. "Questions about what?"

There was a moment's silence. "I don't know." Bettina's voice was apprehensive. "I guess about Rona Jean. About— you know. Who it was might have wanted to . . . kill her."

Beulah laughed lightly. "I don't know what makes Buddy Norris think you know anything about *that*." She paused, then couldn't help asking, "You don't, do you?" What a silly question. Of course Bettina didn't know anything. What could she possibly know?

There was another silence. Bettina took a breath. "Anyway, I'll be in as soon as the sheriff is finished with his questions. I hope it won't be too long."

Now, Earlynne met Beulah's eyes in the mirror. "Murder is a terrible thing," she said in a significant tone. "I sincerely hope Bettina isn't involved."

"I can't think of a reason why she should be," Beulah replied evenly, plying her scissors and comb.

"The two of them were living together, weren't they?" Leona Ruth put in. To Beulah's annoyance, she got up, walked across the room, and plunked herself down in Bettina's empty haircutting chair, where she turned one of the fans directly on herself.

"Yes, but that doesn't mean Bettina is in on any of Rona Jean's secrets." Quietly, Beulah reached for the fan and moved it to its original position. She didn't like to disagree with her customers—clients, she preferred to call them. She believed that true beauty came from within. It was produced by a harmony of spirit, and disagreements were definitely inharmonious. But Leona Ruth was disagreeable and mean-spirited. She could start an argument all by herself in an empty room, and

Beulah had long since given up on making her truly beautiful. The most she could do was keep Leona Ruth's hair curled, and even that was a challenge.

"Well, I hope not." Leona Ruth pursed her lips and looked down her long, thin nose. "If you're interested, I can tell you that Rona Jean herself was keeping a secret or two." With a knowing look, she hummed a bar or two of "Say It Isn't So."

"A secret or two?" Bessie lowered her magazine and regarded Leona Ruth with a frown. "What makes you say that?"

"Oh, no special reason," Leona Ruth replied with an elaborate carelessness. Shoving with the toe of her leather lace-up pump, she rotated Bettina's chair so she could look at Bessie. "Everybody has secrets, Bessie. Lots of them."

Aunt Hetty pushed up the hair dryer, scowling. "Other folks' secrets have nothing to do with Rona Jean Hancock getting murdered, Leona Ruth. If you are going to tell us something, say it straight out. Don't imply. It isn't polite." Aunt Hetty, who was past eighty and Darling's acknowledged *grande dame*, was probably the only person in town who dared to talk snippy to Leona Ruth, who wouldn't dare make a retaliatory move against Aunt Hetty.

Leona Ruth folded her arms across her thin chest. "You ladies may not be aware of this," she replied defensively, "but Bettina and Rona Jean live in that little yellow house behind me, on the next street over from Rosemont. My bedroom window looks right across the alley into their kitchen." She dropped her voice. "And their bedrooms."

Beulah stopped snipping. Earlynne took a breath. Aunt Hetty's eyes narrowed.

"So?" Bessie asked. "What are you saying?"

"I am saying that I am an eyewitness," Leona Ruth said. "I can see—"

"Ladies," Beulah intervened hurriedly, "I really don't

think this is any of our business." She knew that—morning, noon, and night, every day including weekends—gossip was Darling's number one favorite entertainment. It even topped Will Rogers' Sunday night radio show. But she didn't believe they ought to be gossiping about Bettina (who wasn't there to stand up for herself) and Rona Jean (who was dead and gone). And she hated to encourage Leona Ruth, who would go straight home and get on the party line, where she'd start spreading her story to all her friends and fellow gossips. She turned up the radio a little louder, hoping to discourage the conversation.

It didn't work. Leona Ruth just raised her voice. "So I can see who's been helping Rona Jean with the dishes, and what they were doing when they finished," she said triumphantly. As an afterthought, she added loudly, "She did pull down the shade in her bedroom, but that all by itself ought to tell you something."

Nobody seemed to know what to say. Finally, Earlynne remarked, in a carefully casual tone, "Well, aren't you going to tell us *who?*"

"Really, ladies," Beulah said. "We shouldn't—"

"I think maybe I should just leave it to your imagination," Leona Ruth said, smiling demurely.

"*I* think you ought to tell the sheriff what you just told us." With a disgusted look, Aunt Hetty retreated under her hair dryer.

Leona Ruth cast her eyes upward. "I have the idea," she said in an offhand tone, "that the sheriff already knows. His part of it, anyway."

Bessie stared at her, aghast. "You're not saying that it was the *sheriff* who . . ."

Leona Ruth looked straight at Bessie. "And not just the sheriff, either." She smiled. "Actually, Rona Jean had *several* male friends, more than you might expect for a girl who wasn't what you might call just real pretty."

"Actually," Earlynne said, "you might want to be just a little bit careful what you say when it comes to naming names."

"Careful?" Leona Ruth asked archly. "Whyever in the world should I be careful, Earlynne?"

Bessie gave Leona a malicious look. "Because we're not talking tiddlywinks here, Leona Ruth. We are talking *murder*. There's been one already. If you don't watch your mouth, you just might be next."

For once, Leona Ruth couldn't think of a thing to say.

# FOUR

# Sheriff Norris Learns a Few Facts

It was nine twenty and the morning air was already heating up when Buddy Norris got out of his Ford in front of the small frame house where Bettina Higgens lived. When he was a deputy, he had ridden his Indian Ace motorcycle on the job. Now that he was sheriff, though, he was driving the department's Model T, which had the advantage of being able to transport prisoners, if he had one—which he didn't, at least, not very often. Just in case, he had installed a strip of hog wire across the back of the front seat, which should take care of anybody who wanted to join him up front. While he was at it, he had added a special boot to hold his shotgun and a box for his handcuffs and extra ammunition. Now he had a patrol car. He couldn't help feeling proud of it, just a little.

Not that he would need handcuffs and the like this morning, since he didn't expect Bettina Higgens to give him any trouble. Buddy knew her the same way he knew most everybody in Darling, which was to say hello to on the street. Well, actually, he was a little better acquainted with her than that, since she had answered the door, twice, when he'd come to pick up Rona Jean. And she had come out on the back porch when they were sitting on the swing, and Rona Jean was getting a little . . . well, passionate.

As he went up the walk, he thought about that, with some discomfort. Rona Jean had been ruthlessly, heartlessly murdered, and he was responsible for finding her killer and seeing that he got exactly what he deserved: a one-way ticket to Kilby Prison in Montgomery and the seat of honor in Yellow Mama, Alabama's electric chair. Buddy had never wanted to see an execution, but by damn, when this one happened, he intended to have a front-row seat.

But Buddy was uncomfortably aware that some people in Darling—Rona Jean's roommate might be one of them— were likely to say that he ought to excuse himself from the case because of his relationship to the victim. They might think it was more . . . well, *intimate* than it was. They might even want him to call in the state police to handle the investigation, which he was definitely not going to do. And it wasn't just because he had kissed Rona Jean a time or two maybe, or maybe even three or four. This was his first important investigation as sheriff—his first real, live *murder* investigation— and there was no way in hell he was handing it off to anybody else.

So after he had seen Rona Jean's body bundled into Lionel Noonan's hearse and headed for the Monroeville Hospital where Doc Roberts would do the autopsy, Buddy had left Wayne to finish up the fingerprinting and phoned Mr. Moseley to ask if he could drop in for a few minutes to talk.

Benton Moseley had represented the district in the legislature up in Montgomery and was a mover and shaker in the

Alabama Democratic Party, and he sometimes drove over to Georgia, to Warm Springs, where he met with President Roosevelt and other Southern politicos. Back home, he was one of Darling's three lawyers. They rotated the job of Cypress County attorney—not a very big job and certainly undeserving of any lawyer's full-time attention—among them. This year, it was Mr. Moseley's turn, and Buddy had decided he'd better get his advice, just in case somebody made any noise about bringing in the state police.

Mr. Moseley didn't meet clients on Saturday, but he was in his office doing some research work, and when Buddy had knocked, he'd called, "Come on in, Sheriff—the door's unlocked."

Buddy hung his brown fedora on the peg by the door. Then he sat down across the desk, described Violet's gruesome morning discovery, and outlined his problem—not in detail, but the general gist.

"I understand." Mr. Moseley pulled his eyebrows together and puffed on his pipe. "And how many times did you say you saw the victim . . . er, socially?"

In his early forties, Moseley was a slender, attractive man with neatly clipped brown hair, regular features, and brown eyes behind dark-rimmed glasses. He had loosened his tie and rolled up the sleeves of his white shirt and was leaning back in his chair, smoking. There weren't many in Darling who smoked a pipe, except Mr. Musgrove, who smoked a corncob stuffed full of Kentucky Planter's. Mr. Moseley's pipe was made of polished wood, with a sleek, sophisticated appearance, and his pipe tobacco had the pleasing aroma of vanilla.

"We went out three times." Buddy counted them off on his fingers. "First was when she invited me to the Methodist pie social. That's where she went to church, and some of her friends saw us together. Another time, she'd been wanting to go to a dance out at the CCC camp, so I said I'd take her, and afterward, we sat out on her back porch for a while." That was when Bettina had come out and found them.

"Ah," Mr. Moseley said. "Yes, well, go on."

"The third time—" Buddy looked away. "She asked me over to her place for supper. Afterward, we . . . well, we hugged and kissed." He paused, feeling his face redden. "We fooled around some, too."

"I see," Mr. Moseley said, through a cloud of blue tobacco smoke. He looked at Buddy over the top of his glasses. "Did the 'fooling around some' include anything more intimate than hugging and kissing?"

Buddy ducked his head, feeling like all kinds of a fool. He knew the facts of life well enough—he just wasn't used to talking about them out loud. He'd skipped the locker room conversations in high school, and since then, the subject hadn't really come up. In a low voice, he said, "If you're asking, did I have sex with her, the answer is no, I didn't."

Mr. Moseley regarded him. After a moment, he said, in a kindly tone, "Why not, if you don't mind my asking? Did the lady turn you down?"

Buddy shook his head, embarrassed. "I was the one who said no, actually." He'd thought later that maybe he should have taken Rona Jean up on her generous offer, since she had been so clearly ready and willing—eager, even. Most of the guys he knew would have jumped at the chance, and yes, Buddy had been sorely, sorely tempted. But there had been something in Rona Jean's eagerness that had made him think it was *not* a good idea.

He cleared his throat. "We were . . . we were going at it pretty hot and heavy, and all of a sudden I got the idea that what Rona Jean was really looking for was somebody to marry her, like right away, and I happened to be the nearest one. If we had sex, I could find myself in front of a preacher real fast. Like Grady Alexander." Grady, who had been all but engaged to Liz Lacy, had to marry Sandra Mann, and now they had a little boy, born six months after the wedding. Grady was the county ag agent and had a steady job, but Buddy had heard they were just barely scraping by.

The corners of Mr. Moseley's mouth tightened at the mention of Grady Alexander, and Buddy remembered, belatedly, that Liz Lacy worked for him. But he only said, "And you're not interested in marriage?"

Buddy cocked his head, considering. "Well, yeah, sure. Marriage and kids. But it's not going to happen until I can afford a nice little house and some acres, so when the kids come, they've got a good place to grow up." He paused, coloring. "The other thing was—well, I had no idea that we were going to . . . that she would let me . . . so I wasn't, you know, prepared."

He was actually fully prepared, with a package of four Neverrip Preventions that he'd bought from under the counter at Lima's Drugs, but they were under his socks in his top bureau drawer, in his room on the other side of town.

"I told Rona Jean it wasn't a good idea, but she said it would be okay to take a chance, since it was the wrong time of the month. But between that and the marriage thing, I was pretty well cooled off." He colored, remembering. "If you know what I mean."

"I do know. Providential, most likely." The corner of Mr. Moseley's mouth quirked. "Commendable, certainly."

Buddy sighed heavily. "I didn't feel that way at the time. And I guess I didn't do a very good job of explaining to Rona Jean. She got it into her head that I didn't like her, that maybe she wasn't pretty enough or something. She was kinda pissed at me."

*Kinda pissed* didn't quite do justice to the height and depth and breadth of Rona Jean's anger or the way she had expressed it to him afterward, but it wasn't important. Mr. Moseley didn't need to know about that, especially since the letter she had written him afterward was all full of lies. There wasn't a grain of truth in it.

"Happens," Mr. Moseley said thoughtfully. "Some women take it personally. When they do, there's not much a fellow can say about it. There are no witnesses. And juries tend to believe the woman. Funny how that works." He puffed on his pipe and the blue smoke rose over his head. "When was this?"

Buddy shifted uncomfortably. "A week or so after the dance at the CCC camp. Which makes it maybe two months ago, I reckon. It was before I was elected sheriff, anyway."

"And you haven't seen her since?"

"Not to talk to," Buddy said. He was glad that Mr. Moseley hadn't asked whether he'd *heard* from her. If so, he would have had to tell him about the letter. But no, he could say truthfully that he hadn't seen her. Not until this morning. Not until he'd seen her dead, with that stocking tight around her neck and her blouse unbuttoned and her legs splayed like she was a common—

Buddy swallowed. He didn't want to think about that.

Mr. Moseley sat forward and put his elbows on his desk. "All right, then, Sheriff, here is the opinion you asked for. Seems like you already know several rather important things about this young lady's *modus operandi*. What you know may be a help as you try to find out who killed her and why, which clearly puts you at an advantage in this investigation. Furthermore, if we bring in the state police, they're going to take matters out of our hands. There's no telling what'll happen after that, or whether they would be any more or less successful than you would be. But I would prefer not to lose local control."

*Modus operandi.* Buddy frowned, remembering that he had read about that in the scientific crime detection manual he had bought. "Her . . . mode of operation?"

"Well, you just reflect on it for a minute, son." Mr. Moseley put his pipe in his mouth and leaned back again. "What makes you think you were the only lucky fella whom this young lady favored with her attentions?"

Now Buddy felt even more foolish. "Yeah," he muttered. Of course. He'd already had the idea that he wasn't the first guy she was with—she was too experienced for that. She knew where to put her hands and what to do with them once she got them there. But he hadn't thought of it as Rona Jean's *modus operandi.* Just an awkward situation that he had gotten himself into and hadn't managed very well. Mr. Moseley's question put what had happened into an entirely different context. He would have to think about it.

Mr. Moseley eyed him. "Doc Roberts is doing an autopsy?"

"Right. We put her in Lionel Noonan's hearse and Lionel drove her over to Monroeville."

"Well, we'll know soon enough, then."

*Know what?* Buddy was still trying to figure that out when Mr. Moseley knocked his pipe into the green glass ashtray on his desk and said, in a formal tone, "With regard to this criminal case, Sheriff Norris, and acting as Cypress County attorney, I am instructing you to go ahead and do whatever has to be done to apprehend Miss Hancock's killer. If anybody gives you any trouble about your relationship with her, don't try to explain, just refer them to me. I'll take care of it."

"Thank you." Buddy felt a great relief. "Thank you, Mr. Moseley," he said again, emphatically. "I really appreciate it."

"That's what they pay me for, although they don't pay me much." Mr. Moseley gave him a cheerful smile. "What've you got planned for today?"

"Well, I've talked to Violet Sims—she found the body. The two of them were real good friends."

"Ah," Mr. Moseley said thoughtfully. "Good friends, were they?"

Buddy nodded. "Next up on the list is Bettina Higgens, the roommate. I'm hoping she can give me a list of girlfriends, names of the men Rona Jean—Miss Hancock—went out with." He colored and added hurriedly, "I'll talk to them, then canvass the neighborhood, find out if anybody saw or heard anything last night or this morning. Also, I'll talk to the girls she worked with at the Exchange. And Myra May," he added.

Mr. Moseley put his pipe into the holder on the desk and gave him a sharp look. "You think Myra May could be involved?" His voice had a particular edge.

"I don't know," Buddy replied, wondering what exactly Mr. Moseley meant by "involved." He spoke tentatively. "Violet told me that Myra May was working in the kitchen until midnight. Maybe she heard something."

Mr. Moseley went on as if he hadn't said anything. "Myra May has a temper and she's possessive about Violet. But she's a smart cookie. If she killed Rona Jean, she wouldn't do it in the front seat of her very own automobile. And leave the body there for Violet to find the next morning."

Buddy was taken aback. He hadn't gone any farther than an undefined suspicion of Myra May, but now that Mr. Moseley had laid it out so clearly, he found himself agreeing. Myra May may not have appreciated the friendship between Violet and Rona Jean, but she was not a suspect.

He nodded and said, "By the time I get all that done, maybe Doc Roberts will have the results of the autopsy."

He shivered at the thought of Rona Jean being cut open. "After that . . . well, I guess I'll have to figure out where to go from there."

Mr. Moseley nodded. "Makes good sense." He smiled slightly. "Tell you what, Sheriff. You go out there and do your job, and when you've finished, I'll do mine." His voice hardened. "You bring me the killer and enough hard evidence for me to make the case, and I'll see that the son of a bitch is convicted."

Buddy stood. "Yes, *sir*," he said, and almost saluted.

Now, holding his hat in one hand and raising his fist to knock at Bettina's front door, he stood tall and confident, knowing that Mr. Moseley was behind him.

Well before the second month's rent was due, Bettina Higgens had understood that agreeing to take Rona Jean Hancock as a roommate was a big, fat mistake.

It was Rona Jean's half of the rent money that had tempted her. For a couple of years, Bettina had lived with her sister and her brother-in-law over on Oak Street, which hadn't been bad, although their apartment was small and there wasn't a lot of privacy. But her sister had gotten a divorce and moved to Atlanta, and Bettina had to hunt for another place to live.

The cheapest place she found was a room at Mrs. Brewster's boardinghouse for young working women on West Plum. But Bettina hadn't liked what she heard about the place from girls who had lived there. Curfew was at nine on weekdays and ten thirty on weekends, and if you weren't in the house on the dot, Mrs. Brewster (the girls called her Dragon Lady behind her back) simply locked the doors and you were stuck outside for the night. If you overslept at breakfast time (six thirty in the morning) or you were late to supper (five thirty at night), you went hungry, for you couldn't use the kitchen or keep food in your room. As for entertaining company—well, that was a joke. You could sit out with a young man on the front porch until it got dark. Then you could sit in the parlor (on separate chairs, with the lights on), but only so long as the door to Mrs. Brewster's sitting room was open.

But bad as Mrs. Brewster's was, Bettina finally decided it was the best she could do, so she called to make the necessary arrangements. She hadn't any more than hung up, however, when the phone rang again, and the switchboard girl at the Telephone Exchange—Rona Jean Hancock—introduced herself. She sincerely apologized for having overheard Bettina's conversation with Mrs. Brewster. She said she would never have done such a thing but she was looking for a roommate, too, and knew of a small house for rent. If Bettina was interested, maybe they could go and look at it together.

That was how Bettina got hooked up with Rona Jean, and when the two of them had first moved in together, she had thought that it would be okay. She certainly enjoyed the little house, and since Rona Jean was gone a lot, she had it mostly to herself, which suited her just fine. After a hard day's work making women beautiful, it was a relief to come home and kick off her shoes and relax.

But it wasn't more than a couple of weeks before Bettina began to see the mistake she had made. First there was the money. Rona Jean was always a couple of weeks late with her share of the rent and was forever asking to borrow fifty cents or a dollar, which Bettina usually felt she had to loan her because she had been broke herself and knew what it felt like.

And then there were the men. Monday through Friday, Rona Jean worked the three-to-eleven shift at the Exchange, so she was never home on those evenings. She wasn't home on the other evenings, either, for she was in the habit of going out *every* weekend night—to the movies, to the new roller skating rink, to the CCC camp for a dance—and staying out until all hours.

And not with the same guy, either. In fact, Bettina had the idea that Rona Jean never went out with the same young man more than twice or three times. Then there were the occasions when Rona Jean had asked Bettina if she would mind going out to a movie so she could entertain a friend—like the night she'd had the sheriff over for supper and there had been that trouble.

And meanwhile, Bettina had no dates at all, which wasn't just embarrassing, it was downright disheartening. She had learned quite a number of neat tricks at the Beauty Bower, and she thought she had improved her appearance. She'd also studied up on style, using the fashion magazines that a client occasionally brought to the Bower, and she'd bought a sewing machine and taught herself to use it. So her clothes were as good as the next girl's—here in Darling, anyway, where everybody was making do and getting along on not very much.

But she never met a man at work (they got their hair cut at Bert's Barbershop, on the square), and the men at the Baptist church, where she went, were already married or engaged or so old they didn't have any spark left in them. There were quite a few CCC boys in town these days, and Rona Jean obviously had no problem making friends with them. But Bettina felt shy and awkward around people she didn't know, and she couldn't for the world imagine herself going up to a man she had never laid eyes on and starting a conversation right out of the blue. Which made her resent Rona Jean's casual way of connecting with men.

And now, Rona Jean was dead. When Myra May had phoned to tell her, she was stunned. She simply couldn't believe what she was hearing. When she put the phone down, she thought she should cry (after all, she and Rona Jean had been *living together* for more than six months), but she couldn't. Whether it was because of the shock or something else, she didn't know. And then she'd gone to stand in the doorway of Rona Jean's small room, which was just as messy as it always was, with her filmy underwear strewn everywhere, and her makeup and face creams and hair curlers piled on the vanity, and her collection of stuffed bears—which she said boys had won for her at fairs and carnivals—waiting for their mistress on the windowsill.

Bettina did cry, then, for the thought of those forlorn pink and orange and purple plush bears forever waiting for someone to come back and hug them and love them—someone who would never come back, someone who was *dead*—was just too overwhelming. She sank down on the unmade bed, buried her face in a pillow scented with Rona Jean's flowery perfume, and burst into tears. She was still crying when the sheriff phoned to say he would be coming over and would she please stay home from work until he'd had a chance to interview her.

Which gave Bettina something else to think about, because of what Rona Jean had told her about him, about the terrible way he had behaved the night he had come over for supper.

And that was what Bettina was remembering when she heard the knock on the door and opened it and came face to face with the sheriff himself, dressed in a khaki shirt and pants, with his star pinned to his shirt and holding his brown fedora in both hands. She was remembering what Rona Jean had told her about him and thinking that it wasn't right that *he* should be investigating her murder.

Buddy sat down on the chair that Bettina Higgens pointed out, and put his hat on the floor beside him. She sat on the edge of the sofa, hands clasped nervously.

"Sorry to have to barge in on you, Miss Higgens," he said. "I'm sure this has got to be really tough for you, so I'll make it as quick as I can." Taking out his notebook, he glanced around. The little parlor was neat but sparsely furnished, and with a few feminine touches here and there— the embroidered pillow on the sofa, the anemic plant on the windowsill, a frilly doily under the lamp.

The young woman on the sofa was tall and thin, with a wide forehead, gray eyes, and high cheekbones. She didn't think she was attractive, Buddy guessed from the way she held her shoulders. She had dressed quickly or carelessly, misbuttoning her red dress, and her shoulder-length brown hair looked as if she hadn't taken the time to comb it since she got out of bed. She clasped and unclasped her hands and then hunched over, wrapping her arms around herself.

"I don't know what I can tell you." Her voice was hesitant, doubtful. "Rona Jean worked three to eleven at the Telephone Exchange five days a week, and I work eight to five at the Beauty Bower every day but Sunday. We weren't what you'd call bosom buddies, I guess. We didn't go places together. To tell the truth, we weren't even home together all that often." She cleared her throat. "To tell the truth, about the only time we talked was when she wanted to borrow money."

Buddy glanced down at his notebook, where he had written *thick as theives*. But she was making it sound as if they were no more than a pair of strangers sharing the same house. Which was right?

"Borrow money?" he asked, remembering that Rona Jean's pocketbook, which he had found on the floor of Myra May's car, had contained one two-dollar bill in a billfold and forty-seven cents in a coin purse, along with the usual comb and makeup items.

Bettina nodded reluctantly. "She was always broke and, most months, behind on the rent."

*Always broke*, Buddy wrote. "Had you been living together long?"

"Four or five months." Bettina frowned. "No, six. We rented this place in January. It was either move in here with Rona Jean or get a room at Mrs. Brewster's." She told the rest of the story simply, as Buddy took notes. When she stopped talking, he jotted down *just roommates*. At least, that's how she'd put it.

He cleared his throat. "What about Miss Hancock's friends?"

Bettina lifted her eyes. "You mean, friends like . . . *you?*" Her expression was unreadable, but there was an unmistakable challenge in her voice. "I bet you didn't call her 'Miss Hancock' the night she had you over here for supper."

Buddy met her eyes without flinching. He wanted to answer her challenge, but now wasn't the time. "Yes, ma'am, friends. Men, women, anybody she spent time with."

Bettina looked away. "Well, in addition to spending time with *you*," she said pointedly, "she also went out with Lamar Lassen—he works over at the sawmill. And Beau Pyle."

Buddy didn't know Lassen, but he'd already had a run-in with young Beau, Bodeen Pyle's brother. The boy—he wasn't any more than eighteen—had a reputation around town as a kid with a bad temper. He got in a fight at Pete's Pool Parlor, and Pete (who wouldn't stand for roughhousing in his joint) told him to leave. More fists flew, a knife was pulled, and Buddy was summoned to settle some hash. It had been his first major test in keeping the peace, and he thought he'd won the respect of Pete's customers. He hadn't made a friend of the Pyles, though. Beau had spent his night in jail getting even by shredding the straw tick mattress and wrecking the wall-hung bunk in his cell, which had earned him an extra two days' incarceration, sleeping on the floor, and a $12.50 fine. His brother Bodeen, with a surly grunt of protest, had paid the fine. In Buddy's opinion, Rona Jean would've done better if she had stayed away from Beau. He was bad news, and in any case, four or five years younger than she was.

"Lassen and Pyle." He wrote their names. "Anybody else?"

Bettina paused. "Well, she was seeing a guy out at the CCC camp. Lately, I mean. In the last few weeks."

Buddy was momentarily distracted by the curve of her pale cheek, half hidden by a lock of brown hair. Her skin was pale and lightly freckled. She was pretty, in a kind of natural, unself-conscious way—which struck Buddy as odd, since she worked at the Beauty Bower, where women went to get themselves prettied up. "Who?" he asked. "Who was she seeing out there?"

"Ray somebody. I don't know his last name, but he's some kind of something out at the camp. Works in an office, I mean."

"How often did she see him?"

"No idea." Bettina lifted her shoulders and let them fall. "Maybe she put it into her diary."

*Diary*, Buddy wrote, and drew a box around the word. "What about girlfriends? I probably need to talk to them." Especially, he thought, since I'm not getting much out of you.

"Girlfriends?" Bettina's mouth quirked. "Rona Jean didn't have a lot of time for girls. There are the ones she worked with at the Exchange—Lenore Looper and Henrietta Conrad—but she didn't see them after hours. She didn't get along with Myra May just real well, but she sometimes went to the movies with Violet. When she wasn't going out with some guy. She liked Violet a lot."

"What was her trouble with Myra May?"

Bettina paused, considering, then said, "I guess mostly it

was because she was friends with Violet. There was some kind of trouble on the switchboard, too. Every now and then, Rona Jean would say that Myra May had warned her that she was going to get fired."

"Why?"

"For listening in on people's conversations. The operators aren't supposed to do that."

"But Rona Jean did?"

Bettina nodded. "Last week, she told me that Myra May got really mad at her about it and threatened to fire her, but Violet wouldn't let Myra May do it." She pulled her eyebrows together, puzzled. "At the time, I thought it was odd. She even said, 'Myra May wouldn't *dare* fire me.' She laughed when she said it. She seemed to think it was funny."

Buddy wrote *listening in* and *MM wouldn't dare* and added two emphatic question marks. He scratched his nose with his pencil.

"So what about last night? Was Rona Jean planning to see anybody after she got off work?" Eleven o'clock was late by Darling standards, but apparently that didn't matter to Rona Jean.

"If that was her plan, she didn't tell me. But then, she didn't tell me she wasn't, either." Bettina gave a half-discernible shake of the head. "Rona Jean was free as a bird, or she liked to think she was. She pretty much came and went as she pleased."

Buddy closed his notebook. Now was the time. "When I asked you a minute ago who were her friends, you said, 'You mean, friends like *you?*' It sounded like you don't think I'm the kind of friend a girl should have." He looked at her steadily. "Is that it? Is that what you were thinking?"

"Well, why wouldn't I?" Bettina was defiant. "After what happened."

"What happened when?"

"When you . . . slapped her around." Bettina dropped her eyes, as if he were too ugly to look at.

"Slapped her around? I never laid a hand on that girl." Buddy colored, remembering where exactly he had laid his hands. "Well, not in anger, anyway," he muttered.

"That's not what she told me," Bettina retorted.

Buddy opened his notebook again. "What *did* she tell you? I want to know."

"Why?" Bettina challenged. "Don't you remember?"

"Come on, Miss Higgens," Buddy said grimly. "This is a murder investigation. What did she tell you? I want it straight. *All* of it."

She stumbled clumsily through it and Buddy wrote down what she said. When she finished, he said, "Thank you."

She cast a doubtful glance in Buddy's direction. "Well?"

"Well what?"

"Aren't you going to . . . deny it or something?"

"No point," Buddy said quietly. "I don't behave like that. Never have, never will. If you knew me, you'd know that without me having to tell you. But since you don't know me, I doubt you'll believe me."

Bettina's eyebrows went up. "But the sleeve of her blouse was torn. There was a bruise on her arm and she was hysterical. She . . ." She swallowed. "You're saying she made it all up? You didn't . . . ?"

Buddy gave her a steady look. "I am saying she *lied* to you, Miss Higgens, pure and simple. It's true that Rona Jean got mad at me after we had supper together, but it wasn't because I slapped her around." He was too much of a gentleman to say that Rona Jean had gotten mad at him because he rejected her advances. "It's also true," he added evenly, "that she wrote me a letter afterward."

Now that he thought about it, he wondered if some of

the things Rona Jean had written to him had come to her mind after she had talked to Bettina. He didn't know much about psychology, but he'd seen hysterical people. Maybe the things she put in the letter began to seem real to her when she told them to her roommate, especially if her roommate believed her and commiserated with her.

"A letter?" Bettina asked uncertainly. "What kind of letter?"

Buddy met her eyes. "Not a nice one, and that's all I'm going to say about it."

It hadn't been out-and-out blackmail—somehow, it was more naïve than that, or maybe she was only half trying. But the letter had ended with several thinly veiled threats that could have been read as blackmail. Buddy wasn't the kind of person who was easily intimidated, but he'd admit to being relieved when that letter wasn't followed by a demand of some sort. Relieved, yes, and angry, too. But mostly angry at himself, for getting into that position. He was just damned lucky. She could have caused all kinds of nasty trouble for him, and since there weren't any witnesses, it would have been hard to defend himself.

And then another thought came to him. If Rona Jean had behaved that way toward him, maybe she had done the same thing with one of the other fellows she was seeing. Maybe the letter to him was just practice, and with her next attempt, she got serious. Something like that—blackmail, more or less—could very well be a motive for murder, couldn't it?

Buddy stood. "You mentioned a diary. I need to see it. I'd like to take a look at her room, too. And then I'll get out of your hair."

Without a word, Bettina got up and left the room. Buddy followed her.

# FIVE

# The Dahlias Do Business

Verna closed the Dahlias' treasurer's ledger and sat back in her chair, satisfied. "Looks to me like we did pretty well, girls. We netted forty-two dollars and seventy-four cents, after expenses. That's not shabby."

"It's a lot better than last time," Liz replied. "And the time before that, we didn't even break even."

"The difference is that we sold a lot more plants," Ophelia put in. "Getting members to commit to the plant sale a couple of months ahead was a real good idea. They had everything potted up and ready to go, and the plants looked great. They practically sold themselves."

Three of the garden club officers (Elizabeth Lacy, president; Ophelia Snow, vice president; and Verna Tidwell, treasurer) were holding an early morning business meeting in the clubhouse kitchen to discuss the results of the recent Dahlias garden club tour and plant sale, held at the beginning of June, when the gardens were at their peak.

Twice a year, the Dahlias—Darling's only garden club—invited the public to tour their famous gardens. They charged a small admission fee and donated the money to the town's relief fund, where it was needed and welcomed. The Depression had hit Darling hard. Businesses had failed, people were out of work, and those who had nothing needed all the help they could get. Of course, it went without saying that nobody wanted to be on government relief. They were all used to working hard and making their own way in the world, and taking money when you hadn't earned it was a terrible blow to a person's pride.

But people did what they had to do to keep their families together, and if that meant accepting help from neighbors and friends . . . well, that seemed somehow different from accepting handouts from Uncle Sam—and better. For one thing, it wasn't called relief, it was called "community assistance." For another, it was a comfort to know that their fellow townspeople cared and were willing to pitch in and help where they could. It meant they weren't alone.

Still, in such dire times, it would be easy to say that the town could do without a garden club. Who cared about pretty flowers when mothers couldn't afford to buy milk? But the Dahlias had proved themselves to be a valuable asset to Darling. Their vegetable garden helped to feed the town's hungry families (on both sides of the L&N tracks). The flowers they tended on the courthouse square kept people's spirits from flagging. And their garden tours raised money for the relief fund. Nobody could say that the Darling Dahlias' interests were purely decorative.

"One more item," Liz reminded them. "The flowers for the Miss Darling float." The Fourth of July parade was coming up next Wednesday, and the Dahlias were responsible for decorating the float that would carry Miss Darling and

Little Miss Darling. This year, it would be a special treat to decorate the float, since Violet's and Myra May's daughter, Cupcake, had been chosen as Little Miss Darling. "Earlynne is in charge of this project. She asked Myra May to call all the club members and remind them that we need their contributions early that morning. If they don't show up by nine o'clock, we can't guarantee that we'll use their stuff."

"I hope Myra May remembers to tell people that potted plants—especially marigolds and zinnias and begonias, annuals with lots of color—are better than cut flowers," Verna remarked. "Especially if it's windy." One year, they had decorated the float entirely with cut flowers and the wind made a mess of everything.

"I'm bringing three big ruffled ferns," Ophelia said. "They'll make a nice display around the throne. And Aunt Hetty promised her parlor palm—the same one she brought last year."

"Sounds good," Liz said. "We need rain, but let's hope it doesn't rain on our parade. The kids always look forward to it. I hate to see them disappointed."

"The WALA weather forecast said we could get thunderstorms today," Ophelia said. "That big storm south of Mobile—the one that crossed Florida and ended up in the Gulf—is predicted to head inland."

"Maybe it'll break the heat," Verna said, pushing her hair off her forehead. "It's another hot one."

The business part of their meeting finished, the officers could relax and chat. Ophelia brought a plate of old-fashioned jam thumbprint cookies to the table. Liz, who was wearing a yellow voile dress with cap sleeves and peasant-style embroidery, put their papers away. And Verna took a pitcher of lemonade out of the refrigerator.

"I guess you heard about Rona Jean Hancock getting killed," she said, refilling everyone's glasses. Stylishly thin, of medium height, Verna had recently adopted a new look, with short, straight, easy-care hair that fitted her head like a glossy dark helmet. Today, she was wearing a khaki shirt-waist dress with pockets in a flared skirt.

"My mother heard it on her party line first thing this morning and hurried across the street to tell me," Liz said. "I didn't really know Rona Jean, but I felt I did, just because she was there on the other end of the telephone line. I was *shocked*."

In a way, Lizzy thought, the girls who worked on the Exchange were the best-known girls in town, even if you didn't always recognize them when you saw them on the street. Everyone could identify their voices when they said, "Number, please," or "Sorry, that line is busy," or "Mrs. Musgrove just went over to the church to help get the tables ready for the supper tonight. If you need her, I'll ring the Baptist parsonage." Every single person in town would be touched by Rona Jean's loss—and wondering who in the world could have killed her, and why.

"It's a tragedy," Verna agreed, sitting down.

Lizzy took a cookie. "Does anybody have more details?" She worked in Mr. Moseley's law office and had learned the truth of what Mr. Moseley liked to say: the devil was truly in the details.

"Charlie told me that Doc Roberts is doing an autopsy," Ophelia replied. Short and nicely rounded, with a cherubic face, flyaway brown hair, and an irrepressible optimism, Ophelia usually wore a wide smile that showed pretty white teeth. She wasn't smiling now, though. "I'm sure that Charlie will handle the story," she added, and if Liz and Verna thought they heard some envy in her voice, they would be right.

Ophelia worked part-time for Charlie Dickens at the *Dispatch*. She operated the Linotype machine, sold advertising, and wrote up stories for the women's page. She was dying to do some serious reporting, but Charlie was in the habit of assigning her to "soft" news—the baby shows and women's club meetings—and keeping the hard news (what there was of it) for himself. When she had started her new part-time job at Camp Briarwood, though, he'd asked her to write a column about the camp's activities. And he'd come up with a new investigative assignment for her that sounded intriguing. In fact, the story was so important that he'd made her swear not to tell anybody—not even her Dahlia friends—about her investigation, which intrigued her even more.

"An autopsy?" Lizzy turned her lemonade glass in her long, slim fingers, her nails clipped short because she spent hours at the typewriter every day. "But they already know how Rona Jean died, don't they? I understand that she was . . . strangled. With her own stocking."

In Benton Moseley's law office, Lizzy often had to deal with the grimier, grittier side of life. But murder wasn't often on the agenda, and it certainly wasn't something she liked to dwell on. She was creative and imaginative, a romantic who preferred to think of things that gave her pleasure, like her sweet little house and her garden and especially her writing— her new book, for instance. At least, she *hoped* it was going to be a new book. She didn't know for sure yet, but she had her fingers crossed.

Liz's best friend Verna, on the other hand, operated out of an entirely different frame of mind. Pragmatic, realistic, and unsentimental, Verna served as the Cypress County probate clerk and newly elected county treasurer—the first woman in the entire state of Alabama to be elected to that important job. From her office on the second floor of the courthouse, she witnessed most of the grimier doings that went on across the county. Just last month, for instance, she had found out that the contractor who had low-bid the new bridge out on the

Jericho Road was billing the county for twice as many steel trusses as the specifications called for. She hadn't let him get away with it, either. She reported it to the county commissioners, who made him return the trusses, reduced his billing accordingly, and levied a sizable fine. Verna's habit of cracking down on wrongdoers didn't earn her a lot of friends, but she never apologized for it.

"Yes, an autopsy." Verna sat back down at the table and took a Pall Mall cigarette out of the handbag hanging on the back of her chair. "To find out if she was sexually assaulted. She was strangled with her stocking and her body was found in a . . . suggestive position. In the front seat of Myra May's car. I heard that from Myra May herself," she added, "when I stopped at the diner for a cup of coffee."

"Oh dear." Lizzy closed her eyes, not wanting to think about it. "Oh, poor Rona Jean."

"Maybe it was just sex," Ophelia remarked hopefully. "Without the assault, I mean. I wonder if Doc Roberts can tell the difference." She made a rueful face. "Either way, of course, Charlie can't print it in the paper. He says that if the *Dispatch* had a motto, it would be 'Only the news that's fit to be read—by your mother.'" She took a cookie for herself.

Liz shook her head. "Poor Charlie. He's a serious newspaperman. I know he hates to leave stuff out."

"Doesn't have to be in the *Dispatch*," Verna reminded them, lighting her cigarette. "You know Darling. News—especially if it's got anything to do with sex—gets around so fast it'll make your head swim. An hour after Doc Roberts is finished, the autopsy result will be all over town."

"Make that half an hour," Ophelia said.

Verna pulled down her mouth. "Unfortunately, getting the news fast doesn't guarantee that it'll be accurate. Somebody will get it wrong, and the next person will get it even more wrong, and so on. The news you hear may not be the *real* news."

"Well, Doc Roberts can set people straight," Lizzy said. "And Buddy Norris. I'm sure he'll get all the facts in his investigation."

"Maybe not Buddy Norris." Verna sipped her lemonade. "I stopped at the post office before I came over here, and I heard that there might be a problem with Buddy Norris working on this case."

Ophelia gave her a puzzled look. "But Buddy Norris is the sheriff. Why *wouldn't* he investigate? And if he doesn't, who else could?"

"That's a good question, Opie," Verna said thoughtfully. "I suppose Deputy Springer might, but—"

"Oh, for goodness' sake, Verna," Ophelia scoffed. "Wayne Springer is new on the job and besides, nobody knows him. He comes from Birmingham. People won't even want to talk to him." She paused. "Anyway, you didn't answer my question. What's wrong with Buddy Norris? He's the sheriff now—why shouldn't he do his job?"

"Because he was involved with the victim." Verna got up to find an ashtray.

"Involved?" Lizzy frowned. "How do you mean?"

Verna put the ashtray on the table and sat back down. "I overheard Leona Ruth Adcock telling Mrs. Magee that she looked through Rona Jean's kitchen window and saw the two of them hugging and kissing. Buddy and Rona Jean, I mean."

"Through the *window*?" Lizzy rolled her eyes. But she wasn't surprised. Leona Ruth had a reputation for looking where she shouldn't be looking and then telling all her friends what she had seen.

Ophelia shook her head disgustedly. "Nobody ever believes

more than half of anything Leona Ruth says. Anyway, even if it's true, there's no law against a kiss or two."

"No, but there could be a problem if the kissee gets killed and the kisser is supposed to find out who dunnit," Verna pointed out. "Some people might suspect a cover-up—or a frame-up."

Taking a second cookie, Lizzy suppressed a smile. Verna was a mystery fan, and her vocabulary sometimes gave her away.

"Anyway," Verna went on, "it doesn't matter whether Leona was telling the truth or not. Mrs. Magee seemed to believe her. She'll probably tell everybody in her Sunday school class tomorrow, and they'll think they got the word from God."

"I hadn't heard about Buddy Norris," Lizzy observed, "but Rona Jean was certainly seeing somebody else. She got quite a few hugs and kisses from that guy, too."

"Oh yeah?" Verna tapped her cigarette ash into the ashtray. "Who was he?"

"Somebody from the CCC camp," Lizzy said. "He was wearing a uniform. Mr. Moseley and I saw the two of them at the movie house over in Monroeville." Just thinking of it made her blush. "They were sitting a couple of rows in front of us."

"The CCC camp," Verna mused. "I wonder . . . Did you recognize him?"

Lizzy shook her head. "I only got a glimpse of him, but he seemed older than the other CCC boys. An officer, maybe."

Ophelia leaned forward. "Let me get this straight, Liz. You're saying you went to the movie with Mr. Moseley? On a *date*?"

Ophelia sounded so incredulous that Lizzy had to chuckle. "I guess you could call it that. But don't go thinking romance, Ophelia. The movie starred Spencer Tracy, and we're both fans, that's all. You know that Mr. Moseley is involved with that girl in Montgomery."

That girl's name was Daphne. She was a very pretty social-ite, very rich, and very divorced (twice). Sometimes Lizzy felt a stirring of jealousy—an unreasonable stirring—when she thought about Daphne. But she always reminded herself that while she and Bent Moseley were friends, as well as employee and employer, the two of them inhabited very different uni-verses. Daphne was in *his* universe, and Lizzy definitely wasn't.

"This CCC guy," Verna said, frowning a little. "Did you get a look at him?"

"Or a name?" Ophelia put in eagerly. "I work at Camp Briarwood three days a week, you know. Maybe I've met him."

Lizzy shook her head. "No name, and not even a very good look. But I can tell you that they weren't there to watch the movie. They were . . . I think it's called petting." At first, it was amusing, but after a while, the kisses got so passionate that Lizzy had been embarrassed. She thought of finding dif-ferent seats, but she was afraid that Bent—Mr. Moseley—would think she was being silly. She was glad when the movie ended and the lights came up.

Verna blew a stream of blue smoke into the air. "When did this happen?"

"Maybe three weeks ago?" Lizzy hazarded. "The movie was really worth seeing—*The Power and the Glory*. If you're curious, you could check the *Monroe Journal* movie ads and see when it was showing."

Ophelia glanced at her wristwatch and pushed her chair back. "Oh golly. Can we adjourn? I've got Sam's baseball team coming for a picnic tonight, and Sarah's birthday is tomorrow. I promised I'd take her to Monroeville shopping this after-noon. I have to stop at Camp Briarwood, too, and pick up a couple of things I left on my desk."

Verna banged her glass in lieu of a gavel. "Meeting adjourned," she pronounced.

"Sarah's birthday?" Lizzy asked. "I've lost track. How old is she?"

"She'll be fifteen—can you believe? She's asking for a new bathing suit, and heaven knows she needs one. She's getting . . ." Ophelia gestured with her hands. "Curvy. I'll help you two clear up, and then I've got to run."

"Go now," Lizzy commanded, pushing her chair back. "We'll clear."

"And take the cookies with you," Verna said. "They're scrumptious. Sam's team will love them."

# SIX

# Verna and Lizzy Make Plans

A few moments later, everything was put away and the kitchen was in order for the next Dahlia group that would be using it. Verna stuck her treasurer's ledger in her handbag and went toward the door. "Are you headed home, Liz?"

"Going to the post office first. I'm hoping for a letter." Lizzy put on her straw hat, turned out the kitchen light, then followed Verna out the back door and waited while she locked it. "From Nadine Fleming—my agent."

"I've got a favor to ask you, so I'll walk with you," Verna said. "And I have to go to the grocery." She put the key under the rock beside the back door and looked up with a smile. "The letter—you're hoping for news about your novel, then?"

"Yes." Wishing it would cool off, Lizzy fell into step beside Verna as they walked up Rosemont in the direction of the courthouse square. The weather had been hot and sultry the past few days, and the gardens were in need of moisture.

But if the storm in the Gulf blew ashore, it might cool things off and bring them some rain. She hoped so.

"Nadine has promised to tell me whether the manuscript is ready to send out," she added, as they stepped around a pair of young girls skipping rope on the sidewalk. "I have my fingers crossed that it is."

As Lizzy said the words, she found herself not quite believing them. Ever since she was a teenager, she had been promising herself that she was going to write a book, and now she had done it. She wrote it during the months she'd been working in Mr. Jackman's law office in Montgomery—"in exile," as Lizzy had thought of it at first. But now, she had to admit that if she hadn't gone into exile, she probably wouldn't have written the book.

It was Mr. Moseley who suggested the job to her, with the idea that it might be better if she got away from Darling for a while. The suggestion was especially kind and generous, for it came right after she had received the shock of her life, when Grady Alexander—Lizzy's longtime all-but-fiancé—had told her that he had to marry Sandra Mann, because they were expecting a baby. In fact, the wedding was planned for that very weekend. To make matters even worse (if that was possible), Lizzy had discovered that Grady and his new bride would be moving into the old Harrison house, just down the block.

Grady's betrayal had come as a terrible blow, and it took all of Lizzy's strength to pretend that it didn't hurt (although of course it did). For several days, she went around making excuses for Grady, holding her head high and wearing an artificial smile that fooled nobody, least of all Mr. Moseley. But at last, she decided to follow up on his suggestion that she take the temporary job with Mr. Jackman in Montgomery.

This decision was made a little easier when it turned out that Ophelia was eager to fill in for Lizzy in Mr. Moseley's office, in addition to her part-time work for the *Dispatch*. At the time, Snow's Farm Supply was barely holding on and money was tight in the Snow household, so every extra dollar was a big help. If Lizzy went to work in Montgomery, Ophelia could take Lizzy's place in Darling.

The interview went well, and Mr. Jackman immediately offered Lizzy the job. She said yes, closed up her house, and set off for Montgomery, the Alabama state capital and the first capital of the Confederacy. There, she began looking for an apartment for herself and her cat, Daffodil, whom she couldn't bear to leave behind.

The adventure turned out much better than Lizzy could possibly have anticipated. She enjoyed her new job, where there was always something different and challenging going on. Mr. Jackman's practice was wide-ranging, and once he learned how competent she was, he delegated more and more tasks to her. He often went out of town on business or spent long days at the legislature, leaving her in charge of the office. Self-confidence had never been Lizzy's strong suit, but working for Mr. Jackman changed that. She couldn't explain it except to say that it was like finding yourself suddenly promoted two grades ahead in school and discovering—to your delighted surprise—that you could do the work with no trouble at all.

What's more, the three-room furnished apartment that Mrs. Jackman had helped her locate suited her to a T. It was at the back of one of the large old homes on a quiet Montgomery street. It had its own private entrance, decent furniture, a bookcase full of books left by the previous tenant, and a cute little kitchenette with a door that opened onto a splendid garden, where she and Daffy could enjoy warm evenings and quiet weekends. Mr. Moseley (now that they weren't working together, he asked her to call him Bent) drove up on weekends to visit Daphne Stewart, with whom he was romantically involved. Occasionally, he would drop in at Jackman's office to ask Lizzy to go out to dinner with him, or to a movie or a concert, and she always said yes. After all, she wasn't working for him, she did enjoy his company, and Grady was out of the picture. Lizzy (who had always treasured stability and predictability) was learning to be comfortable with the idea of "temporary," and it felt temporarily right to spend a few hours every couple of weeks with her former boss.

But aside from seeing Bent, Lizzy didn't go out. Instead, she gave herself permission to do something she'd been wanting to do for a very long time. With her second paycheck (her first went for two pretty dresses, a pair of summer shoes, and a new red leather collar for Daffy), she bought a reconditioned Royal typewriter. She put it on a little table in front of a window overlooking the garden, equipped herself with a comfortable chair, and began to write about the characters who had been living in a corner of her mind like a group of silent friends and neighbors.

Lizzy had always been a good writer. For years, she had written the weekly "Garden Gate" column for the *Dispatch*, including notes about plants in local gardens and wild plants from the woods and fields and streams around Darling. Her readers began sending clippings to their friends in other cities, and it wasn't long before she was receiving letters from all over the South, asking gardening questions or telling her about the writers' experiences with the plants she had written about.

Gardening wasn't Lizzy's only subject, though. She occasionally wrote a feature story for the *Dispatch*, and she kept a small notebook in her purse where she could jot down vignettes of people she met, places that seized her imagination, and events that piqued her curiosity. While nothing very big or exciting ever happened in Darling, there were always more little things to notice than you might expect, surprising crises that poked up unexpectedly out of the quiet surface of everyday life. She cherished the people who lived in her imagination, and deep in her heart, her secret heart, she half believed that if she wrote about them, if she told their stories, they might actually become real. And the only way to find out if this was true was to *do* it.

Writing a book, however, took a more sustained effort than Lizzy had ever devoted to her writing. It simply wouldn't have been possible if she hadn't left Darling and moved to Montgomery, where she had much more time to herself. She didn't have to be in the office until ten each morning, and she was free after five o'clock every afternoon. Somebody else took care of the garden. There were no meetings of the Dahlias to attend, no Grady to go out with, no friends to telephone or people to see—and (best of all, even though she hated to say it) no interfering mother to casually drop in for an hour every single evening, just to see what Lizzy was doing.

Instead, there had been long, lovely stretches of time with no one around but Daffodil and nothing to do but sit at her typewriter and immerse herself in the world of her story. When she had been working for several months, she rather shyly mentioned what she was doing to Mrs. Jackman, who clamored to read the first three chapters. When she did, she was impressed.

"I think this is simply splendid, my dear," she exclaimed. "Coincidentally, my favorite cousin, Nadine Fleming, has her own literary agency in New York City. Please do let me share these chapters with her."

This wonderful coincidence paid huge dividends. After Miss Fleming had seen the first three chapters of Lizzy's book, she asked to see more—and then more, and then more, until finally she had seen the whole thing.

"Surprisingly good, for a first effort," Miss Fleming acknowledged, when she telephoned—long-distance!—to discuss her impressions with Lizzy. "I was involved with your characters from the very first page. I'd like to send you a few suggestions to help you tighten up your narrative and . . ."

Entitled simply *Sabrina*, Lizzy's book was about a young woman who lived on her family's Alabama plantation during the difficult years after the War Between the States. Her young lover had been killed at Gettysburg, and she was being courted by an older man, a neighbor who seemed to offer her freedom from the burden of keeping the plantation going. Marriage was tempting, but—and in that *but*, of course, lay the story.

Lizzy did her best to incorporate the agent's suggestions into what she hoped would be a final draft. When she was finished, she typed it one more time (with two carbons) and sent the manuscript off to New York. Now, Lizzy was waiting for a letter that might tell her whether Miss Fleming liked it or didn't like it—or might like it better if Lizzy revised it yet again.

She was about to ask Verna what it was she wanted to ask when a bicycle bell jangled behind them. "Hello, ladies," came the shouted greeting. "Pretty day, isn't it?"

"Hello, Charlie." Lizzy lifted her hand to wave at Charlie Dickens, who was catching up to them on his old blue bicycle. He was dressed in his summer seersucker suit and straw boater, a cigarette dangling from one corner of his mouth. Charlie, the editor and publisher of the *Dispatch*, was a rather different man since his marriage to Fannie Champaign. He still wore his newsman's cynical skepticism like a hair shirt, but he no longer hung out at Pete's Pool Parlor, he was home most evenings, and he even mustered the occasional smile.

Charlie slowed his bicycle. "Just letting you know that I'm putting out a special edition of the *Dispatch* early next week," he said, raising his voice. "If your garden column is ready, Liz, there'll likely be room for it."

"The special is for Rona Jean's murder?" Verna asked with interest. The *Dispatch* was a weekly, but if there was a big story, Charlie was known to publish an extra edition, which his readers very much appreciated.

"Guessed right the first time," Charlie said cheerfully.

"What's the scoop on the autopsy?" Lizzy asked. "Has Edna Fay heard anything from the hospital?" Charlie's sister, Edna Fay, was married to Doc Roberts, and she sometimes gave her brother the inside story—her version, anyway. Since Charlie was coming from the direction of the Roberts' house, it was a good guess that he had been visiting his sister.

Charlie gave her a crooked grin. "No comment," he replied. He lifted his hat and pedaled away.

"He knows something we don't," Lizzy said, frowning. "I wonder what it is."

"He knows that murder sells newspapers," Verna remarked, waving at Mrs. Donner, who was deadheading her roses.

"You're right about that," Lizzy said. "He doesn't do that many special editions. The last one was back in December, wasn't it?"

Verna nodded. "When the country went wet." The Twenty-first Amendment had finally ended Prohibition, only months after Roosevelt and the Democrats rode into office on a wet ticket. Michigan had been the first state to repeal in April 1933, and Utah was the thirty-sixth in December, making it official. Alabama had ratified in August, although the legislature had played safe and gone for a local option. Cypress County was still dry, of course (the Temperance movement was strong), but that was only on paper. Everybody knew that Bodeen Pyle was making shine down at Briar's Swamp, in the southern part of the county. And now that Mickey LeDoux had finished serving his sentence at the Wetumpka State Penitentiary (where he had been sent after Agent Kinnard broke up his still and busted him for bootlegging), he would likely be in business again shortly.

Verna went back to what they had been discussing before Charlie came along. "I've got my fingers crossed for you, Liz. *Sabrina* is a very good book—and I'm not just saying that to please you."

"Of course, you're not at all prejudiced," Lizzy said wryly. "But it would be silly to get my hopes up. According to Miss Fleming, the publishing business is terrible right now. People don't spend money on books when they don't have enough to buy food or pay rent. Even established writers are having a hard time. They're finding work wherever they can—ghostwriting, movie scripts, advice to the lovelorn."

"I don't know about that," Verna said. "I just finished reading *Murder Must Advertise.*" Verna loved to read mysteries more than anything else, and while the Darling library didn't have much of a book budget, Miss Rogers, the librarian, bought as many as she could. "It's Dorothy Sayers' eighth book."

"But I'm not Dorothy Sayers," Lizzy pointed out. "*Sabrina* is my first book. Miss Fleming says I'm lucky to have a paying job. And now that this book is done, she told me to immediately start writing another. That way, even if *Sabrina* doesn't make it, I'll have something else to send out."

"Sounds like good advice," Verna remarked as they crossed Dauphin Street and came onto the town square, with the imposing brick courthouse in the center. On the far side, Mr.

Greer was sweeping the sidewalk in front of the Palace Theater, getting ready for the afternoon matinee. Above his head, the marquee advertised a double feature: *King Kong*, with Fay Wray, and *Dora's Dunking Doughnuts*, featuring Shirley Temple, the curly-haired little girl that everybody had fallen in love with.

Since it was Saturday, trading day, the square was crowded with people. Farmers and their families had driven their mules and wagons or ancient Model T Fords into town to trade eggs and butter—and live chickens and fresh-picked sweet corn and watermelons—for coffee and sugar and salt and washing powder at Hancock's Grocery. Others had come to buy tools or equipment at Musgrove's Hardware or Mann's Mercantile. Young women, dressed in their best pastel voiles and floral print chiffons and white summer shoes, had come to be seen and admired, while the young men leaning nonchalantly against the storefronts had come to see and admire—and occasionally, to dare a low wolf whistle that the young women in question demurely pretended not to hear.

As Lizzy and Verna paused on the corner, surveying the crowd, Lizzy went back to the subject of the murder. "I'm afraid I can't get Rona Jean out of my mind," she confessed. "It must be awful for Bettina, too, losing her roommate that way. I hope she'll be able to find somebody else to move in with her."

"She'll have to," Verna replied. "She doesn't earn enough at the Bower to afford the rent on that house all by herself." She frowned. "You don't suppose Bettina is somehow involved in the murder, do you? I mean, I could imagine a scenario where a woman stole her roommate's boyfriend and the roommate got angry and killed her. Can't you? Theoretically, I mean."

"I suppose so," Lizzy said, as they were about to cross the street. "But I can't imagine Bettina Higgens doing that. I don't think she's the type to get jealous, even theoretically. Do you, really?"

"Well, still waters run deep, you know. It's very hard to know what's going on inside her. And anyway, she might know something that would give us a clue to Rona Jean's murder."

Give *us* a clue? Lizzy smiled to herself. She understood the way Verna's mind worked. If there was something mysterious going on anywhere, Verna always wanted to know what it was, who was involved, and what they were up to—and she went to great lengths to find out, even when it was none of her business.

"Don't you think Sheriff Norris has already talked to her?" she asked. "I'd imagine that she would be at the top of his interview list." They paused on the sidewalk. Lizzy was going straight ahead, to the post office, and Verna was turning right, to go to the grocery.

"Probably. But that doesn't necessarily mean that she told him everything she knows," Verna remarked. "And she may know something she doesn't know. If you know what I mean."

"Ah," Lizzy said, with a light laugh. That was Verna, always on the case. "You're probably thinking of having a little talk with her, aren't you?"

"I'd like to," Verna said, "but I'm not sure I'll have time today. Which brings me to the favor I wanted to ask you, Liz. Captain Campbell is coming for dinner this evening. That's why I'm going to the grocery. Mrs. Hancock is saving a stewing hen for me—only twenty cents a pound. I'm going to make a chicken pot pie."

"Captain Campbell?" Lizzy asked. "Who's he? Didn't you just tell us you are still seeing Alvin Duffy?"

Verna had been a widow since her husband, Walter, stepped out in front of a Greyhound bus on Route 12. Their marriage had not been a happy one, and she had always sworn that another man was the last thing in the world she wanted. But when she met Alvin Duffy, she had changed her tune. She had updated her hairstyle, gotten several chic new hats from Fannie Champaign, and bought herself some stylish new clothes.

The "new Verna" had definitely impressed Alvin Duffy. Now president of the Darling Savings and Trust, he had taken the position after the previous president, George E. Pickett Johnson, had died of a sudden heart attack. Actually, every citizen of Darling thanked the good Lord that Mr. Alvin Duffy had come along, for he was the man who—practically single-handedly—had kept the town going during the banking crises of the previous year.

"Yes, I'm still seeing Al," Verna replied, with a wave of her hand. "Captain Campbell is a friend of his. He's also the commandant at the CCC camp and *very* good-looking—tall, dark hair, blue eyes, in his forties. His first name is Gordon. And he's a widower. I think you'll like him, Liz, even if he is a Yankee. I'm sure he'll like you."

"*I'll* like him?" Lizzy asked, surprised.

"When you meet him. Tonight." Verna gave her a look that just missed being anxious, and Lizzy understood that for some reason, this was important to Verna. "You will come for dinner, won't you? I mean, four for dinner is much more fun than three. Al speaks *very* highly of the captain. And of course, the CCC is doing important things for Cypress County—and can do much more, with a little encouragement." She shook her head. "It's amazing, what a little government money can do."

"I'm sure it is, Verna, but I don't see what that has to do with my coming to dinner."

But Verna wasn't listening. "You probably already know about the upgrade to the Jericho Road," she went on enthusiastically, "and the new bridge that's been built over Pine Mill Creek, to replace the one that was washed out a couple of years ago. But maybe you haven't heard about the dam they're thinking of constructing out there. Al says it could create a sixty-acre lake. He's hoping that the CCC will build some boating and camping facilities, like the ones they built over at Sipsey River, and maybe even a lodge. Why, it might even become a state park!"

"Oh, really?" Lizzy murmured. "Mr. Duffy is such a cheerleader." She was beginning to get the picture.

"Yes, really!" Verna waved her arms excitedly. "Just think what that would do for Cypress County, Liz! The lake would attract people from all over the state. And everybody would have to drive right through Darling to get there!" She dropped her arms. "Of course, this is all in the thinking stages now, but if it happens, it could change sleepy little Darling forever. It could catapult us into the *future*."

Lizzy wanted to say that she liked sleepy little Darling pretty much the way it was, with its small-town heart planted, like a green and pleasant garden, in the past, not the future. But she was afraid that might sound selfish, especially when Verna was so excited about the possibilities. And maybe she was wishing for something that couldn't be. Maybe a town and its citizens always had to look toward the future, with more people and more businesses and more roads and schools and everything else that went with it. Except, of course, in fiction. Maybe that was why she had set her novel in the past.

She smiled and said what any friend would say. "So you would like me to come to dinner and be sweet to the captain. Make him want to give Darling a lake and boating facilities and a lodge."

"Exactly!" Verna exclaimed, beaming. "Al and I first met him at a town meeting a couple of weeks ago, when he came to report on some of the possibilities for land development that the CCC officials are considering. That's when I thought of having him over for dinner—but Al didn't tell me until this morning that he's available for tonight. Al is going to bring a map of the county and some photographs, to give the captain an idea of the terrain around the new lake."

"It doesn't sound much like a double date," Lizzy said with a little laugh. "It sounds more like a sales meeting—you and Al selling him on the beauties and benefits of Cypress County and the possibilities of a state park."

Verna was unfazed. "Well, you might think of it like that, I suppose. The men are coming about seven. You'll do me a very large favor and come, too? Pretty please?"

Lizzy nodded. "Yes, I'll come. And I'll be sweet as pie to your captain." She narrowed her eyes. "But you are going to owe me, Verna."

"Anything you say." Verna looked vastly relieved. "Oh, and if you see your chance, you could mention that man you saw at the movie with Rona Jean. He might be able to tell us who it was, right off the bat."

"Yes, Miss Marple," Lizzy said. "Can I bring something for dinner? A salad, maybe? I have cucumbers in the garden and the last of the spring lettuce. Oh, and tomatoes."

"Perfect. We'll have chicken pot pie and fresh sweet corn, and Raylene has promised to save one of her famous lemon meringue pies for me."

Lizzy grinned. "Well, gosh, Verna. With all that, you should be able to wrap the captain around your little finger."

"No." Verna returned the grin impishly. "Around *your* little finger."

# SEVEN

# Sheriff Norris Learns a Few Facts of Life

When Buddy followed Bettina into Rona Jean Hancock's bedroom, the first thing he noticed was the heat, for the room had been closed all night and the air was heavy and hot. The second was Rona Jean's perfume, a floral fragrance that tickled the back of his throat and made him want to sneeze.

"Blue Waltz," Bettina replied when he asked. "From Lima's Drugstore." She went to the window and heaved up the sash. "It's a nice perfume, as long as you don't wear too much of it."

He agreed about the "too much" and was glad she had opened the window. The room could stand a good airing. "Maybe you could tell me where she kept her diary."

"I have no idea. She hid it. The bedroom doors don't have any keys, and I guess she didn't trust me not to read it if she left it lying around." She stood awkwardly in the doorway for a moment, arms crossed. "If you don't need me, I'd better go to work. It's a holiday coming up, and Beulah and I are going to be behind. I don't mind if you stay and look for . . . whatever."

"Thank you." He was glad that she wouldn't be standing there, looking over his shoulder. He added, "You've been a big help. I appreciate it."

She looked away. "I owe you an apology. About that slapping business, I mean. I should have known that you wouldn't . . . I mean, being a sheriff and all. It's just that— well, it's happened to me, and to other girls I know. I guess I just thought . . ." She brushed a lock of brown hair off her forehead. "That all men are alike when it comes to that, I mean. It was easy to believe."

For a moment, Buddy was struck by her vulnerability— by the vulnerability of all women. "I'm sorry," he said. "That it happened to you, or to anybody else. That's not right." He wanted to add that being a gentleman had nothing to do with being a sheriff, but he didn't. "Thanks for giving me the benefit of the doubt. I'll lock the front door when I leave."

"Please do," she said, and turned away. A few moments later, he heard the front door close.

He looked around, feeling large and bumbling and intrusive, like a bully on the school playground. Rona Jean's bedroom was messy. The bed was unmade, and clothes were strewn on the floor and the only chair in the room. He tried not to look at the filmy underwear, and the stockings reminded him of how she'd been strangled. There were dresses and blouses and skirts hanging haphazardly in the closet and three or four pairs of shoes on the floor. The closet shelf was crowded with various hats (Rona Jean seemed to be a collector), and a couple of hats hung on hooks on the wall. He recognized one of them, an olive green felt helmet-like affair with a peacock feather trim—the hat she had worn when they went to the Methodist pie social. He remembered it because the preacher's wife had come up and admired it loudly and asked Buddy if he didn't like it, too, and he'd had to say that he did, when he didn't.

He wandered over to the dressing table, with bottles and tubes and little jars of makeup scattered on its top and dance cards and tickets and mementoes stuck into the mirror frame. He noticed a couple of photographs, one of Rona Jean and a man he didn't recognize, the other of Rona Jean and Violet. The photograph with the man had the name *Lamar* written on the back, and a date in the previous month. He took both and put them into his notebook.

A few moments later, he found Rona Jean's red leather diary in the bottom bureau drawer under a blue cardboard box of Kotex. He felt himself blushing as he picked up the box. One end was open and something fell onto the floor, a long and narrow white rectangular pad covered with gauzy stuff with long flaps on both ends. He picked it up quickly and stuffed it back in the box, then noticed a narrow pink elastic belt lying on the floor, probably also fallen out of the box. He picked it up, fingering it curiously and noticing two little cloth tabs with tiny brass safety pins. He had seen ads for Kotex, of course, but he'd had no clear idea what they looked like, or that a girl *pinned* them on. The rig must be pretty damned uncomfortable, he thought. Then, feeling suddenly that he had no right to be looking at something so intimately *female*, he dropped the belt back into the box and put the box in the drawer and pushed it shut.

After the Kotex and belt, the small red leather diary did not seem all that personal, and he sat down on the bed and began to leaf through it. The cover bore a gilt-embossed *1934*, and there was a separate lined page for each day, with the day's date and the day of the week printed at the top. The pages carried the scent of Rona Jean's perfume, and she wrote in purple ink, in a loopy feminine script with a flourish of capitals and small circles for the dots over the letters *i* and *j*—the same ink and the same script in the letter she had sent him.

Unfortunately, Rona Jean had not been a dedicated diarist, and only about half of the pages were filled, mostly with rambling complaints about her work at the Telephone Exchange and her irritation with her roommate, who was (as Rona Jean put it) "not a very fun person to live with and as bad to nag as my mom about keeping things picked up." He would study it in detail later, but he thought he should give it a quick once-over, in case there was something immediately useful. And besides, he was curious, especially about (*admit it, Norris*) what she had written about him.

He went back to April, when he had first taken her out, and found notations of their dates on three consecutive weekends. The first was headed, *Buddy Norris, church pie supper.* On that day, she wrote that she had worn her green dress and green felt hat—he'd forgotten about the dress. *Likes to have me laugh at his jokes, kissed me good night (not a very good kisser).* Buddy squirmed, feeling his face redden. What the hell was wrong with the way he kissed? Other girls had never objected, and *she* had certainly seemed to be enjoying it at the time.

The following weekend, it was, *Buddy, CCC dance, not a very good dancer* (which was undeniably true: he didn't know his right foot from his left) *but got to dance with lots of guys.* He hadn't minded her dancing with lots of guys. In fact, he had thought it was swell that she was having so much fun. Afterward, they'd sat on the back porch where he'd kissed her and a little more, but she didn't write anything about that, whether she thought it was good or bad or just plain indifferent.

The weekend after the dance, the last weekend in April,

was when things changed. *Buddy for supper*, she had written, and under that, contemptuously, *Babe in the woods*, with a frowning face. Well, she had him pegged there, he reckoned, as far as sex was concerned. He wasn't a totally new hand at the game—there was Claudia back in high school and Irma Joy a couple of years ago and a couple of brief encounters that he didn't remember with a great deal of pride or even pleasure. But it was obvious that Rona Jean knew a heckuva lot more about sex than he did. And after his talk with Mr. Moseley this morning, he was relieved that things had turned out the way they had.

That was it for his appearances in her diary. During the first week of June, she wrote that as soon as she got the money for a ticket, she was going to hop on the railroad train and ride it to Nashville or Chicago or New York, or maybe even to San Francisco. But a couple of pages later, she wrote that leaving Darling meant leaving Violet behind, and Violet was her "one true friend." She went on:

> I haven't told Bettina anything about it, because she would only frown and make ugly faces at me. And anyway she won't do a thing but lecture. Violet is the only one I can count on in this whole entire town to help me out of this mess. She says if I go through with it, she'll give me the money for all the bills, before and after, and I can leave it there.
>
> Which means I can save my money for a ticket. But Myra May is right. It's going to take more than just a train ticket. I want to have enough to keep me going until I can find work. Which might take a while, bad as things are these days. So I need to hold out for more.

Puzzled, Buddy took out his notebook and copied both paragraphs, noting the day they were written and underlining *help me out of this mess* and *give me the money for all the bills, before and after, and I can leave it there.* He would have to ask Violet to tell him what kind of mess it was and what kind of before-and-after bills Rona Jean was talking about. Or maybe he should ask Myra May. Or both. He considered. Yeah, maybe it would be good to get them together and ask them both at the same time—surprise them with the question, so they couldn't put their heads together and agree on an explanation. He wanted the *truth*.

He went back to the beginning of the year and noted all the names of friends that he found on the pages, both men and women, along with the dates and places they'd gone, if that was included. There were other notations and abbreviations, too. On the small calendar for December 1933, and in January and February, she had made Xs on five or six of the pages, all during the first week of the month—maybe Bettina would know what that meant, or Violet. And on a couple of the pages on which she had written a name or mentioned going out with someone, she had also drawn a little Valentine heart with an arrow through it in a lower corner of the page. There were no hearts on his pages, though. Another mystery. He would definitely have to ask.

When he was finished, he looked down at his list, seeing the names of two men he knew (not including his own): Beau Pyle and Lamar Lassen, whose photograph had been displayed on Rona Jean's mirror. There were names of two other men he didn't know: Jack Baker and Ray (no last name). There were two others—not clear whether these were men or women—with just initials: B.P., who was mentioned twice, recently; and DR mentioned once, with a phone number over in Monroeville. For Friday night, last night, the night she'd been killed, there was no notation. The last name in the diary was

Violet's. They'd gone to the movies on the Sunday afternoon before Rona Jean was killed.

Buddy put his notebook in his pocket, then began looking through the drawers in the vanity table for stationery and envelopes, hoping to find an address book and maybe even a few letters. He found a flat gold box of the same unlined pink writing paper Rona Jean had used to write the letter to him. But there was no address book, and if she was saving letters other people had written to her, they weren't in the box. But he found something else of even greater interest: a stack of twenty-dollar bills—$140, when Buddy counted them out— with a rubber band around it. He looked down at the money, trying to decide what to do with it. Finally, he put it in his wallet, then wrote out a signed and dated receipt for $140 on one of his notebook pages and stuck it in Rona Jean's dressing table mirror.

He thought for a moment, remembering what Bettina had said about Rona Jean always borrowing from her. But here was $140 in twenties—a lot of money. How had she gotten it? Who gave it to her? Why? And was there more money stashed around the room?

There wasn't, at least not that he could find. A few moments later, taking the diary with him, he put on his hat, locked the front door, and left.

Even though Buddy left the windows rolled down as much as he could, the upholstery in the patrol car still smelled of Sheriff Burns' cigars, the cheap ones Roy bought at Pete's Pool Parlor. Buddy missed the cranky old man who had become his friend as well as his boss, and it saddened him to think he'd gotten the job of sheriff over Roy's dead body, so to speak. Well, that was the way life was, he reckoned. You might could get what you wanted, but it came with strings, some of which you couldn't see until they started pulling on you. Roy hadn't wanted to die down in that creek canyon, Buddy knew that much. But if Roy had had a choice in the matter, Buddy was about 99 percent sure he would have pinned the star on *him.*

He started the car, drove up to the corner, and made a right, then a left on Rosemont, heading toward the square. Today was Saturday, and as he drove past the Cypress County courthouse, the streets were already crowded. The courthouse was an imposing two-story red brick building with a bell tower topped by a white-painted dome. The tower had a clock that struck the quarter hours so regularly you could set your watch by it. Built in 1905 after the big tornado tore down the earlier structure, the courthouse was surrounded on all four sides by an apron of green grass bordered with pretty yellow and orange flowers planted by the Darling Dahlias. The club maintained several gardens around town, on the theory that when times were hard, a few pretty flowers went a long way toward uplifting people's low spirits. And when times were better, the same pretty flowers made people feel like celebrating the fact that they lived in a town where other people cared enough to keep things looking spiffy.

The square looked even spiffier than usual, Buddy thought. In honor of the Fourth of July celebration next week, the members of the American Legion Post had already planted a festive row of little American flags around the courthouse. They had also hung rug-size American and Confederate flags from the courthouse windows, draped bunting from the streetlights around the square, and slung a big banner across Robert E. Lee Street, declaring, DARLING: THE BEST LITTLE TOWN IN THE SOUTH.

The Fourth was always a crackerjack day, featuring a

swell parade, with the Academy marching band, veterans of the War Between the States (sadly, they were fewer in number every year), and a float featuring Miss Darling and Little Miss Darling. And best of all, the CCC camp boys, nearly two hundred of them, would be there to march, wearing their uniforms and carrying shovels over their shoulders instead of guns—"Roosevelt's Tree Army," people were calling it. President Roosevelt was a tree man himself, it was said, having reforested his family's depleted land on the Hudson River by planting hundreds of thousands of trees.

Darling itself had a great many trees, which helped to make it beautiful. While Buddy was no expert on the matter, he subscribed to the opinion that when a town's surroundings were clean and pleasant, people were more contented and less likely to commit crimes. Of course, there would always be a few malcontents complaining about this and that and the other thing, and occasional terrible crimes, like what had happened to Rona Jean. But for the most part, people thought their little town was a fine place to live, especially now that the camp was established and there were more jobs and more money to spend. And soon there would be more trees, thanks to the CCC boys.

Trees had been an important part of Darling's life from the very beginning. The town was nestled in the gently rolling hills a few miles east of the Alabama River and seventy miles north of Mobile. Buddy had often heard Bessie Bloodworth, the town's historian, tell the story of its founding. According to her, it had been established in the early 1800s by Joseph P. Darling, a Virginian who was following a faint wagon trail through the area. With him were his wife, five children, two slaves, a team of oxen, a pair of milk cows, and a horse. Joseph P. was on his way to create a cotton plantation on the Mississippi River, but his wife was sick and tired of bouncing along in that wagon day in and day out, baking biscuits over a campfire and washing diapers in a lard bucket. At this point in her story, Bessie would repeat what she thought Mrs. Darling might have said.

"You can do as you like, Mr. Darling, but I am not ridin' another mile in that blessed wagon. If you're lookin' for your meals and your washin' to be done reg'lar, right here is where you'll find 'em."

Mr. Darling (who was fond of his grub and liked a clean shirt every now and then) surveyed the dense stands of timber and the fertile soils, the nearby river and the fast-flowing creek beside which they were camped, and—all things considered, but especially the grub—decided that the little valley might be a good place to live, after all. He cut down enough pine trees to build a barn and two log cabins, a big one for his family and a small one for his slaves. Then (because Mr. Darling's interests took an entrepreneurial turn) he cut down more trees and built the Darling General Store (now Mann's Mercantile). Then he ordered some store stock, put on an apron, and waited for the customers to come.

And come they did. In those early days, the hills were covered with a virgin forest of loblolly and longleaf pines, with sweet gum and tulip trees in the river bottom, and magnolia and sassafras and sycamore and pecan anywhere their roots could find good water. Hearing that the timber was so fine, Mr. Darling's cousin came from Virginia to build a sawmill, so that all those pine trees could be turned into boards for houses and barns. And houses and barns were needed, because the settlers who had also heard of the plentiful timber and fertile soil were also on their way.

Since the settlers were mostly farmers, they cleared the land for crops by cutting even more trees. In fact, over the next few decades, lumber became a very profitable business, in part because the Alabama River could be used to float the logs in huge rafts down to the port city of Mobile, on Mobile Bay. Before long, the lumber industry in Mobile was loading millions of feet of sawn boards on ships bound for Cuba, Europe, South America, and even the California gold fields. About the same time, the demand for paper began to rise, and paper mills sprouted like mushrooms throughout Alabama's forests, turning the low-grade timber to paper and shipping it via the newly built railroads to major cities all over the country.

But since it never occurred to anybody that they ought to plant more trees to replace the trees that had been cut down, it wasn't long before pretty much all of the original forest had totally disappeared. The hillsides were starkly denuded, the soil was eroding, and even people who didn't know a loblolly from a longleaf had begun to understand that something had to be done to save the land.

Which was, Buddy thought as he slowed to let a little girl holding on to a big red balloon skip across the street in front of him, maybe the biggest reason to be grateful to the CCC. Speaking at a recent town meeting, the commandant had announced that over the next two years, the camp was scheduled to receive half a million pine seedlings, fifty thousand black locusts, two thousand five hundred catalpa, and (to help control soil erosion) a quarter of a million kudzu crowns. The pines would mostly be fast-growing loblollies that could put on a couple of feet of height a year. This meant that within a decade, the trees would be twenty feet tall and ready for harvest—a more selective harvest this time, which would leave enough trees standing to prevent erosion and ensure the continuity of the forest. The CCC boys would begin planting in January (tree-planting time), on several thousand cut-over acres out by Briar's Swamp. When they were finished with that section, they would go on to others. This had been welcome news, and the commandant (Buddy had forgotten his name) had been given a big round of applause.

Buddy shifted into second gear and made a left turn onto Franklin. He drove west for half a block and turned right into the alley behind Snow's Farm Supply. The sheriff's office was located in what had been a small frame house on the back of the lot, and the jail was upstairs over the Farm Supply. This handy arrangement made it easy to keep an eye on the jail, which was usually occupied only on Saturday night and Sunday by one or two of the local fellows who had indulged a little too freely in the local moonshine. Following the practice of his predecessor, Buddy booked them on drunk and disorderly, let them sleep it off overnight, then released them on Sunday in time to get cleaned up and shaved and make it to morning worship at the church of their choice—in lieu of a fine. Sheriff Burns (himself a fervent Methodist) had liked to brag that some of his D and Ds had gotten saved and sworn off the bottle, at least for a while.

Wayne Springer's old 1927 Chevy was parked on the gravel strip in front of the office, and the COME IN sign hung face out on the front door, which meant that the office was open. Buddy went in and slung his hat onto the wall peg.

"Yo, Springer," he called. The place smelled like fresh coffee.

"Back here," Wayne replied.

Buddy found his deputy hunched with a magnifying glass over fingerprint cards, at the scarred pine-topped table in what once had been the back bedroom, now a workroom and conference room. A Royal typewriter sat on the table (the deputy was a pretty good typist), and on a shelf beside the table, a radio was playing "Oh, You Beautiful Doll." Wayne reached over and turned down the volume. The coffee percolator was burping on the hot plate beside it, and

Buddy poured himself a mug. He liked it black and strong, which was a good thing, because when Wayne brewed it, that's how it was. Strong enough to lift a locomotive.

Wayne Springer was tall and rail-thin, with a beaked nose that looked as if he had inherited it from a Cherokee ancestor (which he had), in a narrow, sun-darkened face, and he preferred a battered felt cowboy hat to his deputy's uniform cap. Buddy had hired him because he had five years of experience as a deputy over in Jefferson County, where he'd worked with a bigger and more up-to-date sheriff's office and had gone through a law enforcement training program.

But what was even more important to Buddy's way of thinking was the fact that Wayne came from Birmingham. He had no local baggage or history or kin, unlike the dozen or so other men who had applied for the job, five or six of them with daddies who had political muscle in the county and fully expected to be hired. Buddy thought it would be better to bring in somebody who was essentially unknown and didn't have any special friends or foes. Wayne had smarts and he definitely knew his business. He also had more experience than Buddy, especially when it came to handling a .38 Special, the standard cop gun. (Buddy was a fair shot when it came to pinging cans on a fence, but he'd never gotten used to the idea that he might actually have to shoot *somebody*.) And so far, Wayne had been easy to work with. But they were still trying each other out.

Buddy peered over Wayne's shoulder. The deputy had dusted the dark surfaces of Myra May's car with Chemist Gray Powder made of mercury and chalk, then lifted the prints with strips of that handy new Scotch cellulose tape. Still at the scene, he had transferred the print tapes to individual cards and labeled them with the site where he'd lifted them (the steering wheel, the gearshift, the door handle) and the date and time. Now, he was sorting and classifying them, getting ready to make comparisons.

Wayne sniffed. "You been usin' *perfume?*"

"I was searching the victim's bedroom," Buddy said. "Is it bad?"

"Not as long as you don't get too close."

Buddy stepped back. Looking down at Wayne's work, he said, "You get the prints of the ladies at the diner and the Telephone Exchange?"

"Yeah." Wayne nodded at a thin stack of cards at the corner of the table. "From all the weepin' and moanin' that went on, you'da thought their fingers would be purple forever." The fingerprint kit contained a purple ink pad that some people objected to using.

"Females are like that," Buddy remarked. "Where you at on that job?"

"Just getting organized. There were lots of prints on that car, but I'm focusing on the doors, the front seat area, and the dashboard. Miss Mosswell is supposed to be giving me a list of everybody that's been in that car in the past month— could be three or four more, on top of the ladies I printed this morning. They'll all have to be excluded." Wayne's voice was flat, uninflected, unexcited. Buddy liked that about him. "Anything that's left could belong to our man. There's a good one on the driver's side door handle that I haven't found a match for yet. A thumbprint with a scar."

"Yeah. Well, stay with it, Wayne," Buddy said, congratulating himself on hiring somebody precise and methodical enough to do a picky job like matching prints. "Could be what's needed to get a conviction."

He went into his office, in what had once been the dining room of the house, and set the coffee mug on the corner of his desk. Taking down a large brown envelope and a smaller white envelope from a supply shelf, he slid Rona Jean's diary into the brown one and the $140 in twenties into the white one, labeled both, and dated them. He raised his voice, speaking through the open door.

"Nothing from Doc Roberts yet, I reckon?" He was asking just to be sure. Even if the doctor had gotten to Rona Jean first thing, he wouldn't call with the results until after he'd written the report—unless there was something extra special he wanted to pass on.

"Nope," Wayne replied. "Nothing. Been quiet as the grave since I got here. Except for the weather report, just before you came in. Might want to keep an eye on the sky today."

"Oh yeah?" Buddy opened the top drawer of the scarred wooden desk and slid the envelopes into it. "What's happening?"

"Storm pushin' in off the Gulf right about now. Could be a hurricane."

"Just what we need," Buddy said darkly, remembering the last hurricane that had blown through Darling, maybe ten years before. It had crossed the Gulf Coast west of Mobile, ripped the roof off Jake Pritchard's Standard Oil station, blown in windows and torn up fine old trees all over town, and sent Pine Mill Creek out of its banks, flooding pastures and drowning old Tate Haggard's cows. Buddy had been in high school then, and remembered that the sheriff had imposed a curfew and helped the mayor organize the cleanup. He probably ought to talk to Jed Snow, the current mayor, and figure out what they should do if this storm turned out to be a bad one.

He was reaching for the phone to call Jed when it rang. "Sheriff's Office," he said. He always liked what came next. "Sheriff Norris speakin'."

"Buddy, this is Edna Fay Roberts," a woman's voice said. "Doc called a little while ago. He wanted me to call you."

Buddy sat down, picked up a pencil, and pulled a piece of scratch paper toward him. Edna Fay was the doctor's nurse as well as his wife. She might have news about the autopsy. "Is he finished?"

"Yes." Then, in a louder voice, she said, "Henrietta Conrad, if you're still on the line, I'll thank you to get off, if you don't mind." There was a pause and then a click, as the Exchange operator broke the connection. "Those switchboard girls," Edna Fay said, in a tsk-tsk voice. "Myra May tells them it's against the rules for them to listen in, but they do it anyway, especially on the doctor's line. Probably on the sheriff's line, too. They like to think they're getting the latest news hot off the wire."

"That's the truth," Buddy remarked pleasantly, putting down the pencil and taking a sip of coffee. He had known Edna Fay since he was a kid, for he'd been accident prone and frequently ended up in Doc Roberts' office getting stitched and splinted. In his experience, the lady was a talker. If you gave her an inch, she'd take the rest of the morning, and by noon, you'd be no wiser. But there was no hurrying her. She had to go at her own pace.

"It purely is," Edna Fay said. "Anyway, Doc said to tell you that she was hit on the head—the right temple, actually. Hard enough to produce a skull fracture. He says it was probably something like a beer bottle."

"Hit on the head?" Buddy picked up a pencil and wrote *hit on the head* on the scratch paper. Then: *beer bottle.* "I missed that."

"Doc said it'd be easy to miss," Edna Fay said. "It was in the hairline. And yes, she was strangled, no surprise there. But not with her stocking."

"Wait a minute," he said, frowning. "I saw the body myself. There was a stocking around her neck."

"Yes. There was a stocking around her neck. But she was strangled with a rope. A hemp rope. Doc said he could tell by the bruises, and by some hemp fibers that broke off and got embedded in her skin. The stocking came later. Afterward."

"Ah," Buddy said. "I see." The stocking might have been added to make it look more like a sexual assault. He jotted the words *hemp rope* on the scratch paper.

"Doc said it wasn't just real easy to fix a time of death," Edna Fay said. "He guesses it's around midnight, give or take. But he also found——"

She broke off and Buddy drew a circle on his scratch paper. "Darla Ann," she said in an exasperated tone to some-body on her end of the line, "I thought you were supposed to be hanging those sheets out. What are you waitin' for?"

Buddy put clock hands inside the circle, pointing to five minutes to twelve o'clock. There was a murmuring voice and a pause, then Edna Fay said, "Well, go next door and see if Mrs. Barker has any clothespins you can borrow until I can get over to Mann's to buy another package." To Buddy, she said, "I swear, that girl breaks more clothespins every wash day than a normal person would in a month." She paused. "Where were we?"

"Yes'm," Buddy said, and drew a diamond around the clock. "You were saying that Rona Jean—Miss Hancock—was hit on the head and then strangled with a rope, not her stocking. What about assault?" He reminded himself that Edna Fay was a nurse. "Sexual assault," he added.

"No evidence of sexual assault, is what he said," Edna Fay replied cheerily. "And——" She broke off. "Lord, Darla Ann, what is it *now*?"

This time the murmur was louder and more querulous and the pause was longer. While he waited, Buddy wrote *no assalt* under the diamond. He frowned at the word, which didn't look right, crossed it out, and wrote *assallt*. He was glad, for Rona Jean's sake. But if she hadn't been killed fighting off her killer's advances, why had she been killed?

Edna Fay was back on the line, and this time, she was fit to be tied.

"Buddy, you are not going to believe this, but Darla Ann knocked out the prop and down came the clothesline, with all the clean sheets and towels on it. Right down in the dirt, and of course they were still sopping wet, which means they are *muddy*."

"Sorry 'bout that," Buddy said, and drew a big square around the diamond. "You said there was no evidence of assault and—" He paused, hoping she'd fill in the blank.

"Yes, no assault," Edna Fay said. "And no evidence of recent intercourse. But he was surprised when he saw that—" She raised her voice. "Darla Ann, I'll be out there in a minute, soon as I finish on this phone. You start unpinning them off the line and put them in the basket. Shake off as much of that mud as you can. I don't want to have to wash them again if we don't have to."

*Intercourse?* Buddy was shocked. He had read the word, of course, and he knew what it meant, in his own experience. But the guys he knew used other words for it, and he had never heard anybody—let alone a woman—actually utter the word. But then, Edna Fay was a nurse and probably used to talking that way. *No intercorse*, he wrote, and drew two heavy lines under it. "You were saying that when he did the autopsy, Doc was surprised," he prompted. "Surprised about what?"

"I was saying?" She sounded distracted. "Oh, yes. He said she was about four months. Now, if you'll excuse me, that poor girl I've got workin' for me has absolutely no brains in her head at all. I am going to have to get out there and rescue those sheets myself."

*Four months*, Buddy wrote. He frowned. "Four months? Four months what?"

Edna Fay's laugh tinkled over the telephone wire. "Oh, Buddy, you are so *funny*. Why, four months pregnant, of course."

Buddy's pencil lead snapped.

# EIGHT

# Charlie Dickens: A Newsman in Search of a Story

Whistling the cheerful refrain of "Dixie," Charlie Dickens pushed his bicycle through the front door of the *Dispatch* office and leaned it against the inside sill of the wide front window. He was hanging his straw boater and light blue seersucker suit coat on the coat tree in the corner when he heard a male voice.

"Mornin', Mr. Dickens. Wasn't lookin' for you to come in today—it bein' Saturday and all."

Taking a deep breath of the combined fragrances of ink, kerosene, and newsprint that always hit him when he came into the office, Charlie turned to see Purley Mann leaning on a broom, an inky rag sticking out of the rear pocket of his overalls. Purley's fine, silvery blond hair, cherubic face, and mild manner had earned him the nickname Baby when he was a kid, and he'd never outgrown it. Folks said that Baby hadn't been at the head of the line when the Lord was handing out smarts, but Charlie had found him to be a good worker. He kept the place clean and helped operate the presses—the arthritic Prouty job press that had to be coaxed into producing handbills and advertisements and the like and the demonic Babcock that shook the floors and rattled the windows. The blasted thing had always given Charlie heartburn, but for Baby, who spent hours fixing and fine-tuning and polishing it, the Babcock purred like a kitten.

Ophelia Snow was Charlie's other helper. To his surprise, she had proved to be a whiz at the Linotype, a balky machine that women weren't supposed to have the strength to operate. She was a good writer and willing to report on the Darling social events—women's clubs, church events, and bridal and baby showers—that Charlie himself hated to cover. And recently, she'd taken a part-time office job at the CCC camp, so Charlie had given her a weekly assignment, "The Camp Briarwood News," under her byline. She had already written three columns and was doing a commendable job, picking up little anecdotes here and there and weaving them into a read-able, often amusing little story. And yesterday, Charlie had talked her into doing some extra investigating on the side.

"Wasn't lookin' to come in today, Baby," Charlie replied, going to his desk. "But then I got the news about Rona Jean's murder. Figured it might be a good idea to put out a special edition. So let's get ready for an extra print run on Tuesday." He pulled a handkerchief out of his back pocket and wiped the sweat off his face. It was another hot day, after too many hot days. The radio had mentioned the possibility of a storm. A good thing, if it would break the heat.

Baby had brightened at the mention of a special edition. The Babcock was his pet and he loved to run it. But then he remembered what the special edition was about and put on a doleful expression. "Terrible thing, that murder."

"That's right," Charlie said. *Terrible for Rona Jean*, he

thought—*but good for circulation.* There was nothing like a murder to entice folks to read the newspaper. He could charge thirty-five cents for the special edition, and who knows? They might sell as many as three or four hundred papers, and the only out-of-pocket cost would be the extra ink and newsprint.

Charlie had grown up in Darling and returned after a long and successful career as an investigative reporter. He had worked for the *Baltimore Sun* and the Cleveland *Plain Dealer* and the *Fort Worth Star-Telegram*, assignments sandwiched between a couple of stretches in the Associated Press wire service office in New York. He could smell a story a mile off and refused to rest until he had tracked it down, no matter how far he had to go or what he had to do to get it. The stories that paid off in the most column inches were sensational crime stories, of course—murders, kidnappings, bank robberies—and stories about fraud or political corruption. Crime made scorching front-page news, and Charlie had scrapbooks crammed with his bylined clips to prove it.

But lately, he had begun to fear that he was losing his newshound's nose for a good story. There was very little crime in Darling, a tame, two-bit town that was a newsman's arid desert. For months on end, what happened was so unexciting, so unremarkable and utterly non-newsworthy that Charlie could write the stories in his sleep.

And if Darling was a two-bit town, it had to be said that the *Dispatch* was a two-bit newspaper. Charlie had inherited it when his editor-publisher father died of cancer. He had never intended to keep it, planning to invest just enough effort to keep it going until he found a buyer for it. That plan might have worked, too, but then the Crash came and nobody wanted to put scarce money into a small-town newspaper with a serious shortage of paid advertising and an even greater shortage of news. Like it or not, Charlie was stranded here in

Darling, a realization that had not done wonders for his disposition—until Fannie Champaign had agreed to marry him, that is. After that, things were noticeably different. Better. Much better.

Now, Charlie loosened his tie, rolled up his sleeves, put on his green celluloid eyeshade, and sat down at his battered old wooden desk. He opened the bottom right-hand drawer and pulled out a bottle—a bottle of warm, flat Hires Root Beer. Last year at this time, it would have been a bottle of Mickey LeDoux's best, but not now. For one thing, Mickey's still had been busted and a young boy killed (that was the last big news story Charlie had written), and Mickey had spent eleven months or so in the slammer. He would be up and shining again in a few weeks, though, and many in Darling would raise their glasses in celebration. But Charlie wouldn't be celebrating. He would be drinking Hires. He had promised Fannie to leave the booze alone, and he meant to keep his promise.

Charlie swigged his warm root beer, shaking his head at the thought of himself, a crusty bachelor newspaper reporter who had lived to chase stories and who had never had the least intention of settling down, now a married man who had sworn off the hard stuff. His nomadic experiences had given him a slantwise, skeptical view of settled, small-town life, and he'd seen too many bad marriages to be anything but skeptical about the possibility of marital happiness. But now that he and Fannie were married, he was by God going to make her happy and hope that some of it would rub off on him.

He polished off the last of the root beer and tossed the bottle into the wastebasket with a loud clank. And maybe, just maybe, one of the stories he was chasing right now would turn out to be *the* story. The story he'd been waiting for ever since he'd been marooned in Darling by his father's death.

And it just might happen. For the astonishing fact was that at this very moment, Charlie had *two* stories to work on, either or both of which might prove to be a real doozy, something that the AP or UP wire services would pick up and distribute around the country. Or, better, that he could sell as a bylined special to the *Atlanta Constitution*.

The first story, of course, was Rona Jean Hancock's murder. The minute he got the word, Charlie had picked up his camera and raced for the scene of the crime, where he'd managed to snap a half-dozen photos before the sheriff—the *new* sheriff, Buddy Norris—showed up and told him to knock it off. He couldn't print the photos in the *Dispatch*, which was a family newspaper. But he could use them in his *Constitution* piece or sell them to one of the wire services, which had recently run those dramatic death photos of Bonnie Parker and Clyde Barrow. Bonnie and Clyde had been ambushed and shot to death six weeks before, over in the piney woods of Louisiana. The crowd that had gathered got quickly out of control and the scene turned into a circus. A woman whacked off bloody locks of Bonnie's hair and pieces of her dress to sell as souvenirs. A man tried to cut off Clyde's trigger finger, and others pulled off pieces of the stolen Ford V8 that the pair had been driving. Photos of the bullet-riddled bodies of the notorious pair were plastered across newspapers and magazines coast to coast.

Rona Jean was no gun moll (or if she was, that fact had not yet come to light), and her murder wasn't anywhere near as dramatic as the death of Bonnie Parker. But the photos that Charlie had taken were sensational, to say the least. Not to be insensitive about it, but the fact that the girl—a telephone operator—had been strangled with her very own silk stocking would make for excellent copy. Charlie could see the headline now: *Hello Central, Give Me Heaven.*

And with this story, Charlie was going to break a Darling rule. Up until now, the *Dispatch* would not have dared to report to its readers the news that Doc Roberts' autopsy had revealed that the unmarried victim was pregnant. (Yes, his sister, Edna Fay, who was married to the doctor, had let him in on the secret.) "Only the news that's fit to be read— by your mother," Charlie's father used to grumble, when he couldn't print everything he wanted to print. "Or your grandmother. Or your little sister. It's a curse. It's an obscene, profane, dad-blamed blasphemy, is what it is. No newspaperman worth his salt ought to put up with it." With a sigh, he would add, "But I do. 'Cause if I don't, I get canceled subscriptions from the Baptists and the Methodists and the Catholics and letters to the editor from the rest of 'em."

But Rona Jean's murder was the story *du jour*, and Charlie had decided that it was high time the *Dispatch* joined the modern newspaper world. It was a true fact, attested to by a reliable physician, that the victim was pregnant. And regardless of the unspoken prohibition against printing the word "pregnant" in the *Dispatch*, that fact, and that word, was exactly what he intended to print. He wouldn't put it in the headline, out of deference to tender sensibilities, but it would be there. All by itself, that word would make readers blink and make Rona Jean's murder a very big story, worthy of a special edition.

But the killing of Rona Jean Hancock wasn't the only story Charlie had up his sleeve. In fact, the other one might be even bigger, because of its possible national repercussions. It had come to him the week before via a telephone tip from an anonymous source—a woman—who claimed that there was something seriously fishy and definitely illegal going on at Camp Briarwood. The voice sounded familiar, but Charlie couldn't quite put his finger on who it was.

Anyway, he had been in the newspaper business long enough to know that nine times out of ten, an anonymous tip wasn't worth a plugged nickel.

But then the second tip had come in, from the same source but by mail this time, in the form of a handwritten note. In four sentences, it spelled out what the tipster had said on the phone. It was signed with an obvious pseudonym: *Mata Hari*. Charlie did a double take when he saw that. Mata Hari was a famous exotic dancer accused of being a spy during the Great War.

Now, confronted with these serious claims, Charlie realized that *this* could be his big story, an exposé, exactly the kind of story he needed to get him back into the newspaper game. If he investigated and found out that the charges were true, somebody ought to clean house at the camp and throw out whoever was playing dirty. But who could do that? It couldn't be the camp commander, who might be in on the scheme, and it definitely wasn't a job for Sheriff Norris, who had no jurisdiction. It had to be somebody in the government, didn't it? But how would he get word to the right person?

Charlie had no answers, but he knew someone who might. Using the long-distance line, he tracked down Lorena Hickok—Hick, her friends called her—who had been the top female reporter for the Associated Press when Charlie was working for the wire service in New York. Hick had left the AP the year before and gone to work as a roving chief investigator for Harry Hopkins. Hopkins was head of the Federal Emergency Relief Administration, one of FDR's most important New Deal programs, and responsible for funneling half a billion dollars into federally funded, state-run work projects. FERA's money was government money, big money, and that kind of funding always invited fraud and misuse. Hopkins, who was no dummy, was understandably eager to make sure it was going where it was supposed to go. So he had hired Hick as an investigator-at-large and ordered her to travel around the country, assess the operation of the programs, and report back to him.

Charlie had caught up with Hick late one evening the week before, at the Peabody Hotel in Memphis, where she was staying. As a political reporter during the Tammany Hall bribery scandals of the late 1920s, she'd had plenty of experience investigating bribery and kickbacks. She had listened to Charlie's abbreviated version of Mata Hari's allegations, asked a couple of probing questions, and told him point-blank that he ought to drop whatever else he was doing and start following up on the tip.

"I've seen a few instances of that kind of monkey business in the FERA programs," she said in her gritty, cigarette-roughened voice, "and there's no reason to think the CCC is any cleaner. Sounds like you're onto something, Charlie my boy. Handle it right, and you've got yourself a story—a *big* story." Helpfully, she added, "If you latch onto something, give me a call. I know somebody who hates this kind of dirty dealing, who could maybe pass the word to the top."

"Oh yeah?" Charlie asked. "Who would that be?"

He'd heard that Hick was a close friend of Mrs. Roosevelt's, and everybody knew that the First Lady liked to stick her nose into all of her husband's New Deal programs. "Eleanor Everywhere," people called her. If she got interested in Camp Briarwood, he would *really* have a big story on his hands. Maybe it would even win a Pulitzer, every newspaperman's dream of glory.

"Never mind who." Hick chuckled. "That's my business. You let me know what you've got, and I'll take it from there. But you be careful," she cautioned. "It's no secret that there are bad guys who have their hands in Uncle Sam's pockets. We don't live in a perfect world."

Hick's response had convinced Charlie that he had to go ahead. But this wasn't an investigation he could handle by himself. He needed somebody who had legitimate access to the camp and who could do some surreptitious on-the-scene investigating. And luckily, he knew just the person: Ophelia Snow, who worked part-time in the quartermaster's office out there and knew her way around the camp.

So yesterday, he had asked Ophelia if she would agree to do some "research" for him as an investigative journalist. He had told her that he didn't have the vaguest idea who Mata Hari was, and that while her claims sounded legitimate, he couldn't be sure. That's what Ophelia's investigation was designed to prove. She had been reluctant at first, but he had reminded her how important Camp Briarwood was to Darling and suggested that if there was something crooked going on out there, it could endanger the success of the camp and might even result in its closing. (He didn't really think so, but it was a possibility, wasn't it?) She had finally said yes. Charlie glanced up at the clock. In fact, if all was going according to plan, she might be getting started right about now.

And here in the *Dispatch* office, it was time to get started on the story of Rona Jean's murder. Charlie rolled a sheet of paper into his typewriter, lifted his elbows, flexed his fingers, and leaned forward. The juices were flowing now, and he was ready to write.

He'd been working steadily for ten or fifteen minutes when the telephone on his desk jangled. Charlie raised his voice. "Hey, Baby, pick up that call. I'm busy." He'd had a second phone installed in the composing area, to save steps.

"Oh, yessir," Baby said importantly. He loved answering

the phone. Charlie heard him say, "*Dispatch* office, Purley Mann speakin'. Speak your piece."

Charlie made a mental note to talk to Baby about his telephone manners, then stopped listening and went back to his typing. But after a moment, he heard a scuffling sound.

"Not now, Baby," he said. "I'm working on a story for the special edition. Get a number and I'll call him back this afternoon."

Baby ducked his head and shifted his feet. "Uh, Mr. Dickens, it's a lady. She says it's important. Says it cain't wait."

Charlie kept his eyes on his work and his fingers going, rat-tat-tat. "Tell her to call back in ten minutes, then. I need to finish this first."

Baby disappeared, but a moment later he was back again. "Says she cain't call back, 'cause of where she's callin' from. Says she's gotta talk to you this minute or not at all, and if you don't, you'll be plenty sorry."

"Damn," Charlie growled. "Who the hell is it?"

"Nobody I ever heard of." Baby cleared his throat apologetically. "Says her name is Miz Mattie Harry."

Charlie stopped typing and reached for the phone.

# NINE

# Sheriff Norris Learns More
# Facts of Life

Edna Fay's revelation had thrown Buddy for a loop. *Four months?* Catching his breath, he thought for a moment, then pulled Roy's desk calendar toward him and flipped back to April. He and Rona Jean had their last date on Saturday, April 28—the night that she had invited him over for supper. If Doc Roberts was right, at that point she would have been just about two months along. Maybe she suspected she was pregnant and already knew that she didn't want to marry the father. She'd rather marry *him.* He shivered, feeling he had escaped by the skin of his teeth.

Or maybe she didn't just suspect. Maybe she knew for sure. He opened the top drawer, took out the brown envelope, and slid the diary onto the desk. He opened to April and thumbed through the month until he came to April 23. On that day, she had written *DR* and a Monroeville phone number. April 23, five days before their last date.

With the diary open on the desk before him, he picked

up the phone and gave the Monroeville number to the operator. When it began to ring, he said mildly, "Henrietta, honey, this is sheriff's business. I'd appreciate it if you'd click off right about now." He smiled when she did.

"Doctor DuBois' office," a pleasant-voiced woman said into his ear. "This is Linda June speaking. If you're calling about seeing the doctor, just to let you know, we're full up today, but if it can wait till tomorrow, we can fit you in then."

Buddy pulled in his breath. He'd guessed right. *DR* wasn't somebody's initials, it was the abbreviation for "doctor." "Ma'am, this is Sheriff Norris, over in Darling. We've had ourselves a murder here. I'd like to speak to the doctor about it."

"Oh dear," Linda June said. "Oh, my goodness gracious, that is just too bad. Well, if you'll hold on, Sheriff, I'll see if I can get him to the phone."

A moment later, Buddy was talking to an elderly doctor with a deep, rumbling voice and a persistent cough. "Sheriff Norris?" Dr. DuBois boomed. "So Roy Burns finally retired, did he? Been telling him for years he oughta quit and take it easy." He coughed. "You got a lot to live up to, son. Roy Burns was the best damn sheriff in the whole state of Alabama."

"I'm afraid he's gone, sir." Buddy cleared his throat, feeling suddenly and unaccountably guilty for having the nerve to think he could step into the shoes of the best damn sheriff in the state. "Dead, I mean. Got bit on the wrist by a rattlesnake down in Horsetail Gorge when he was fishing."

"Aw, hell." There was a silence, then, "Wonder how I missed hearing 'bout that. Must've been out of town and nobody thought to tell me." Another silence, another cough. "Well, that's the way I'd like to go when my time comes. So, Sheriff, Linda June says you've had a murder over there in Darling. Somebody go crazy with this heat and start shooting up his favorite saloon? Seems like it happens at least once every summer now."

"Nothing like that, sir," Buddy said. "The victim's name is Rona Jean Hancock. She was strangled. With her stocking." He didn't mention the rope. He had asked Edna Fay to tell Doc Roberts to keep it quiet, too, so the killer would be the only other person who had that important little detail. You never knew when something like that might come in handy.

"Strangled?" the doctor said, in a raised-eyebrow voice. "Well, that'll sure spoil your day."

"Yessir. According to Doc Roberts' autopsy report, she was four months pregnant. Her diary says she had an appointment with you on April 23. I'm wondering if she said anything at all about who the baby's father was. Gave a name, maybe." He could feel the apprehension lance through him. What if she had given *his* name? It wouldn't have been true, but he would have no defense.

"Ah." A long exhale, and a cough. "Well, you just hold your horses, Sheriff, and I'll have a look." A moment later, Buddy heard the squeak of a chair being moved and the rustle of papers, and DuBois was back on the line. "April 23, yes. Rona Jean. Pregnant, yes, some seven weeks, maybe eight— hard to be sure at that stage, but that's my guess. Health, good, a little anemic but nothing to worry about. First pregnancy, says here she was unmarried. I don't remember any mention of the father, and there's nothing in the file. Back when I was a young man, you know, the girl's father would have her namin' a name, and her and the boy would be up in front of the preacher faster'n green grass through a goose." He sighed. "These days, modern girls and all that, it's diff'rent. It's nobody's business but theirs. So no, she didn't name the father and I didn't ask."

Buddy let out his breath. He hadn't known he'd been holding it. "Did she seem upset when you told her about the . . . pregnancy?" Today was a day of firsts, Buddy thought. *Pregnancy.* He couldn't remember ever saying that word out loud.

"No, the way I remember it, she seemed pretty much unconcerned. She didn't volunteer any information about her situation, and I didn't ask." There was a pause. "So she's dead. I'm sorry to hear that. Strangled, you say? A man's crime, although I remember once—it was down in Mobile, as I recall—a woman strangled her husband's mistress. I always wondered about that one. Must've been one helluva strong female. An Amazon, wouldn't you guess?"

"Yes, sir." An image of Myra May flashed through Buddy's mind. He had seen her carrying trays loaded with a tableful of crockery. She was plenty strong.

Another cough, followed by a reflective sigh. "You said Roy was fishing? Too damn bad, but it comes to us all in the end. Remember me to his missus next time you see her. We were in school together, about a hundred years ago."

"I will, sir, and thanks." They exchanged good-byes and Buddy replaced the receiver on the telephone hook. He looked down at the diary. *Seven weeks, maybe eight.* Flipping the pages, he counted back from April 23 to early March. The first weekend, Rona Jean noted that she had gone to the movies with Beau Pyle. According to the diary, they drove over to Monroeville to see *Today We Live*, starring Joan Crawford and Gary Cooper. Rona Jean had worn her purple dress with the polka dots, and Beau was a good (underlined twice) kisser. The next night, Sunday night, she had gone to the Roller Palace with Lamar Lassen, where she also skated with Jack Baker, whom she apparently met for the first time at the rink. The next Saturday night, she'd gone out with Baker, who (she noted) was from nearby Thomasville and was *a swell skater, even better than Lamar, but not much of a kisser.*

So it could've been Pyle, Lassen, or Baker—but maybe not Baker, who wasn't much of a kisser. And then he noticed that on the pages that mentioned Beau Pyle and Lamar Lassen, Rona Jean had drawn those little Valentine hearts. Staring at them, a realization flickered. Rona Jean had been twice as experienced as he had imagined, for both Beau Pyle and Lamar Lassen were candidates for fatherhood. Was there anybody else?

He glanced through the previous weeks, and while both Pyle and Lassen were mentioned, he saw no other men's names, and no hearts. Then he paged through the rest of March and April, remembering that Doc Dubois had said that it was "hard to be sure at that stage." Baker's name appeared again, and there was somebody named Ray. But none of those names had been awarded the Valentine heart. The symbol of Rona Jean's sexual favors belonged exclusively to Lassen and Pyle.

Buddy closed the diary and regarded it for a moment, imagining Mr. Moseley holding it up in court for all to see: *Your Honor, we have here People's Exhibit One—the document that gave Sheriff Norris the facts he used to solve this horrific crime.* Buddy smiled, picturing the jurors leafing through it, reading Rona Jean's entries, and drawing the same conclusion he had drawn.

Then he reddened, remembering that she hadn't written very favorably about *him* and imagining the jurors' reactions to her comment that he wasn't a very good kisser. At the same time, and contradictorily, he felt grateful to whatever caution had kept him from accepting Rona Jean's invitation to go to bed with her. There was no Valentine heart on *his* page.

He put the diary back in its envelope and locked it in the drawer and sat for a moment, thinking. His job now: find out which of the two men—Lassen or Pyle—had fathered Rona Jean's baby, since he would be the likeliest candidate for the killer.

Buddy frowned, feeling confused. But that wouldn't work. Unless one of them upped and confessed and the other one said that it couldn't be him because he'd used protection, there was no way to know, let alone prove, which of the two was the actual father. What he had to find out was which of the two *Rona Jean* had fingered as the father, which might or might not be the same thing. And he'd better get on it right away, which meant that he'd need to assign Wayne to the job of checking the garage for rope and something that could've been used to hit Rona Jean on the head. And he was going to have to interview the neighbors, to see if anybody saw or heard anything around the time of death.

The phone rang again, and Buddy picked it up. The woman on the other end of the line was screaming, half hysterical. It took a while to calm her down long enough to get the details. When he did, he stepped to the door and spoke to his deputy.

"Wayne, Miz Parker out on the Livermore Road claims her neighbor stole her old brown mare, and she's promising to take a shotgun and go over to his place and settle his hash." He held out the card on which he'd written the directions. The one drawback to Wayne, so far, was that he didn't know the country. "You better hightail it out to the Parkers' and take care of whatever the hell is going on. I'd go, but I need to talk to a couple of suspects in the Hancock case. Oh, and when you get back, stop at the garage where Miss Hancock was killed and look around for some rope. Hemp rope. Doc Roberts says she was strangled with a rope, not the stocking."

"Oh yeah?" Wayne said, raising both eyebrows. "The stocking was to make it look like a sexual assault, huh?"

"Yeah. But it wasn't. There wasn't any sexual assault." Buddy thought of telling him about the pregnancy, but didn't—why, he wasn't sure. Instead, he said, "While you're there, look around for something the killer could have used to hit her with. She was conked on the right temple, Doc says, hard enough to give her a skull fracture. Maybe a beer bottle, something like that."

"Got it, boss." Wayne stood, reaching for the gun belt that was slung on the back of his chair. "On my way."

Buddy watched him buckle on his belt, feeling regretful. He supposed it would be smart to wear his .38 when he went to see Lassen and Pyle, just in case. And now that he thought of it, he wished he could take Wayne with him, too.

Lassen lived at Mrs. Meeks' boardinghouse on Railroad Street, two blocks from the rail yard and depot, and since it was Saturday, he was likely to be there. The Meeks place was a two-story frame house that had been recently painted a bilious shade of green (a batch of paint Mr. Musgrove had on sale). There were eight small rooms upstairs, on both sides of a long hall, which Mrs. Meeks rented as sleeping rooms (usually two or three to a room, so there wasn't much space for anything *except* sleeping) to men who worked at Ozzie Sherman's sawmill or on the railroad.

Buddy knew the place well, because he'd lived there after his dad got so cranky he thought it would be better if he moved out. The rooms were clean, if crowded, and the sheets were washed once a week, regular. You got out of bed in the mornings to eggs, bacon, oatmeal, hot buttered biscuits, and coffee, and came home in the evenings to beef stew and dumplings or meat loaf and biscuits and sometimes baked ham and mashed potatoes, plus green apple pie or stewed pears or even chocolate cake. And all this, including the room, for just $9.50 a week plus $2 for laundry, extra for ironing. Or $35, if you took it by the month and did your own washing and ironing. It was, Buddy thought, a sweet deal for a man who didn't much like to cook and do his own washing.

Lassen apparently had the day off, because he was still asleep upstairs when Buddy knocked at Mrs. Meeks' front door and explained what he wanted. She invited him into the parlor, but he opted for the front porch. The thermometer on the porch wall said it was eighty-eight, but there was a breeze. He cast an eye toward the sky, remembering what Wayne had said about the storm. It was a flat, pale gray, with a kind of silvery sheen to it. A storm sky, his old man would call it. But if there was a storm coming, it wasn't there yet.

Five minutes later, Lassen came downstairs, rubbing the sleep out of his eyes. He was broad-shouldered and bulky, with gingery hair, a round, ruddy face, and muscular arms. From the size of him Buddy judged that he was making the most of Mrs. Meeks' generous boardinghouse table. His brown wash pants were held up with red suspenders, and he wore a blue, coffee-stained shirt with the shirttail untucked, and brown leather work boots. A bent and misshapen cigarette, hastily hand-rolled, dangled from one corner of his mouth. He seemed surprised to see Buddy and even more surprised—genuinely shocked, Buddy thought—when the two of them went out on the front porch, where it was marginally cooler than the parlor, and Buddy told him, coming out with it hard and fast and without any cushion, that Rona Jean Hancock was dead.

"Dead?" Lassen took a step backward, as if Buddy had pushed him in the chest, and his mouth worked around the cigarette. "Dead how? Accident? She liked to drive fast whenever she could get her pretty little hands on a steering wheel."

"She was murdered. Where were you last night?"

"Murdered?" Lassen's eyes widened and his jaw dropped. "Murdered? Aw, jeez. Jeeeeez!" The last word was a long exhale. Lassen sat down hard in the porch swing and dropped his elbows on his knees.

"Where were you last night?" Buddy repeated, giving his voice an edge.

There was no answer. Lassen's head was bowed. He seemed dumbstruck.

"Mr. Lassen," Buddy said sharply. "Where were you last night?"

"Me?" Lassen looked up, blinking, and Buddy saw that there were tears in his eyes. "Well, I'll tell you where I wasn't. I sure as hell wasn't out there killin' . . ." He swallowed. "Killin' Rona Jean. I was here, if you gotta know. Howie and Nick and Mr. Meeks and me was playin' poker from after supper to twelve thirty or one. I won the pot. Two bucks." His eyes went to the holstered .38 on Buddy's hip and he licked his lips. "Murdered . . . murdered how?"

Buddy folded his arms across his chest. "What'd you do after you won the pot?"

"Went to bed. Me'n Howie share the room at the top of the stairs. Tough to sleep in this heat, though." He shook his head and kept on shaking it, as if trying to get rid of what he had heard. "I stopped seeing her, you know," he muttered, and pulled his cigarette out of his mouth, holding it between two fingers. "Rona Jean, I mean."

"When was the last time?"

A sour look crossed Lassen's face. "It was before she started hanging out with you, I reckon. She didn't want to see me no more." He dropped the cigarette and ground it out with the toe of his work boot. His voice hardened. "How'd she get killed? You know who done it? If you do, tell me and I'll save the county the cost of a trial."

Buddy ignored the questions. "When did she tell you she was pregnant and that you were the father?"

The sour look was replaced with a look of pure surprise, and Lassen reared back. "How'd you know? Where'd you hear about that?"

"Come on, Lassen," Buddy said, pushing it. "When?"

Lassen's mouth worked. He was silent for a moment. A tear welled up and ran down his cheek. "Last week of April, sometime around there. She phoned me up, asked me to come over to her house so we could talk." He stopped, as if he were trying to remember.

The last week of April, which would be after Buddy had taken himself out of the running as a potential husband by declining to take Rona Jean to bed. "Go on," Buddy said. "What did she want to talk about?"

Lassen looked down. The words came slowly at first, then faster, as if a plug had been pulled and it was all spilling out. "She said she was pregnant and wanted money to get rid of it, but I told her nothing doing. I wasn't giving her a cent to get an abortion. I told her that what we was gonna do was get married, just as quick as we could. Ozzie don't pay me near enough to support a wife and family, but I could hit him up for a little more, and I figured we'd make it some way or another. Folks do, y'know. My folks did. They never had one nickel to rub against another, but they raised seven kids okay." His voice cracked. "And I wanted to get married, I really did. I told her I'd be damned if I was gonna let a boy of mine be born without my name on him."

Buddy felt a tug of compassion for the man before him. No doubt about it, he was hurting. "And she said—?"

"She said that what she really wanted was the money but she'd think about what I said, about gettin' married, I mean. But a couple days later, she phoned me up here at the boardinghouse and said she was wrong. It was a false alarm—there wasn't gonna be no baby—and I didn't need to worry no more about it." He swallowed. "I was . . . well, I was disappointed, I guess. I'd got my head around gettin' married and I was likin' the idea—having a wife to come home to and home cookin' and all that. So I kinda pushed her on it, but she just kept saying she'd been wrong, it was a false alarm."

Caught by surprise, Buddy stared at him. Rona Jean had lied to Lassen about being pregnant. But why? Because he had refused to give her money for an abortion and was instead insisting on getting married? Because she had approached the other candidate, Beau Pyle, and gotten money for the abortion from him? Or because she had decided that abortion was too dangerous? It was strictly illegal and often fatal. In fact, he had read somewhere that in 1932 alone, some fifteen thousand women had died from abortions or complications afterward.

Whatever the reason, though, Rona Jean must have decided against an abortion, or maybe she hadn't been able to find anybody to pay for it, because she was still carrying the baby when she was killed. He thought of the stack of twenties he had found in her room. Maybe somebody had given her the money to get rid of the baby, but she had decided to have it anyway—and was asking for more money. Was *that* why she had been killed?

Lassen was going on, the words coming faster now, tumbling out in a rush. "I gotta say I was glad we didn't have to get married right away. But I'd kind of got myself used to the idea, you know?" He looked beseechingly at Buddy. "And Rona Jean, she was right pretty and lots of fun to be with and I figgered she'd make a good wife. But when I asked her to go out with me again, she said no, and that there was no point in me askin' again. It hurt me like a knife in the gut, but if she wouldn't, she wouldn't, and that's all there was to it."

Buddy could hear the pain in his voice. Rejection was hard, whoever you were. "You haven't seen her since?" he asked, and followed that with another of the questions he had come to ask. "Did she . . . did she write you any letters?"

"No, sir, Sheriff," Lassen said emphatically. "Haven't talked to her since she called me on the phone, and I don't know why she'd be writing me letters. Sayin' she was sorry she wasn't going to have that baby after all? Wouldn't of been no point." He looked up, his eyes glittering with tears. "Let me tell you, when you get that guy, you better put him somewhere else than in that tin pot jail of yours, 'cause if he's where I can get at him, I'll kill him." His voice was like a file rasping against bare metal. "I swear to God I'll kill him."

Buddy knew he wasn't being professional, but he did it anyway. He put his hand on Lassen's shoulder and said, "For what it's worth, Lamar, I understand how you feel. Go get yourself a bottle and get drunk. And when you've slept it off, forget about killing anybody. It's not worth it. Believe me, it's not worth it." He wanted to say *she's not worth it*, but he knew if he did, Lassen would throw a punch.

When he got back to his car, he took out his notebook and scratched Lassen's name off his list.

Buddy's route across town took him down Robert E. Lee, past the courthouse. As he drove, he spotted Verna Tidwell, carrying two brown paper shopping bags, walking toward her house. He slowed and hailed her.

"It's too hot to be walking, Verna, and that's a big load. You want a ride? I'm going right past your place. Or I'll be glad to take you wherever you want to go."

"I'm heading home," Verna said gratefully, getting in.

"Thanks for the offer." She put one bag on the floor between her knees and held the other on her lap. "You going to your dad's?"

When Buddy was a young teen, he and his father had moved into the house next door to Verna, and the old man still lived there, so Verna was a longtime family friend. She kept an eye on Buddy's dad, who was now in his eighties, and sometimes even shopped for him.

"Tonight, maybe," Buddy said. "Right now, I have to see a guy."

Verna regarded him curiously. "About Rona Jean's murder?"

"Well . . ." Buddy shifted into first gear and they started off. He was frowning, not sure how much he ought to say.

"That's okay," Verna said comfortingly. "It's different, now that you're sheriff and not just the boy next door." She chuckled, then turned serious. "But there's something you ought to know about Rona Jean, if you don't already."

"Oh yeah?" Buddy was remembering that Sheriff Burns had never liked it when Verna stuck her nose into one of his cases. *That damn Tidwell woman again*, he'd groan. *A pain in the patootie.* But he would add that he couldn't very well tell her to butt out when she might know something he ought to know and didn't, which she always seemed to do. Roy had even been forced to thank her once or twice. "Like what?" Buddy added cautiously.

"Well, Ophelia Snow and Liz Lacy and I were talking about her murder, and Liz said she saw Rona Jean with a CCC guy at the movie house in Monroeville a few weeks back. It was one of the nights they showed *The Power and the Glory*." She chuckled. "Liz said the two of them were getting into some pretty powerful passion of their own."

"Huh," Buddy said. Mentally, he added Liz to his list of

people to talk to, although if his calculations (and Rona Jean's diary) were correct, the CCC guy wasn't the father of Rona Jean's baby. "Any idea who the guy was?"

"Liz said she thought he was an officer, but that's about all she could say."

"I'll talk to her," Buddy said. "Thanks for the tip."

Casually, Verna said, "I suppose you've already talked to Rona Jean's roommate. Bettina Higgens."

"Yep. Did that first thing." He gave Verna a crooked grin, wondering if Verna and her friends—didn't all three of them belong to that garden club, the Dahlias?—did nothing all day but sit around and trade gossip. Too bad they couldn't put all that time and energy and imagination to work solving real crimes.

"And that you're making a list of the men Rona Jean was seeing."

"Uh-huh."

"And that—"

"Verna," Buddy said, "I respect your interest in this case. I truly do. Everybody in town ought to be concerned when a girl gets murdered right here in our very midst. I appreciate your telling me about what Miss Lacy saw at the movie show. But I'd prefer that you leave the investigating to me and my deputy. If you don't mind." They had reached Verna's house, next door to his dad's place, and he pulled over to the curb and stopped. Without giving her time to respond, he said, "Hope I didn't offend. You need a hand with those grocery bags?"

"Thanks, I can manage. And no, you didn't offend. Roy Burns usually said pretty much the same thing whenever I offered my assistance." She turned to him as if she had suddenly thought of something. "How would you like to come for supper tonight, Buddy? I'm asking because the commandant of Camp Briarwood is coming—Captain Campbell. If you haven't met him already, you should. Mr. Duffy will be here, too, and Liz Lacy. We're having chicken pot pie," she added.

He didn't have to think twice. It was time he met Captain Campbell, and he always enjoyed Mr. Duffy, who had Darling's best interests at heart. "Thank you, Verna. You know how I feel about your chicken pot pie. I appreciate the invitation. What time?"

"Seven," she said, and got out of the car. "Thanks for the lift, Buddy—see you then."

On the porch of the house next door, Buddy saw his father sitting hunched in his rocking chair, his dog Zach—one part hound, one part beagle, and two parts something else—lying across his feet. It was a hot day, the temperature close to ninety, but the old man wore a crocheted afghan across his shoulders and was staring blankly into space. With a stab of guilt, Buddy thought he ought to stop and talk for a few minutes, see how the old guy was doing. He hadn't been too well lately.

But Buddy could do that tonight, before he went to Verna's house for dinner. Right now, he had to talk to Beau Pyle. So he put the car in gear and drove off, waving to his father.

His father didn't wave back. Buddy didn't think he even saw him.

Beau lived with his mother on the south edge of town, down Robert E. Lee to Natchez, east on Natchez six blocks to Pleasant View, and south to the end of the narrow dirt street. The street—not much more than an alley, really—was misnamed, for there was nothing pleasant about the view. It was lined on both sides by forlorn houses, some leaning one way, some leaning the other, their front yards filled with junked cars, piles of rusting equipment, energetic chickens, laconic dogs.

Buddy pulled to a stop behind a shiny 1932 black Ford three-window coupe with all four fenders stripped off. Buddy knew that Beau had dropped a V8 into it, giving him the kind of horsepower and torque that allowed him to outrun a sheriff's car any day—or night—of the week. It was a lot of car for a kid, but then Beau was a lot of kid, eighteen going on twenty-eight and touchier than a hog that'd stepped down hard on a section of barbed wire and couldn't shake it off. The Ford was parked in front of a dilapidated one-story frame house with a rusted metal roof, set up on stacks of bricks a couple feet high, in the middle of a bare dirt yard.

Buddy looked at the house for a moment, wondering who was in there and whether whoever-it-was was likely to give him any trouble. He considered leaving his gun in the car, on the theory that, if he wasn't armed, he'd be less likely to shoot somebody with it, and maybe less likely to be shot. Young Beau had a short fuse, and the three other male Pyles—Bodeen; his older brother, Rankin; and old man Pyle (who right now was serving a five-year prison sentence in Wetumpka State Penitentiary for killing a man in a fight over in Monroeville)—were known to be easily riled. Buddy had had no dealings with the female Pyles, but guessed that they wouldn't win a be-nice contest, either.

He gave up trying to decide about his gun and left it where it was, holstered on his right hip. With a sigh, he got out of the car and made his way across the dirt yard to climb the step and rap on the screen door, scattering a half-dozen squawking red hens as he went. The exterior of the house had once been painted white but was now beaten by the weather into a subdued gray. The front step was a wide board propped on a couple of large rocks, and the porch sagged despairingly, as if it were anxious to separate itself from the house. The screen door had a big hole in the bottom panel where a dog had gone through it once and then kept right on using it as his own personal door. The dog in question, a mournful looking coonhound, came around the corner of the porch and stood watching him, head and tail down, too dispirited to bark.

A woman in her sixties answered Buddy's knock. Standing on the other side of the screen door, she wore a blue cotton housedress that hung loosely from her shoulders, a feed sack apron, rayon stockings that had slipped down around her ankles, and felt house slippers. Her gray hair was piled in a loose bun on top of her head, and the tendrils straggled down over her neck. She was missing several front teeth.

Her eyes went to the star pinned to Buddy's khaki shirt pocket, down to the holster on his hip, back up to his face. "He ain't here," she said, in a thin, querulous voice. "Nobody home but me."

Buddy took off his fedora and pretended she hadn't spoken. "I'm Sheriff Norris, Miz Pyle," he said politely. "I need to talk to your boy Beau. It's important."

"Beau ain't here," the woman said, pointedly hooking the screen door. "No point in you lookin'. Him and Bodeen went down to Mobile and won't be back till—"

A male voice came from somewhere inside. "Ma, if that's Tubbs, tell him I'll meet him at the pool parlor in half an hour."

"It's not Tubbs, Beau," Buddy said loudly. "It's Sheriff Norris. I need to see you. Now."

"Aw, hell," Beau said disgustedly. Something slammed, hard. Not a door, a boot, maybe, against a wall.

Buddy waited. When nothing else happened, he raised his voice but kept it even, easy. "No foolin', Beau. You come on out now. We need to talk."

"Got nothin' to say, Sheriff. Nothin' to do with it, neither."

So he knew that Rona Jean was dead. "I hear you," Buddy said. "Need to talk to you anyway. And I don't think your mother wants me to come in and get you."

The woman straightened her shoulders. "Beau," she said sharply. "You, Beau! You get out here, right now. I ain't havin' no trouble in this here house, you hear?"

If Beau Pyle was afraid of anybody in this world, Buddy thought, it must be his mother, since he was out on the porch a moment later, pulling on a boot. He was a handsome kid, with a shock of black hair that fell across a broad forehead, a dark complexion and high cheekbones, a hard jaw, and a don't-give-a-damn air. He got his boot on, then lit a Camel with a match flicked against his thumbnail and propped one shoulder against a porch post, mouth pulled down and petulant, a dangerously seductive bad boy.

Buddy understood why Rona Jean had found Beau attractive, even though at eighteen, he was four years or so younger than she had been. He was dressed in a blue work shirt with the sleeves rolled up, jeans, and smart-looking leather boots, and the chain he twirled around his finger was most likely gold, Buddy had to allow. Beau worked his brother Bodeen's still out by Briar's Swamp. After Mickey LeDoux was arrested and sent to prison, Bodeen's moonshine was all there was in Cypress County, so if you wanted tiger spit these days, it was the Pyles' tiger spit you got. The Pyle brothers made no secret of the fact that they had plenty of money to spend, witness Beau's late-model Ford coupe parked in front of the house, fenderless and stripped down for the speed he needed to outrun the Revenuers.

Limping, the hound dog climbed the porch steps, dropped down heavily in front of the screen door, and began to lick his sore paw. Buddy fished a toothpick out of his shirt pocket and stuck it in his mouth. He hooked his thumbs in his belt and leaned against the other porch post. "So you've heard about Rona Jean."

"Yeah. Bodeen was over at the diner for breakfast and heard tell of it."

Buddy regarded him mildly. "News to you, was it?"

"Well, sure." He looked offended. "O' course it was news to me. What'd you think—that I did it?"

"The thought did cross my mind," Buddy admitted. "When did she tell you she was pregnant?"

The question was an obvious surprise. Beau stared at him, dark eyes glittering. "How'd you—" He bit it off, reining himself in. "She never," he said sullenly.

Buddy chuckled. "What? You were hopin' it was some kinda secret?" He flicked the toothpick to the other side of his mouth. "You think you're the only one?"

The boy's head came up and his voice hardened in an ugly line. "Well, yeah, there was *you*."

Buddy shrugged it off. "Maybe. But she didn't tell me she was havin' my baby. When did she tell *you* that?"

Beau turned his head away, muscles tightening in his neck, lips pressed hard together.

"Don't jack me around, Beau," Buddy said, letting the impatience show in his voice. "We're talking murder here. And the girl kept a diary—with your name in it."

"I had nothin' to do with no murder," Beau flared angrily. He pulled on his cigarette.

Buddy made his voice soft. "Seems to me you're a pretty good candidate. Man gets a woman pregnant, doesn't want to be bothered with the baby or with *her*. Gets tired of being hounded for money, gets mad and puts an end to—"

"It wasn't like that," Beau growled, his face working. "That's not how it was."

"How was it?"

"She told me she was pregnant but—"

"When?"

"When?" He scowled, thinking. "End of April, maybe," he hazarded. "It was a while back. Wanted me to give her money to get rid of it. I told her she could get lost. She wasn't goin' to get a nickel out of me. How was I to know it was mine? Like you say, there was others." His voice was hard-edged, almost savage. If he'd used it on Rona Jean, Buddy thought, he'd likely scared the starch out of her. And maybe he'd used more than his voice. Maybe he'd used the back of his hand.

"What happened after that?" Buddy asked.

Beau flicked the cigarette, sending it arcing into the dirt of the yard. "A week or so later, I saw her out at the Roller Palace and she told me it was all a mistake. She wasn't, after all. Or so she said." He grunted. "Women. You never can tell whether they're tellin' you straight or tryin' to pull a fast one."

"Yeah." Buddy wondered if Rona Jean had decided that trying to get money out of Beau was too dangerous. "Did you go out with her after that?" There was no mention of it in the diary, but maybe Rona Jean hadn't kept an accurate record.

"You kiddin'?" Beau laughed shortly. "I ain't goin' out with no woman who thinks she can shake me down."

But something about the way he said it made Buddy think that it might just as easily have happened the other way: that Rona Jean, maybe frightened for her safety, had decided she didn't want to see Beau again. How would a kid with a tinderbox temper take a rejection like that? Would he have blown his stack? Lost control and throttled her?

But that was all conjecture, and he for sure wasn't going to get answers to those questions out of Beau himself. "One more thing about Rona Jean," Buddy said. "Did she write you any letters?"

"Letters? Nah. Why would she do that? I'd already told her I wasn't givin' her a red cent. She could've got down on her knees and begged, and it wouldn't do her no good." He fished another Camel out of his pocket and lit it with a match. "Damn, it's hot," he said.

Down the street, a child cried shrilly. A woman yelled, and the crying stopped. The old dog lifted his head at the sound, then went back to licking his sore paw. Buddy let the silence stretch out. Finally, in a casual tone, he asked, "So where were you last night?"

"Last night?" Beau took a long, hard pull on his cigarette, letting out the smoke before he spoke. "Well, if you gotta know, I was down at the still." He slanted Buddy a hard, defiant look. "You got a problem with that, Sheriff?"

Buddy had the same attitude toward Bodeen Pyle's still that Sheriff Burns had had toward Mickey LeDoux's larger and more successful operation, before Agent Kinnard and his boys had shut it down. The sheriff's words had been frequently and publically repeated. *Far as I'm concerned, them boys can cook up whatever they want so long as they live decent and don't go to killin' other folks. Some of them shiners couldn't feed their kids if they couldn't make moon.* The sheriff had said a true thing, in Buddy's estimation, and that was the way he intended to do business in Cypress County.

Of course, the situation was different now, with Prohibition repealed, Alabama local option, and Cypress County dry. But that didn't mean that Mickey and Bodeen and their kin were out of a job. No, not by a long shot. The only legal booze a man could drink now was the stuff that was brewed in taxpaying distilleries, and the bottles bore the stamp that proved that Uncle Sam had taken his cut, which added about two dollars a gallon to the cost of the whiskey. Bootleggers didn't pay taxes, so their homemade stuff was still illegal. But they didn't give a damn. They had a bone-deep contempt for the government and the laws it slapped on their moonshine.

And so did the people who drank it. Over the years since 1919, when the Eighteenth Amendment criminalized the making and drinking of alcohol, Darling drinkers had developed a strong preference for their neighbors' swamp-brewed white lightning. For one thing, the local boys didn't make the kind of alcohol that would pickle a person's insides, like the poisonous bathtub gin that had killed all those drinkers in New York and Chicago. Mickey and Bodeen made good corn whiskey, which in Darling's view was just as true and right and American as grits, peanut butter, and home-cured bacon. For another, the money that Darlingians forked over for their drink stayed right here in the Alabama county where their neighbors made it, rather than going into the pockets of some rich distillery owner up in Kentucky or Tennessee. And for a third, Darlingians felt that drinking the local white lightning was a pleasurable way of thumbing their noses at the Yankee bureaucracy, up north in Washington, D.C.

So instead of shutting down the Cypress County moonshiners, Repeal had given them what looked to be a longer, stronger life, and Buddy was taking a leaf from his predecessor's book. He had no intention of getting in their way. Live and let live, he'd decided, as long as there wasn't any shooting. Or strangling.

"I don't have a problem with you being out at the still," Buddy replied, "If that's where you were. So how long were you out there? Was there anybody else around?"

Beau blew smoke hard out of his nostrils. "I went out to take over the fire at six yesterday evening. I was out there all by myself. It don't take two to mind the fire, if the wood's cut and ready."

Buddy knew that keeping the wood fires burning under the pot stills at the right heat and intensity was an art in itself, just one of the many minor arts that went into the larger art of cooking mash. Fire tending wasn't a job that was taken lightly, and Bodeen would've come down hard on Beau if he'd let the fire go out.

"You were out there all night?" Buddy asked.

"Until six this morning." Beau's chin jutted out. "But I didn't leave and drive back into town and strangle Rona Jean, if that's what you're thinking. Didn't have no cause."

Buddy grunted, a grunt that might have said, *Now, that is purely a crock*, or *Yeah, reckon I can accept that.* He didn't know which it was, since there was nobody to confirm or dispute Beau's alibi. The boy could've planned ahead and paid one of the Pyle cousins to tend the fire for a few hours. And he was certainly capable of killing Rona Jean. But on impulse, Buddy thought. It wouldn't have been according to a plan.

He cocked his head and asked: "How'd you know she was strangled?"

"Got it from Bodeen. Strangled with her stocking. He got it from Myra May while he was having breakfast this morning." His lip curled in a mirthless smile. "Said it damn near spoiled his grits and sausage."

That rang a bell. Buddy frowned and took his notebook out of his shirt pocket, flicking to the page where he'd made the list of the people Rona Jean had mentioned in her diary. He ran his thumb down the list. *B.P. Bodeen Pyle?*

"Bodeen," he said, looking up. "He ever take Rona Jean out?"

"Not that I know of," Beau said. His voice took on a jagged edge. "Not that I better find out, anyway."

*Like that, was it?* Buddy thought. Maybe there was a new angle here. What if Rona Jean hadn't been killed because of the pregnancy? What if she had told Beau she was finished with him and turned right around and started seeing Beau's brother? What if one of the brothers had killed her in a jealous rage? He drew a line under the initials and added a question mark. He'd have to check and see when the mentions of *B.P.* occurred, and how often. He closed his notebook and pocketed it, took out the toothpick, and stuck it in his shirt pocket, too.

"Reckon that's it for now," he said. "Don't you be goin' down to Mobile until I get this business straightened out. Or anywhere else." He tightened his voice. "You hear?"

Beau nodded sullenly.

"Where will I find Bodeen?"

"Out at the still, I reckon," Beau said, and pushed himself erect. He turned to look full at Buddy. "You think she was puttin' the arm on somebody else? Was that why she got killed?"

*Putting the arm on Bodeen? Was that what he meant?* "Your guess is as good as mine." Buddy gave Beau a stern look. "I'm going to talk to your brother. I'd appreciate it if you'd keep your mouth shut about this conversation until I've seen him."

Beau shrugged carelessly. "Yeah. Okay by me. Bodeen and me ain't talkin' much anyway, these days."

*Yes, like that,* Buddy thought.

Back in the car, he sat for a moment, thinking. Then he opened his notebook and thumbed through the pages. If he had read Rona Jean's Valentine heart code accurately, Lamar and Beau were the only candidates for paternity. But what if he hadn't read it right? Or what if she had left somebody out, either accidentally or on purpose?

And it wasn't smart to trust Beau. The boy might be lying about tending that fire all night, and unless he could get some confirmation, one way or another, Buddy knew he'd be a fool to put any faith in what Beau said. He'd seen the evidence of Beau's rage: the shredded jail-cell mattress and the wrecked bunk. He was perfectly capable of flying into a rage and throttling Rona Jean, and then of lying about it.

But Beau had raised a good point. Rona Jean could expect both Lamar and Beau to believe that they were the father; she'd had sex with both of them, so it made sense to try to get money out of them. And there was that threatening letter she had written to *him*. Her charges—that he'd slapped her, torn her clothes—were false, but he'd be the first to admit that it would have been tough to dispute them if she had pushed it somehow. He was just damned lucky she hadn't demanded money from him.

But maybe she'd pulled that trick on somebody else. Maybe she wrote a similar letter to him, making similar charges, similarly false, and threatening to go public if he didn't pay up. The evidence? That stack of twenties, $140 in all, which was a lot more than she could have saved out of her paycheck, especially since she was always broke, according to Bettina. Blackmail payoff, was it? Maybe she squeezed it out of some poor sucker—or for that matter, out of more than one poor sucker, using the same technique she had tried out first on *him*.

And maybe she had been killed for it.

Frowning, Buddy thought some more about this angle. He went back to the top of his notebook list. With this new possibility in mind, who should he talk to next? He stopped at Violet's name, remembering that Rona Jean had written something about Violet in her diary. He flipped back through his notebook and found that he had copied a line out of the diary entry for June 5: Violet had promised Rona Jean to give her the money for all the bills, *before and after*, she had written, *and I can leave it there*. When he first read that, he'd been totally in the dark. He'd had no idea what before-and-after bills she was writing about or what the "it" was that she could "leave."

Now, knowing about the baby, it made sense. The "before and after" part, anyway. He needed to talk to Violet and find out what she knew. And Myra May, as well.

He put the notebook into his shirt pocket. Bodeen Pyle might be important, especially if there was some jealousy involved between the two brothers. But Bodeen could wait until Buddy had filled in some more of the details. He turned the key in the Ford's ignition and drove off.

# TEN

# Lizzy's Prayer Is Answered—But Which One?

Lizzy went up the path to her house, carrying her handbag as carefully as if it contained a dozen new-laid eggs. In it was a letter from Nadine Fleming, her literary agent—still sealed because Lizzy hadn't wanted to open it in the post office or on the street. It might contain good news about *Sabrina*, in which case she would probably have disgraced herself by bursting into tears of delight. Or bad news, in which case she'd be crying tears of disappointment. One way or the other, Lizzy knew she was going to cry. She preferred to do it in private.

Home was a tiny yellow-painted frame bungalow on Jefferson Davis Street, a block off Franklin and two blocks from Mr. Moseley's office, close enough to walk back and forth to work. The house, which Lizzy had owned for three years or so, was just big enough for one person—a doll's house, really. But as if to make up for its small size, it was surrounded with a large and very pretty yard. In the front, there were azaleas, hibiscus, and a dogwood tree that was lovely in the spring. In the back, there was a grassy lawn, and a perennial border where eleven o'clock ladies sprang up among the lilies and irises in April and May; pink roses covered the trellis in June; and sunflowers bloomed along the fence in July and August. A small kitchen garden, fenced with a low white picket fence against hungry bunnies, provided fresh vegetables and herbs all summer long. The yard was perfect for a gardener, and gardening was Lizzy's favorite hobby—next to writing, of course.

In fact, as far as Lizzy was concerned, this absolutely perfect house and its perfect garden had only one drawback. It was right across the street from her mother's house, which meant that it was close enough for Mrs. Lacy—a quarrelsome, bossy woman who wanted nothing more than to manage her only daughter's life—to run over once or twice a day to "visit."

Lizzy, a dutiful daughter, felt a half-guilty, half-loving obligation to her mother, which was why she continued to live within shouting distance. After all, her mother was a widow and otherwise alone in the world. She was an only child and a daughter, and it was well understood that Darling daughters (*only* daughters, in particular) had a special responsibility to their mothers. When Lizzy was a girl, her mother had been fond of remarking that so-and-so had never married, in order to stay at home and help her mother. (She had a large catalog of so-and-sos, updated every few months.) And that Great-aunt Polly had refused all beaus and took care of her invalid mother to her dying day. To Great-aunt Polly's dying day, that is: she took such good care of her mother that the irascible old woman outlived her acquiescent daughter by six years.

But while Lizzy felt she was duty-bound to look after her mother, she had no intention of following Great-aunt Polly's example to the grave. So, feeling strong and *almost* rebellious, she had bought her own house and steadfastly refused to give her mother a key. (After all, a grown person needed *some* privacy!) And without a key, Mrs. Lacy couldn't drop in just any old time, which she would have done, since the plain truth was that she was not only bossy and argumentative, but also a snoop. Lacking a key, she had to wait by the parlor window until she saw her daughter come home—and *then* she came over.

Just now, Lizzy was praying that her mother would stay away long enough for her to read her letter and have her cry in private. And that privacy—her solitude—was Lizzy's deepest joy. If she wanted company, she had plenty of books, including the one she was writing. And if she wanted to hear a human voice, why, she could listen to her own. She could talk to her orange tabby cat, Daffodil, who never ever talked back.

Lizzy went up the steps to the front porch, where Daffy was waiting on the porch swing, keeping cool in the breeze that filtered through the honeysuckle at the end of the porch. He jumped down and wound himself around her ankles, purring a loud welcome. She unlocked the front door and stepped into the small entry hall. On the left, a flight of polished wooden stairs led up to two small bedrooms. On the right, a wide doorway opened into a parlor that was just large enough for a fireplace and built-in bookcases, a Mission-style leather sofa, a dark brown corduroy-covered chair, and a Tiffany-style lamp with a stained glass shade that had cost Lizzy the enormous sum of seven dollars and fifty cents. It was much too much to pay for a lamp, but she loved its soft amber-colored light, which gleamed richly against the refinished pine floors.

She hung her straw hat on the wall peg in the hallway, then went past the parlor and into the compact kitchen. She had left the windows open, and the room was cooler than the out of doors. Nervously, thinking about the letter (so *much* seemed to hang on it), she filled a kettle with water and set it on the gas stove and got out her Brown Betty teapot and the ceramic canister of tea she had bought in that cute little tea shop in Montgomery and measured the fragrant tea into the strainer in the teapot. Her fingers trembling, she took Nadine's envelope out of her purse and slit it carefully, then laid it on the oilcloth-covered table in the small dining nook. The nook looked out on the garden and was one of her favorite places in the house—one of her *comfort* places, especially when the window was open to the honeysuckle-scented breeze, as it was now.

When the tea was ready, she poured herself a cup, added a spoonful of honey, and sat down. Steeling herself to read the letter—*bad news or good?*—she took it out of the envelope and said a tiny silent prayer for the courage to face whatever came. She had just begun to unfold it when she heard a sharp rapping at the back door. She looked up to see her mother peering through the glass.

"Damn and *blast*," she muttered, and quickly slid the folded letter under the oilcloth. With a long sigh of resignation, she got up and opened the door.

"Oh, hello, Mama," she said brightly. "I was just sitting down to a cup of tea. Would you like to join me?" She was going to do it anyway, Lizzy thought. She might as well be invited.

"I waited for you to telephone me when you got home," Mrs. Lacy said accusingly. "But you didn't." She puffed out her breath. "Lord sakes, it is *hot*. Comin' across the street in that sunshine is like walking across a bed of coals."

"Then maybe you'd rather have lemonade," Lizzy said. "It might cool you off."

"I'll have lemonade," Mrs. Lacy said, as if she had thought of it herself, and went to the refrigerator to get it, taking the opportunity to look on the shelves to see what Lizzy was eating. Mrs. Lacy was an oversized woman with an oversized voice and ample bosom and hips. She was wearing a wide-brimmed orange straw hat and a red rayon chiffon dress splashed with large orange and yellow flowers that made her appear even bulkier than usual. Her smile was just a little smug. "I have some important news, in case you're interested." She put the pitcher on the table.

"Of course I'm interested," Lizzy said. Since the kitchen was quite small and Mrs. Lacy was quite large and loud, she took up more than her share of the space, leaving very little room—and not quite enough air—for Lizzy. Now, Lizzy moved her teacup and the teapot to the round kitchen table and took a glass out of the cupboard for her mother. The one time her mother had tried to squeeze into the dining nook, she'd gotten stuck and Lizzy had had to move the table so she could get out.

Lizzy was often tempted to feel sorry for her mother, but that was difficult, because she had been so foolish. Five years before, she had put up her small annuity and her paid-for house as collateral against a bank loan to buy stocks in the booming stock market, planning (like everybody else in America) to get rich quick and be set for life. When the stock bubble burst and Wall Street crashed, she lost everything. Mr. Johnson, at the bank, carried the note on her house as long as he could (he had done that for a great many Darlingians), but he finally had to foreclose.

Unfazed, Mrs. Lacy declared that the bank could take the house and she would move in with her daughter, which, as Lizzy saw it, would be a disaster of titanic proportions. Her little dollhouse wasn't large enough for two normal-sized people. If her mother moved in, there wouldn't be any room for *her*—and not one shred of privacy.

Lizzy had gone into action to avert this calamity. She had been saving for a car, so she went to the bank and put the money down on a loan to buy her mother's house. Now, Mrs. Lacy worked a couple of days a week at Mr. Dunlap's Five and Dime and helped Fannie Champaign to make hats. Out of her earnings, she was able to buy groceries and give her daughter a few dollars a month for rent. It wasn't enough to cover the payment to the bank, and Lizzy still had no car. An ideal solution, of course, would be for her mother to marry, and Lizzy had often addressed the Almighty on that very question. But the Almighty wasn't listening—at least, He wasn't listening yet. And in the meantime, it was worth every dollar it cost to keep her mother on the other side of the street.

With an air of mystery, Mrs. Lacy sat down at the table, picked up the pitcher of lemonade, and poured a glass for herself. "I'll save my own personal news for last, because I've got something else on my mind. It's about the murder," she said in a conspiratorial tone. "Rona Jean Hancock's murder. You've heard she was strangled, I suppose. In Myra May Mosswell's car. With her *stocking*. Which is what happens to girls who fool around."

"Yes, Mama, I know," Lizzy said with a sigh. "Such a terrible thing." She picked up a folded napkin and fanned herself with it, wondering briefly if maybe the killer had been driven mad with the heat. She'd read about things like that happening. It might make an interesting story.

"But that isn't all," her mother went on, eyes sparkling, quivering with barely suppressed excitement. She looked, Lizzy thought, as if she was enjoying herself. "Ouida Bennett says that the girl was *pregnant*."

"Oh dear!" Lizzy said, completely taken aback. So there wasn't just one death—there were two. Rona Jean and her unborn baby. She frowned. "Are you sure that's true, Mama? Where did Mrs. Bennett hear—"

"Oh yes, it is definitely true," Mrs. Lacy said, picking up her glass and drinking deeply. "Ouida heard it at Mann's Mercantile. Mrs. Mann's cousin Agnes works over at the Monroeville Hospital, where Doc Roberts did the autopsy on Rona Jean. Agnes heard it from a records clerk over there and phoned Mrs. Mann right away. Ouida happened to be in the store when the call came." Mrs. Lacy dropped her voice confidingly. "Poor Ouida has been putting on so much weight lately that she had to buy some new elastic to repair the waist of her unmentionables. Anyway, she got an earful as soon as Mrs. Mann hung up."

*I'll bet she did*, Lizzy thought darkly. *And then she delivered that earful to everybody she met on the way home.* She shook her head. There was no way on God's green earth to keep a secret in Darling.

"And if you ask me—" Mrs. Lacy leaned even closer and lowered her voice almost to a whisper, as if she were afraid that somebody might be listening at the open window. "If you ask me, it's *entirely* likely that whoever it was put that bun in Rona Jean's oven was the one who killed her."

"I suppose it's possible," Lizzy acknowledged cautiously. "But—"

Her mother sat back. "And what's more, it could very well be the *sheriff* who got her in the family way—and who could have done the awful deed himself. The very person who is supposed to be investigating this crime!" She threw up her hands. "What this world is coming to, I don't know. When we can't trust the law to—"

"Mama, stop!" Lizzy said firmly. "Facts are one thing, but

gossip is something else again. It can wreck a person's career, and even his whole life. I wish you wouldn't—"

"But it's *not* gossip!" her mother exclaimed, offended. "It's the truth, Elizabeth, the bare-bones truth. Leona Ruth Adcock saw Rona Jean and Buddy Norris hugging and kissing with her very own eyes, right there at Rona Jean's kitchen sink. Of course, he wasn't sheriff then, but he *was* a deputy sheriff and—"

"And Leona Ruth's eyes aren't what they used to be," Lizzy said sharply. "Unfortunately, there's nothing wrong with her tongue, except that it flaps on both ends."

Her mother gave her a reproachful look. "I don't know why you'd want to defend Buddy Norris, Elizabeth. He's a man, just like all the rest of them." She took another drink of lemonade. "He wouldn't even be sheriff today if it weren't for poor Roy Burns gettin' bit by that rattlesnake and dyin' such an untimely death. And bein' sheriff doesn't make a person holy. Sheriffs can chase around just like anybody else. In fact, Roy Burns himself used to—"

"I didn't say it made him holy, Mama," Lizzy protested.

But in a way, her mother was right. Having worked for Mr. Moseley for quite a few years, Lizzy had a respectful attitude toward the law and anybody who enforced it. It seemed to her that the law put up a barrier between the civilized and the savage—a necessary barrier that separated the good from the bad. Mr. Moseley was always telling her that it wasn't as simple as that, that good people often did bad—that is, unlawful or immoral—things, and vice versa. And she knew from her own experience that it didn't take much black mixed in with the white to make a fuzzy-looking gray.

But as far as she was concerned, anybody who enforced the law stood for justice and order, and justice not just for some but for everybody, which right now, meant justice for Rona

Jean Hancock, who had been murdered. And Buddy Norris had been elected to stand up for Rona Jean, find out who had killed her, and assemble the evidence that would allow Mr. Moseley (who was county attorney this year) to get a conviction. Buddy was only a man, yes, and young and inexperienced at that. But she knew him well enough to know that it was ridiculous to think that he'd killed Rona Jean. He had an important job to do, and out of a sense of fairness, Lizzy didn't think people should be saying things that made his job even harder.

Her mother turned her glass in her fingers. "Well, of course, the sheriff wasn't the only one who was fooling around with Rona Jean. Adele Hart says she was sitting out on her front porch one night this week and saw a man waiting around the back of the diner for Rona Jean to go off her shift at eleven."

Lizzy thought about that. Adele Hart and her husband, Artis, owned Hart's Peerless Laundry, at the corner of Franklin and Robert E. Lee, across from Musgrove's Hardware. The Harts lived in the house next door to the laundry, which was convenient because they both had to get up well before dawn to get their help started on the day's washing, as well as manage the three grandchildren who had recently come to live with them. Lizzy and Adele worked together on the Darling Christmas pageant every year, and Lizzy sometimes stopped in for a cup of tea when Adele wasn't too busy. She knew that the Harts could see the vegetable garden behind the diner—and the garage where Rona Jean's body was found.

"Did Adele say who it was?" Lizzy asked.

Mrs. Lacy shook her head. "Just that she thought he was from the camp."

*From the camp*, Lizzy thought. And the man she had seen with Rona Jean at the movies was a CCC man, maybe even an officer. Was he the same person?

Her mother was getting her teeth into the subject of the camp. "Those men out there—I swear, they're makin' trouble all over. Have you heard about Lucy Murphy?"

Lucy was a Dahlia who lived on a small farm on the Jericho Road and worked at the camp. Her husband, Ralph, had a railroad job. He was gone all week and didn't usually make it home until late Saturday.

"Lucy?" Lizzy felt a flare of concern. "She's all right, isn't she?" Lizzy had always thought of Darling as a safe little town, but after what happened to Rona Jean, she was thinking that women who spent a lot of time alone—women like herself and Lucy—ought to be extra watchful. It was an unsettling thought.

"Depends on what you mean by 'all right.'" Her mother pressed her lips together disapprovingly. "Ouida's widowed sister, Erma Rae—the one that lives out on the Jericho Road— saw her riding on the back of one of those Army motorcycles." She lowered her voice. "Just at dark, it was. Last Wednesday night, when Ralph was gone on the railroad. And Erma Rae said she's heard that motorcycle before, comin' and goin' late at night, only she didn't know who it was until she saw her. Lucy Murphy, I mean."

"Oh, Mama," Lizzy sighed. "There you go again. I wish you wouldn't—"

"I am just sayin' that—no matter how many good things everybody says that camp is doing for Darling—it's not all one hundred percent positive. Those boys are flirty. I've heard 'em whistling at girls on the square, and who knows what else they're getting up to. Why, the very idea of a Yankee taking a married lady for a motorcycle ride after dark. It's sinful, is what it is."

Lizzy wondered whether the greater sin lay in being a Yankee or giving a motorcycle ride to a married lady. "Lucy manages the kitchen at Camp Briarwood," she said evenly. "Maybe she had to work late and somebody gave her a lift home."

"Maybe, and maybe not," Mrs. Lacy said, pulling her eyebrows together. "You're too trusting, Elizabeth. Too naïve. If you ask me, it was one of those CCC boys that got Rona Jean Hancock pregnant, although she herself wasn't any better than she should be. It could have been one of them that killed her, too, especially considering who it was that Adele Hart says she saw out there behind the diner."

"I wonder if the sheriff knows about that," Lizzy said thoughtfully.

"Not unless he's been at the laundry in the last hour or so. Adele told me when I took in my damask tablecloth to be washed and ironed." She made a face. "For things like that tablecloth, I surely miss my Sally-Lou. Catsup and mustard stains never did faze her."

Sally-Lou had been Mrs. Lacy's maid ever since Lizzy was a girl, but when the money was gone and Mrs. Lacy had to go to work, she'd had to let Sally-Lou go. Now, for the first time in her adult life, Mrs. Lacy had to do her own housework, which Lizzy thought might turn out to be a good thing. It gave her something to do in the evenings, at least— something other than walk across the street and pester Lizzy.

There was a silence. Mrs. Lacy seemed to be waiting for something. At last, she put her cup down. "Well, do you want to hear my news or not?"

"What?" Lizzy had been thinking that maybe she'd call the sheriff's office and tell him what she saw at the movie show and also suggest that he drop in and have a talk with Adele Hart. "Oh, I'm sorry, Mama. You *did* say that you had something important to tell me. Yes, of course I want to hear your news. What is it?"

Mrs. Lacy smiled smugly. "Mr. Dunlap has asked me to marry him. And I've said yes."

Lizzy gasped, feeling as if she'd been socked in the stomach and the air had just been knocked out of her. "*Marry* Mr. Dunlap?" she repeated stupidly. "Mr. Dunlap at the Five and Dime?"

"Well, yes." Mrs. Lacy narrowed her eyes. "Is there anything wrong with that?"

Lizzy wanted to leap up and cry, *No, nothing wrong! The Almighty has just answered my prayers, that's all. Now you'll be Mr. Dunlap's problem!*

But she couldn't, so she said, as calmly as she could, "Of course not, Mama, if that's what you want to do. It's just . . . it's just a little sudden, that's all. I need a minute to catch my breath."

"Not sudden at all," Mrs. Lacy said smartly. "Of course, we were church friends before I went to work for him at the Five and Dime. I've always enjoyed hearing him sing in the choir—he has such a lovely tenor voice. After I began working at the store, we got friendlier and friendlier and . . . well, things just developed, that's all."

"And you kept it a secret," Lizzy marveled. That by itself was a huge surprise, since her mother had never before demonstrated any ability to keep a secret. The minute she heard anything interesting, she ran right over to tell Ouida Bennett. And *this* was certainly interesting.

"Mr. Dunlap thought it would be better to wait until we were sure," Mrs. Lacy said shyly. "He's telling his children this weekend." She smiled, and Lizzy thought it was one of the first genuine smiles she had seen on her mother's face in a very long time. "He really is a very dear man, Elizabeth, once you get to know him."

"I'm sure he is," Lizzy said. "I'm looking forward to getting better acquainted." This was the honest truth, for the Mr. Dunlap she knew was a meek, mousy little man—a widower with two grown children—who would scarcely say boo to a goose. She couldn't imagine how he had gotten up the nerve to kiss her mother, much less propose to her. But maybe things had happened the other way around: the proposal first, the kiss second. Or maybe her mother had cornered him, kissed him, and proposed. Lizzy had no difficulty imagining *that*.

"To tell the truth," her mother said, "Mr. Dunlap is a *tiger*." She smiled. "If you know what I mean."

Lizzy blinked. "Not exactly." She added hurriedly (to forestall an explanation), "Have you set a date for the wedding? And have you decided where you will live?" Mr. Dunlap, she knew, lived in a house behind the Five and Dime—a small house, no bigger than her own. She didn't think there was room for her mother there.

"We're having a church wedding next month. You'll be my bridesmaid, won't you?" Without waiting for an answer, Mrs. Lacy went on, "And we've decided to live in my house." She made a face. "His house is a shoebox. Mine is larger, and *so* much nicer."

Actually, it was Lizzy's house now, but she was so happy about this new development that she didn't remind her mother of their arrangement. "I would love to be your bridesmaid," she said, with a heartfelt enthusiasm. "We'll have to put our heads together about dresses. And flowers. And the reception. It'll be *fun*, Mama!"

Mrs. Lacy's eyes were misty. "Do you think it would be too gauche of me to wear white, with a veil? Your father and I eloped, and I so wanted a white wedding. But at my age, and having been married before and with a full-grown daughter . . ."

Lizzy got up, went around the table, and hugged her

mother. "You can absolutely wear white if you want to, Mama. If anybody complains, I'll—" She stopped, trying to think of something appropriate. "I'll have Mr. Moseley send them an official cease-and-desist letter," she finished triumphantly, and they both laughed.

"Well," her mother said, and pushed her chair back, "enough of that. Mr. Dunlap is coming over for supper this evening—why don't you join us?"

Lizzy frowned. She really wanted to meet Mr. Dunlap informally and let him know how *glad* she was that he was marrying her mother, but it wasn't going to be this evening.

"I'd love to," she lied, "but I promised Verna I'd have supper with her. Thanks, anyway." After what her mother had said about the CCC camp, she wasn't going to tell her that Captain Campbell was expected for supper, too. And that she was supposed to be sweet to him so he would do more good things for Darling.

Mrs. Lacy frowned and shook her head. "It's all very well to have girlfriends, Elizabeth, but I do wish you would make an effort to find a nice young man." She went to the door and stood with her hand on the knob, looking down her nose. "Ever since Grady Alexander had to get married . . ."

Mrs. Lacy let her voice trail away sadly. Lizzy knew that she had never been quite forgiven for allowing Grady Alexander to marry Sandra Mann—not that she could have done anything about it, of course. Well, that wasn't exactly true, Lizzy reminded herself ruefully. If she had let Grady do what he wanted to do, he might not have done what he wanted to do with Sandra Mann—and gotten her pregnant. On balance, Lizzy was glad that she had held the line where sex was concerned, but she often wondered how Sandra felt. If she had it to do over, would she? Of course, Sandra had a baby *and* a husband, so she might think she'd gotten the best part of the bargain.

"And now they live just down the block," Mrs. Lacy said in an accusing tone, reinforcing her implication that Grady's defection was entirely Lizzy's fault. "I suppose you know that they're expecting again?"

Lizzy pulled in her breath. "Actually, I didn't," she said evenly, "but I'm glad to hear it." The first baby had been a little boy, Grady Junior. "I hope the next one will be a girl. That would be nice for Sandra."

"She's not well, you know," Mrs. Lacy said with a meaningful glance. "Her aunt Twyla says she's very sick."

"That's too bad. I hope her health improves."

"Oh, of course. For the sake of her *two* little children." Mrs. Lacy heaved a dramatic sigh. "And to think that you could have—"

"No, Mama," Lizzy said firmly. "I couldn't. And I didn't. And I'm glad." She pushed the door open for her mother. "Oh, and congratulations again. I just can't tell you how *delighted* I am for you and Mr. Dunlap. I know you'll be very happy together."

She shut the door firmly and stood with her back to it for a moment, thinking back over their conversation, past the fascinating news that Mr. Dunlap was about to take her mother off her hands—forever, she hoped—and back to what her mother had said about Adele Hart. Then she went into the entry hallway and picked up the candlestick phone that sat on the little table under the mirror. She rang the operator and heard a young woman saying, "Number, please."

"Lenore, is that you? Will you ring the sheriff's office for me, please?"

"It's me, Henrietta," the operator said. "I can ring the

office, but the sheriff isn't there. He's upstairs here at the diner, talking to Violet and Myra May."

"Well, ring the office anyway," Lizzy said. "Maybe the deputy is there."

A moment later, Lizzy was talking to Wayne Springer, telling him that she had seen Rona Jean Hancock at the Monroeville movie theater with a man who might have been a CCC officer. "They were a little . . . well, passionate," she said in an explanatory tone. She added that her mother had told her that Adele Hart had seen somebody—a man in a CCC uniform—waiting for Rona Jean outside the diner. "I thought this was something the sheriff should maybe look into. Will you tell him, please?"

"Thank you, ma'am," the deputy said. "I'll do that." He paused. "That's H-a-r-t?"

"Yes. Adele Hart. Artis Hart is her husband. They live next door to the laundry, but if the sheriff stops in during the day, she'll probably be at work. He should go there first."

There. She had done her good deed for the day. Lizzy put the phone down and stood for a moment, thinking. She had promised Verna she would bring a salad for supper tonight, so she ought to go out to the garden and see what she had in the way of salad fixings—the last of the lettuce, if the heat hadn't done it in. But she knew there were some tomatoes, a cucumber or two, and a few green onions. She looked out of the window, noticing that the sky had grown darker and that there were thunderclouds piling up to the southwest. She probably ought to get the salad makings now, before it rained. And since she had the rest of the afternoon free, she should finish up the "Garden Gate" column she'd been working on, in case Charlie had room for it in the special edition of the *Dispatch*.

But first, there was Nadine Fleming's letter.

Back in the kitchen, Lizzy slid into the dining nook, lifted the oilcloth, and took out the letter. She sat down holding it for a moment, thinking about prayers and wondering whether—and how—her life might be changed by what the letter held or whether she would go on doing just what she was doing now, for the rest of her days. Then she unfolded it and read the first few lines.

And burst into tears.

# ELEVEN

## THE GARDEN GATE

#### BY ELIZABETH LACY

    At a recent meeting of the Darling Dahlias, Miss Rogers (Darling's devoted librarian and noted plant historian) gave a talk on old-fashioned flowering bulbs that thrive in Southern gardens. Among the plants she recommended were eleven o'clock ladies, naked ladies, chives and garlic chives, gladiolas, starflowers, and snowflakes, as well as caladium and elephant ear, which are grown for their decorative leaves. Of course, Miss Rogers gave us the correct Latin names, which she recommends that we use to avoid confusing one plant with another. We have a list of those, if you want them. Just ask.

❧ It's been a busy summer for the Dahlias Canning Kettle Ladies (Bessie Bloodworth, team captain, with Earlynne Biddle, Aunt Hetty Little, and Beulah Trivette). They have been putting up extra produce donated by gardeners all over town, to share with our Darling needy folk in the winter. The team is using the two new big pressure cookers the Dahlias bought with the money they earned from the quilt raffle. (Big thanks to Mildred Kilgore and Alice Ann Walker for organizing the raffle!) The Canning Kettle Ladies put up dozens of jars of green beans, corn, tomatoes and tomato sauce, peaches, and pickles. The residents of the Magnolia Manor will be helping to distribute the canned goods, so if you want to put your name on the list (or the name of a needy neighbor), let Bessie Bloodworth know, or call the Magnolia Manor at 477 and leave a message. Come November and December, you'll be glad you did. It'll be like eating summer out of a jar.

❧ Mildred Kilgore gave a demonstration on how to make an old-fashioned rose jar to the Methodist Ladies last week. Several ladies from other churches have expressed their regret that her demonstration was limited to their Methodist friends and have requested her how-to instructions. She says to take a pint of dried rose petals (red are prettiest) and pack them in a jar, sprinkling each layer with coarse salt. Put a lid on it and put it on a closet shelf for a month. Then find a big bowl and mix in 1/4 ounce of orris root, 2 teaspoons each of powdered ginger, nutmeg, and allspice, and 4 tablespoons each of dried lavender and lemon verbena. Dump in the rose petals and mix it all together very well with a big spoon. Put everything back in the jar and put the jar back in the closet for another month. To use, put in a pretty bowl, stir every so often, and take a deep sniff when you walk past.

🦢 The Dahlias, under the direction of Verna Tidwell, have compiled a companion booklet to their very popular "Makin' Do" booklet. This one is called "The Dahlias' Household Magic: A Baker's Dozen Ways to Do It Easier, Faster, Better." You may pick up a copy free at the *Dispatch* office. (Mrs. Albert says she's going to include it in her latest book, which Miss Rogers has promised to get for the Darling Library. She says that you should put your name on the waiting list now if you want to read it. It'll probably be a very long list.)

🦢 Aunt Hetty Little is inviting everyone to her garden to see the very strange Voodoo Lily (*Dracunculus vulgaris*, according to Miss Rogers), which is blooming now. It has impressively large (12") deep purple flowers that last about a week. But you might want to bring a perfumed hanky to cover your nose. The Voodoo Lily (a.k.a. Stink Lily) smells like something crawled under the porch and died. Mildred, who collects exotic plants, reports that the plant produces this smell on purpose, to attract the flies that pollinate the huge blossoms. "Some plants are very clever that way," she says.

🦢 We were cleaning up Mrs. Dahlia Blackstone's papers recently (Mrs. Blackstone was the founder of our garden club, as you probably know), and found this lovely clipping that we want to share with you. It's been around for so long that nobody knows who wrote it. We hope it will be around for a long time to come.

### Recipe for Preserving Children

Take one grassy field, 1/2 dozen children, 3 small dogs, a pinch of a brook, and some pebbles. Mix the children and dogs well together and put them in the field, stirring constantly. Pour the brook over the pebbles. Sprinkle the field with flowers, spread over all a deep blue sky, and bake in a hot sun. When brown, remove the children and set away to cool in a bathtub.

# TWELVE

# Ophelia Goes Undercover

Ophelia took one look at her daughter's choice of a birthday present and knew that Jed would *not* approve. Sarah, a long-legged, gray-eyed blonde with developing curves and a liberal peppering of freckles, had found the swimsuit she wanted on the second floor of Katz Department Store on the south side of the square in Monroeville. The suit was a bright red clingy wool knit, cut high in the legs and low in the bust. When he saw it, Jed would have a conniption fit.

But even though she felt a little disloyal to her husband, Ophelia went ahead and bought the swimsuit anyway. Times had changed—jeepers, had they ever!—and the swimsuits she had worn when *she* was a teenager (and which Jed would certainly approve) would be laughed at today. She remembered one fetching number her mother had bought her when she was twelve, before the Great War. It had a blousy, button-to-the-chin black top with elbow-length sleeves and a calf-length black-and-white striped skirt, and she wore it with black stockings, lace-up rubber shoes, and a frilly turban. Sarah was a sensitive young girl, and she ought to have what her friends had. In Ophelia's opinion, the worst thing that could happen to a young girl was to feel *different* from all the other girls.

With the idea of somehow making it up to Jed, Ophelia went down to the men's department and picked out a shirt for him—another boring blue plaid cotton, but it was the kind he liked and it was on sale for ninety-nine cents. She also bought a tee shirt for Sam (thirty-nine cents) and splurged on a white blouse for herself, tailored, with pearl buttons and short sleeves. It was $1.09, but well made and worth the money, she thought, and anyway she needed it, now that she was working five days a week, three of them out at Camp Briarwood, where she met a great many strangers and liked to look nice.

Then, with Sam's baseball team picnic in mind, she shopped for hamburger (fifteen cents a pound) and hot dogs (eight cents a pound) at Haynes' Meat Market, and got a frying chicken for twenty cents a pound for Sunday dinner. Kitty-corner across the street at the Value Rite grocery, she bought cabbage for slaw (ten cents a pound), yellow cheese to top the hamburgers (nineteen cents a pound), buns for the hamburgers and hot dogs (eight cents a package), and a dozen and a half lemons (fifteen cents a dozen) for lemonade. She had already made two apple pies for dessert, with apples that the Dahlias had canned last fall. And she had saved back a dozen eggs for an angel food cake—Sarah's favorite—for her birthday dinner tomorrow. She didn't have any cake flour, but she had a box of cornstarch and a bag of all-purpose flour and she knew how to make a very decent substitute for the more expensive cake flour.

As she and Sarah got in the family Ford and drove back toward Darling, Ophelia was still worrying about what Jed was going to say when he saw Sarah's bathing suit. Maybe she would just casually mention it to him at the same time she gave him his new plaid shirt, and bank on his usual lack of curiosity about things she bought for the kids. At least she hadn't had to ask him for the money to buy it. She had her own money to spend, which she counted as a hundred blessings, one for every penny in the dollar.

Ophelia was able to buy clothes and groceries—as well as put tires on the family's old blue Ford and finish paying for the living room suite she had foolishly bought on time out of the Sears and Roebuck catalog—because she had gotten a really lucky break. During the months that her friend Liz was working in Montgomery, Mr. Moseley had hired her to take Liz's place three days a week in his office. She'd still been able to work for Charlie at the *Dispatch* on the other two days, so between them she was working five days a week. Then, when Liz came back and reclaimed her desk in Mr. Moseley's office, Ophelia had gotten a three-day-a-week job at Camp Briarwood: another lucky break. A *very* lucky break, especially given how slow the feed business was.

Unfortunately, Jed didn't quite see it that way. His masculine pride had been stung by Ophelia's success, and he kept muttering that it was *his* responsibility to support the family and his wife should stay home where God had put her. Ophelia didn't know about God, but she understood Jed's feelings about her working. He came from a conservative family, and none of his womenfolk—his mother and aunts and cousins—had ever held a paying job outside the home. Women just *didn't*; that was all. It was no wonder he hated to see her go out the door every morning, all dressed up and with lipstick on and heels, like she was going to the picture show.

But while Jed would never admit it, Ophelia knew that the money she brought home every week had been a lifesaver. Snow's Farm Supply, the family business Jed had inherited from his father, had been in deep trouble for the last few years. Farmers were scrambling to find the money for seed and equipment, and Jed (who had a hard head but a soft heart) had extended too much credit to his customers. The Snows had been scraping the bottom of the barrel, and Ophelia—who never felt very secure, even in the best of times—lived in constant dread that he would come home one day and tell her that the business was finished and that they were going to lose their house. And their car. And everything they had worked for since they got married.

Through all those dark months, it was Ophelia's earnings that had kept the family afloat and supported Jed's parents, too, both of whom were too old and too sick to work. She didn't mind helping them, of course. She accepted it as her obligation. Jed was their only child, so they had nowhere else to turn—except the county poor farm, and she and Jed would never let *that* happen, not in a million years. But where else could old folks turn if they didn't have any children and couldn't pay the rent or doctor or dentist bills, or buy enough fatback and beans to keep them alive? For many, it was a desperate situation.

Just recently, though, Ophelia had read that President Roosevelt had sent a message to Congress about something he was calling "social security," which was designed to give older people a little something to live on when they couldn't work any longer. There seemed to be a lot of opposition to it—some were calling it socialism or even communism—but when Ophelia paid Mother Snow's doctor bill and bought Dad Snow a pair of new dentures, she felt it would be a godsend if it passed. If it didn't, she was hoping that Senator Huey P. Long, a Democrat from Louisiana who had a bigger mouth and even bigger ideas than Franklin Roosevelt, would win the 1936 presidential election. She often heard the senator talking on the radio about his plan to make every man a king, and she thought it was grand. If Senator Long was elected, he promised to limit rich people's annual incomes to a million dollars. The government would take the rest and use the money to guarantee every family two thousand dollars a year and every person over sixty an old-age pension. Ophelia had declared that she was personally ready to cast her vote for Huey P. Long if President Roosevelt couldn't get his social security program through Congress.

She and Sarah were halfway back to Darling and the turn-off to Camp Briarwood was in sight when Ophelia said, "I want to stop at the camp for a few minutes. I left some papers on my desk, and I need to take them home and work on them." (That was what Charlie Dickens called her "cover story," what she would say to anybody who happened to come into the office while she was getting the files that Charlie wanted.) She turned to glance at Sarah. "And you haven't seen the camp yet, honey, or the building where I work. Let's take a quick detour."

"Do we *have* to?" Sarah asked, pouting. "Really, it's too hot to be out driving around. I want to get home and show my swell new bathing suit to Connie. It'll knock her eyes out." She hugged the swimsuit sack. "The one her mother got her has a skirt on it. A ruffled skirt that comes halfway down to her knees. Of course Connie hates it." Connie, who lived next door, was Sarah's best friend.

Sarah was right about it being *hot*, Ophelia thought. She glanced up at the sky, which was clouding up. It looked like the weather forecast might be right. They might have rain, in which case they might have to move the picnic onto the back porch, if it didn't come down too hard. Or indoors, if it did.

"We won't be there very long," she promised, making

the turn. She shifted into second gear and headed down the bumpy graveled road that led to the camp, a mile away. She smiled over at Sarah. "Don't pout, sweetie. Your face might get stuck that way, and then you won't look very pretty in your red swimsuit. Which is going to turn your father a dozen shades of purple, you know. He would rather it had a skirt on it—all the way down to your ankles."

That brought a giggle. "Poor Daddy," Sarah said, rolling her eyes. "He is such an old fogy. What makes him be that way?"

"Love." Ophelia reached out and patted Sarah's arm. "He loves you, hon. He doesn't want you to grow up and go away from home."

Sarah was silent for a moment, looking out the window. "Daddy's an old fogy about your job out here, too, isn't he? I guess maybe he doesn't want *you* to go away from home, either."

Ophelia sighed. Sarah was an uncommonly perceptive young woman. She had sensed the tension that the Camp Briarwood job was creating in the family. Jed hadn't been happy with the *Dispatch* job or the work in Mr. Moseley's law office, but (as Ophelia had often pointed out), she was just a half block from the farm supply store and only a few blocks from home. Jed knew and liked Charlie and Mr. Moseley, he knew exactly where to find her, and she was always available to him and the children on a moment's notice.

None of that was true with her new three-day-a-week job at the CCC camp, which was five miles out of town. She left early in the morning and barely got home in time to put supper on the table. (Jed was always complaining that they never had dessert on weeknights, and when they did, it was Jell-O, which he wasn't crazy about.) She couldn't be reached very easily, which was bad enough. But probably more important, Jed didn't know the people she worked for. It wouldn't be right to say that her husband was jealous, exactly, because she never gave him any reason for jealousy. But it would certainly be fair to say that he was uneasy at the idea of her working among so many strange men—strange men in uniform, and Yankees, to boot. She suspected that it was the Yankee part that bothered him the most. Jed's grandfather had been a captain in a Confederate regiment. To Jed, Yankees wearing uniforms—even if they were CCC uniforms and didn't look much like the regular military—were soldiers in an invading army.

But while Ophelia kept a wary eye on the Yankees, she loved working at the camp. She was on the job at the *Dispatch* on Wednesday and Thursday, helping Charlie put the paper together for Thursday night printing and Friday mailing. But on Monday, Tuesday, and Friday, she got up early, put the family's breakfast on the table, then rushed to catch the bus to Camp Briarwood, where she worked as a liaison between the camp and the local people who supplied it with goods, equipment, and services—an important job, and she was the right one to do it.

Jed's mood had improved somewhat when she handed him her first pay envelope, but he was still acting surly about it. "You watch out for those damn Yankees," he'd muttered. "You can't trust a one of 'em any farther than you can throw him."

Charlie's reaction, on the other hand, was entirely different. When Ophelia told him about her new job, he had thought it was a grand idea. He even improved on it, coming up with the suggestion that she should start writing a weekly newspaper column about the camp. He would pay her a dollar fifty for each column, which was the same amount he paid Liz for the "Garden Gate" column she wrote for him.

"We'll call it 'Camp Briarwood News,'" he said. "Folks are curious about what's going on out there. You can tell them what's happening. And if you've got enough material for a feature story, we can run that, too." And then just yesterday, he had come up with the more interesting undercover investigative assignment, but that was a different matter. A different matter entirely.

Ophelia was delighted to be writing the column, and not just because of the money. It gave her a chance to satisfy her curiosity and find out much more about the camp than she could have learned just by working there. For her first column, she had interviewed Captain Gordon Campbell, the camp commander, who heartily approved of Charlie's idea for a newspaper column. He was eager, he said, for the local folk to learn about the camp's activities and its plans.

"Our work will go a lot more smoothly if we can count on local cooperation," he had said. "And people will be better able to cooperate if they know what's going on out here, especially now that we're employing a few townspeople." Ophelia got the feeling that Captain Campbell really cared about making his camp successful and that the camp's success could depend on the support it got from Darling. The captain was pleased by the letters that people wrote to the editor about that first column, and told Ophelia that if he could help in any way, all she had to do was let him know.

"Well, here we are," Ophelia said, slowing the car at the top of the small hill that overlooked the camp, beside a large wooden sign.

> *Welcome to Camp Briarwood*
> *Civilian Conservation Corps*
> *Company 432, Camp SCS-8*

"Golly," Sarah said, her eyes widening. She sat up and looked through the windshield at the camp below them. "It's huge, Mom! It's a lot bigger than I thought."

"One of the biggest camps in the state," Ophelia replied proudly. "It's really something, isn't it?"

Camp Briarwood sprawled like a small city across about twenty acres of open meadow, a mile or so from the eastern edge of Briar's Swamp. On the flat plain below them lay an orderly arrangement of two dozen wooden buildings of similar construction, all single story, each painted a dark forest green with a brown shingled roof. They were laid out around a large rectangular parade ground, its grass neatly clipped, with a graveled road that traced another rectangle around the perimeter of the buildings. The place looked like a military compound, which it was, partly. That is, it was run by Army officers, and there was enough military discipline to keep the young men organized and working in an orderly way, although not as much as they would have encountered in a real Army camp.

As they would in the Army, though, the "enrollees" (that's what the boys were called) were given free dental and medical care, free inoculations, and free meals and lodging and clothing. They received a wage of $30 a month, $25 of which was automatically sent home to their families, all of whom were on relief. For that, each boy traded eight hours of labor, five days a week. Everybody was there, as Captain Campbell said firmly, to do a job. An important job.

"Those are the administration buildings," Ophelia said, pointing to two identical structures on the right. "And those are the barracks where the enrollees sleep." She pointed to the left, to a row of four long green-painted frame buildings with doors at either end, each capable of housing fifty young men. "Beyond them are the officers' quarters and the camp guesthouse. When I began working here, there were already 192 enrollees with more on the way, along with a half-dozen officers. Before the barracks were built, the boys lived in tents."

She chuckled. "I'm told that they were glad to move out of those tents. The barracks don't leak. And they're heated." Which mattered in January, when the temperature could go as low as ten or fifteen degrees above zero.

"What do the guys do all day?" Sarah asked wonderingly. "Do they go to school, maybe?"

"They *work*," Ophelia said, remembering what the captain had told her. "That's what they're here for."

Ophelia knew that when the boys arrived, most of them had never held a steady job—and their dads weren't holding steady jobs, either, thanks (or no thanks) to the Depression. Many of them had roamed around the country, catching rides on freight trains, which meant avoiding the railroad cops, sleeping in cardboard boxes in hobo jungles beside the tracks, picking up whatever work they could find in return for something to eat. Ophelia found it frightening that a whole generation of young American men had grown up with no experience of making or building or creating something lasting, or trading their labor for a regular paycheck.

So for the enrollees, the camp's regular daily and weekly work schedule was a crucial part of their learning. Monday through Friday, they were awakened before dawn by the camp bugler blowing reveille. Dressed, beds made, they went for calisthenics, then breakfast in the mess hall. Then they picked up their equipment and climbed into trucks that drove them wherever they were scheduled to work that day. At noon, the mess wagon took lunch to the job site. The trucks brought them back in time to wash up and get ready for supper, announced with another bugle call.

The camp had been built just a short distance from Briar's Swamp for an important reason, Ophelia had learned. According to the "Mission Statement" posted on the wall in the quartermaster's office, the first big work project was to drain the swamp to control the mosquitos and "to put the land into condition for continuous production of timber." One or two people in Darling—including Bessie Bloodworth—were strongly opposed, since the swamp was a natural feature of the land and draining it would mean denying a home to many different species of wildlife. But that was definitely a minority opinion, and the mission was going forward. To get that job done, the boys spent their workdays digging drainage ditches, building roads, and clearing firebreaks. Once finished with that, there were other projects on the camp's agenda.

"But they don't work all the time," Ophelia added. "The boys eat supper in the mess hall, over there." She pointed. "After supper, they can go to the rec hall—that's the building next to the mess hall. Or they can take classes in the education building. That's the shop building, behind it. Or they can catch a ride into town for a movie, as long as they're back by lights-out."

On weekdays, the bugle call for lights-out came at ten p.m. Saturday mornings were reserved for camp cleanup and personal chores. On Saturday afternoons, there were organized sports, or trucks took the boys into town for a matinee movie and a stroll around the square, or dropped them off at the Roller Palace. On Saturday nights there was a dance, to which the townspeople were invited. Some of the enrollees had brought their clarinets and saxophones and trumpets and trombones, and formed a dance band, calling themselves the Briarwood Boogie Boys. Ophelia hadn't been to any of the dances yet—Jed wasn't much for dancing—so she hadn't heard them. But everybody said that while the Boogie Boys weren't quite Benny Goodman, they were really quite good. Ophelia wished she could get Jed to at least come and listen. It sounded like fun.

"Looks like they're playing baseball," Sarah said, pointing

to a game that was underway on a diamond just behind the rec hall.

"It's a tournament," Ophelia replied. "It's been going on all month, among six or seven of the camps in this part of the state." One of the camp officers was in charge of organized sports—baseball, basketball, boxing, horseshoes, footraces, and even table tennis and pool, played in the rec hall. There was a drill team, too, and a flag team and regular calisthenics. When Ophelia interviewed Captain Campbell, he had mentioned that the sports and games weren't just designed to keep the enrollees occupied and out of trouble. They were an important part of the plan to put more meat and muscle on the young men, many of whom had been underweight and malnourished when they arrived at the camp. For many, food hadn't been easy to come by when they were living at home or hopping freight trains to get from here to there, in hopes of more opportunities.

Ophelia reached over and ruffled her daughter's hair. "I wrote about the baseball tournament in my newspaper column last week. Bet you didn't read it, did you?"

"I'm afraid not," Sarah said, laughing ruefully. "But now that I know what it's like out here, I'll try to do better." A deeply tanned young man in a khaki uniform with the sleeves rolled up walked past the car and turned to wave at Sarah with a wink and a broad grin. Sarah, blushing, waved back. "Golly," she breathed. "He's cute!"

Ophelia couldn't help smiling. Last year, boys had been the object of Sarah's scorn. Now, it was different. Sarah was definitely growing up. Ophelia put the car in gear, and they started down the hill, bearing right, toward the administration buildings. Through the open car windows, they heard the whack of a ball being solidly hit and a chorus of wild yells—the rebel yell—as the hitter rounded the bases. It sounded as if somebody had just scored a home run.

"Hey." Sarah sat up straight. "Can I go watch the base-ball game while you get your stuff?"

Ophelia shook her head firmly. "Not a good idea, dear. Some of these boys haven't seen a girl in a while. You'd be mobbed."

Sarah gave her a long-suffering look. "That's the idea, Mom. Being mobbed by a few boys wouldn't hurt a bit. I'll bet it would be fun. Pretty please?"

"Not on your life," Ophelia said. "You know what your father would say to *that* idea." She turned right at the main camp signpost, followed the gravel road a quarter of the way around the parade ground, and parked behind the far-thest administration building. "If you don't want to come in with me, you can stay out here and read." She turned off the ignition. "You did bring a book, didn't you?" She really didn't have to ask. Sarah was a bookworm. She always had a book with her.

"Yeah," Sarah said and pulled a book out of the satchel on the floor. "Nancy Drew. Miss Rogers got it for me at the library." She held it up. *"The Secret of Red Gate Farm."*

"Oh, good," Ophelia said. Grown-up that she was, she enjoyed reading the Nancy Drew books, and she always reached for them when Sarah was finished. "What's it about?"

"Nancy, Bess, and George are conducting an undercover investigation to get the scoop on a counterfeit money ring and turn the information over to federal agents. I can't wait to see what's going to happen next—looks like Nancy is about to be captured by the counterfeiters." Sarah grinned mischievously. "Maybe they'll torture her to get her to give up the secret code she stole."

*An undercover investigation?* Ophelia was startled, since those were the same words—the very same!—that Charlie had used to describe the assignment he had given her. It was unsettling to hear that Nancy Drew, who was usually so astute and careful, had gone undercover and was about to be captured. And *tortured?* Surely not. She frowned. Anyway, that was a story, just fiction. It had nothing at all to do with real life. Still, maybe there was more to this undercover stuff than she had thought. Maybe—

Ophelia pushed the thought away, opened the door, and got out of the car, taking her large handbag with her. "I won't be too long, Sarah. Please wait for me here. And don't leave the car," she added through the open window. She trusted her daughter, but she knew that the baseball game might be tempting.

"I won't," Sarah said, opening her book. "I want to see if Nancy actually gets captured. It's kind of scary, actually. These counterfeiters are dangerous people. If Nancy can get the goods on them, it'll shoot down their whole operation, so they've got a lot at stake. She'll have to be careful."

And for the first time, Ophelia (an optimistic person who liked to look on the bright side of things) thought of the dangers she might face—and the consequences—if somebody caught her doing what Charlie had asked her to do. She felt a cold knot of apprehension, almost of fear, tightening somewhere deep inside, and she shivered. She hadn't thought of it before, but she could lose her job! And if she was accused of taking records she wasn't supposed to have access to, she might even go to jail. But worse, if she was caught by whoever—

Ophelia was startled out of her frightened thoughts by footsteps on gravel and looked up to see a familiar figure coming toward her. It was Lucy Murphy, one of the Dahlias.

Lucy had started working at the camp six months ago as a part-time kitchen helper, but she soon showed what she was made of and had been promoted several times. Now, she managed the entire food service for the camp, planning meals, making up the grocery and supplies orders, and supervising the enrollee kitchen helpers who did the prep work, cooked, baked, and cleaned up. Ophelia put Lucy's menus in the *Dispatch* every week, so the mothers of local boys could see how well their sons were eating—fried chicken, meat loaf, pot roast, pulled pork, and macaroni and cheese, which they probably didn't get at home on a regular basis.

"Hey, Lucy," Ophelia said, raising her hand in a greeting. Trim and athletic, Lucy was wearing a green short-sleeved blouse and khaki-colored slacks, her flaming red hair tied back with a matching green ribbon, a purse swinging from one shoulder. Her cheeks were flushed—as a redhead, she had porcelain skin—and she looked unusually attractive.

For a moment, Ophelia thought Lucy might turn and go the other way, almost as if she wanted to avoid a conversation. But then she changed her mind and came forward. Studying her, Ophelia sighed, wishing she dared to wear slacks. A couple of weeks before, she had seen a pair she liked in the women's department at Katz's. She had bought them on impulse, but she hadn't had the courage to wear them yet. Jed would put up a big fuss. He didn't mind her wearing coveralls when she was working on the Linotype and helping Charlie around the newspaper press, but he was dead set against women wearing men's clothes in public.

"Hey, Ophelia." Lucy wore an unusually sober expression— that is, unusual for Lucy, who never let anything bother her. "You've heard what happened to Rona Jean?"

Ophelia nodded. "I know about the murder, but that's about the size of it. A sad thing."

"Yes. Do you think . . . do they know . . ." Lucy swallowed. "Have they caught the guy yet?"

"Not so far as I know," Ophelia said, thinking that Lucy seemed awfully apprehensive. But then, Ralph was on the railroad and she spent a lot of evenings alone. Rona Jean's murder probably made her feel vulnerable. "I'm sure the sheriff's doing an investigation," she added.

"I *hope* so," Lucy said, in an odd voice. "We can't have somebody running around killing people. I mean, it's downright scary, is what it is."

Uncomfortably, Ophelia changed the subject. "I didn't think you worked on Saturday." Five days a week, the camp had hot meals, but on the weekends, the enrollees set out cereals for breakfast and sandwich and salad fixings for lunch and supper, and everybody helped themselves. "I figured you'd be home with Ralph today, working in your garden."

"I'm not here, usually," Lucy said in an offhand way. "But Ralph had to make a run to Nashville, and I had a stack of orders to finish."

She cleared her throat, her eyes sliding away, and Ophelia, with a startling conviction, thought, *She's not telling the truth!* Or maybe she was remembering the gossip that had cropped up lately. Lucy was an attractive woman, and Ralph's railroad job took him out of town at least five days a week, and sometimes weekends, too. In fact, Ouida Bennett's sister, Erma Rae, who lived just up the road from the Murphys, had told Mother Snow that she had seen Lucy on the back of an Army motorcycle, late in the evening, and that she'd heard that motorcycle several other nights. It didn't look good, Erma Rae had said, especially with Ralph out of town. Mother Snow had told Ophelia, who had immediately pooh-poohed the idea that Lucy was running around.

But now she wasn't so sure. Was it possible that Lucy

and her motorcycle man had been having a tryst this afternoon? Were they romantically involved? Yes, of course it was possible. In fact, looking at Lucy's flushed cheeks, she'd say it was entirely likely. But if they were, Ophelia reminded herself, it was none of her business. Whatever Lucy was up to was between her and Ralph and nobody else.

"Anyway," Lucy was going on, "I thought I'd just go ahead and get it done today, while nobody's around. Weekdays are always such a madhouse in that kitchen. And there's always too much paperwork—the CCC may be doing good things, but it's a huge bureaucracy."

"That's certainly true," Ophelia said emphatically. The Civilian Conservation Corps was jointly run by the secretaries of war, agriculture, labor, and interior, and there were so many reports to compile and send that it made Olivia dizzy. "I often wonder if anybody actually reads that stuff or whether it's just stuck in a file drawer in an office somewhere in Washington." Which, as Charlie had explained when he offered her the undercover assignment, might make it all too easy for somebody to cheat the system.

Lucy gave Ophelia a sideways glance. "But you're not usually here on weekends, either. Right?"

Ophelia nodded warily. "I left some papers on my desk that I meant to take home, so I stopped to pick them up." It was the second time she had said this out loud, and she thought it sounded more or less authentic.

But she knew it wasn't true. Did she suspect Lucy of lying because *she* was lying?

Lucy was studying her, frowning. "You work in the quartermaster's office with Corporal Andrews, don't you? Managing the supply orders from local people?"

Ophelia was guiltily aware of her undercover assignment. "That's right. I'm the liaison person, between the camp and the local suppliers. Corporal Andrews arranges the contracts, and he and Sergeant Webb supervise the deliveries, manage the payments, and make sure that the camp gets what it pays for." She hesitated. What was behind Lucy's question? "Why are you asking?"

"Oh, I was just wondering," Lucy said casually—too casually, Ophelia thought. "I've met Corporal Andrews a time or two. He's nice."

"He is," Ophelia said. She suddenly remembered that Corporal Andrews rode an Army motorcycle on his various rounds of the local suppliers. Was *he* the guy Lucy was involved with? Assuming she was involved with anybody, that is, which might not be the case at all. And of course, the corporal wasn't the only one who rode a motorcycle. The camp had a motor pool, and there were a couple of motorcycles in it, and she frequently heard them buzzing past her office. Hurriedly, she changed the subject. "Are you headed home? I'll be going back to Darling in a few minutes. I'd be glad to drop you."

Lucy smiled. "Thanks, but I've got Ralph's car. He let me take it while he's gone, for once, although I'm sure he doesn't expect to get it back in one piece. He keeps saying that women don't know how to drive." Lucy's eyes were bright, and to Ophelia, she seemed unusually vivacious. "Anyway, Bessie is over at the garden, keeping an eye on the boys who are picking the first batch of early sweet corn. I told her I'd give her a lift back to town."

Bessie Bloodworth, another Dahlia and an experienced vegetable gardener, came out to the camp three days a week to supervise the planning and maintenance of the large garden. Captain Campbell had assigned a half-dozen strong young men to do the heavy work—plowing and harrowing with the camp mules and doing the planting, hoeing, irrigating, and picking. Bessie decided what they were going to plant and how much and when, and when it was ready for harvest. Bessie had told Ophelia that she thought the garden was going to be the best she'd ever seen. "We've already got ripe watermelons," she'd said, "and it looks like we'll soon have all the sweet corn the boys can eat."

But Ophelia, Lucy, and Bessie weren't the only Darling people working at the camp—and not the only Dahlias, either. The enrollees were expected to do most of the labor, but experienced local people, both men and women, were hired to help manage some of the operations. Since jobs were so scarce in Cypress County, there was plenty of competition for every position, even for jobs in the camp laundry and kitchen. The camp was about five miles outside of town, and most of the workers didn't have their own transportation, so Captain Campbell had arranged for the camp jitney to pick up the employees each morning in front of the Darling courthouse and bring them back to town at the end of the day, at no charge.

The Dahlias who happened to be around at lunchtime often ate together at one of the tables in the mess hall. They agreed that Darling was much better off now that the camp had brought more money into the community, and that the building projects and roads and tree plantings and erosion controls were going to make a big difference in Cypress County.

But they agreed that there were also plenty of personal benefits. Working at the camp gave each woman her very own salary, several of them for the first time in their lives. Bessie Bloodworth, for instance, owned a boardinghouse called the Magnolia Manor, but she had never earned a regular paycheck working for somebody else. And while Lucy sold the fruit and vegetables she and Ralph raised in their market garden, the money went into Ralph's pocket, and he handed over whatever he thought she needed for household expenses. Working at the camp gave all of them their very own paycheck and a new feeling of personal independence.

And, as Miss Dorothy Rogers frequently said, working with people who came from somewhere else—like the Yankee officers at the camp and the young men who came from out of state—was "broadening." Miss Rogers, Darling's long-time librarian, was now managing the Camp Briarwood library. In the column Ophelia had written about the library, she had quoted Miss Rogers as saying that "the boys always seem thrilled to find the latest magazines and paperback books." Off the record, Miss Rogers had told her that Captain Campbell had given her a surprisingly large budget for library materials and had hinted that once the camp had finished its work and made plans to pack up and leave, the books and magazines would be donated to Darling.

Earlynne Biddle, Verna Tidwell, and Liz Lacy were the other Dahlias who worked at the camp, part-time, as teachers. Since one of the goals of the CCC program was to give the boys as many learning opportunities as possible, Briarwood offered a full-scale educational program, with classes taught by local people. It included basic reading, writing, and arithmetic, as well as wood shop (taught by Ozzie Sherman, who ran the sawmill), welding shop (taught by Jesse Maxwell, who had recently converted his Darling blacksmith's forge into a welding operation), and auto shop (taught by Jake Pritchard's son, who helped his dad run the Standard Oil station).

Verna taught arithmetic and a small advanced course in basic accounting. Earlynne and Liz shared the reading and writing classes. When Ophelia interviewed Earlynne for her column, she said she'd been astonished to learn how many of the CCC boys hadn't stayed in school long enough to learn to read and write properly. Now was their chance, and many of them were taking advantage of it. All of the classes were held in the education building, which contained the camp library and reading room as well as the classrooms. The vocational classes were taught in the adjacent shop building.

Lucy shifted her bag to the other shoulder. "It looks like almost all the Dahlias are out here today. Bessie is waiting for me, and I saw Earlynne and Miss Rogers a little while ago, on their way to the education building. And here you are. Haven't seen Verna, though, or Liz." She glanced in the direction of Ophelia's car. "Sarah's with you?"

Ophelia nodded. "Tomorrow is her fifteenth birthday. She and I drove over to Monroeville to get her birthday present—a new red swimsuit that'll likely make Jed blow his stack." She laughed.

Lucy rolled her eyes. "Fifteen. It doesn't seem possible, Opie. Seems like that little girl should still be climbing trees and jumping rope."

"I know." Ophelia made a mournful face. "Next thing you know, she'll be all grown up." Sam, too—he was two years older. When the kids were gone, she and Jed would just rattle around the empty house.

"Sarah is so smart," Lucy said with a serious look. "I hope she'll go to college." Lucy had told Ophelia that she had wanted to go to college, but she'd wanted to marry Ralph even more and didn't think he'd wait for her. She wished now that she'd gone for at least two years, Ralph or no Ralph. But of course it was too late. Women her age didn't go to college, even if they had the money.

"I don't think we can afford it," Ophelia said. "Sam graduates next year, and Jed is hoping he'll be able to go. He says there's not much future in the farm supply business. But Sarah's a girl and—" She gave a little shrug. "Jed thinks college for girls is a waste of money. He says she'll just get married."

Lucy leaned forward, her face intent. "Don't you believe

everything that man tells you, Ophelia Snow. Girls have every bit as much right to a college education as boys do. Every woman ought to have a shot at independence. At freedom." Her voice was low and fierce, and there was a kind of longing in it that Ophelia had never heard before.

"Freedom?" Ophelia asked uneasily. "What kind of freedom?"

Lucy came from Atlanta, so she had a somewhat different view of the world than women who had lived in Darling all their lives. She was different in other ways, too. She said what she thought and felt without holding back, and she was . . . well, romantic. Ralph had complained once that she wore her heart on her sleeve where it could get knocked around and hurt, and Ophelia thought that was probably true. It might also account for some of the gossip about her.

Lucy bit her lip, as if she wished she could bite back what she had said. And when she spoke, she didn't quite answer Ophelia's question.

"I just mean . . . well, things are getting better now. There's finally some hope, when we've all been feeling hopeless for so long." She took a breath. "You don't want Sarah stuck in Darling for her whole entire life, do you? She ought to get a college degree so she can get a decent job if she wants one, or a career. So she can go places and *do* things. And doesn't have to depend on a husband to support her."

That last sentence startled Ophelia, and she suddenly saw what Lucy was driving at. She shifted uncomfortably. She was holding down two jobs and helping to support the family, and she thought of herself as a modern mother—modern enough, anyway, to buy that red swimsuit for Sarah, even if she didn't dare put on a pair of slacks.

But she hadn't given a lot of thought to Sarah's future. She had assumed, more or less unconsciously, that her daughter would get married, settle down right here in Darling, and start having babies. Ophelia had always wanted *lots* of grandbabies to hold in her lap. To croon to and cuddle. And that's what girls wanted, too, wasn't it?

But maybe she ought to think beyond that, for Sarah. For the sake of Sarah's future. Maybe college—

Lucy drew back. "Sorry," she muttered. "I'm probably way out of line. Sometimes I wish I could have done it differently myself, that's all." She sighed and waggled a hand, resigned. "Well, you know, Opie. Water under the bridge. We can't have everything we want out of life. And maybe I'm just depressed, thinking about what happened to Rona Jean. It seems so awful, dying like that, so young. She never had a chance to see the world or go to college or anything. Just think of all she's missed."

Ophelia studied Lucy's face sympathetically. Lucy didn't have many friends, even among the Dahlias, because she lived outside of town. But since Ralph was Jed's cousin, she and Lucy had occasionally talked, and she knew it wasn't the first time Lucy had felt stuck in her marriage. But people in Darling always said that when you've made your bed, you have to lie in it. That was what most folks did, as best they could, even though they might not like it. Not all of it, anyway, and not always. The thing about Lucy, though— the thing that made her different from everybody else— was that she didn't *pretend* to like it.

"I appreciate what you were saying about Sarah and college," Ophelia said quietly. "I'll start thinking about it and see if I can't put a little more in the cookie jar, without telling Jed. Then when the time comes, maybe Sarah will have an option."

That made her feel . . . well, disloyal, like buying their daughter a bathing suit she knew Jed wouldn't like, only more so. College was a bigger, more consequential thing than the bathing suit, but either way, she was going against his wishes. Still, she ought to be thinking of what was best for Sarah, which probably wasn't what Sarah's father—or her mother, for that matter—might like.

She glanced down at her wristwatch. "Gosh, look at the time! I'd better get what I came for and head home. We're having a backyard picnic for Sam's baseball team tonight. If the rain holds off, that is." She glanced toward the southwest. Did the sky look more menacing? "It might be a back porch picnic, if it doesn't."

Lucy nodded. "Thanks for listening, Opie." She raised her hand. "I suppose I'll see you at the clubhouse early on the Fourth." The Dahlias were decorating the Miss Darling float that morning, for the parade.

"Count on it," Ophelia said. She waved good-bye, reached into her handbag, and took out the key to her office, which also unlocked the front door. Like the other buildings, this one was so new that it still smelled of fresh pine, roofing tar, and paint. No effort had been made to pretty it up or make it anything other than functional. Inside, the pent-up heat was stifling. The hallway went through the middle of the building, with offices on either side. Lit only by a dim bulb hanging from the ceiling midway to the far end, it was hot and dark and . . . well, creepy.

It was silent, too, and Ophelia's heels tapped on the bare wooden floor. Suddenly aware of the clatter, she stopped, slipped out of her shoes, and picked them up. Nobody worked on weekends if they could help it, which meant that there was nobody around to hear her footsteps—and nobody around to catch her doing what she was about to do, which now struck her as more than a little dangerous, and risky, too. It might not be strictly illegal—after all, government records were public records, weren't they? But it was definitely not in her job description, and if she got caught, it was probably a firing offense.

A shiver started at her tailbone and ran up her spine to her shoulders. The place seemed different than it did on weekdays, when all the lights were on, the office doors were open, and the hallway was bustling with busy people. The conversation with Lucy, unsettling as it was, had pushed Ophelia's earlier apprehension to the back of her mind. Now, it returned in a chilly flood, heightened by the darkness and shadows. Why hadn't she thought to ask Lucy to come in with her? Lucy would have no idea what she was doing, and two women would surely be safer than one woman alone. Being alone meant that there was nobody around to hear if she called for help—although, of course, that wouldn't be necessary. Would it?

And then, with a sudden chill, she thought of Rona Jean Hancock. Rona Jean must have struggled, must even have called for help, but there was nobody around to hear—except her killer.

Of course, there was no connection between the murder and the job Charlie had sent her to do. But the thought of Rona Jean made Ophelia's breath come fast and her heart pound so hard she could feel the thudding in her bones, and she broke into a run toward the safety of her office at the far end of the hall. Her hands shaking, she stuck the key in the lock and fumbled it open. Then she shut and locked the door behind her, leaning against it and breathing hard, her eyes squeezed shut.

In here, at least, she felt safer.

# THIRTEEN

# Sheriff Norris Collects More Clues

Before Buddy went into the diner for lunch, he paused at the wire newspaper rack beside the front door to read the front-page headline of the *Mobile Register*. It announced, in big, bold letters: *Roosevelt Orders $150,000,000 Spent in Drought Relief.*

Buddy had been following the news about the Dust Bowl in Oklahoma and Nebraska, and thought that nature had suddenly thrown a temper tantrum and was making it very hard for people who just wanted to grow their crops and their cows and their kids and get on with their lives. The federal money sounded like a good idea, even though the smaller headline noted that FDR had "borrowed" it from the $525,000,000 fund to support CCC camps. Buddy hoped the president wouldn't "borrow" any money from Camp Briarwood, which seemed to be doing good things for Cypress County. He was looking forward to meeting the camp commander at Verna's house that night.

The lunch rush was just tapering off when Buddy took his usual place at the counter, right in front of the big black Emerson electric fan, where it could blow directly on him and cool him off. The day was hot and sultry and—unless you were sitting in front of a fan—the air wasn't moving.

He always had meat loaf on Saturdays, but today the liver and onions sounded good, so he ordered that, with mashed potatoes and skillet corn and cabbage slaw and a piece of Raylene's lemon chess pie, all for thirty-five cents. He ate to the accompaniment of the weather report from radio station WALA (which was supposed to stand for "We Are Loyal Alabamians") down in Mobile. A ship out in the Gulf had registered a barometric low of 979 millibars, and winds of 85 miles an hour had been reported at a nearby weather station. Hurricane flags were flying for Mobile Bay and the northern Gulf of Mexico. Inland, the forecast was for rain and plenty of it, which was good, Buddy thought. The crops and pastures needed it—as long as they didn't get too much. There were miles of unimproved roads in the county, and rain turned them into bottomless goo.

The weather report was followed, as usual, by the noon market report: pork bellies were up, feeder calves were down, corn and beans were both down. And then the national news. FDR had just signed something called a "credit union" act, whatever that was. The Yankees had beaten the White Sox 13 to 2 in Yankee Stadium, with Lou Gehrig—who had a .366 batting average for the season—slamming a double, a triple, and a home run. And the mayor of Shreveport, Louisiana, had threatened to organize a lynching party for Senator Huey P. ("Kingfish") Long. "If it is necessary to teach him decency at the end of a hempen rope," the mayor cried, "I, for one, am willing to swing the rope!" Buddy, who had heard from law enforcement friends in Louisiana that the Kingfish ran a mighty corrupt shop over there, thought that in this case, lynching might be acceptable.

While Buddy listened and ate, he fielded questions about the murder from Mr. Dunlap, owner of the Five and Dime, and old J.D. Henderson, who helped Mr. Musgrove at the hardware store next door. They wanted to know when he was going to catch Rona Jean's killer and what was slowing him down—as if they thought he should pull the murderer out of his hat, like some vaudeville stage magician or a slick cop in a detective story. Well, real life was nothing like that. In real life, there weren't any parlor tricks and nobody was standing there, feeding you the clues one at a time so all you had to do was put them together, like a jigsaw puzzle. In real life, each clue led off in a different direction, and there was so much confusion and contradiction (as there was in his head right now) that it was a wonder *any* crime got solved, let alone a murder.

Finally, he got fed up with the questions. He threw down his fork and yelled, "Will you two just quit the heck pestering me? You'll find out who killed her when I do, and not a durn minute sooner."

A couple of ladies he didn't recognize—visitors from out of town, probably—stared wide-eyed at him from a table in the corner, then put their heads together, murmuring apprehensively, as Buddy hunched his shoulders and began on his pie.

When the customers had mostly cleared out, Violet and Myra May left Henrietta on the switchboard and Raylene and her helper, Holiness Hatfield, to clean up the kitchen, then took Buddy upstairs. But before they could begin their talk, Violet had to put Cupcake down for her afternoon nap, which took a little while because Cupcake resented taking a nap while her two moms were having an interesting conversation with a man in the kitchen. And Myra May was called back downstairs to solve an urgent culinary mystery involving a missing mess of catfish that had been brought in by Old Zeke, who sold them his day's catch twice a week. It turned out that Zeke had put the fish in a burlap bag with some ice in the old soda pop cooler beside the back door without telling anybody where they were.

But at last the three of them were together, sitting around the kitchen table. Violet and Myra May were drinking coffee, and Buddy was finishing the orange Nehi (his favorite soda pop) that he had carried upstairs and was wishing he had brought another piece of pie upstairs with him.

For Buddy, the green and white kitchen was a familiar place. When old Mrs. Hooper ran the diner (years ago, before Myra May and Violet bought it), she used to pay Buddy a nickel an hour to weed her vegetable garden. He'd been about ten years old then, and when he was finished pulling weeds, she'd sit him down at the kitchen table—the very same table where he was sitting now—and give him a plate of cookies and a glass of milk. Then she'd open the window wide so the breeze would cool him off, and pat him on the shoulder and say, "Buddy, you did a real good job with those weeds. But you know how fast they sprout back up. I hope you'll come back and tackle them next week."

Now, the window was open and the breeze carried the delightful fragrance of the apple pie that Raylene was baking downstairs, along with the distant sound of the diner's radio, playing "I Got Rhythm." But even in that pleasant setting, he didn't get the questioning off to a very good start. "I was wanting to see you both together because I . . . well, because—" He stopped, feeling clumsy.

"Because you didn't want us comparing stories," Violet offered helpfully. She had put on a fresh pale green dress with puffy little sleeves and was looking much better than she had that morning.

"Because you want to surprise us with your questions, and you don't want us putting our heads together to agree on an answer." Myra May reached into the pocket of her slacks for her cigarette packet and tapped out a Lucky Strike. "That's how they do it in detective stories."

Buddy grinned sheepishly. "Actually, what I want from you is a little help. There are some things I don't understand."

To tell the truth, there were quite a few things he didn't understand, but "some" would do to start with. He took out his notebook and flipped to the page where he had copied the passage from Rona Jean's diary.

"This morning, I found something Rona Jean had written. She said that Violet was the only person she could count on to help her out of the mess she was in. Is that true?"

"Yes," Myra May said shortly. "She took advantage of Violet."

Violet shook her head. "I didn't exactly see it that way. She was in trouble and I felt sorry for her. I wanted to help, even though she didn't always take my advice."

"What kind of trouble?" Buddy asked.

"Gosh, we figured you knew that already," Violet said. She traded glances with Myra May. "From Doc Roberts' autopsy report."

"About Rona Jean being pregnant," Myra May clarified. "You're the sheriff, Buddy. You must have heard about the report even before we did."

"Not necessarily," Buddy said. "You know how fast news gets around this town. So being pregnant—that's the 'mess' she was thinking of when she wrote that?"

Violet said, "Yes, but there was more, of course."

"Violet is saying," Myra May added, "that Rona Jean had a knack for making things even more of a mess than they really were." She took out a match, scratched it with her thumbnail, and lit her Lucky Strike.

"What does that mean, exactly?" Buddy asked, finding a new page in his notebook and taking his pencil out of his pocket. He liked Myra May. She might be gruff and sometimes a little short with people, but she didn't beat around the bush. She said what she meant and she meant what she said.

Violet answered. "It means that Rona Jean was . . . well, she was pretty mixed up about herself and . . ." Her voice trailed off.

"Promiscuous," Myra May said darkly, and breathed out twin streams of tobacco smoke.

"Excuse me?" Buddy asked, wondering how that was spelled.

"Fast, as my mother would say," Violet added, and went on. "When she found out she was going to have a baby, the first thing she thought about was getting married."

Myra May pulled on her cigarette. "But there were two guys, and she wasn't sure which one was the father."

"And when she thought about marrying one of them," Violet said, "it didn't seem like such a good idea. I couldn't blame her," she added candidly. "I wouldn't have wanted to marry either one of them, myself."

"Their names?" He knew—at least he knew what Rona Jean had written in her diary—but he wanted to know what *they* knew.

Violet hesitated. Myra May reached out and touched her hand. "Tell him, Violet. He's just doing his job."

"She said it was Lamar Lassen and Beau Pyle," Violet said reluctantly.

Myra May gave Buddy a direct look. "She said it wasn't you, in case you were wondering."

"I wasn't," Buddy said. "I *knew* it wasn't me." He spoke emphatically, but inside, he was shivering as he thought again of his narrow escape. If he had accepted Rona Jean's invitation to tumble into bed with her, she might have tried to convince him that the baby was his, and his guilty conscience would have prodded him into believing her. He might have married her and ended up raising some other man's baby.

There was a light tap on the kitchen door and Raylene came in. "This is for Buddy," she said, and put a piece of lemon chess pie on the table in front of him, with a fork and a paper napkin.

Buddy looked up at her, shaking his head at her ability to know what people wanted. "Miz Riggs, you do beat all." He picked up his fork. "Thank you."

"You're welcome," she said with a little smile, and left.

Myra May picked up the story. "After Rona Jean decided she wasn't going to marry anybody, she decided she'd get an abortion. She knew how dangerous it is, but that didn't matter—Rona Jean was the kind who thought it was fun to take risks. She thought she could get Lamar or Beau or both to pay for it, but that didn't work out. Lamar said no because he wanted to get married, and anyway, he didn't have any money. Beau's always got money in his pocket, but he was too smart to give her any."

"Those were the only two she asked?" Buddy asked, around a bite of pie. He was remembering the stack of twenties he'd found in Rona Jean's room. The money hadn't come from Lassen or Pyle, so where *did* it come from?

"They were, so far as we know," Violet said. "But Rona Jean wasn't . . ." She shrugged. "Well, she wasn't always very careful with the truth. It wasn't that she lied, exactly," she added hastily. "It was . . . well, she mixed up what she wanted to happen with what was actually happening, if that makes any sense. She sometimes convinced herself, and then she wasn't lying—to her way of thinking, anyway."

Buddy nodded, understanding. He had met other people who operated that way. But that still didn't explain where the money came from. He put down his fork and opened his notebook. "She wrote in her diary that if she went through with it—the pregnancy, I guess—that Violet would give her the money to pay her bills, before and after." He glanced back up at Violet. "Is that right?"

"Not quite." Violet shook her head. "I mean, we talked about doing it that way, but—"

"But we decided against it," Myra May interrupted. "We paid Dr. DuBois, the doctor she saw over in Monroeville. And we were planning to pay the hospital for her expenses. But we didn't want to give *her* the money, because we weren't sure . . ."

"Because *Myra May* wasn't sure," Violet said pointedly, "that she would actually use it to pay the bills."

"You agreed," Myra May said, frowning.

"I let you talk me into it," Violet retorted. "But I still think we should have trusted her."

Myra May rolled her eyes. "That's because you're such a sweet and softhearted person, Violet. If we had given Rona Jean the money, she would have left town and we'd never have seen her again."

"That's what *you* say," Violet replied. "I don't agree."

"I found a hundred and forty dollars in her room," Buddy said, breaking into the argument. "Do you have any idea where it came from?"

"A hundred and forty dollars!" Violet blinked, startled. "Gosh. That's a *lot* of money! Where did it come from?"

Myra May frowned at Violet. "You didn't—"

"I did *not*," Violet replied hotly. "Where in the world would I get a hundred and forty dollars without you knowing about it? Out of the cash register downstairs?" She crossed her arms. "I don't think so."

Myra May's frown deepened. "Well, then, where *did* she get it?"

"From another . . . boyfriend?" Buddy flipped a page in his notebook. "I copied down a couple of names from her diary. Do they mean anything to you? Jack Baker and Ray—no last name."

"She mentioned Jack Baker," Violet said. "She met him at the Roller Palace. She said she thought he was cute. And funny."

"Is he from the CCC camp?" Buddy asked.

"I don't think so," Violet said. "From somewhere close by, though. Thomasville, maybe? He might work at the sawmill."

"What about . . ." He looked down at his notes. "What about Ray?"

"Ray *was* at the camp," Myra May said. "I caught her talking to him one afternoon when she was on the switchboard. I had to remind her that the operators aren't supposed to be using the phone to do personal business when they're working." She frowned. "It didn't sound like they were making a date, though. It sounded more like a . . . well, an argument. At least on her end. I couldn't hear him."

Buddy circled *Ray* and wrote *argument*. "Any idea of his last name?"

Both women shook their heads.

He went back to his notebook. "How about B.P.?" He thought that might be Bodeen Pyle, but they were looking blank.

"I'm still trying to figure out how Rona Jean got that

much money." Myra May pulled a saucer toward her and used it for an ashtray. "She was working for us, of course, and we pay our Exchange operators a decent wage—more than they get most places here in Darling. But there's no way she could have saved that much out of her salary. Somebody must have given it to her. But *who*? And why?"

Those were the right questions, Buddy thought, but it was clear that neither Myra May nor Violet had an answer, and he certainly didn't. He closed his notebook. "One last thing. Rona Jean says in her diary that Violet would be taking care of the bills, before and after. Before the birth, I assume, and afterward." He looked up. Violet was nodding. "And then she wrote, 'And I can leave it there.' Leave what?"

Myra May ground out her cigarette in the ashtray. "Ask us a hard one, why don't you, Buddy?" Her laugh was brittle.

Violet was smiling sadly. "Leave the baby, of course," she said. "With us."

"Oh," Buddy said. "I see."

Of course. The baby. It explained a lot of things. Like why Violet had befriended Rona Jean and why Myra May was willing to pay the bills. And why Rona Jean had told Bettina Higgens that Myra May wouldn't dare fire her, and why Violet had been so upset by Rona Jean's death. Violet hadn't just lost a friend, she had lost a baby—the baby she hoped would become her own. He felt like all kinds of a fool for not figuring this out for himself.

Violet sighed. "Rona Jean didn't have any way to take care of a baby—she didn't *want* a baby. But we do." She looked at Myra May. "We adopted Cupcake after my sister died and Cupcake's father couldn't take care of her. We don't want our little girl to grow up as an only child. We would just love to give her a little brother or sister. We thought . . . I mean, we were hoping . . ." She shrugged and sighed again.

"So in return for letting us have her baby," Myra May said in a hard, flat voice, "we were paying Rona Jean's bills. And she was holding our feet to the fire."

"Myra May," Violet said plaintively, "I really wish you wouldn't—"

"Well, she *was*, Violet. That girl listened in on the switchboard and there wasn't a damn thing I could do about it. She knew it was against the rules, but I couldn't stop her and I couldn't fire her, because if I did, she'd leave town. And you wanted the baby." Myra May raised her hand as if to ward off Violet's protest. "I know, I know, dear—I wanted the baby, too. Both of us did. But that doesn't change the fact that Rona Jean was blackmailing us."

"No, no," Violet protested. "That's not how I saw it. Not at all."

"That's *exactly* how it was, Violet." Myra May mimicked Rona Jean's Southern drawl. "'You pay my bills, you let me do what I want, and I'll give you my baby. *Maybe* I'll give you my baby, if I don't decide to leave town first.' It was blackmail, pure and simple."

Buddy picked up his fork and went back to his pie. He was now convinced that the money he had found—the $140— was a blackmail payoff of some kind. But whose? And what for, exactly? Blackmail was a powerful motive for murder, he reminded himself. Answer those questions and you'd probably have the killer.

He finished his pie, picked up his notebook and pencil, and put them in his shirt pocket. "Thanks," he said. "You've been a big help. If you think of anything else I should know, please get in touch."

"We will," Violet said. She leaned forward with a wry little smile. "To tell the honest truth, Buddy, we were kind of disappointed when Rona Jean told us that the baby wasn't yours. Myra May and I would have been proud to raise your child."

That was almost too much for Buddy, who for the life of him couldn't think what to say. He was grateful for the knock on the kitchen door that prevented him from saying anything.

It was Raylene again. "Buddy, there's a phone call for you on the switchboard. It's your deputy." She hesitated. "And I wonder if you'd stop in the kitchen on your way out. There's something I need to tell you."

"Tell Henrietta to ring the phone upstairs, so Buddy can talk to his deputy up here," Myra May said, and stood up. To Buddy, she said, "Raylene and I made up that list of people who've been in my car in the last few weeks. You can pick it up from her before you leave."

"I'll be down as soon as Cupcake wakes up," Violet said, and disappeared into the bedroom.

Still feeling bewildered about what Violet had said, Buddy picked up the phone when it rang. "Yeah, Wayne, what's up?"

"Somebody named Liz Lacy just called," Wayne replied. "She said you should maybe talk to the woman who runs the laundry—Adele Hart, her name is. Seems that Miz Hart told somebody, who told Miss Lacy, that she saw one of the CCC guys hanging out behind the diner. Not clear whether it was last night or another night. But it sounds like it's worth looking into."

"I'll check it out," Buddy said. "How'd it work out over at Miz Parker's? You're back at the office, I reckon."

"Yeah, I'm here. Miz Parker's got her mare back. The neighbor—Bob Denny—claims she owes him for a fence her bull broke down and a sow and eleven piglets that got loose and haven't been seen since. That's why he took the mare. Denny's going to file a complaint in magistrate's court about the fence and the pigs. That way, the judge can settle it."

"Yeah. Did you check out the garage? Any sign of a bottle or something like that the killer might have used to hit Rona Jean?"

"Matter of fact, I did find something," Wayne said. "It was layin' under the car—a Dr Pepper bottle. I took a couple of photos of it, then brought it back here. There are prints on the neck, the way you'd hold a bottle like that to use it as a weapon. Most are smudged, but I'm still working on it."

"Keep at it," Buddy said. "Good work, Wayne."

"Thanks. Oh, and I found a couple of lengths of rope. Could be what we're looking for." He paused. "How's the investigation going?"

"Complications," Buddy said. He was still struggling with Violet's remark. Did she mean . . . No, he was sure she didn't. "I'll go across the street to the laundry and talk to Miz Hart. You need anything?"

"That list of people who've been in the car when you can get it. I want to be sure I've got comparison prints from everybody."

"I'm picking it up in a minute or two," Buddy said. "You'll have it when I get back to the office."

In the kitchen, he scanned the list Raylene handed him. It contained eight names, four of whom he knew hadn't been fingerprinted. "Thanks," he said, folding it into his notebook. "Looks like we've got our work cut out for us. I'll get my deputy started on this right away."

Myra May's mother was a tall, competent-looking woman, with penetrating eyes under heavy brows, a firm mouth and chin, and short auburn hair streaked with gray. When Buddy looked at her, he knew he was seeing Myra May, in another twenty years. He was seeing something else, too, in her eyes.

"Excuse me, Miz Riggs," he said hesitantly, "but I'm wondering . . ." Her "gift," as Aunt Hetty Little called it, was known to everyone in Darling. Buddy couldn't help thinking that she must have some knowledge about what had happened in the garage the night before.

"Yes, I do," Raylene said, as if she had read his mind (as she probably had). "I don't know as much as you think I do, but I have the feeling that this wasn't about Rona Jean's baby. It was about somebody—more than one person, I think—paying money to somebody to get more money. And about knowing too much, and trying to sell that knowledge." Her voice seemed to take on an odd resonance, as if she were speaking in a cave. "Selling what you know can cause big problems. I've seen people do that, and it's always dangerous. In this case, I'm afraid it was . . . deadly."

That last word seemed to hang in the air between them. Buddy stared at her, wishing she wouldn't talk in riddles. If she'd just come straight out with it— He sighed. "Thanks," he said, even though he wasn't quite sure what he was thanking her for.

"Oh, and Buddy," she said, frowning a little. "You be sure and keep your eye on the weather, will you?"

Hart's Peerless Laundry was on the other side of Robert E. Lee, across from Musgrove's Hardware. Outside, it was hot as the vestibule of Hades, as Buddy's grandfather used to say, and the dark clouds piled up to the south gave the sky an ominous tint. But inside, it was just plain hot as hell, and the air was so heavy with the steamy smell of soap and bleach that Buddy could hardly draw a full breath. Behind the counter, Adele Hart, a plump, cheerful-looking woman in her early fifties, was folding a big basket of fluffy white towels marked "Old Alabama Hotel." She wore a brown dress covered with a big white apron, and her face was flushed beet red.

"Oh, hello, Buddy," she said, looking up. She laughed a

little. "Oopsie, guess I should be callin' you 'Sheriff,' huh? Seems kinda funny, since I can remember when you used to haul you and your daddy's wash in your red wagon. You were a cute little boy—you had that funny cowlick, and your hair used to stick straight up."

Buddy blushed, wishing that people would stop reminding him that he'd once been a kid. But she was right about the wagon, anyway. After his mother died, his father would load their dirty clothes into a big wicker basket, and Buddy would put it in his wagon and haul it up the street to the laundry, where Mrs. Hart, then a young woman, would wait on him. A day or two later, he'd pick up the clothes and towels and sheets, all clean and folded neatly into the basket, and haul them back home.

Buddy went straight to business. "Liz Lacy says she thinks maybe you saw somebody hanging around behind the diner at night. Is that right?"

Mrs. Hart wiped her sweaty forehead with her sleeve. "Word gets around, don't it? I was sayin' that very thing to Liz's ma, just a couple of hours ago, when she brought in her damask tablecloth." She tut-tutted. "Catsup and mustard both. Had to tell her I didn't think we could get it all out, especially the mustard. If you don't get on it right away, mustard'll stain worse than almost anything. But at least it's in the middle, where she can put a doily on it." She picked up another towel, shook it out, and began to fold it. "And, yes, I reckon I did see a fella, late at night. Wouldn't have thought much of it, but he was wearin' one of them CCC uniforms. I heard those boys have to be in bed by ten, and I wondered if he was goin' to get in trouble for being late."

Buddy took out his notebook. "When did you see him?" Hopefully, he added, "Was it last night?"

"No, wasn't last night." She heaved a resigned sigh. "Poor

little Mikey was throwing up last night, and I was sitting up with him until way past midnight, in the back bedroom. Mikey is my Bert's youngest," she added in a confiding tone. "We're keeping all three of Bert's kids just now. Junie died last year of TB—remember Junie Plunkett? She was Bert's wife, and a real nice girl, gave her heart and soul to those kids. Bert's gone over to Atlanta, trying to find work." She shook her head regretfully. "Hard for fam'lies these days. Tears Bert up to be away from his babies."

Not last night? Buddy felt disappointed. But the fact that Mrs. Hart hadn't seen the man didn't mean that he hadn't been there.

"What day did you see him, then?" he asked. "What time?"

Mrs. Hart pushed her wispy brown hair off her forehead. "Let's see—last night was Friday, right? So it would have been the night before, which would make it Thursday. And right after eleven, because my Artis had just got back from his poker game over at the Meeks' place and gone into the house and up to bed. The kids were all asleep, and I was sittin' on the porch, enjoying the cool, such as it was, and the whip-poor-will that sings from Mr. Vader's big old willow across the street. We can see the back of the diner and the garden and the garage from our porch, you know. There was a right good moon that night, and I saw that girl— Rona Jean, the one that got killed—come out of the back of the diner and meet the man in the alley by the garage."

"Had you seen this man before?" Buddy asked. "Would you recognize him if you saw him again?"

"I don't think so." Mrs. Hart pushed her lips in and out. "Far as I know, he ain't been in the laundry, at least when I've been up front here. He's kinda built big, like my Artis, with big shoulders." She illustrated with both hands.

*Built big, big shoulders.* Buddy was taking notes. It wasn't a very good description. But most of the young men he had seen out at the CCC camp were thin and underweight. Someone with a big build and wide shoulders might stand out. "Height?"

She eyed Buddy. "About as tall as you, maybe."

Buddy wrote down *5'10"*. "When you saw Miss Hancock and this man on Thursday night, did they seem . . . were they . . . well, friendly?"

Mrs. Hart frowned. "If you mean, were they huggin' and kissin'—no, they weren't. They were mostly talking, and neither of 'em seemed any too happy about it, either."

*Not happy.* "Arguing?"

"Maybe," she said slowly. "I couldn't hear. They were serious, is all I can say. They weren't funnin' around."

"How long did they talk?"

She considered. "Maybe four, five minutes. Then she walked off and he climbed on his motorcycle and rode away." She frowned. "Blasted the night to smithereens, he did, revvin' up that engine. Rode away mad was the way it looked to me."

*Motorcycle.* Of course. "Can you describe the motorcycle?"

"Well, I couldn't see it too good that night, but I've seen it before," she said. "Around town, I mean. Green, with U.S. Army painted on it, and a rack on the back, and saddlebags. Leather saddlebags, with buckles."

Instantly, Buddy knew the motorcycle she was describing. He had noticed it, too, here and there: an olive-drab 1930 Harley-Davidson, about the same size as his Indian Ace.

Mrs. Hart was going on. "Mostly when I see that motorcycle, it's parked—like, out in front of the diner or the movie theater." Her hand went to her mouth and she gave him a round-eyed look. "Are you thinking that maybe the one that drives it is the one that *killed* her?"

"Could be," Buddy said. "If you see him or the motorcycle again, could you call the sheriff's office right away?"

"Oh, I will, Sheriff," she said. "I surely will." She regarded him, shaking her head a little, marveling. "You know, I just can't help remembering how you used to come in here, pulling that little red wagon piled up with your dirty underpants and socks. And just look at you now, all grown up and a *sheriff*." She was beaming. "My, my, you have done us all *proud*."

Buddy ducked his head, feeling himself coloring. He tried to think of something to say, but the best he could do was, "Yes, ma'am. Thank you."

Her smile faded and she cocked her head, regarding him sternly. "Well, maybe I oughtta say that you'll do us proud when you catch that killer and lock him up. We can't have folks goin' around stranglin' other folks here in Darling. It ain't right, Buddy. It just ain't right at *all*. I'm sure your daddy has told you that."

"Yes, ma'am," Buddy said contritely.

# FOURTEEN

# Ophelia Collects What She Came For

Breathing heavily, Ophelia leaned against her office door, taking comfort from the familiar surroundings where she spent her workdays and trying to push the thought of Rona Jean—dead, *murdered*—out of her mind. Rona Jean's murder had nothing to do with Charlie's investigative assignment. There was nothing to be afraid of. Here in her office, the door firmly locked, she was safe.

The large bush outside the window filtered a greenish light into the room, pale but bright enough so that she didn't have to turn on the bare 60-watt electric bulb that hung from the ceiling. Her wooden desk, with its covered Remington typewriter, neat stacks of manila file folders, and a gilt-framed photograph of Jed and the kids, sat against the white-painted beadboard wall to her left, her chair pushed under it. Corporal Andrews' desk—the top clear except for a black dial telephone and a Cypress County phone book—sat against the opposite wall, under a sign that said, NO PERSONAL CALLS. Large area maps were pinned on the walls over both desks. There was a tall, three-drawer wooden filing cabinet; a narrow worktable under the window; and a shelf of thick, paperbound CCC operations manuals. And two doors—the door Ophelia had just closed and locked behind her, and the door that opened into the office that belonged to her boss, the camp quartermaster, Sergeant Luther Webb.

Like most of the other officers at Briarwood and other camps, Sergeant Webb was regular Army. Some people were alarmed by this and declared that the presence of the Army officers (both active duty and reserve) made the camps look like a fascist militia, like what that fellow Hitler was cooking up in Germany. Most Americans were isolationists who, after the experience of being dragged into the Great War by a president who had promised that America would not get involved, were unwilling to support a militia of any description. They liked the idea of a permanent civilian corps that would train young men for work and give them a healthy outdoor life, although they would prefer that it be managed by the Forest Service. But for now, the Army managed the camps, and it looked like it was going to be that way for a long time to come.

Ophelia didn't much like Sergeant Webb. He was a slender, upright man with a square jaw, a hard eye, and an authoritative air, who made it a rule to follow *all* rules to the letter. Every document he signed (and there were plenty of them) had to be letter-perfect. If it wasn't perfect the first time, it had to be redone until it was. He even had his own typewriter, a twin of Ophelia's standard-issue Remington, and often typed his own reports. That way, he said (somewhat self-importantly, Ophelia thought), he would know it was done right. It wasn't easy for Ophelia to satisfy his requirements for exactitude, and when he was in the office (thankfully, this was only a few hours a day), the air often crackled with his disapproval.

Ophelia very much liked Corporal Andrews, though, and appreciated his informality—they were on a first-name basis—and his relaxed way of working. The corporal was well built, with crisp brown hair, pale blue eyes, and a flash of ironic humor in a face that could be as hard as a nut. He was quite good-looking, Ophelia thought. No wonder Lucy was interested in him—*if* she was. The corporal was a Yankee from the big city of Chicago, with a Yankee's quick, staccato speech. But while he sometimes seemed secretly amused by Darling's small-town ways, his pleasant friendliness made him easy to like. Ophelia especially appreciated his infectious laugh, which took some of the sting out of Sergeant Webb's by-the-book style and his daily demand that they get the job done fast and get it done *right*.

Which wasn't easy. Measured by the reams of paperwork that crossed their desks and flew on to the various offices in Washington, the quartermaster's office was the busiest in the camp. It handled the arrangements for buying or leasing all the materials and supplies and equipment necessary to build and maintain the camp and carry out its mission. The office operated under a single cardinal rule, as it was spelled out by the sign on the office wall: BUY LOCAL.

As Sergeant Webb had explained to Ophelia and Corporal Andrews, although it wasn't discussed much publically, one of the goals of the Civilian Conservation Corps program was to pump money into the economically crippled towns and villages around the camps. As much as possible, the camp's supplies were supposed to be purchased locally. Orders that had to be filled outside the local area had to go through the office of the camp commandant, and Captain Campbell had made it clear that he didn't want to see them.

But while buying local was proving to be an economic windfall for Cypress County, it could be a challenge. When Camp Briarwood was first established, everyone had lived in tents while the permanent buildings were built. This construction had required an enormous amount of milled lumber, which was hauled out to the camp from Ozzie Sherman's sawmill and from three or four smaller sawmills elsewhere in the county. Musgrove's Hardware and Mann's Mercantile had supplied sacks of concrete, rolls of tar-paper roofing, and all the tools for clearing and construction—shovels and axes and hammers and saws and carpenters' planes. To get all this material out to the camp, a new road had to be built, using mule teams and equipment rented or leased from local farmers and teamsters. Native stone and gravel was used where possible; where it wasn't, Carruthers Gravel Pit had provided what was needed. For all this work, the supplies had to get where they were needed and get there fast, which was often hard to do, for the local merchants and suppliers were geared to a lower demand and a slower pace.

And that wasn't the end of it. When the initial camp construction was finished, it was time to get started on the projects. The first was the new bridge over Pine Mill Creek and a couple of concrete bridges on the road that led to the camp. After that, they had built six new fire towers. There was talk of even bigger projects, like the dam on Pine Mill Creek, which could create a sixty-acre lake for fishing and boating. If that happened, they might build recreation facilities around the lake to attract tourists. All of this building required more materials—obtained locally wherever possible and paid for through the quartermaster's office.

In the meantime, of course, everybody at the camp had to be fed three meals a day, every single day of the year. The Army sent in some of the staples—flour and sugar and coffee.

And some of the fresh vegetables were grown in the garden that Bessie managed. But the rest of it had to be found locally, and merchants and farmers from Darling and Cypress County were granted contracts to supply meat, vegetables, fruits, milk, eggs, and bread. The quartermaster handled the payments for that, as well.

As Camp Briarwood's liaison officer, Ophelia had played a vital role in finding the right suppliers and contractors. She had spent all her life in Cypress County and could confidently boast that she knew every single merchant, businessman, farmer, orchardist, and plantation owner, as well as all their fathers, brothers, cousins, and friends. So when somebody put in a bid to become a supplier, Ophelia was responsible for assessing the capability of his (or her) dairy herd to supply milk, cream, and butter; or an orchard to produce peaches and plums; or a garden to provide fresh vegetables; or a herd of pigs or beef cattle to furnish the kitchen with steaks, hamburger, bacon, and ribs. She did a good job, too. She had been able to find local suppliers who were qualified to fill more than 90 percent of the orders Sergeant Webb gave her.

Of course, Ophelia didn't do the purchasing itself, or handle any of the billing or the payments. Corporal Andrews negotiated the contracts with the suppliers. Sergeant Webb prepared and managed the invoices that went to the appropriate federal offices in Washington, D.C., where payment was approved and the checks sent to the camp for disbursement. They were held in a locked drawer of the quartermaster's desk until the suppliers picked them up. The system was straightforward enough, Ophelia had thought, and—at least as far as she could tell—it seemed to be working perfectly. There was hardly ever a hitch in the supply schedule, and none of the suppliers had ever complained that they weren't paid on time.

But somebody—a woman, he said, calling herself Mata

Hari—had tipped Charlie Dickens that something fishy was going on in the quartermaster's office, and he had asked Ophelia to help him find out whether the tipster was telling the truth. Now that she was here, though, in this deserted, creepy building, Ophelia was getting cold feet. And recalling the story of Mata Hari, she seemed to remember that the woman, an exotic dancer, had been executed for being a German spy. All of a sudden, her excuse for coming—that she had to pick up some paperwork—didn't seem very plausible. What did she have to get off her desk that was so pressing and urgent that it couldn't wait until Monday morning?

But she was here, and she should do what she had come to do and get out as fast as she could. There was a sheaf of papers on her desk—that was her excuse for being here, if anybody asked. But what she was really after was a file folder that was kept in the locked top drawer of the gray metal file cabinet in Sergeant Webb's office. In it was an up-to-date list she had recently typed of the vouchers that had been prepared for payment to the merchants, farmers, and other suppliers from whom the camp had purchased goods and services. She couldn't for the life of her think why Charlie Dickens would want that voucher list, and when she asked him, he had only said something vague about "checking" with a few of the suppliers. But he'd insisted that it was important to get it, and she would do her best.

Nervously, she went to the sergeant's door and pushed it open. The quartermaster's office was windowless and airless and black as pitch, and smelled of the sergeant's pipe tobacco. She reached up and pulled the chain on the light bulb that hung from the ceiling. When it came on, the bulb swung back and forth, casting swaying shadows across the walls and the bare pine floor. The sergeant's desk was scrupulously neat, the papers stacked with their edges aligned, two pencils lying perfectly parallel, a calendar displaying the day's date, a small gold clock displaying the time, a wooden name plaque displaying its owner's title and name: Sgt. Luther T. Webb, U.S. Army. On a shelf behind the desk were several Army purchasing manuals, a couple of sharpshooting award plaques, and a framed photograph of a pretty blond woman and two small girls in party dresses standing in front of a well-kept home with palm trees in the background—the sergeant's wife and children, who lived in St. Petersburg. He never spoke of them, though, and she had never seen any letters going back and forth or known him to take leave to go to St. Pete for a visit.

Ordinarily, Ophelia was only allowed in Sergeant Webb's office when he was there, and she rarely had a reason to open his filing cabinet, which he kept locked. But a few days before, he had asked her to return a file to the top drawer, and she noticed that he had taken the key out of the top drawer of his desk.

Feeling guilty and more than a little apprehensive (*What if somebody came in and caught her?*), she opened the desk drawer (*Lucky it wasn't locked, too!*), found the key, and hurried to the filing cabinet. It only took a minute to locate the file Charlie wanted: a manila folder labeled "Local Suppliers." She was familiar with it because she herself had typed the voucher list for the sergeant just last week, and she found it easily, in the very front of the folder. She had alphabetized the suppliers' names, addresses, and amounts. The single-spaced list was numbered, with thirty names on the first page, twenty-two on the second page, and the pages were stapled together in the upper-left corner. Charlie had suggested that she take the list home and copy it out by hand. She could give him the copy, then replace the original in the file when she went to the office on Monday morning. She figured that would work, since the sergeant never showed up before ten o'clock.

But as she was replacing the manila folder in the filing cabinet drawer, Ophelia happened to see that the folder contained a second typed, single-spaced list of vouchers, also labeled "Local Suppliers." The sergeant must have typed this one, however, since she hadn't, and she and the sergeant were the only ones in the office who typed. The list was made up of three stapled pages, not two, and contained not fifty-two typed names, addresses, and amounts, but seventy. *Seventy?* Puzzled, Ophelia scanned it, noticing that on the list were quite a few names she didn't recognize—eighteen in all, it looked like.

But according to the addresses, these people, eighteen of them, lived in Cypress County. Who were they? Why weren't they on *her* list? Had she somehow missed that many names? If she had, when Sergeant Webb got around to noticing what a mess she had made of the task, he'd be furious. She had better do something about it, like maybe retype her list and add his names. And the sooner she did that, the better— *before* he found out. She would take both lists home with her, and bring them both back on Monday morning. The risk would be no greater for one than for two, she told herself. Or as her grandmother used to say, *You might as well be hung for a sheep as a lamb.*

But she had collected what she came for and it was time to get out. She replaced the file, closed and locked the drawer, and replaced the key, then went back into her own office, shutting the sergeant's door behind her. At her desk, she slipped the two lists into her large handbag. And just in the nick of time. She heard a heavy step in the hall and the rattle of a key in the lock, and the door opened. Ophelia turned, sucking in her breath and feeling her stomach lurch. But the figure was a familiar one.

"Raymond!" she gasped. "Gosh, I'm glad it's you! You scared the living bejeebers out of me!"

Corporal Andrews laughed. "Who did you think it was? King Kong come to carry you away?"

A man of thirty-five, maybe forty, he was out of uniform and dressed in jeans and a cotton shirt the same pale blue as his eyes, with the sleeves rolled to his elbows. Ophelia thought again how good-looking he was. He turned on the light.

"I must say, you're a bit of a surprise, too, Ophelia. What are you doing here in the dark? Getting in some overtime?"

Ophelia picked up the thin sheaf of papers from her desk. "A little job I didn't quite finish yesterday," she said glibly, waving the papers. "My daughter and I were shopping in Monroeville this afternoon, and I wanted to show her the camp. While we were here, I thought of the job and just popped in to pick it up." She grinned—disarmingly, she hoped—and made a show of putting the papers into her handbag. "I've been in Sergeant Webb's doghouse so often the past week or two, I figured I'd try to burnish my image by having this stuff on his desk when he comes in on Monday morning. Maybe even get a little raise."

To her great relief, Corporal Andrews didn't question her excuse. He chuckled wryly. "I don't know about a raise, but if you find the key to that man's heart, I hope you'll let me know what it is. I'm in his doghouse as much as you are, maybe more. You can type and I can't, you know. My image could sure use a little burnishing."

Ophelia laughed a little. "Well, don't say I haven't tried to teach you."

It was true. The sergeant could type, and often prepared his own reports. He had told the corporal to learn to type. It hadn't quite been an order, but almost, and both Corporal Andrews and Ophelia had made a good-faith effort. But the corporal seemed to be all thumbs. He just couldn't get the hang of the typewriter. The best he could do was hunt-and-peck, and even that was full of errors, which didn't please the sergeant, either. They had both finally given it up as a bad job.

"You gave it your all," the corporal said, "and I'm grateful. I guess I was just never meant to type." He gave her a curious look. "That pretty girl I saw out there in the car— you're not going to tell me you're her *mother*?"

Ophelia nodded proudly. "That's my Sarah."

Andrews shook his head. "I am amazed," he said with an admiring look. "Honest to Pete, Ophelia. You can't possibly be old enough to have a teenaged daughter!"

"You're sweet." Ophelia laughed lightly. "Actually, I'm glad to hear that she followed my orders and stayed in the car with her Nancy Drew mystery. She made noises about wanting to walk over and watch the baseball game, which I strictly forbade."

"Smart mama," Andrews said approvingly. "A pretty girl like that—those boys would lose their heads." He went to his desk. "Well, I won't keep you. Hope you and Sarah have a great afternoon."

"You, too, Raymond," Ophelia said. As she went back down the hall, she couldn't help remembering what he had said—*You can't possibly be old enough to have a teenaged daughter!*—and feeling a small, warm glow deep down inside. She loved her husband very much, even if he was a bit old-fashioned. But she had to admit that it was nice to be admired, especially by such a good-looking man as Corporal Andrews. Even if he was involved with Lucy Murphy.

# FIFTEEN

# Charlie Dickens Has Lunch with His Wife and Is Enlightened

The telephone conversation that Charlie had held with Mata Hari (or Mattie Harry, as Baby Mann called her) had been brief and intriguing. She had to talk to him in person, she said, and it *had* to be today, no *ifs*, *ands*, or *buts* about it. She told him to meet her at two thirty that afternoon, out at the old Loblolly School. Which left him plenty of time to finish the piece he was writing, then put on his hat and walk home through the oppressive noontime heat, for a leisurely lunch with his wife.

When he had returned to Darling to take over his father's newspaper, Charlie had fallen into the habit of eating lunch at the diner, where he caught up on the news that hadn't yet reached the *Dispatch* office. But now that he and Fannie were married, he almost always went home for lunch—an easy walk, kitty-cornered across the courthouse square to the small apartment above Fannie's Darling Chapeaux shop, where the newlyweds lived.

Charlie's life had changed in several other ways, major and minor, now that he and Fannie were married. He still played poker with the boys, but only once a month, instead of once a week. He only occasionally dropped in at Pete's Pool Parlor, rather than making it his regular Saturday night stop. He only smoked at the office, because Fannie didn't like the smell of cigarettes. And instead of his local white lightning, one of Fannie's Atlanta friends kept them supplied with several good dinner wines, which they shared over Fannie's good meals.

His weekends had changed, too. They used to be primarily valuable for sleeping off hangovers and having some of the hair of the dog that bit him. But now, when the weather was good, he and Fannie liked to get out into the countryside and ride around in his old blue roadster, stopping to pick flowers and admire the scenery. When it rained or was chilly, they stayed home and puttered around their neat little apartment, Charlie reading aloud to Fannie, while she cooked something special for him. Or they might listen to the *Palmolive Beauty Box Theater* on the radio (sentimental crap, Charlie thought, but he never said so for fear of hurting Fannie's feelings), or play dance records on the Victrola. Charlie wasn't much of a dancer, but he liked band music, and dancing gave him an excuse to hold Fannie, who fit so sweetly into his arms and was light as a feather on her feet. After a nice dinner (with wine), they could often be found dancing to "More Than You Know" and "It's Only a Paper Moon" in their attractive living room, which Fannie had tastefully decorated, with stylish furniture, airy curtains, and art prints on the ivory-painted walls.

This weekend, though, Fannie was working, finishing a large order in the small workroom behind her shop, where she made the most amazing hats. That Charlie thought they were amazing should come as no surprise to anyone. (He was, after all, a fond husband.) But it was true that other people were genuinely impressed with her work. Lilly Daché, for example, a glamorous French milliner who had discovered Fannie's work at a shop in Atlanta and now sold her hats on commission in her famous Daché shop on New York's Fifth Avenue. Mme Daché also provided custom-made hats for the Hollywood studios. Thus, most amazingly of all, film stars (Marie Dressler, for instance, in *Dinner at Eight*) were wearing Fannie's hats in the movies! Which meant that even though the *Dispatch* still paid only a few dollars a week to its editor and publisher, Fannie Dickens was bringing in a pretty penny every month, and Mr. and Mrs. Dickens were living quite comfortably—especially since Fannie had bought the building they lived in and they didn't have to pay any rent.

But Fannie's success was a two-edged sword, and Charlie felt its bitter blade all too keenly. She was bringing in most of the money, while—financially speaking—Charlie was a loser, tethered to a small-town newspaper that would never bring him anything but grief. Charlie hated the thought that he couldn't support his new wife—that she had to work to keep their little family afloat. Although he had lost maybe thirty pounds in the past year and wasn't as thick around the middle as he had been, he was well into middle age, with thinning hair, wire-rimmed glasses, and (he couldn't help it) a newsman's skeptical frown. He could not for the life of him figure out what sweet, attractive, clever, *successful* Fannie Champaign had seen in him, or why she wanted to marry him. Add to that his fear that he had lost his reporter's nose for a good story, and it wasn't any wonder that beneath Charlie's more or less contented exterior lurked a discontented soul. Discontented, that is, with himself, and not in the slightest with his new wife, whom he loved to distraction and desperately wanted to please.

Which in part accounted for Charlie's mood when he sat down to lunch at the small table in front of the open window that overlooked the courthouse square. Fannie liked to have things looking nice, so their luncheon table was covered with a flower-printed luncheon cloth and centered with a glass bowl of red roses. She had made Charlie's favorite grilled cheese, tomato, onion, and bacon sandwich and served it with a cup of her homemade tomato soup—better, even, Charlie thought, than the tomato soup he got at the diner, which was pretty doggone good—and glasses of cold lemonade.

As Charlie sat down across from Fannie and bowed his head while she said grace, he thought again how lucky he was to have found her, how smart he was to have married her, and how *much* he would like to impress her by getting at least one of his two big stories on the wire. He allowed himself one swift moment of fantasy, like a gossamer dream, with President Roosevelt introducing him to an assembled throng at the White House (with Fannie, of course, in the front row), and praising him for having broken the Pulitzer Prize–winning story of—

"It's just the saddest thing about Rona Jean," Fannie said, unfolding her napkin in her lap. "Have they captured the man who killed her?"

She seemed troubled, Charlie thought, and looked at her more closely. Her eyes were red. He could swear that she had been crying. But then, Fannie was a compassionate person. She had a soft heart. Sad things, like the death of a friend, affected her deeply—although he hadn't been aware that she knew Rona Jean, except as a voice on the other end of the telephone line, saying, "Number, please," and "I have your party now."

"If they have, I haven't heard," Charlie replied. "I asked the deputy to phone the newspaper when they caught him." He picked up his sandwich. "I got some swell photos of the victim, though. Before the sheriff showed up and made me stop."

Fannie's response was not what he expected. "Photos?" Her brown eyes widened. "You took photos of Rona Jean? After she was *dead*?"

Charlie nodded, his mouth full of delicious sandwich. When he could, he said, "I was lucky to get them, too."

"Well, I certainly hope you're not going to use them," Fannie said in a low voice.

"Not in the *Dispatch*." Charlie licked mayonnaise off his fingers. "I'm planning to send the best of them to both the AP and the UP, though, along with my story. I'm betting both wire services will run them, which would mean—"

Fannie dropped her spoon and it splashed into her soup bowl. "Oh, dear, oh, Charlie, please *don't*!" she exclaimed.

Charlie was nonplussed. "Don't? But why? It's a great story, Fannie. And the photos make it *real*. Without them, it's just another murder—"

"Because it's . . . it's disrespectful, that's why. And it's not just another murder. She was . . ." Fannie's voice trembled. "She was going to be a mother. That's pretty special, you know."

"Yes, I know, but . . ." Charlie frowned. "Wait a minute. How did you know she was pregnant? Did Edna Fay tell you? Doc told her not to talk about it with anybody but me and the sheriff." Of course, the news could be all over Darling by now. But Fannie had spent the morning in her workroom, out of touch with the normal gossip networks.

Fannie shook her head. "No, it wasn't your sister. She told me herself. Rona Jean, I mean."

Charlie leaned forward, his eyes on her face. "*She* told you? When?"

Fannie's eyes met his with something like defiance. "She

liked hats. She said they made her feel pretty and special. I knew she didn't have much money so I always gave her a bit of a discount. She bought a new one a couple of weeks ago—a pretty little peach-colored straw with pink and white silk flowers. That's when she told me that she was having a baby." She looked away. "She said she didn't like the baby's father well enough to marry him."

Charlie was surprised at this, and then he wasn't. Fannie was a good listener, and supportive. The more she listened, the more you wanted to talk, and the more things you thought of to tell her about. At least, that had been Charlie's experience. It probably wasn't any different for her clients.

"Who *was* the father?" Charlie asked. "Did she say?" *Did she know?* he wondered.

Fannie picked up her spoon again. "You're not going to put it in your story, are you?"

"No," Charlie said thoughtfully. "No, I wouldn't do that."

"She wasn't sure," Fannie said. "It was either Lamar Lassen or the youngest Pyle boy. Beau, he's called. She didn't want to marry *either* of them—and I couldn't say I blamed her."

Charlie raised his eyebrows. "*Two* possibilities? My goodness. She was a busy girl. Not to mention working three to eleven on the switchboard."

"I don't think she was brought up right," Fannie said with a sigh. "She didn't seem to feel she had done anything terribly evil, although I'm sure that when people find out she was pregnant, some will say she got what she deserved. *I* don't feel that way. I feel that she was just a mixed-up young woman who made a mistake. Twice."

*At* least *twice*, Charlie thought. Aloud, he said, "I won't name names in the story, of course. But the sheriff ought to know who they are. He might want to question them." *Because one of them*, he thought grimly, *is likely the killer.*

"He's already talked to Lamar Lassen," Fannie said. "I ran into Mrs. Meeks at the grocery this morning. Lamar Lassen boards with her. The sheriff came by to see him this morning. If he knows about Lamar, he probably knows about Beau, too. But give him the names, if you think that's the best thing to do." Not looking at him, she took a spoonful of soup. "When I heard that Rona Jean was dead, I decided I didn't have to tell you. But now that we're talking about it, I think I'd better. Because of the money, you see."

"Didn't have to tell me *what*?" Charlie felt he had somehow lost track of the conversation. "What money are you talking about? Fannie, you're not making sense. You—"

She pushed her soup bowl away and clasped her hands on the table in front of her. "Rona Jean was going to give us her baby."

Charlie stared at her, speechless. Finally, with a croak, he managed, "Give *us* her baby?"

Fannie nodded, her mouth trembling. "I knew you wouldn't be in favor of it. That's why I didn't tell you. Right away, I mean. Of course I was going to tell you, before he arrived. Or she. And in plenty of time for you to get used to the idea."

Charlie shook his head, now feeling entirely in the dark. "I don't understand, Fannie. *Why* was this girl going to give us her baby?"

"Because." Fannie's eyes were bright with tears. "Because she didn't want a baby, and *I* do."

And all of a sudden, the light dawned. Like any couple about to be married, he and Fannie had talked about having a family. But Fannie had told him, tearfully, that this was out of the question for her; if he wanted children, he would have to find another wife. Charlie hadn't asked for the details, so he didn't know why this was true. But to tell the honest truth, he was just as glad. He was old enough to be somebody's grandfather. All he knew about little babies was that they cried a lot and monopolized their mother's attention and created mountains of dirty diapers. Having been perfectly happy as a career bachelor for over two decades, he wasn't eager to take on a young family. And anyway, he didn't want another wife, he wanted Fannie, and there was nothing more to be said. In fact, he had thought the question was firmly settled, so this confession—*she didn't want a baby, and I do*—was . . . well, it was baffling, that's what it was.

He frowned, not sure what to ask next. "So what kind of arrangements did you make with her?"

She half turned away. "She had been to a doctor in Monroeville, Dr. DuBois. She needed to pay his bill. She was going to need money for the hospital, of course, and a train ticket, and money to start a new life—somewhere else, which I thought was a good idea. I didn't want to risk her seeing the baby, *our* baby, and deciding that she wanted to take him back. Or her." She pressed her lips together, and Charlie saw how close she was to tears. "So I . . . I gave . . ." She couldn't finish the sentence.

"So you gave her money," Charlie said gently. "How much?" After a moment, he added, not quite so gently: "And when were you going to tell me about . . . this new addition to our family?"

Fannie bit her lip. "I was waiting for the right moment. I thought. . . I was hoping that when you saw how happy it made me, you would . . . well, soften toward the idea." She paused. Not looking at him, she added, in a low voice, "I gave her a hundred and twenty-five dollars. She said she would probably need another hundred and fifty or two hundred." She swallowed. "I know it's a lot of money, but I'd just gotten a check from Lilly Daché, and I . . . well, I cashed it and gave her what she needed."

Charlie was stunned. A hundred and twenty-five was

more than he made in two months, and Fannie had just handed it over, with no assurance that Rona Jean would keep her end of the bargain. No wonder she hadn't wanted to tell him. It wasn't just the baby. It was the money she had paid for it.

"Did you mention anything about this to anybody else?" he asked.

Fannie shook her head. "Why?"

Charlie could think of all kinds of reasons, but he settled for one. "Because I'm not sure that it's legal to buy a baby in the state of Alabama."

"I didn't *buy* a baby." Fannie swallowed hard. "Rona Jean didn't want to be a mother. She wouldn't have been a *good* mother, Charlie, and the baby would have no father. I knew we could give it a home—a good home."

"You *paid* for the child, Fannie. How could you be sure that she wouldn't just take the money and—"

"Please stop," Fannie said despairingly. "Anyway, it doesn't matter. Rona Jean is dead, and the baby's dead, too. And I wanted the baby!" She dropped her face into her hands and began to cry. Charlie got up from his chair, went around the table, and leaned against her back, wrapping his arms around her and resting his cheek on her hair.

"I'm sorry," he said, and knew he was telling the truth. He was sorry that Fannie was unhappy. He was sorry that Rona Jean was dead, and the baby was dead, and they weren't going to have the baby for their own. "I wish . . . I'm just sorry, Fannie."

"Thank you," Fannie said, her voice muffled. She turned on her chair, sheltering herself in his arms. "Do you think maybe you should tell Sheriff Norris? About the money, I mean. He may be looking through her things. If he finds it, he'll wonder who gave it to her. It might help if he knew."

"Do you want the money back?" Charlie asked. *Assuming that Rona Jean hadn't already spent it.*

"I don't know," she said helplessly. "Whatever . . . whatever seems right to you and the sheriff." She wiped her eyes on his sleeve. "I'm sorry about doing this behind your back, Charlie. When you and I discussed not having children, I got the idea that you really didn't want a family, which at the time, I appreciated. But then this came up, and I suddenly realized that I *wanted* a child. It seemed like the right thing to do—a good solution for her and for us, too. I know I should have talked to you before I made any arrangements, but I was afraid if I waited, she would change her mind. I thought I had to act fast."

"I understand," Charlie said gruffly. He put his fingers under her chin, lifted her face, and kissed her mouth. "It's okay, really it is, Fannie. Let's talk about this again, later. Now that I know how you really feel, maybe we can consider some other options. I mean—"

He stopped, not sure of what he meant, just sure that he wanted her to be happy. And if a baby was what it took, they could surely find a baby. The *right* baby.

"Oh, Charlie," she sighed. "Oh, Charlie, I do love you." She looked up at him, her eyes shining, and he knew that she understood what he wasn't yet able to say.


When Charlie left their apartment, the flags that hung from the courthouse windows were limp and listless, and the afternoon heat felt solid, like a damp sponge pressing down. Charlie had missed the noon weather forecast, but he wondered if the storm that had been brewing for several days had finally come alive and was gathering the strength to blow onshore. Looking to the southwest, he saw thunderheads building up, dark against the pale afternoon sky. The farmers' fields and gardens could certainly use some rain, so a storm wouldn't be a bad thing, as long as there wasn't any wind.

He glanced at his watch. It wasn't one thirty yet, and the sheriff's office was less than a block away from the apartment, so he thought he'd walk over there first, before he drove out to the old Loblolly School to meet Mata Hari. He was troubled about Rona Jean's willingness to trade her baby for Fannie's money, and the sooner he told Buddy Norris about it, the better he would feel. But there was more to it than that, of course. He hadn't seen the sheriff since early that morning, and there might be new developments that would affect the story he was already writing in his head.

And something else, too. Fannie's compassion for Rona Jean and her difficult situation had turned his attention away from the mechanics of the murder and the murder investigation, and he found himself wanting to know more about Rona Jean herself. Beyond being "Hello, Central" and an unwed expectant mother, who *was* she? The first sentence of a story began to take shape in his mind. *The victim—a dedicated telephone operator— was killed not long after she left the Telephone Exchange at the end of her eleven o'clock shift at the switchboard.* Which gave him the idea for a title, "The Eleven O'clock Lady."

And with the title came a spurt of energy, the kind of energy Charlie had always felt when he began to get his teeth into a story, a really *good* story. This wouldn't just be a story about a murder. It would be a personality story, a story about the victim, about Rona Jean: where she grew up, where she went to school, who her people were, how she'd gotten her job at the Exchange—maybe even the motive for her killing, if Buddy managed to find it out before the paper went to press. He could interview the other "Hello, Central" girls at the Exchange and write an appealing description of how they all worked closely together, night and day, every day of the week, to keep the Darling telephones plugged in. And, of course, he could include a couple of paragraphs about Violet Sims, that hardworking young mother and co-owner of the Exchange, who had discovered the body when she was picking beans in the garden early in the morning. (That would be a nice, earthy touch.) And Myra May Mosswell, who not only owned the Exchange with her friend Violet, but owned the car where Violet found the body and where the murder had likely taken place.

In fact, that old green Chevrolet touring car (Myra May called her "Big Bertha" and treated her like one of the family) was already famous locally. Big Bertha had been bought new back in 1920 by Myra May's daddy, a much-loved Darling doctor who had driven it to deliver babies and visit deathbeds all over Cypress County. Lots of Darlingians no doubt cherished fond memories of Bertha and would be saddened to know that one of their "Hello, Central" girls had died on her front seat. He could also mention the fact that Myra May took loving care of Bertha and did all the repair work on the car herself, including changing her oil and spark plugs. Yes, Charlie thought, the car, as the scene of the murder, would make a fascinating story all on her own.

He was still thinking of the stories he would write for the *Dispatch*—and sell to the *Atlanta Constitution* as a bylined special—when he reached the sheriff's office, opened the door, and walked in. Buddy and his new deputy, Wayne Springer, were looking at a Dr Pepper bottle and talking about getting fingerprints of the people who had recently been in Myra May's car. They broke off when Charlie came in.

"Well, hey, if it isn't the press." Buddy stuck his hands in his pockets and cocked his head to one side. "I hear you're putting out a special edition on the murder."

"Word gets around, doesn't it?" Charlie said, noticing that Buddy wore a holster on his hip and that the deputy was armed, too. Roy Burns had rarely worn a weapon—Darling didn't seem the place for it. But maybe the new sheriff and his deputy were a different breed of lawmen. Or maybe Darling was becoming a different place, now that the CCC camp had moved in. Did Rona Jean's murder mark a turning point in the town's history? Maybe that was yet *another* story.

"And when will that be coming out?" Buddy asked curiously. "The special edition, I mean."

"I'm figuring on Tuesday, so there'll be copies on the Fourth, when everybody comes to town for the big parade. There'll be plenty of room for late-breaking news, so keep me posted on developments." Charlie paused, raising an expectant eyebrow. "Got any?"

"If you're asking has anybody been arrested," Buddy said, "the answer is no." His grin was crooked. "As Sheriff Burns used to say, 'We ain't caught up with that damn son of a gun yet, but we're a-fixin' to just as quick as he slows down.'"

Charlie remembered Roy Burns saying that, and had even quoted him once in print, which had made the sheriff laugh out loud—a memorable occasion, since Burns was notoriously surly. "I guess I won't hold my breath, then," he said. "In the meantime, I've got something I think you might want to know. About Rona Jean Hancock and that baby."

"You mean, you're not here to pump *me* for information for your story?" Buddy's eyebrows went up. "Well, now, that's a switch. Come on in here and let's talk."

He led the way into his office and pointed Charlie to a chair. Charlie hung his straw boater on the wall hook and took the chair, looking around at the bare office, thinking how many times he'd sat across this very desk from Roy Burns. He would be trying to pry story details out of the sheriff and Roy would keep saying, "No comment." Roy was like that. He never wanted anybody looking over his shoulder, trying to see his hand. He had a poker face, too. You never knew what he was thinking—and you usually didn't want to.

Now, Charlie wondered whether Buddy Norris would hold his cards close the way Roy had. He was young for a sheriff, and he was a Darling boy, which was both an advantage and a disadvantage. On the one hand, he'd grown up with the town's secrets and knew where all the skeletons were hidden, so to speak. It'd be a lot harder to pull the wool over his eyes. But people—especially the older folks—might not be inclined to take a hometown boy seriously, especially one who hadn't seen his thirtieth birthday yet. This might just be Buddy Norris' make-or-break case, the most important case of his career.

Buddy pulled out a lower desk drawer and swung one boot onto it. "So what's this about Rona Jean and her baby? You here to pass along some gossip, or you got something to add to the case?" He spoke with a smile and mildly, but the question was a deliberate challenge.

Charlie decided not to pick up the gauntlet. "I guess you'll have to be the judge of that," he replied, equally mild. "Fannie—my wife—just told me that Rona Jean was one of her regular customers. The young lady liked hats, it seems."

"That's the truth," Buddy said, more to himself than to Charlie. "That girl did have a passel of hats."

Charlie nodded and went on. "A couple of weeks ago, the two of them had a conversation. Rona Jean told Fannie she was pregnant and that she didn't want to keep the baby. She wasn't keen on Darling, either. What she wanted was to get out of town and make a new life for herself somewhere else. So Fannie gave her some money in return for her promise to give us the baby." At the look on Buddy's face, he added, "I know—it was a dumb thing to do. We've talked, and Fannie understands that. But she can't have children, and she felt sorry for a baby whose mother didn't want him. Fannie did—want him, I mean. She wanted him very much."

Buddy gave him a look he couldn't read. "Just how much did Miz Dickens give Rona Jean?"

"A lot, I'm afraid." Charlie gave him a rueful look. "A hundred and twenty-five dollars. Rona Jean said she needed it to pay a doctor over in Monroeville and to handle the hospital. Fannie told her she could come up with more, if she needed it. We thought . . . Fannie and I thought we'd better tell you, in case you found some of that money in Rona Jean's possession and wondered where she got it. And I thought you might want to know what she was up to."

Buddy whistled. "A real con artist, wasn't she?" There was an edge to his voice. "That girl was playing all the angles. It's beginning to sound like one of her shakedown tricks caught up with her."

"Con artist?" Charlie frowned. "All the angles? What angles?"

Buddy pursed his lips, thinking. After a moment, he said, "Are we off the record?"

"If that's how you want it," Charlie said. Of course, when he got something off the record, he could always try to get somebody else to confirm it. He'd played that little trick any number of times. And in Darling, nothing was *truly* off the record. Secrets had wings. And mouths. And legs.

"That's how I *need* it," Buddy said. "I'm not telling you this because you're a newsman, Charlie. I'm telling you because your wife got caught in a con. Y'see, Rona Jean didn't promise that baby just to Miz Dickens. She promised it to Violet and Myra May."

"She *what*?" As the information sank in, Charlie felt a hot, mounting anger. "How much did *they* pay her?"

"They hadn't given her any money directly, at least not yet. But they paid the doctor—Dr. DuBois, his name is—over in Monroeville. And they told her they'd pay the hospital and give her money to get a new start somewhere else. Like your wife, they wanted her baby." Buddy picked up a pencil and tapped the eraser end on the desk. "At least, Violet did. Myra May maybe just went along to keep Violet happy." He kept his eyes on the pencil. "Violet's the one who wants kids."

"*Damn* it!" Charlie shook his head. "I don't think I can tell Fannie this, Buddy. She really wanted that baby, and she wanted to help Rona Jean. I don't want her ever to know that she was the victim of a shakedown artist. That's just going to rub salt into the wound."

He stopped. But if he was going to write Rona Jean's story, the *whole* story, this was just another part of it, wasn't it? This was who she was—the kind of person she had been—as Buddy said, a woman who played all the angles. Or maybe, to put it more charitably, a woman who was dealt a bad hand in life and then played whatever cards she had, hoping to improve her hand. Maybe she didn't play those cards fairly or honestly, but if he was going to write about her, he had to see things from her point of view and tell her side of the story, too. And even though Buddy had given him the information off the record, Darling was a small town. Rona Jean's arrangement with Violet and Myra May was bound to come out, one way or another. Fannie would have to know, and it would be best if she heard it from him, rather than from somebody at the post office or the grocery store.

Buddy was tapping his pencil on the desk, perhaps keeping time with his thoughts. "The thing is, Charlie, that pair at the diner and your missus may not be the only ones who thought they were helping her out. Once Rona Jean got the idea that she could get money from people who wanted the baby, there was nothing to stop her from making the same promise to other people. In fact . . ." He frowned, then went on in a lower voice, thinking out loud. "In fact, that's maybe what got her killed."

"Got her killed?" Charlie asked uneasily.

Buddy was going on. "So Rona Jean figured out that she had this one thing to sell, this baby, and she was selling it to different people, and all of them thought they had a claim on it. If one found out about the others and threatened to blow the whistle . . ." He shrugged. "I guess you can see where I'm going with this."

Charlie stared at him for a moment. As the idea sank in, he didn't like it. "Well, you can count Fannie out as a suspect," he said curtly. "There's no way she'd have the strength to wrap a stocking around Rona Jean's neck. And for what it's worth, I can tell you that she was home in bed with me from ten o'clock until past daylight this morning."

"I don't doubt you," Buddy said, swinging both feet onto the floor. "I don't doubt you one bit." He opened a desk drawer and took out an envelope. "How much did your wife give Rona Jean?"

"A hundred twenty-five, but—" He stopped as the sheriff opened the envelope and began to count twenties.

"Here's a hundred and twenty," Buddy said, pushing the money across the desk. "The rest of this is twenties, and I don't have any change. I'll have to owe you five."

Charlie shook his head. "I really don't think you need to—"

"Money's tight these days." Buddy pulled the desk calendar toward him and tore off the day's page. "You take it and keep your mouth shut." He pushed the page toward Charlie, with the pencil. "Just you write me a receipt, signed and dated. That'll take care of it."

"If you insist," Charlie said, and wrote the receipt. "Thanks,

Buddy. I appreciate it." He took the money and folded it into his wallet. "Rona Jean also told Fannie the names of the men she'd been with, either of whom could have been the father. She named Lamar Lassen and Beau Pyle."

"Yeah, those are the names I have." Buddy paused. "Did she mention Bodeen Pyle?"

Charlie shook his head. "No, but I don't suppose that means much. There could be somebody else. Somebody who couldn't marry her because he was already married. Maybe she threatened to tell his wife if he didn't cough up enough to take care of her and the kid. Maybe he was trying to protect his reputation—and his job. Maybe—"

Buddy sighed. "All that, too," he said. "Look, Charlie, I know you're a newspaperman and you like to print stories, and even speculations, when they fit your story."

*That's true*, Charlie thought. Sometimes speculations *were* the story. And sometimes a speculation could itself be a fact, even a *valuable* fact.

"But I'm in law enforcement," the sheriff went on, "and speculation isn't enough for me. I need real facts—who did what, when, how, that kind of thing. If you've got any facts, I'll be glad to hear them." He paused, pushing his lips in and out. "Especially anything connecting Rona Jean with somebody out at the CCC camp."

Charlie raised both eyebrows. "You think maybe some fellow out there—"

"Not namin' names," Buddy said. "But I've been told that Rona Jean was seeing some guy who rides one of those Army motorcycles. You see that bike around town, you give me a holler. Okay?"

"Okay," Charlie said, then added, "I was in the diner yesterday and heard somebody talking about a motor pool out at the camp. Maybe that's something you could check out."

"Oh yeah?" Buddy said. "Sure. I can do that. Thanks for the suggestion."

Charlie stood up, thinking that Buddy Norris, hometown boy or not, had the makings of a pretty fine sheriff, after all. He thought briefly of mentioning Mata Hari's tip, then decided against it. Buddy might think he should be involved, and Charlie wasn't ready to hand any part of his story to anybody else—at least, not yet. Anyway, it wasn't connected to the Hancock murder. And that's what Buddy had to focus on right now.

"Thanks, Sheriff," he added. "And yes, you'll hear from me if I turn up anything that's connected to your case." He chuckled ruefully. "But don't count on it. I just report the news. I don't make it."

Charlie didn't know it, of course, but he couldn't have been more wrong.

After Charlie left, Buddy picked up his hat and went into the workroom. To his deputy, he said, "What I was saying when Charlie Dickens came in was that Miz Hart saw somebody from the camp over behind the diner, night before last. He rode off on a green military Harley. I'm going out to the CCC camp. If there's a motor pool out there, maybe there's a log or some way of checking out vehicles. If I can find out who drove a motorcycle into town last night, I'll bring him back with me." He grinned crookedly. "I'd rather question him here than at the camp, where he might have friends."

"If you're bringing a suspect in, you might need backup." Wayne cocked an eyebrow. "Want me to come with you?"

Personally, Buddy would have been glad of the backup, but there were other things to consider. He shook his head. "Better you stay here and keep the radio on, Wayne. Last time we had a big storm blow through, maybe seven, eight years ago, Pine Mill Creek came up and flooded half the town. The sheriff and the mayor teamed up to make sure people were okay, so we'll be doing that again. The Exchange has a list of old folks to call and find out if they need any help. The Methodist church basement is a good place for people who don't feel good about staying in their houses. If the mayor stops in while I'm gone, tell him we'll do whatever we can if things get bad."

Wayne nodded. "Maybe you could also check with the head man out at the camp. There are a lot of young guys out there who could give us a hand if we need them. And we might, if there's much flooding."

"Good idea," Buddy said, thinking that—whether it was smart planning or just plain luck—he had hired a deputy who had his head on straight. "Actually, I'm supposed to have dinner with that guy tonight, over at Verna Tidwell's house. Campbell, his name is. Captain Campbell."

Wayne smacked the side of his head with his hand. "Damn," he said. "I knew I should have written it down. Miz Tidwell called just before you got back from talking to Miz Hart. Tonight's dinner is off, because of the storm. She'll let you know when it's rescheduled."

"Just my luck," Buddy said ruefully, reaching for his black rubber raincoat. "I lived next door to that woman when I was growing up. Nobody in the world makes a better chicken pot pie."

# SIXTEEN

# Charlie Dickens Meets Mata Hari and Is Enlightened

The sun had been shining fitfully when Charlie went home for lunch. An hour later, when he walked across the street to the sheriff's office, the clouds were piling up in the southwest. By the time he got in his car to drive out of town to meet his informant, the air was so sultry and heavy with heat and humidity that it was difficult to breathe, and the sunlight seemed to have been leached from the sky. The storm clouds now filled the southern horizon, and lightning lanced from one towering thunderhead to another. It was going to rain before long, he guessed, and rain hard.

The abandoned schoolhouse where Charlie had agreed to meet Mata Hari was some seven miles west of town, on Loblolly Road. The narrow, rutted dirt road had once led to a sawmill down by the river, but the area had been logged over, and the sawmill, too, was abandoned. The one-room school had never enrolled more than a couple of dozen students at one time and had been closed seven or eight years before, when Cypress County created a consolidated school district.

Now, with almost no traffic and no county maintenance, Loblolly Road was a narrow green tunnel through arching trees, the roadsides overgrown with blackberry bushes and giant ragweed. The electricity and the telephone lines had once run from the county road to the school and the sawmill, but every fourth or fifth utility pole was leaning at a steep angle and the wires were down. Charlie guessed that his informant had chosen the out-of-the-way place to give them some privacy for their conversation—but they could have gotten the same privacy at the *Dispatch* office, couldn't they? When he had been sitting behind his desk back in Darling, meeting at the old school hadn't seemed like such a bad idea. But as he drove down Loblolly Road, the isolation felt so nearly overwhelming that he wished they had settled on a meeting place closer to civilization, especially in view of the deteriorating weather.

Loblolly School stood in a clearing that the unruly forest, like a tropical jungle, was threatening to swallow whole. It was a one-room frame building, constructed on wooden piers that raised it a couple of feet above the ground—pier and beam construction, common to rural buildings in the area. It stood the test of time, too, for the piers were usually cypress, a dense, durable wood that resisted rot.

But the building itself wasn't standing time's test very well. Once painted white, the pine siding had weathered to a pale gray, with wild vines clambering up the walls. The surrounding schoolyard was unmowed, and the whole place wore a derelict look, some of the windows broken, half the shingles blown or rotted off the roof, the peaked belfry empty, its bell carted away long ago to serve another purpose.

Charlie pulled up on the gravel apron in front and turned

off the ignition. The parking area was empty—no other vehicle. The woman he was meeting, whoever she was, could not have walked to this remote place, and the road was too rutted for a bicycle. He congratulated himself on being the first to arrive. It gave him a measure of confidence and a sense of control.

Until now, curiosity had been the driving force behind Charlie's eagerness for this meeting—curiosity and a newspaperman's instinctive desire to see his byline on a big story. Mata Hari's claims were shocking, yes. And deeply disturbing, too, for if her allegations were true, it meant that the system that supplied the CCC camps—not just here but everywhere—was easily manipulated. There was a lot at stake here, as he'd told Lorena Hickok, his friend from the old Associated Press days. Because of these wider implications, this story could be big—much bigger, even, than Rona Jean's murder, tragic as that was.

But as he parked and turned off the ignition, Charlie thought again that agreeing to meet his informant in this isolated spot was *not* the best idea he'd come up with all week. He knew he didn't frighten easily. He had distinguished himself for bravery under artillery fire during the Great War, and he'd behaved more or less admirably in several close calls during his reporting career. But at the moment, curiosity and instinct were trumped by apprehension, and he found himself remembering Rona Jean, dead in the front seat of Myra May's car. He should have told Fannie where he was going. Or the sheriff, although he had deliberately *not* mentioned this meeting to Buddy, who (he suspected) might want a piece of the action. But keeping it to himself might have been a mistake. If something happened out here, it might be a while before anybody found him.

*Don't be ridiculous*, he reprimanded himself impatiently.

*What's going to happen? Somebody's going to show up with a gun and shoot both of us? That kind of thing only happens in Sam Spade novels. Or if you're Clyde Barrow, with Bonnie Parker riding shotgun.* He got out of the car, took off his jacket and straw boater, and put both on the passenger seat, then loosened his tie and rolled up his sleeves. The back of his shirt was already wet with sweat. A breeze was beginning to lift the leaves on the huge sycamore that stood next to the schoolhouse, showing the leaves' pale green undersides, so that the whole tree seemed to be shot through with twists of silver. To the south, he glimpsed a bright flicker of lightning and heard a rumble of thunder, and the air was laden with the fresh scent of rain. He rolled up the windows before he left the car, thinking that, if nothing else, a storm might at least break the heat.

The wooden front door had once been locked, but the padlock had been wrenched off long ago and the door hung crookedly from a top hinge. Charlie climbed the three wooden steps, pushed the door open, and went in. A bird fluttered wildly in the rafters, and from a corner came the scratch-scratch of a rat, or maybe even a possum. The scent of mildew and chalk and children's sweaty bodies lingered, mirage-like, on the heavy air.

Charlie looked around. He felt as if the clock had suddenly been turned back some four decades and he had stepped into one of the schoolrooms he remembered (not very pleasantly) from his childhood. As he paused in the door to light a cigarette, he could almost hear the angry ridicule of the teacher who had caught him and another boy smoking behind the school's privy one spring afternoon. The voice was so real that he had to remind himself: he wasn't that little kid now—he was a grown-up, and smart and capable, and that teacher had long ago gone to her reward. He pulled on his cigarette and deliberately blew out a stream of smoke.

(*Take that, you old witch!*) A ghostly, greenish light filtered through the fly-specked windows, illuminating the four rows of empty wooden desks, each attached to the one in front of it; the dusty wooden floor, scarred by decades of children's feet; and the aisle down the center of the room.

Midway down the room on the wall to Charlie's right stood a rusty potbellied stove, the ghost of winters past. Its stovepipe poked through the roof, and a few sticks of wood and a kerosene can lay on the floor beside it. The teacher's desk and chair stood on a scarred wooden platform at the front of the room, with a blackboard on the wall behind it, topped with a frieze of large, precisely formed alphabet letters in Spencerian script, designed to show the children how to make their ABCs.

Above the blackboard hung several grimy rolls of pull-down maps; beside it hung pictures of an Egyptian pyramid and the Taj Mahal and a framed photograph of a sour-looking Calvin Coolidge, president from 1923 to 1929. "Silent Cal," he'd been called, because he said very little and smiled less. Charlie half grinned at a story he remembered, about a society matron who was seated beside the president at a dinner. To Coolidge, she said, "Mr. President, I made a bet today that I could get more than two words out of you." He replied, "You lose," and returned his attention to his potato. Charlie thought with pity of the poor children who had to do their schoolwork in this gloomy room, under the president's sour stare.

There were door openings at either side of the back wall, bookending the blackboard. These were the entries to the cloakroom, Charlie knew, which ran across the back of the building. Rows of big hooks on the walls waited for the children to hang up their sweaters and coats, and several long shelves offered space for stowing books, boots, and sack lunches: peanut butter and jelly sandwiches (if they were lucky), or split biscuits smeared with lard and sprinkled with sugar, or chunks of cold corn pone and baked sweet potato. The luckiest ones got a tomato or a peach or an apple and sometimes a cookie.

The carpet of thick dust that stretched the length of the aisle was undisturbed. He'd wait at the teacher's desk, Charlie decided, where he could see his informant as she came in. Now that he was here and thinking about the meeting, his curiosity was overcoming his apprehension. He had been puzzling about the identity of this woman for days now, and at last he was going to meet her. Who *was* she? She had to be somebody from town, somebody he already knew, since he knew everybody in Darling. But what was her connection to the camp? How had she come by the details that she was— presumably—about to share with him?

He began walking to the front of the room, his steps echoing hollowly on the wooden floor. He had almost reached the teacher's platform when a woman spoke. Her voice was slightly muffled, but her words were quite clear.

"That's far enough, Mr. Dickens. Why don't you just sit down on one of those kids' desks, and we'll have ourselves a talk."

Charlie pulled in his breath, startled, and the gooseflesh raised on his arms. Mata Hari—he would have to call her that until he found out who she really was—was in the cloakroom. She had likely come in through a back door, and he chastised himself for not having gone around to the back of the building where her car was probably parked. She must be able to see him, he thought, and he searched the wall on either side of the blackboard for what he knew was there: a peephole. His teachers had had one, so if they retired briefly to the cloakroom, they could keep an eye out for misbehaving pupils. After a moment, he spotted it, beneath Calvin Coolidge's photograph. Just a round hole in the wall, an inch or so in diameter. He couldn't see an eye at that hole, watching, but he knew it was there, and it made him wary. And apprehensive.

"Sit down, Mr. Dickens," Mata Hari said sharply. "Right there."

"Whatever you say," Charlie agreed, trying to sound casual. He pulled out his handkerchief and brushed the dust off a desk next to the aisle. He sat on the desk, his feet on the bench of the desk in front, directly in line with the peephole. He took a drag on his cigarette and leaned forward, his elbows on his knees.

"But you are gonna come out here and talk to me, aren't you?" he asked. "I sure would like to know who you are." As if to emphasize his remark, there was a sudden, electric-blue flash of lightning, bright enough to briefly illuminate the room, which had grown perceptibly darker since he had come in.

In answer, he heard a ripple of amused laughter. "Not on your life, Mr. Dickens. If I'd've wanted you to know who I am, I would've told you before now. I'm staying back here in the cloakroom and *you* are staying right where you are." Her words were punctuated by the loud clap of thunder that followed the lightning. It rattled the glass in the old building's windows—what was left of them.

The cloakroom. So that was why they were meeting here, Charlie realized. She had deliberately chosen this place so she could conceal herself while they talked and watch him through that peephole. He was disappointed, but he reminded himself that this was only the opening inning of their little game. Just because Mata Hari intended to get things started this way didn't mean they had to end this way. No question about it, he needed to know who she was and what her connection was to the camp. His story would carry a lot more weight if he could quote his source and say how she got her knowledge. But to entice her out where he could see her, he first needed to make a move that would establish *him* as in control of their meeting.

"Any way you want it," he said with a shrug of one shoulder. He dropped his cigarette into the dust of the aisle, got off the desk and stepped on it, and sat back down again. "Personally, I think it'd be friendlier if we could talk eye to eye. You know, friend to friend. But you can stay back there if that's how you want it."

"That's generous of you," she said with a dry irony.

"Yeah. I'm a generous person." He pulled out his wallet and removed the handwritten four-sentence note she had sent him earlier. "Let's start off with what you wrote to me. It's actually pretty explosive stuff." He unfolded it and read aloud, raising his voice over another growl of thunder.

*Dear Mr. Dickens,*

*I think you ought to know that the purchasing program at the CCC camp is totally crooked. To get a contract, a farmer or supplier has to hand over a percentage of what he expects to get paid. Sometimes it's ten percent, sometimes fifteen or even twenty, but he has to pay it before he gets the contract. Nobody dares to blow the whistle on this dirty dealing because everybody wants the money they get for whatever they're selling.*

There. That was it. That was what they were here to discuss. Corruption in the federal program. Kickbacks at Camp Briarwood.

"So tell me, Mata Hari." He glanced up at the peephole under Silent Cal. "Far as you're concerned, those claims are all still true?" He chuckled loudly, so she could hear him.

"By the way, 'Mata Hari' is pretty cute. You got my attention with that one."

She disregarded the compliment, if that's what it was. "Yes, it's true," she said grimly. "It's been going on ever since the camp started buying milled lumber for the buildings. It's still going on."

Charlie reached into his shirt pocket for his notebook and pencil. "Hope you don't mind if I take a few notes. My recollection's not as good as it used to be."

As he found a clean page in his notebook, he was sorting through his memories of women's voices, trying to place this one. It wasn't easy, though. Southern women tended to sound alike. This voice was familiar—it belonged to one of the Dahlias, he thought. That garden club seemed to get tangled up in everything that went on in Darling. But whose was it? From what he'd heard, half of the club members were working or teaching out there at the camp and could be expected to know something about what was going on. Ophelia, of course, but also Bessie Bloodworth, Verna Tidwell, Liz Lacy, Lucy Murphy, Earlynne Biddle, Miss Rogers, and maybe a couple of others he didn't know about. Mata Hari could be any one of them. Well, not Miss Rogers, who was a prissy old thing with a voice like a squeaky violin string. No, definitely not her. But any one of the rest. Verna Tidwell was the most likely, he thought.

"Take all the notes you please," Mata Hari said. "It's important that you get it right."

Her words were followed by a lightning flash that made Charlie blink, and the thunderclap followed in seconds. The sky outside the windows was darker, too, and the wind, gusting across the stovepipe, had set up an eerie, vibrating wail, like a kid blowing across a bottle. The storm was getting closer.

"Okay." He held his pencil poised. "To start with, how come you didn't contact the sheriff instead of sending that note to me? What we're talking about here is a crime. Shouldn't you have gone to Buddy Norris?"

There was a silence. "If I'd known what I know now, I would have." Mata Hari's voice was bleak. "Given what's happened, I wish I had. I think . . . I'm afraid you'll have to."

He was about to ask why, but she drew a regretful breath and sighed it out. "You see, when I wrote to you, I was thinking that this was a *federal* thing, involving a federal employee, and maybe more than one. Yes, there are some local people involved, but mostly it's federal. So the sheriff wasn't . . . well, he wasn't relevant."

"Wait a minute," Charlie said, looking up at Silent Cal. "What do you mean, what you know *now*? What's changed?"

"We'll get to that. But later." There was a moment's silence. "Anyway, I was thinking that Buddy Norris is a pretty nice boy, but he's new on the job, you know, with almost no experience, and no connections out there at the camp. So what's he going to do but go straight to the head guy? And for all I know, Captain Campbell himself might be in on this. It may be his idea. He may be taking a big cut."

She paused, and Charlie asked, "Do you have any evidence that he is?"

"No, and I'm not saying he is. But if he doesn't know anything about it, people will say that he *should*, since it's his camp and he's responsible for what happens in it. Either way, it's bad for him. His reputation is at stake. He won't want anybody poking around, especially the local law. Give him half a chance and he'd probably sweep the whole thing under the rug." She paused again. "And go after anybody who might have squealed." With the last sentence, her voice had changed, almost imperceptibly. It held something that Charlie thought sounded like fear.

"I see." Charlie was scribbling fast, trying to get her words down verbatim. "So you wrote to me instead of the sheriff. You didn't stop to think that *I* might go straight to the head guy?"

But he now had a different, and rather unsettling, perspective. He was looking at the situation from her point of view. Whoever she was—and she could be any one of a half-dozen women—her knowledge made her vulnerable. It put her in danger, like . . . The image of the woman he had seen this morning, dead, strangled, flashed into his mind, and he frowned. Why had he thought of that? There wasn't any connection between Rona Jean Hancock and what was going on at the camp. Was there?

Mata Hari gave a humorless chuckle. "Of course you won't go to the head guy. You won't go to anybody, not on this. You don't want to solve a crime or put somebody in jail. You don't get paid—or get elected—for doing that. You just want a *story*. And that's what I want, too. If you write this up the way I tell you and run it in the *Dispatch*, they won't be able to ignore it out there at the camp, or pretend that it's not happening. What's more, that'll keep me safe. The bad guy—or guys, or whatever—might suspect me of telling, but they won't dare touch me."

Charlie wondered at that. There could be a lot riding on this. Why wouldn't the "bad guy" (singular or plural) try to silence her, to keep her from telling what she knew? He started to say this, but a heavy thud of thunder interrupted him, and when the reverberations had died away, Mata Hari was hurrying on.

"But even better, if you do a really, *really* good story on this, it might get picked up by a bigger paper. Maybe somebody will start an investigation. And when that happens, this swindle will *stop*. There won't be any more kickbacks." Half under her breath, she added, "At least, that's what I was thinking when I wrote you that note."

"It's good thinking," Charlie said approvingly. It was. She had thought this all the way through, and her conclusions were pretty much in line with his own thoughts on the matter. "But if I'm going to run a story, I can't do it just on your say-so. I don't even know who the hell you are, or whether what you're telling me is the truth or a passel of lies. I have to run a background check on your information. I have to confirm it with other sources, the more, the better. But first, I'm going to need everything you've got—names, dates, amounts, everything you know. Don't hold anything back. And let's start with your name. Your *real* name."

Of course, Charlie had already begun to work on that background check. That was why he'd put Ophelia Snow on special assignment and why she was out there at the camp today, getting the confirmation he needed. At least, that's what she was supposed to do, assuming that everything was going according to plan. Which it didn't always.

The wind blew eerily down the stovepipe again, and ashes puffed out into the room, wraith-like, the ghostly remains of long-dead fires. Somewhere toward the entry to the building— in the belfry, maybe—a board pulled loose and took up an annoying arrhythmic banging.

"No," Mata Hari said in a determined voice. "I am *not* going to tell you who I am. But I'll tell you everything else I know. Get your pencil and start writing."

And for the next few moments, while the lightning flickered, the thunder banged like an orchestra's percussion section, and the wind—and now and then the rain—whipped against the old building, that's what she did, reciting the names of a half-dozen local suppliers who had paid kickback fees, the amount they had forked over, and the kind of items that were being supplied to the camp. Charlie—who hadn't known what to expect in the way of serious information, *real* information—was impressed. Whoever she was, she knew her stuff. He was talking to an insider.

When she paused for breath, he said, "How did you get all this? The names, I mean. The amounts. I need to know what kind of access you had."

"You don't *want* to know," she said. "And I don't want to tell you."

He frowned. "Why?"

She didn't answer right away, and when she did, she spoke reluctantly, as if she would rather not answer the question but felt compelled to. "It wasn't . . . it wasn't honest, what I did. I didn't play fair."

He frowned, wondering what she had done that she was ashamed of and wanting to make her feel better, to reassure her. "Look, *Mata Hari*." He gave the name a special emphasis. "You've given yourself a spy's name, and maybe you're thinking there's something dishonorable about spying. But the kickback scheme—it's dishonest, start to finish. Illegal and immoral, too. So what does it matter if you didn't play fair?"

"It matters to me," she said quietly. "I didn't set out to be a spy. I only did what I felt I had to do. So don't ask how I did it. Just believe me. Give me credit for telling the truth. If you could get the records, you'd see that everything I'm telling you is accurate."

"Well, then, how about the way the scheme operated?" Charlie said, moving on. After all, Ophelia was supposed to be getting the records. With luck, he'd have plenty of corroborating material, maybe as early as this evening. "Give me the big picture."

She seemed happier to talk about that part of it, in the intervals between the lightning and thunder, which seemed to be coming at an accelerating clip. But she was focused on what she was saying, and she ignored the storm. At the camp, the various departments and divisions turned in their orders to the quartermaster's office, which ran a regular advertisement in the *Dispatch* for what was needed. (Charlie knew all about this, of course. Corporal Andrews, the quartermaster's assistant, brought the ads in a couple of times a month. The additional advertising revenue was definitely welcome.) The advertisement spelled out what was needed and invited bidders. Once the bids were in, the liaison officer (Ophelia Snow, as Charlie also knew) went to work, "qualifying" the bidders, who were then selected by the quartermaster.

"Sometimes they're picked on price," she said. "The low bidder gets it. But as time goes on, they're usually picked on the basis of performance on a previous contract. That is, if your vegetables were fresh and good and you delivered on time, you'd get another contract. If you were still the low bidder, that is. It's been pretty competitive."

It sounded like a standard operation, Charlie thought. "You're a supplier, I take it," he said.

"Yes." She hesitated, then in a lower voice, said, "No. Not now."

Charlie heard the change in her tone. "Not now," he repeated. "Why is that?"

She sighed. "Just listen," she said, and went on to tell him in detail how the kickback system worked. The contract would be offered to the supplier, who would be told before he signed it that there was a fee involved, which would have to be paid out of the proceeds. If the supplier balked at this or seemed reluctant, he would be told that the contract would go to the next person on the list. There was nothing overtly intimidating about any of this, the woman said. It was presented to the would-be supplier as a simple step in the process and delivered with a friendly smile, so that people would think that this was just the way business was normally done in the CCC.

"And of course, once the suppliers have accepted the terms," Mata Hari said, "they've broken the law, too. They've become criminals, and if they balk, they'll be reminded of that fact." Charlie could hear the bitterness in her voice. "Which means that nobody's going to tell what he's done. Everybody will keep on bidding and keep on paying the bribe. Even if they don't get another contract, they'll keep their mouths shut."

Charlie fished in his shirt pocket for a cigarette and his pants pocket for his lighter. *You scratch my back, I'll scratch yours* was the rule everywhere. But when it came to government funds, quid pro quo was strictly illegal. Of course the supplier would keep his mouth shut. Bribery was a two-edged sword. Both the person who gave the bribe and the person who accepted it were equally guilty, under the law.

But still . . . He flicked a flame to his cigarette and pulled on it. "What if somebody decides not to play? What happens then?"

She laughed ironically. "Who do you think you're talking to?"

"Ah," Charlie said, pocketing the lighter. And then, "Isn't that . . . kind of dangerous?"

"I haven't told him yet," she said simply. "I'm hoping you'll run the story and then it'll all be out in the open and everything will change."

*Him. Him who?* Now they were getting to the interesting part. "Okay," Charlie said, "we've gotten to the part where you name names. I need to know who's setting this up, who's taking the bribes. I'll be careful how I use the information, but you're going to have to tell me."

Something heavy smashed against the building—a limb off that old sycamore, maybe—and Charlie heard a window shatter. By the time the storm was over, he thought, every pane of glass would be gone.

"I'll tell you," she said flatly. "But not yet."

Charlie scowled at Silent Cal, whose gaze seemed more sour than ever before. "Why not tell me *now*?"

She cleared her throat. "Because it's bigger than I've said. It's . . . this is the part where it gets really bad."

"Sounds pretty bad already." Charlie looked down at his notes. "I don't know what the sentence is for bribery, but we're talking multiple counts." And if the man was Army, which he almost certainly was, he wouldn't be tried in a civilian court. There would be a military court-martial, and the sentence was likely to be stiffer—not to mention that he'd be doing time in a military prison. Charlie made a note. "Any idea how many contracts we're talking about?"

"Not really. He didn't put the bite on all the bidders, just on the ones he thought would pay up. Where there was a lot of competition among bidders. Or where the contract was really big and he thought the bidder was anxious to get it. The first lumber contract alone, I know, was worth ten thousand dollars."

"Yeah," he said ironically. "Pretty damned big. He must be raking it in by the thousands, getting ready to do a quick fade." He made another note. *The money—in cash somewhere, in a bank account?* In cash, if the man was smart. Bank accounts were easily traced. "Do you know where he's keeping it?"

She didn't answer the question. Instead, she said, "But

when I say it got bad, I don't mean that it just got *big*. I mean—" She broke off. When she spoke again, Charlie could hear the tears in her voice. She was speaking so low that he almost couldn't hear what she said next. "This is where it gets to be more than just a newspaper story, Mr. Dickens. This is the part where I think you have to go to the sheriff."

Charlie stopped writing. It had been hot when he arrived, and he'd left his jacket in the car. The storm had dropped the temperature dramatically, and his sweaty shirt was as cold against his shoulders as if he'd just taken it out of Fannie's icebox. He shivered.

"Go to the sheriff? But a minute ago you said—"

"I know what I said." There was a long silence. Outside, the wind was pushing like a live thing, a savage thing, against the building, and Charlie thought he could feel it shudder.

At last she said, "Look. I sent you that note the day I told my husband that I wasn't going to bid on another contract. I didn't tell him why, just that I didn't want to do it anymore."

*Her husband*, Charlie thought. Well, that let Verna Tidwell out, and Liz Lacy and Bessie, none of whom were married. Earlynne Biddle? Could Mata Hari be Earlynne? Maybe— her husband ran the Coca-Cola bottling plant outside of town, and Charlie knew that Earlynne worked part-time in the office there. The bottling plant very likely had a contract to supply soft drinks to the camp.

She was going on. "I could afford to stop bidding because my husband has a good job and I'm working, too. But most people can't afford to get out. They need the money to buy shoes for the kids or put food on the table. They're forced to become criminals just to stay afloat. And it doesn't have to be that way! If it's honestly run, the contract system will work for everybody. For the camp, for the suppliers, for Darling."

She dropped her voice. "When I wrote that note, I was hoping that all I had to do was give you a little push and get you started on the story, and you'd do the rest. You'd see that the system got fixed and I wouldn't have to be involved." She was silent for a moment, as if putting a period to that sentence. "That's what I thought. Until this morning."

"This morning?" Charlie asked. "What happened this morning?" And then he remembered. An icy finger began to tickle his spine, from his nape down to his tailbone. "You mean, when you heard about—"

"Yes," Mata Hari said, in a very low voice. "That's why I had to talk to you *today*."

A blinding flash of blue-white light illuminated the classroom for an instant and was gone just as quickly. The lightning was followed a heartbeat later by a bone-rattling clap of thunder.

He sucked in his breath. "You're telling me that this bribery business out at the camp is connected to Rona Jean Hancock's *murder*?" In his mind, he was putting two and two together—what Fannie had told him about Rona Jean's willingness to trade her baby for money, what the sheriff had told him about the deal she'd made with Violet and Myra May—and it was beginning to add up. Maybe.

He licked his lips. "You're saying that Rona Jean found out what was going on? That she blackmailed the guy who was running the kickback system?" He swallowed hard, trying to get rid of the lump in the middle of his gullet. "That she was killed to shut her up?"

As he said this, he thought how ridiculous it sounded, like a page out of an Ellery Queen mystery. But it wasn't ridiculous at all. It was utterly reasonable, given the way Rona Jean operated. She knew how to manipulate people, how to turn their desires—Fannie's longing for a child,

Violet's wish for a sister or brother for her daughter—into weapons she could use. She knew what *she* wanted and she wasn't afraid to go after it. And that kind of audacity could be dangerous. It could even be deadly.

"Yes," Mata Hari said. "I think she was killed to keep her quiet." Her voice was very low. "She knew what was going on. As for the other thing, the blackmail, I don't know that for sure. I think so, but—"

"But how did she find out?" Charlie interrupted urgently. "She wouldn't have been a supplier. How did she know—"

Another sudden gust of wind slammed the old building. This time, Charlie *knew* he could feel it shudder, and he wondered how solid the old piers were underneath the building. Or more to the point, how solid the frame construction was on top of the piers. Another gust or two like that one and the whole thing could—

"Think about it," Mata Hari commanded sharply. "Where did Rona Jean work?"

"Well, she worked at the . . ." And then Charlie understood. "Of course. She worked at the Exchange. She listened in on a telephone call." It was against the rules, of course, and not all the operators did it. But some did, especially at night, when the traffic was slow and they had nothing else to do. People in Darling knew, and if they had something they didn't want anybody to hear, they didn't trust it to the telephone. But somebody from out of town, somebody who was used to privacy on the phone, wouldn't know this. He might—

"Yes," Mata Hari said. "That's how it happened. She listened in on a telephone call. I'm sure it wasn't the first time for her. She figured out what he was doing and snooped around until she discovered who he was, and when she did, I'm sure she thought she'd found herself a gold mine. She got herself introduced to him." Her voice became bitter.

"From then on, it wasn't hard at all. He was a pushover—for her, anyway."

Charlie had stopped writing now and was listening hard, listening to the story but also listening between the lines, listening to the woman who was telling it. And beginning to guess at another reason for her refusal to let him know who she was. The man she was talking about had been her friend. No, more than that, she had been in love with him, married woman or not. Maybe she had even been thinking of leaving her husband for him, leaving Darling and starting a new life somewhere else. And maybe he'd been in love with her, too, a lot or a little. Or maybe he was just taking advantage of her interest in him, finding her willing, even eager for kisses and whatever else he wanted. Which had maybe been just fine, for both of them.

Until Rona Jean had come along and changed the equation.

"I couldn't figure out what he saw in her." Mata Hari went on, now speaking flatly, mechanically. "She wasn't all that pretty, but there was something . . . I don't know, seductive maybe. They went to the movies over in Monroeville, and to the roller rink and the dances at the camp. I could see that he was getting in over his head and I tried to warn him, but he thought he was in charge where women were concerned and he wouldn't listen. Until she told him what she wanted."

Almost playfully, lightning skipped and skittered outside the window. The wind pummeled the building. "What was that?" Charlie asked. "What did she want? Marriage?"

She laughed abruptly. "No. Not that. She might have wanted a husband in the beginning, but somewhere along the way she changed her mind. What she wanted was a lump-sum payoff—a substantial payoff—to keep quiet. She wanted to leave Darling and get a new start somewhere else.

She demanded money. Five hundred dollars. And when he heard that—" A blast of wind and rain rattling against the windows blotted out the rest of her sentence.

Charlie waited until the assault quieted. "When he heard that, he *what?*" he prompted.

Her voice flattened out, lost all inflection. "I don't really know, because I wasn't . . . because after that we didn't . . . we didn't talk anymore." In her pause, Charlie heard a final chapter of aching regret, the ending of a love affair, the beginning of a new and painful understanding.

After a moment, she went on. "I don't know, but I can guess. He decided he couldn't trust her. He was afraid that once he gave her anything, there'd never be an end to it. She'd keep coming back to him, asking him for money, for the rest of his life. He isn't the kind of man who could live with somebody holding something over his head. I hate the thought of it, and I almost can't believe I'm saying this, but I think . . ." Her words were swallowed by a sob.

"You think he killed her." Charlie was suddenly frozen in the understanding that his two big stories—Rona Jean's murder and the kickback scheme—were one single story, a story that was bigger than anything he had ever written.

"Yes," she said. "I think so. I don't know for sure, but I think so." She was struggling with the words. "I don't think he planned it, though. I think she taunted him until he got so angry that he lost his head and just . . . just *did* it. I can't prove any of this—I don't have even a single clue, except what I know about her demand. But I know him and I heard what happened to her and I can't live with myself if I don't tell what I know." She took a deep breath. "I'll tell you his name. But I can't go to the sheriff. You'll have to do that for me." Another breath. "Please."

*She's desperate*, Charlie thought, understanding. *She's try-ing to do the right thing, but she's scared. She wants to see justice done, but she doesn't want anybody in Darling to know that she's been romantically involved with a man who isn't her husband, who is running a kickback racket, who might even be a killer. She's hoping to go back to her marriage without being found out. She's using me as a conduit to law enforcement—and a screen to hide behind.*

But he couldn't blame her for any of this, could he? He had fallen in love unwisely a time or two himself, and he understood the desperation she must be feeling. She'd paid a bribe, yes—but so had dozens of other people. And she had come forward with her suspicions about the murder, and about the suspect's possible motive, even though she might still care for him. She could have kept quiet, but she hadn't. He had to give her credit for that.

He leaned forward, elbows on knees, hands clasped in front of him. "Okay. But I still think the sheriff will want to talk to you. He won't take my word for any of this, because it's secondhand. It's . . ." He groped for the legal term. "It's hearsay. He'll be looking for evidence. He'll need—"

"No, please!" she cried. "I can't talk to him. I can't! I have to stay out of it entirely." She hurried on. "You've got everything you need to expose the kickbacks and print your story. For Rona Jean's murder, you can tell the sheriff that you got an anonymous tip that he should question Corporal Raymond Andrews, out at Camp Briarwood. And if he needs evidence, tell him to take a look at the motorcycle pool roster at the camp. Ray had to check the motorcycle out every time he drove it to town and check it in when he brought it back. He didn't have any other way to get around."

*Corporal Andrews?* Charlie was surprised. And then he

wasn't. The quartermaster's assistant, the man who placed the ads every couple of weeks, was a good-looking man, mid-thirties, maybe forty, affable and quite charming. He was the kind of guy who could ask for a bribe and make it seem like he was doing the other person a big favor.

"Corporal Andrews," he said aloud. "I see."

"Yes," she said. He could hear the muffled misery in her voice. "Tell the sheriff everything, if you want, and take all the glory. For breaking the story, for giving the sheriff a lead to the man who might have killed Rona Jean. But leave me out of it, *please*."

Blue-white lightning flared like popping flashbulbs, and thunder was an almost constant stutter. Rain was sheeting down the closed windows and pouring in buckets through those that were broken. Water was spreading across the floor, and the smell of wet dust hung on the air.

"I understand," Charlie said, raising his voice above the storm. "But it would be better if you'd come with me to talk to the sheriff. I know Buddy Norris. He's a good guy. He'll keep your part in this confidential. He's got ways to handle stuff like this, if you'll just trust him." He hoped it sounded like he knew what he was talking about. "Look. All you have to do is get in the car with me. We'll drive to town, and you can tell Buddy everything you've told me." He made himself laugh. "Hell, we can even put a bag over your head if you don't want anybody to see your face. So what do you say? The deputy is working on fingerprints now, and they may be able to get a match. If they do, it'll make the case. You won't have to—"

But the rest of what he had intended to say was annihilated by a blinding flash of lightning and a simultaneous explosion, as lightning struck the old sycamore next to the building. The tree exploded like a detonating artillery shell, dropping two massive limbs squarely on the school building's roof and hurling showers of sparks and torso-sized chunks of splintered, flaming wood through the windows. The school's belfry toppled onto the roof, and the roof collapsed on the desks with a deafening roar, as if a giant hand had broken its spine. The stovepipe came down and the Acme stove crashed over onto its side. The schoolroom filled with a haze of dust and old ashes—and smoke and the smell of burning kerosene.

The explosion had flung Charlie forward and onto the floor in front of the teacher's platform. He tried to get to his feet, but he couldn't and crouched there, covering his head with his arms, stunned, his ears ringing, his heart pounding like a trip hammer. Dazed, he heard the crackle of flames and got to his knees, turning to look over his shoulder. The fire was spreading across the floor, ignited by the lightning strike and fueled by the kerosene that had spilled out of the can beside the stove. Tongues of flame licked hungrily at the walls and the wooden desks. If it weren't for the pelting rain that sought out the fire and doused it with a hiss and a sizzle, the old tinderbox would have gone up in an instant. As it was, it was likely to smolder for hours.

But the building no longer provided any shelter. Charlie scrambled to his feet. "Mata Hari?" he yelled, and sucked in a lungful of choking dust and smoke. He coughed. "Mata Hari?"

The only answer was the wail of the wind and the groan of the walls under the weight of the collapsed roof. The teacher's desk still stood on the platform in front of the blackboard, but part of the wall was gone. Charlie picked his way through broken boards and roof shingles toward the nearest cloakroom door, and stepped into a splintered chaos. The roof of the back part of the building had collapsed, and most of the back wall. The rain was pouring down in a drenching torrent. The woman lay on the floor, pinned under a beam, her eyes closed, face ashen, head bleeding. Charlie recognized her immediately and bent over her, taking her hand. Her fingers were limp and cold.

"Lucy," he said urgently. "Lucy, answer me. Are you all right? *Lucy?*"

There was no answer.

# SEVENTEEN

# In Which Several Important Things Happen at Once to Different People

As Ophelia drove home from the camp, the southwestern sky was dark and ominous, and she knew that the coming storm was likely to be a bad one. After she and Sarah got home and carried their purchases into the house, the first thing she did was turn on the parlor radio to try and catch a weather forecast. Ten minutes later, the announcer on WALA was reporting that the storm that had been hanging around out in the Gulf had finally crossed the coast and was picking up speed. It was moving inland west of Mobile on a curving path that took it in a northerly direction. The announcer warned of torrential rain, lightning, and winds of over a hundred miles an hour, higher in gusts.

Ophelia, who had weathered a great many storms, didn't need to look at a map to know that Darling was on the edges of the path and that they were about to be brushed by a hurricane. She telephoned Jed to alert him to the situation, then summoned Sam and put him to the task of telephoning the boys on his baseball team to tell them that their picnic was postponed, since the whole town would be hunkering down until the storm had blown over. She called Sarah down from upstairs (where she had been trying on her new bathing suit) and put her to work collecting all the candles and oil lamps in the house so they could be easily located when the lights went out, which was sure to happen. Darling's power went off when the wind blew hard or when there was ice on the wires, and it was sometimes days before the electricity was restored. Ophelia filled gallon jugs with water from the faucet, since Darling's water pumps wouldn't work without power.

The big worry was the food in the icebox. The ice that had been delivered that morning and kept the food cold throughout the weekend would normally be replaced on Monday. But the Darling Ice Company depended on the Darling Power Company and the Darling Water Company. If the electricity went out, the ice company wouldn't be making ice over the weekend, which meant no Monday deliveries—or Tuesday or Wednesday, either, if the power was out for a long time. Ophelia tied a length of bright red yarn to the icebox handle to remind everybody not to leave it open when they took food out of it.

At two o'clock, Jed closed the Farm Supply and came home. He and Sam fastened wooden shutters over the windows while Ophelia went down the street and persuaded Mother and Dad Snow to come and ride out the storm with them. Their house was one of the sturdiest in the neighborhood and had weathered several bad blows over the years, with only minor damage. They would all be relatively safe there, and it was good for the family to be together.

But while she was tending to her storm preparations, Ophelia was thinking about the situation at the camp. The boys would likely be confined to barracks for the duration of the storm, but the buildings were designed as temporary structures, and she wasn't sure that they would weather a big blow without a lot of damage. She hoped everyone would be safe.

But mostly, she was thinking about those two voucher lists she had taken from the quartermaster's filing cabinet earlier that day—the people, with names, addresses, and amounts, who were due to receive contract payment checks from the government. For the life of her, she still couldn't figure out why the *second list*, the one Sergeant Webb had typed, contained so many more names than the list she herself had typed. It didn't make sense, she thought. It just didn't make sense.

So after she had settled Dad Snow for a game of checkers with Sarah and persuaded Mother Snow to lie down for a nap on the double bed in the bedroom she and Jed shared, Ophelia sat down at the kitchen table with a cup of coffee and the two lists. She studied them carefully, then (since she couldn't mark the originals) made a list of the names—eighteen of them—that were on the sergeant's list but not on hers. She included the voucher amounts and totaled them, a little over $22,000. Then she picked up the thin telephone directory for Cypress County and began to look up the names. Fifteen minutes later, as the sky outside the kitchen window grew darker and thunder growled and grumbled in the distance, she gave it up as a bad job. None of the eighteen—not a single one!—was in the telephone directory.

She was still sitting there, thinking about this, when Jed came in from his last-minute outdoor preparations. "It's beginning to blow pretty hard out there," he said, taking off his yellow storm slicker and hanging it, dripping, on the hook beside the back door. "Looks like we lost a limb off the peach tree. And who knows what else we'll lose in the next few hours. We may be lucky to hang on to the roof—and the chimney."

Ophelia sighed as she got up to get the coffeepot. They'd had to rebuild their chimney a couple of times already. "Is everything taken care of in town?" she asked.

"I think so." Jed pulled out a chair and sat down at the table, and Ophelia poured him a fresh cup of coffee. "After you called, I went over to the sheriff's office to let them know about the forecast. Buddy had gone out to the camp, but Springer was there. That new deputy has a lot on the ball. He'd heard the forecast and was already making plans. The sheriff's office will be storm headquarters, and the Exchange will relay emergency messages there."

"Out to the camp?" Ophelia asked.

"Yeah. Springer wouldn't tell me why, but I'm guessing that it has something to do with the Hancock murder." He pulled out a handkerchief and mopped his face. "After that, I went over to the courthouse and told Hezzy to ring the storm bell and take all the flags in, then stopped in at the Exchange to make sure that Myra May's diesel generator is ready to fire up if the power fails. She had already heard the WALA weather forecast and had brought in a couple of her extra girls to call the older people in town—the ones with no families or near neighbors—to see if they need any help getting over to the Methodist basement. And all the party lines are going full tilt, of course. Everybody should get the word."

As mayor of Darling, it was Jed's responsibility to monitor emergency situations. Hezzy was Hezekiah, the colored man who managed the flags and wound the clock and rang the courthouse bell, which could be heard from one end of Darling to the other. The storm bell was a peal of five rings and a pause, then three and a pause, then five. By the time Hezzy finished pulling the bell rope thirteen times, everybody in town would know that a bad storm was on the way. If they missed that warning, Hezzy would ring it again thirty minutes later. Those who weren't sure that their houses could stand a big blow were welcome to go to the Methodist church, where the deacons and their wives were organizing the basement as a storm shelter. If people needed a ride to the church, they could call the switchboard (which could be powered by a diesel generator if the electricity went out), and somebody would go and get them. In a difficult situation, Darling always took care of its own.

"I'm sure you've done everything you could do," Ophelia said. She sat down and pushed her list of eighteen names across the table. "If you've got a minute, I wonder—would you mind taking a look at this, Jed?"

He glanced down at it, then picked up his coffee and drank. "What am I looking at?"

"It's supposed to be a list of people who are due to get government checks through our office at the camp. But I don't recognize a single name. Do you?" As the owner and manager of the Farm Supply, Jed had business dealings with every farm family in the county, while Ophelia knew everybody in town and most of the people in the county. If *he* didn't know them and *she* didn't know them, they didn't exist. It was as simple as that.

He frowned down at the list. "Can't say that I do, Opie. And the addresses—well, they're just plain crazy. Some of them are the right names—I mean, they're the names of county roads—but the numbers are all wrong. And some of the others, I've never heard of. Rider Road, for instance. Where the heck is that?" Frowning, he put his finger on the total she had written at the bottom. "These people are collecting twenty-two thousand dollars in government checks? But who the devil *are* they? Nobody I know."

Ophelia sat back in her chair. There was only one way to answer Jed's question, but she almost didn't believe it, and she didn't trust herself to give it voice. She was still trying to think of what to say when Sarah came skipping into the kitchen. She was wearing one of her brother's shirts over her new red wool bathing suit. The loose shirt covered her neck and arms, but her legs were long and lovely—and bare.

Jed blinked. "What in the . . . ?" he barked. "What's that you're wearing, Sarah?"

Ophelia thought of Lucy and her slacks and everything she had said. She took a deep breath and replied, with the greatest calmness, "It's Sarah's birthday present, Jed. Isn't it just the most *practical* bathing suit you ever saw? It's designed so that a girl can go swimming without worrying about skirts getting all bunched up and twisted. It really didn't cost that much, and there was enough left over from my last paycheck to take care of it." To Sarah, she said, "Sarah, honey, thank your father for the present."

Sarah bent over the back of her father's chair and put her arms around him. "Thank you, Daddy," she whispered, with her cheek against his. "It's exactly what I wanted—and the very best birthday present ever."

To the end of her life, Ophelia would be grateful to Jed for swallowing down his objections. She could see what an effort it took, but he managed it. Patting Sarah's hands against his chest, he said, "I'm glad you got what you wanted, honey. As long as your mother thinks it's okay, it's fine with me." With a crooked grin, he looked across the table at Ophelia. "Remind me, wife. How old is this one? Twenty-one? Twenty-two? Thirty? I always lose track."

"Oh, Daddy," Sarah scoffed, cuffing him playfully. "You are such a tease. I'm still just a *girl*, not a grown-up! I just turned *fifteen*."

Jed held out his fingers and pretended to count on them.

"Well, by golly, you're right," he said, as if he was marveling at the fact. "You're still just fifteen."

He got up from his chair and put his arms around his daughter. "And see that you remember it," he added with mock sternness against her hair, and with a wink at Ophelia.


The rain was coming down hard when Buddy drove into Camp Briarwood and stopped at the main camp signpost to look for directions to the motor pool. He saw what he was looking for, then turned left and followed the gravel road until he reached a graveled lot on which were parked a couple of trucks, a tractor, and three staff cars. One Harley-Davidson motorcycle and a smaller Indian Ace were parked in a wood-frame shed, where they were out of the rain. Next to the shed was a shack with a sign that said MOTOR POOL over the door.

Before Buddy got out of his patrol car, he checked the gun in his holster, then took the handcuffs out of the box on the floor and clipped them to his belt. Wishful thinking, he told himself. He probably wouldn't need them. But just in case—

A uniformed young man in his late teens, his blond hair clipped so close to his scalp that he looked almost bald, was sitting on a stool in the motor pool shack, reading. When Buddy opened the door, the man looked up from his comic book—*Famous Funnies*—and frowned.

"The vehicles in this lot are for—" He saw the badge and blinked.

"Sheriff Norris," Buddy said, and took out his official wallet ID. Sheriff Burns had never bothered with identification, since everybody in Cypress County knew him. But it had come in handy for Buddy a time or two, as it did now. The young man put the comic book aside and straightened his shoulders.

"Yessir," he said. "Lookin' for something in particular?"

"A log of the vehicles that are checked out. You got one?"

"Yessir." The young man hesitated. "But maybe you should ask Captain Campbell."

"I can do that," Buddy said. "Or I can get a warrant. But all I really want right now is just to take a quick look. That okay with you?"

The young man considered. "You're the law," he said after a moment. He reached behind him, took a canvas-covered ledger off a shelf, and handed it over.

"Thanks," Buddy said. He raised an eyebrow. "You got a name?"

"Homer," the young man said. "Homer Kennedy. Sir."

"Thanks, Homer." Buddy opened the ledger to the most recent entries and ran his finger down the ruled columns. Yes, there it was, he saw, with mounting excitement. On Thursday night, one of the motorcycles—the Harley—had been checked out at seven thirty p.m. and checked in at eleven forty p.m. Next to that entry was the pencil signature *R. Andrews.* Last night, the Harley had gone out at eight fifteen. There was no name next to the Harley checkout time, though, and it hadn't been checked back in.

Buddy looked up. "You on duty last night, Homer?"

"Yessir." The young man sighed and rubbed his short-clipped hair. "Just my luck. I was goin' to town to play some pool. But Jerry—he was supposed to be here last night—cut his foot on a shovel real bad and had to go to the infirmary. So I got his duty. Three to eleven."

"No curfew?" Buddy asked. "No specific time these vehicles have to be back in?"

"You kiddin'?" Homer laughed shortly. "Not for the Army guys. They pretty much come and go as they please. Us CCC boys, we got rules. We got to take the bus."

Buddy turned the book so Homer could see the empty space next to the Friday night entry. "Who took the Harley out last night?"

Homer scowled down at the page. "Must've forgot to sign for it when he took it out. Reckon he brought it back after I went off duty last night, 'cause it was here this morning." He pointed toward the motorcycle shed. "That's it, the one on the left, the big one. It's what he always rides." He opened a drawer and looked inside. "He put the ignition key back where it belongs, too. So we're square. But I'll remind him to sign before he takes it out again."

"And who was that?" Buddy asked, although he already knew.

"Corporal Andrews," Homer answered. "Same one who took it out on Thursday night. Like I said, he likes to ride that Harley." He cast a judicious eye to the sky. "Reckon he won't be takin' it out today, though. Not unless he figures on gettin' wet."

"You're a good man, Homer," Buddy said, handing the ledger back. "I'm going to need this. Don't let anybody walk off with it." He paused, thinking out his next steps, since this was about to become very official. "Where can I find your camp commander?"

"Captain's quarters," Homer said promptly, stowing the ledger. "He brought one of the cars back thirty minutes ago, and I saw him hoofin' it back to his place." He pointed. "Over that way, second building on the left."

The rain was coming down harder now, and the wind was beginning to blow in gusts that whipped tree branches and whirled flying leaves through the air. Buddy drove to the small cabin and ducked through the rain to the porch, where he knocked on the captain's door. The man who opened it was a slender forty-five or so with round wire-rimmed glasses, thick brown hair, and a precisely trimmed mustache. He was wearing a neatly pressed uniform.

"Captain Campbell?" Buddy asked, and pulled out his ID. "Buddy Norris, sheriff over at Darling. Need to talk to you about a problem we've got in town."

"Sheriff," the captain said in a clipped Yankee accent, and put out his hand. "Looks like you and I won't be having dinner together tonight, after all. I just learned that Mrs. Tidwell has postponed our little party because of the storm."

"So I heard," Buddy said, shaking the captain's hand. "Too bad for us. That lady makes the best chicken pot pie in town."

"About your problem," the captain said. "I was about to call and offer our assistance. It looks like the worst of the storm will stay south of us, but there'll be plenty of rain. If you anticipate any flooding in Darling, I can send some of our boys to help out—equipment, too, depending on what you need."

"Thanks," Buddy said. "I may take you up on the offer. But the storm isn't my problem, Captain. At least, it's not my only problem." He took a deep breath, feeling rattled. "I mean, it's not what I'm here for. We had a murder in Darling last night. I have reason to suspect that one of your men may be involved."

"A murder?" the captain asked, startled. He took his glasses off and regarded Buddy with concern. "One of my men? Who? Are you *sure*? What's your evidence?"

"No, I'm not sure. Not yet. And the evidence is mainly circumstantial—at this point, anyway. That's why I need to talk to him." Buddy outlined the situation briefly, ending with, "I would like to take your motor pool log as evidence.

And I want to take Corporal Andrews back to the sheriff's office in Darling for questioning, and for fingerprinting."

"Andrews?" With a troubled look, the captain put his glasses back on. "There were fingerprints at the scene of the crime?"

"Yes," Buddy said truthfully. There were, indeed, quite a few fingerprints. It was not yet clear whether the murderer's prints were among them.

He added, "If you feel that you need to send an officer with the corporal, or accompany him yourself, I have no problem with that." He wasn't sure about Army protocol or where federal law fit into this—he'd have to ask Mr. Moseley. But he was damn sure that a murder in Darling was *his* business, and that it was an Alabama law that had been violated.

A muscle twitched in the captain's jaw. "I'd like to take a look at that log first. Andrews is here at the camp—I saw him heading for the mess hall a little while ago. I'll go with him when you're ready to take him into town." He took down the khaki-colored raincoat that hung on the rack beside the door. "I'm hoping it's all just a mistake, and that Corporal Andrews is innocent. But of course I want to see it straightened out, and the guilty man brought to justice."

"I do, too, Captain," Buddy said fervently. "And the sooner the better."

A few moments later, the two of them were in the shack next to the motor pool parking lot, their raincoats streaming water onto the floor. They were looking at the log, with Homer standing at attention, blinking. The afternoon had darkened to the point where he had gotten out an oil lamp and lit it, since the shack had no electricity. Outside, the lightning flared and the wind was blowing the rain almost horizontal.

"Yessir, Captain," Homer said, in answer to Captain Campbell's question. "Corporal Andrews forgot to sign for the

Harley, but I was here when he took it out last night. He brought it back after I went off duty at eleven. He had it on Thursday night, too, the way the log says." He glanced up and through the window and his face brightened. "Say, here he comes now. You can ask him yourself. He'll tell you."

The door opened with a gust of wet wind that nearly blew out the lamp, and a broad-shouldered, well-built man stepped inside. He had pale blue eyes and close-clipped brown hair. He was wearing civilian clothes—a plaid shirt, jeans, and rubber boots—under a half-open hooded yellow slicker, and carrying a duffel bag over his shoulder. He closed the door behind him and dropped the heavy bag on the floor.

"Hey, Homer," he said, "I'm going to need a—" He broke off when he saw the captain and Buddy. "Sorry. I see you're busy." He stooped to pick up the duffel bag. "I'll come back later."

"Corporal Anderson," the captain said crisply, "this is Sheriff Norris, from Darling. He's investigating an unfortunate incident that took place in town last night, and I'm placing you in his custody. You can leave that duffel bag here. I'll have somebody stow it in your quarters."

The corporal straightened up and looked at Buddy, whose open raincoat showed the sheriff's badge pinned to his shirt pocket. His mouth dropped open, snapped shut. There was an instant's sheer panic in his pale eyes, then determination. His face hardened, and he whirled on one foot, yanked the door open, and bolted through it into the rain.

"Hey!" Homer yelled. "You forgot to sign the Harley in last night!"

"Corporal Andrews!" the captain shouted. "Stop! That's an order! The sheriff wants to talk to you about—"

But the corporal didn't obey the order and Buddy wasn't wasting his breath on talk. He sprinted through the open door and out onto the parking lot. Andrews was hotfooting it across the open space, dodging puddles and aiming for a patch of woods on the other side of the road. But Buddy had been a champion sprinter in high school, and he had never failed to win the hundred-yard dash. He may not have run much in the past few years, but he still had the legs and the wind, and he was younger. And definitely faster.

Andrews vaulted a split-rail fence that ran along the road. He stumbled, staggered, caught himself, and half turned, shoving a hand into his raincoat pocket. He pulled out a handgun and raised it to fire, then turned, gun in hand, and kept running across the road, toward the nearby woods.

Buddy cleared the fence easily. He caught up with Andrews, threw a flying tackle at the back of his knees, and brought him facedown, hard, in a patch of gravel. The gun went flying and skidded under a flowering clump of Joe Pye weed. Swearing, Andrews struggled to push himself up, but Buddy scrambled to his feet, pushed the struggling man's shoulders down, and planted a knee squarely in the middle of his back. Breathing hard—the sprint across the parking lot was more exercise than he'd had for a while—he unclipped the handcuffs from his belt, pulled Andrews' arms together behind his back, and cuffed his wrists.

Captain Campbell ran up. He took one arm and Buddy the other, and together they pulled Andrews to his feet. His forehead, nose, and mouth were bleeding where he had slammed into the gravel. His head was hanging and he was gulping air, but he still had some fire left in him.

"What the devil—" he sputtered. He raised his head and licked the blood off his lips. "What's all this? Why did you—?"

"Because you ran," Buddy said. "It would have been smart not to, Andrews. And smart not to draw a gun on a police officer. It's a good way to get yourself shot." He retrieved the gun, a Colt 1911 automatic, and handed it to Captain Campbell. In his official voice, he added, "I'm taking you in for questioning in the murder of Rona Jean Hancock."

"Murder? The hell you say!" Face working, eyes wide and showing panic, Andrews appealed to the captain. "I'm innocent, Captain! I don't even *know* Rona Jean Hancock!"

"Then you won't object to having your fingerprints taken and answering the sheriff's questions," the captain replied calmly.

"Fingerprints?" Andrews sounded surprised.

"Yeah." Buddy chuckled. "Darling may be a rinky-dink town, but that doesn't mean it's got a rinky-dink police force."

The captain pocketed the Colt. "I'm confiscating your weapon, Corporal. You may retrieve it when the sheriff clears you and returns you to the camp."

Buddy felt the hair on the back of his neck tingle. A bolt of electric-blue lightning split the air and was followed immediately by a deafening thunderclap. The storm was getting too close for comfort.

"Let's get out of here," he said, and pushed his hand-cuffed prisoner toward the patrol car.

By the time Charlie had dragged the fallen schoolhouse roof timbers off Lucy Murphy, her eyes were open and she was able, shakily, to get to her feet. "I guess there's no need for fake names now," she said disconsolately. "You know who I am."

It was true. Charlie knew Lucy—and knew her husband, Ralph, who worked on the railroad and was gone during the week. "I understand why you didn't want to reveal yourself," he said. "I've always protected my confidential sources, and I'm not changing that practice now. But you've *got* to talk to the sheriff, Lucy. He needs to know what you know. It might mean the difference between catching Rona Jean's killer and losing him."

"What you said about that bag over my head," Lucy said, leaning on Charlie's arm. Her hair was wet and her blouse stuck to her revealingly. "Maybe I could do that?" She chuckled wryly, to show that she was joking.

"I hope you won't want to," Charlie said in a neutral tone. "The sheriff will see that your part in this is kept confidential. I'm sure of it."

"I hope you're right." Lucy was glum. "I'd do anything to keep Ralph from finding out what a fool I've been."

A tree had fallen across the car Lucy had parked back of the building, so they took Charlie's, leaving the ruins of the school behind. It should have been a short drive to town, but the storm was howling around them and the few miles seemed to take forever. The wind rocked the car, the lightning struck perilously close, and the rain sheeted down so heavily that the windshield wipers were powerless to clear the glass. Driving was like running an obstacle course. At several points, downed pine trees made Loblolly Road impassable, and Charlie had to get out and slog through the driving rain and the thick, gooey mud to pull the fallen limbs and small trees out of the way. Lucy took the wheel and drove cautiously behind him, struggling to keep the car from sliding sideways off the slick track.

But at last they managed to get to the highway. Soaked to the skin, with mud up to his knees, Charlie crawled behind the wheel and drove the rest of the way to town. The streets were flooding, and trees and utility wires—electric and telephone— were down everywhere. By the time Charlie pulled up in front of the sheriff's office, next to the sheriff's patrol car, he was shaking.

"You ready?" he asked Lucy, who was huddled in the front seat beside him.

"No." She sighed. "But I don't think I have any choice. At this point, all I want to do is keep this from Ralph, if I can."

"Hmm." He considered this for a moment. "Look, Lucy. I think you should wait out here. I'll go in and . . . kind of lay the groundwork. That might make it easier for you. But you've got to promise not to run off," he added.

She threw up her hands with a despairing laugh. "On a day like this? You've got to be kidding."

Inside the sheriff's office, the electricity was out and the deputy was at his table, working by the light of a kerosene lamp. There was an empty Dr Pepper bottle in front of him, covered with dark gray fingerprint dust. He turned to look at Charlie. "Man, oh, man, you are *wet.*"

"Yeah. It's pretty bad out there," Charlie said, shaking rain out of his hair. "Some of the roads are blocked. I was lucky to get back to town." He paused, looking around. "Sheriff Norris here?"

"He's questioning a suspect in the Hancock murder," the deputy said, nodding toward a closed door. "An Army corporal, from the CCC camp. Andrews, his name is."

"Corporal? Corporal Raymond Andrews?" Charlie was surprised—and then immediately relieved. The sheriff must have some other evidence against the man. Lucy's evidence about the motive for the murder would be corroborating, which might mean that she wouldn't have to testify if he was brought to trial.

"Yeah." Springer turned and one eyebrow went up. "That's who it is. Andrews. His commanding officer is in there, too. Captain Campbell. Seems like he has his head screwed on straight." He stopped, frowning. "Say, Dickens, you know this guy? Andrews, I mean. You maybe got something on him?"

"Yeah," Charlie said. "Matter of fact, I have. She's out in the car."

"*She?*" Both eyebrows disappeared under Springer's hair.

Charlie nodded. "If you'll ask the sheriff to step out here for a minute, I'll be glad to explain the whole thing. It might give him some extra leverage with Andrews."

It took more than a minute for Charlie to summarize what Lucy had told him about the kickback racket Andrews was running. In fact, it took more like three or four minutes, because the scheme had so many moving parts. But the note he'd gotten from Mata Hari a few days before spelled it out pretty well, and the sheriff grasped its significance as soon as he read it. And even before Charlie had finished, Buddy was guessing how Rona Jean Hancock had gotten involved.

"She found out what was going on by listening in on the telephone," the sheriff said, narrowing his eyes. "She figured since there was money involved, she'd get a piece of the action. She hit Andrews up for money, but he saw her as a loose cannon. He killed her to keep her mouth shut about his bribery scheme. Is that it?"

"That's about the size of it," Charlie admitted.

"Then it looks like we've got a case," Buddy said with satisfaction. "We've got testimony that puts him with Rona Jean after her shift on Thursday night. We've got his scarred thumbprint on the car door handle. And now we've got a motive."

"We've also got the same thumbprint on the Dr Pepper bottle," Wayne put in, gesturing to the bottle on the table. "Just confirmed, Sheriff. On the neck of the bottle, exactly where you'd hold it if you were going to use it to knock somebody out."

Buddy clapped the deputy on the shoulder. "That's my man!" he exclaimed. "More than enough for an arrest!"

Charlie grinned, thinking what a great story this was going to make, with or without Lucy Murphy. Which reminded him that she was sitting out front in the car. "I think Lucy would prefer not to confront Andrews, at least right now," he said. "But maybe if one of you could go out to the car and take her statement, you might be able to use it to pry a confession out of him."

"Yeah." Buddy's smile lit up his whole face. "But we don't need to do it out in the car. Wayne, you go out and get Miz Murphy, and you and her go in the kitchen and shut the door. Get it all written down and signed and dated—you can type it up later. Oh, and if she can come up with the names of some of the folks that have been paying these bribes, that would be great. We're going to need to talk to them. I'm thinking maybe Mr. Moseley will want to trade immunity for testimony."

"I may have something on that," Charlie said. "Ophelia Snow, who works at the *Dispatch*, also works in the quartermaster's office. With any luck, she's getting the full list."

"Ah." Buddy looked at him. "Doing a little spy work on the side, are you, Dickens?" He grinned. "Got an angle on a story?"

"I have," Charlie agreed. "But I didn't reckon on setting foot in the middle of a murder investigation."

"Snow," Wayne muttered, taking a handful of pink slips off his table. "Snow. Ophelia Snow. There's a message here somewhere— Here it is." He handed the pink slip to Charlie. "Said she called your apartment and your wife told her you headed here after lunch, so she left a message."

Charlie took the pink slip. On it, the deputy had written: *Mrs. Snow's got the list Dickens asked for and something else he didn't. Call her or go over there as quick as you can.* He looked up at Wayne.

"Something else? Something I didn't ask for?" he asked curiously. "Did she say what it was?"

"Nope. She was pretty excited about it, though." Wayne picked up a yellow tablet and headed for the door. "On my way to take care of the Murphy interview."

The sheriff put out his hand. "Thanks, Dickens. I owe you. I'm going back in the office and lay out what you've given us. Andrews is pretty spooked just now. This might be all we need to get a confession out of him."

Charlie grinned. "You owe me. That must mean that I get the story. Right?"

"That's what it means," Buddy said. "You get the story."


Charlie left Lucy at the sheriff's office, then drove around the corner to the apartment to let Fannie know that he was safe. But despite her entreaties, he couldn't stay. He changed into some dry clothes and drove through the pouring rain and branch-littered streets to Ophelia's house.

"Charlie!" she gasped when she opened the door. "You shouldn't have come out in this! It's terrible out there!"

"It's not as bad as it was earlier this afternoon," Charlie said, thinking of what he and Lucy Murphy had been through. "The wind has died down and people are starting to clear their streets. I think the worst of the storm missed us. But there are still a lot of limbs down."

"And wires," Ophelia said, leading him into the parlor. "Our lights have been out for several hours." She took matches out of a drawer and lit a kerosene lamp on the table next to the overstuffed chair and another on the coffee table in front of the sofa. "The family's in the kitchen playing cards, so we'll talk in here. But first I'll go and get the papers I want to show you. And something for us to drink."

A few moments later she was back with a sheaf of papers under her arm and a tray with two cups, a teapot, and a sugar bowl. She sat down next to Charlie on the sofa and poured their tea.

"I went to the quartermaster's office this morning and got what you asked for—a list of all the suppliers who are due to get checks. I knew what to look for, because it's the voucher list I typed last week. Here it is." She put down a two-page list.

"Swell!" Charlie said with enthusiasm. "That's what I was hoping you'd get." He picked up the list and flipped through it. "The sheriff can use it to corroborate Lucy's claims about the bribery."

"What?" Ophelia frowned at him, puzzled. "The sheriff? What bribery? And how is Lucy Murphy involved in this?"

"It's a long story," Charlie said, feeling that he'd jumped the gun. "Let's finish this part of it first."

"Well . . ." Still frowning, Ophelia put down another typed list. "When I took my list out of the file, I found this one there, too. It had to have been typed by Sergeant Webb, because I didn't do it, and Corporal Andrews doesn't type." She smiled ruefully. "Sergeant Webb asked me to teach him, but the poor guy just can't seem to get the hang of it. It's a real problem for him."

"Mmm," Charlie said, thinking that the corporal's inability to type was the least of his problems now. He was facing indictment for murder. He could get the death penalty.

"Anyway," Ophelia went on, "you can see that the sergeant's list is longer than mine. It has more names on it. Eighteen more, to be exact." She put another list down, this one handwritten. "These eighteen people are due some twenty-two thousand dollars."

"Huh." Charlie frowned down at the list. "Well, maybe

you didn't get everybody. Maybe you skipped some. Maybe the sergeant saw the problem and typed up a correct list."

"Or maybe not." Ophelia produced a Cypress County telephone directory. "Here. Pick a few names at random and look up their phone numbers."

Charlie chose one, checked for the listing, and couldn't find it. Ditto for his second and third attempts. "Hey," he said, frowning. "What gives? What's going on here?"

"Exactly my question," Ophelia said triumphantly. "*None* of those eighteen people are listed as having telephones, Charlie. What's more, I don't recognize a single name on that list, and neither does Jed. Plus, he doesn't recognize any of the addresses. He says they're fakes."

"Fakes!" Charlie blinked. "But that means . . ." He stopped, considering, and put his finger on the bottom line. $22,000. "Okay. Tell me how the process works, Opie. How are these checks distributed?"

"Exactly the right question," Ophelia said. "Every few months, I type up a voucher list like this one." She tapped her list. "The checks are mailed in a batch to the quartermaster's office. Sergeant Webb keeps them in his desk until the individual suppliers come in and pick them up."

"Ah," Charlie said. "And the sergeant will keep any that are not picked up."

"I suppose." Ophelia shook her head, frowning. "I hate to say it, Charlie, but this looks like a case of fraud. I wouldn't have thought it of Sergeant Webb, who is such a by-the-book kind of guy, but I don't see any other way to explain it." Her frown deepened to a scowl. "And I don't see how this is connected to the story you wanted me to help you with. Mata Hari's tip was about a bribery scheme, wasn't it? *This*—" She tapped the list again. "This isn't bribery. It's something else. So maybe Sergeant Webb was running both a bribery scheme and this . . . this voucher fraud?"

"No," Charlie said, thinking that the plot was thickening at a rate he could barely keep up with. "Sergeant Webb wasn't involved in the bribery, at least so far as we know. That was Corporal Andrews."

"Corporal Andrews?" Ophelia pressed her lips together, shaking her head. Then she said, reluctantly, "I should have guessed, though. He was the one with the opportunity, since he was the one who arranged the contracts. I'm afraid I just didn't see through his charm." She gave him an uncertain look. "You've got evidence, I suppose. You're sure?"

Charlie nodded. "There's evidence. And yes, I'm sure. And it's worse than bribery," he added quietly. "He's also a killer."

"No!" Staring at him, Ophelia set her teacup down with a rattle. "You mean . . . *Ray* killed Rona Jean Hancock? But why? Were they having an affair? How—"

Charlie raised his hand. "Just be quiet for a moment and I'll tell you." He went through the whole thing, except for Lucy's romantic escapade, which he kept mostly to himself. He ended with, "And that's as much as I know, now. The sheriff has agreed to give me more of the details later. Maybe I'll be able to include them in the special edition."

"I . . . I just can't believe it," Ophelia said, biting her lip. "He seemed like such a nice guy. I was completely taken in."

"You and a lot of other people, apparently," Charlie said. He looked down at Ophelia's lists. "And now there's this. Which seems at the moment to be a separate thing entirely."

Ophelia just sat there, shaking her head. "But what do we do now, Charlie? This fraud—or whatever you call it— it's a government matter, isn't it? But I'm not sure who at the camp we can trust."

Charlie thought back to Deputy Springer's comment that

Captain Campbell, the commandant at Camp Briarwood, had his head screwed on straight. "I think we should take this to Captain Campbell," he said. "I hear he's a pretty good guy."

And, he was thinking to himself, he would place a call to Lorena Hickok. Maybe, when this was all over, they would even get a visit from Eleanor Everywhere.

# EIGHTEEN

# The Dahlias Celebrate the Fourth

The storm that brushed past Darling during the weekend took off a few roofs, knocked down several chicken coops, disrupted the electricity and telephone, and rearranged the furniture on some lawns, but it wasn't bad enough to wreck Darling's big midweek celebration on the Fourth of July. By that time, the flooding had subsided, the fallen branches and trees had been cleared away, the electric and phone wires were repaired, and the people who had lost this and that were very glad they hadn't lost the whole kit and caboodle. While some had been stranded by flooding and impassable roads (Alabama mud is reputed to be the gooiest mud on earth), most had simply hunkered down with families and neighbors and waited for the wind and rain to blow past. When the sun peered over the eastern horizon on the morning of the Fourth, it smiled down on a brave, resilient little town that had weathered yet another storm and was getting ready to celebrate the founding of the nation to which it proudly belonged.

After the War Between the States, many towns of the Confederacy debated whether to celebrate the Fourth or ignore it. To some, it felt like a Union holiday—a day that commemorated the birth of the government from which they had seceded. Others felt that the South should claim the Fourth, arguing that the Declaration of Independence was drafted by a Southerner (Thomas Jefferson) and defended by a Southerner (George Washington). Vicksburg, Mississippi, of course, had its own separate opinion, for the Fourth marked the town's bitter surrender to Union general Ulysses S. Grant, who had besieged and bombarded Vicksburg for seven long weeks. To escape the shelling, the starving residents had lived in caves and were reduced to eating dogs and cats and even rats. Vicksburg had vowed it would never again celebrate the Fourth except as a day of mourning, and so far, the citizens had kept their vow.

Darling had compromised. It celebrated Confederate Day on the fourth Monday of April, a day set aside to mark the last major Confederate offensive of the war and the surrender of Confederate general Joseph E. Johnston to Union general William Tecumseh Sherman, on April 26, 1865. There was always a solemn parade and speeches and a town picnic at the cemetery, where Confederate flags were placed on soldiers' graves. Many Darlingians (although perhaps fewer every year) felt that Confederate Day was the most patriotic day of the year.

But Darling had long ago decided that the Fourth should be celebrated as a Southern holiday, and it seemed that the event became larger and more exuberant with each passing year, with a jubilant parade through the town and around the square, speeches (and speeches and more speeches) on the courthouse steps, and a picnic, entertainment, and fireworks at the fairgrounds.

The parade was the main event of the morning. The storm had pretty well wrecked the flags and bunting that decorated the courthouse, so they had been replaced and a new banner hung over Robert E. Lee Street declaring, DARLING: THE BEST LITTLE TOWN IN THE SOUTH. The townspeople, cheering and waving flags, lined the streets for a full half hour before the parade began, and a great menagerie of small boys, dogs, cats, and chickens were caught up and moved along by the celebratory throng.

At ten o'clock, the parade began. Playing "You're a Grand Old Flag," the Academy band marched down Robert E. Lee from the staging area near the sawmill, circled twice around the square, then lined up beside the platform in front of the courthouse to provide music for the rest of the marchers.

The grand marshal came next, riding in Andy Stanton's blue 1928 Franklin touring car, polished and gleaming and draped with red, white, and blue streamers. This year, the town council had unanimously chosen Sheriff Buddy Norris as grand marshal, in honor of his recent achievement in solving the murder of Miss Rona Jean Hancock, memorialized as the Eleven O'clock Lady in Tuesday's special edition of the *Dispatch*. When Buddy's car stopped briefly in front of the courthouse, the band swung into a splendidly spirited "Alexander's Ragtime Band." People shouted "Speech! Speech!"

Buddy only grinned shyly, waved to the crowd, and told Mr. Stanton to drive on. But privately, he couldn't help feeling that he had indeed proved himself. He had cleared his first difficult hurdle and achieved his first major success in his new job as sheriff. He had proved himself to the town and— perhaps more importantly—to himself. And he had personally captured Rona Jean's killer, who was still locked up in the Darling jail awaiting indictment on a charge of murder.

Following the grand marshal came the three surviving veterans of the War Between the States, dressed in their best Confederate gray uniforms, which smelled strongly of the camphor chests where they were stored all year. The veterans were riding in Roger Kilgore's burgundy-colored 1933 Dodge convertible (which you could buy at Kilgore Motors, if you could lay your hands on $645, or $64 down and $35.50 a month for two years). Roger stopped the car in front of the courthouse, the veterans got out and stood a little shakily at attention, while Eva Pearl Hennepin, wearing a plantation ball gown and a big white straw hat with a swag of red and blue feathers (created by Fannie Champaign Dickens), sang a reverent a cappella rendition of "Dixie."

> *I wish I was in the land of cotton,*
> *Old times they are not forgotten;*
> *Look away! Look away! Look away! Dixie Land.*
> *In Dixie Land where I was born in,*
> *Early on one frosty mornin',*
> *Look away! Look away! Look away! Dixie Land.*

If it had been April and Confederate Day, Mrs. Hennepin would have gone on to sing, to the same melody, all three verses of the Confederate States of America war song, beginning with:

> *Southern men the thunders mutter!*
> *Northern flags in South winds flutter!*
> *To arms! To arms! To arms, in Dixie!*
> *Send them back your fierce defiance!*
> *Stamp upon the cursed alliance!*
> *To arms! To arms! To arms, in Dixie!*

But since today was the Fourth of July, this verse wasn't appropriate, and as the quavering notes died away, everybody cheered and waved the Stars and Stripes.

Following the veterans in gray came two dozen khaki-clad doughboys who had served in the War to End All Wars. As the band played "Over There," they marched in four columns behind the American flag. Several of them carried Bonus Army flags, a poignant reminder of their sad defeat two years before by General Douglas MacArthur and Major George S. Patton, acting under President Hoover's orders.

After the veterans came what everybody had been waiting for: the float featuring Miss Darling (AnnaBelle Claiborne, daughter of Mr. and Mrs. Junior Claiborne) and Little Miss Darling (Cupcake, the daughter of Violet Sims and Myra May Mosswell), pulled by county commissioner Amos Tombull's oldest grandson driving a Ford tractor decorated with colorful streamers. The two Misses Darling, surrounded by pots of blooming flowers, were dressed in beautiful white ruffled dresses and twirled decorated parasols over their shoulders. They smiled and blew kisses at the crowd while the band played "Did You Ever See a Dream Walking?"

As it turned out, the Dahlias had faced a huge challenge when it came to decorating the float, since Saturday's storm had shredded the summer flowers blooming in Darlings' gardens. But the Dahlias, thinking ahead, had brought pots of marigolds, begonias, zinnias, petunias, and geraniums indoors, for protection from the storm, so on Wednesday, there were plenty of pretty potted plants for the float. Ophelia had contributed three large ruffled ferns, which made a nice display around Miss Darling's throne (an ornate gold and red velvet antique chair borrowed from Mrs. Voleen Johnson), and Aunt Hetty's parlor palm stood tall behind the throne. Everyone agreed that it was the most beautiful Miss Darling float they had ever seen.

And if that weren't glory enough, the delightful Misses Darling were followed by the entire company of CCC camp boys, wearing neatly pressed uniforms and polished boots, and carrying shovels over their shoulders. The thunderous roar that greeted them almost drowned out the Academy band, which was playing "Happy Days Are Here Again"—as they were, thanks in large part to the economic boost Camp Briarwood had given the town. The company was led by Captain Campbell himself, looking proud and handsome in his Army uniform, and followed by the other camp officers. A careful observer, however, might have noticed that two men were missing. Corporal Raymond Andrews was in the Darling jail, while Sergeant Luther Webb was under guard at Camp Briarwood, awaiting a military hearing and likely court-martial on multiple counts of fraud and attempted fraud. It was reported that the higher-ups in Washington already knew of the situation and were planning an inquiry.

The parade continued with the children's pet parade, the Darling Bicycle Club, the Ladies Guild Flag Twirling Team, the Darling Fire Brigade. Mr. Musgrove, the owner of Musgrove's Hardware, dressed as Uncle Sam, in red-and-white-striped trousers, red waistcoat, and blue jacket, with a stovepipe hat decorated with stars and stripes. He was accompanied by Mrs. Musgrove, dressed like the Goddess of Liberty in a pale green toga and spiked crown, and carrying a flaming (well, smoking) torch in one hand and a copy of the Declaration of Independence in the other. When the Musgroves reached the courthouse steps, Eva Pearl Hennepin sang "God Bless America" and then the band played "The Star-Spangled Banner." (Eva Pearl was meant to sing the anthem with the band, but she inhaled a wasp as she was reaching for a high note in "God Bless America" and had to be helped from the podium.)

After the parade, most of the crowd lingered to hear the speeches (of which there were many), and when the last one was finished, everyone trekked to the fairgrounds, where neighbors and families and extended families met for picnics, games, swimming, dancing, music, and the fireworks. It was going to be a long and happy day, in the very best Southern tradition.

At the fairgrounds, the Dahlias pulled together several picnic tables under a couple of large live oaks and assembled their families there, loading the tables with the food they had brought. Platters were heaped high with Myra May's fried catfish and Raylene's barbecued spareribs and Alice Ann Walker's home-cured ham. Big earthenware crocks were filled with Earlynne Biddle's corn pudding; Aunt Hetty Little's stewed okra with bacon, tomatoes, and corn; Verna Tidwell's green beans cooked with fatback; and Mildred Kilgore's coleslaw with pecans. There were plates of Miss Rogers' deviled eggs and pints of Bessie Bloodworth's pickles and gallons of iced tea and lemonade. The meal was topped off by desserts: cobblers and cookies, a key lime pie, Beulah's red velvet cake, two pecan pies, and Lucy Murphy's Jefferson Davis pie, proudly baked from a recipe that had been in her Atlanta family (who claimed kin with the Confederate president) for generations.

The Dahlias' picnic went on for hour after lazy hour, while everyone ate a little bit of every single thing and then—in honor of their friends' marvelous cooking—ate a little bit more. After they had finally finished and returned the very few leftovers to the picnic baskets, they were all free to enjoy themselves. The men went off to toss horseshoes or watch the Darling baseball team play the Camp Briarwood boys. The young people ran off to the swimming hole or walked to the pavilion to listen to a group of folk singers that sounded just like the Carter Family. Some of the Dahlias took glasses of iced tea and their knitting or crocheting and relaxed in the shade of the oak trees, where they could enjoy the music. Other women, feeling the need of a little after-dinner exercise, went for a stroll.

Ophelia and Lucy walked over to the swimming hole, where Ophelia could keep an eye on Sarah, who was wearing her new red swimming suit. Ophelia herself was wearing a short-sleeved, silky red blouse and a brand-new pair of tan cotton slacks, flared at the bottoms. She had told herself that a woman who was brave enough to carry out an undercover investigative journalism assignment was surely brave enough to wear whatever she wanted. When she put them on that morning, Jed pulled his eyebrows together, shook his head, and said, "Woman, darned if you don't beat all." She had turned around in front of the mirror, smoothing the fabric over her hips, and replied, "Yes, I do, don't I?" It was a grand moment.

The women found a picnic table in the shade of a large sycamore tree, brushed the leaves off the benches, and sat down. Lucy lit a cigarette. "Charlie told me what you were doing at the camp on Saturday, Ophelia." Looking down, she turned her cigarette lighter in her fingers. "I thought I ought to explain about Corporal Andrews and me and what I—"

"That's really not necessary, Lucy," Ophelia said, not wanting to embarrass her friend. She had heard only a hint of the story from Charlie, and it seemed terribly private.

Lucy met Ophelia's eyes. "Well, maybe I just want to get it off my chest. The truth . . . the sad truth is that Ray Andrews and I had a romantic fling. For a while, I even considered leaving Ralph and going off with him when he got reassigned to another camp. I might have, too, if Rona Jean hadn't come along and . . . well, distracted him." She sighed. "I was at the camp on Saturday because I had come to tell him I was through."

"So that's why you were so nervous," Ophelia said, thinking she understood.

"Well, that, yes. But there's more. When Ray and I were talking, he said something that made me suspect that he had killed Rona Jean, and I was just plain scared. When I saw you, I had just come from telephoning Charlie Dickens, at the *Dispatch*, to arrange a meeting. I'd already written to him about the bribery, but when I realized that Ray might have done something much, much worse, I wanted Charlie to go to the sheriff and tell him what I suspected. I was hoping that, if Charlie would do it, I could stay out of it, and nobody would find out that I had been involved with a . . . a killer." Lucy's eyes filled with tears. "I was a coward, Opie. And stupid. Falling for Ray was so terribly *foolish*. I'm ashamed."

"We're all foolish sometimes, Lucy," Ophelia said quietly. "And I can testify to Corporal Andrews' personal magnetism. I felt it myself. Whatever else he is, the man is a charmer." She paused. "But look at it this way. If you hadn't gotten close to him, you wouldn't have known what he was doing. That kickback racket he was running, I mean. And you wouldn't have known that he and Rona Jean even knew each other, so you couldn't have suspected that he killed her." She reached across the table and took Lucy's hand. "If it weren't for you, he might have gotten away with it."

"I don't know about that," Lucy said doubtfully. "Buddy Norris says he's got fingerprint evidence."

"Yes, but maybe Buddy would never have thought to fingerprint the corporal. And you were the one who supplied the motive. Mr. Moseley said that motive is the important key here—that when it comes to building the case for trial, it's just as important as the fingerprints."

Ophelia waved away a pesky fly. "I hope you won't have to testify at the trial."

"Me, too." Lucy sighed heavily. "But of course I will if I have to. I've told Ralph everything, and he says he's forgiven me. So keeping it from him isn't an issue any longer." She managed a small smile. "He even wanted to take some of the blame for himself. He says he's going to try to get his railroad shift assignments changed so he can be home more often. I've been wanting that for a long time. So something good might come of this, after all."

"Charlie got what he wanted, too," Ophelia said. "He told me this morning that the special edition of the *Dispatch* was a sellout. What's more, he's sold his story 'The Eleven O'clock Lady' to both wire services, and to the *Atlanta Constitution*, as well." She smiled. Charlie had been more excited than she had ever seen him. She had the feeling that this story was more than just a story to him. It was some kind of personal test. "He's also talked to an old friend of his from his days with the Associated Press," she added. "Miss Hickok doesn't normally investigate CCC camps, but her boss wants her to come down here and report on the situation. Charlie's even hoping that she invites her friend, Mrs. Roosevelt. Wouldn't that be *exciting*?"

Lucy nodded. "I guess the only people who didn't get what they wanted were the ones who hoped that Rona Jean would give them her baby. Fannie Dickens, for one. Violet and Myra May, too."

"I know," Ophelia said sadly. "Charlie says that Fannie is terribly disappointed, but that they've started to talk about adopting a child. Which I guess is another good outcome of this." She looked up and waved at Sarah, who was poised at the end of the diving board, looking beautiful in her new red bathing suit. Daughters were wonderful creatures, she thought proudly. She was going to see that Sarah had all the opportunities that her brother did—and that included college.

"There's one more good outcome, if you're keeping score." Lucy chuckled. "Guess who came to the picnic together this afternoon."

"Uncle Sam and the Goddess of Liberty?" Ophelia rolled her eyes. "I'm terrible at guessing games, Lucy. *Tell* me."

"Buddy Norris and Bettina Higgens, that's who! It seems the sheriff is dating Rona Jean's roommate."

"Oh, my gosh!" Ophelia exclaimed. "I suppose they met during the investigation, huh? Beulah says that since Bettina works at the Beauty Bower, she doesn't have much of a chance to meet men."

"I'm sure that's true," Lucy said. "Anyway, I saw them together after the parade, and then the two of them settled down over there under the big weeping willow for lunch. A little while ago, I saw them walking along the creek." She chuckled. "They were holding hands. They both looked rather shy, I thought. And romantic."

"How sweet," Ophelia said, smiling. "And speaking of romance, here's a 'guess-who' for you. Guess who's getting married!"

Lucy pinched her lips together, thinking. "Getting married . . . getting married . . . Sorry, I don't have a clue. Who?"

"Liz Lacy's mother and Mr. Dunlap, of the Five and Dime! Liz told me about it while we were putting out the picnic food. They're planning a big church wedding, and then they're moving into Liz's mother's house."

"Mr. Dunlap?" Lucy asked, blinking. "He's always struck me as . . . well, sort of rabbitish. And Mrs. Lacy is—" She hesitated. "Managerial. A bossy sheepdog."

"Too true," Ophelia agreed with a laugh. "But Liz told me that her mother says that in private, Mr. Dunlap is a *tiger.*"

"Well, you can't beat that," Lucy said. "And speak of the devil, here comes Liz. And Verna."

"Hello, girls," Verna said. She was carrying a bottle of ginger ale in one hand and four paper Dixie cups in the other. "Is this a private confab, or do you have room for us?"

"There's plenty of room," Ophelia said, eyeing the bottle. "I see you brought refreshments. That wouldn't be bubbly, would it?"

"Don't I wish," Verna said, laughing. "Just plain old ginger ale. But suitable for toasting." She began filling cups for everybody.

"What's the grand occasion?" Lucy asked, reaching for a cup.

Verna grinned and slid onto the picnic table bench next to Ophelia. "It's Liz's occasion. And it's not just grand, it's spectacular!"

Liz sat down beside Lucy. "It's a miracle, is what it is," she said, all smiles. "On Saturday, I got a letter from my literary agent, Nadine Fleming. She wrote that she liked *Sabrina* very much, just as it was, and planned to show it to an editor she knows. Last night, she called long-distance to tell me that she had showed it to him and he's agreed to publish it! And Nadine says I need to begin another one, right away." She shook her head. "I still can't believe this is happening. Maybe I'm just dreaming it."

"You're not dreaming!" Lucy cried, flinging an arm around Liz's shoulders. "It's all real—and all wonderful!"

"Liz, that's so exciting!" Ophelia exclaimed. "I can't wait to read it!"

"I'll bet it wouldn't have happened if you had married

Grady," Verna muttered knowingly. "You'd be having babies instead of books."

Ophelia glanced over to the swimming hole, where Sarah was executing a perfect dive. "There's something to be said for babies, you know."

"Of course there is," Lucy agreed. "There's *everything* to be said for babies. But we're glad that Liz is having a book, instead. At least, this year." She lifted her Dixie cup. "Here's to you, Liz. And to *Sabrina*."

Verna stood up. "To Liz and *Sabrina*," she said.

They all rose. "To Liz and *Sabrina*," they said in unison, and lifted their Dixie cups together.

# Historical Note

Like the other books in the Darling Dahlias series, this sixth mystery takes place during the Depression. The previous book, *The Darling Dahlias and the Silver Dollar Bush*, was set in spring 1933, shortly after the March inauguration of Franklin Delano Roosevelt, to whom the nation had turned for salvation (that isn't too strong a word) from the disastrous economic situation in which America found itself. Banks were flat broke, people were out of work, businesses were out of customers, families were out of money for food and rent, and almost everybody in the country was out of luck. The song "Brother, Can You Spare a Dime?" which depicted the nation's anger at the destruction of the American dream, was on many people's lips.

But by the summer of 1934, things were looking up for the fictional town of Darling—and for real towns all over the United States—partly because of the impact of the Civilian Conservation Corps. The CCC was the New Deal's earliest and best solution to the most baffling riddle of the Depression: how to create meaningful work for unemployed men and ensure that their wages went to support their families. A public works program, the CCC operated from 1933 to 1942, employing young unmarried men from relief families in conservation and natural resource development projects on rural land owned by federal, state, and local governments, and on some private lands. By President Roosevelt's executive order, the CCC also employed veterans of World War I, many of whom were destitute and had joined the 1932 Bonus Army, attempting to persuade Congress to give them the promised bonuses they weren't scheduled to receive until 1945. In return for their labor, the men received shelter, clothing, food, and a stipend of $30 a month, $25 of which was automatically sent home to their families.

Throughout the nine-year life of the program, nearly three million men lived in some 2,600 CCC work camps in every state and territory. The workers planted more than three billion trees, constructed or upgraded more than eight hundred parks nationwide, fought forest fires, built dams, and constructed service buildings and public roads. Administered by the U.S. Army and staffed by Army officers, the camps imposed a quasi-military discipline that took some getting used to. But the food was probably better—and certainly more ample—than the workers got back home. Most of the young men discovered that the daily physical labor required by the CCC projects improved their physical conditions, raised their spirits, and, best of all, taught them employable skills.

The camps also benefitted the areas around them. Camp administrators brought in some bulk supplies, but purchased butter, chickens, eggs, milk, bread, beef, pork, potatoes, and fresh vegetables from the local farmers, who were also invited to put in bids for the use of their teams and equipment to help with camp projects. Materials were purchased from local sawmills, gravel pits, and rock quarries. Local women and men supervised the camp kitchens, laundries, and repair shops and administered the educational programs that were such a vital part of the program. And while the CCC boys didn't have a lot of spare change, they were always glad to spend whatever they had when they went to town on Saturday night for a game of pool, a movie, a milk shake, or a trinket for their best girl. The camp officers, too, were frequent town visitors, and they had more money to spend. In communities close to the camps, these purchases contributed from $5,000 to $7,000 a month to the local economies, saving many small businesses from failure and giving the towns a welcome new lease on life.

FDR had put a great deal of effort into the reforestation of his family estate in Hyde Park, and that became the first emphasis of the CCC, which quickly came to be called "Roosevelt's Tree Army." The enrollees were put to work planting natively adapted tree seedlings in logged-over areas and badly eroded fields. This relatively brief nine-year effort, directed by the U.S. Forest Service, was so extensive and so successful that modern conservationists believe that it was responsible for more than half the total public and private reforestation that has been achieved in the nation's entire history.

But when the Dust Bowl hit in 1934, the need for soil conservation was on everyone's mind, and the CCC was put to work to remedy the environmental and human disaster created by fifty years of poor agricultural practice. The number of camps was dramatically expanded, most of them located in the Dust Bowl region, under the direction of the Soil Conservation Service, and the CCC set to work plowing hundreds of miles of contour terraces to reduce slope erosion (some of which I can still see on our own Central Texas homestead), building farm ponds, controlling gullies, and planting soil-holding crops. In some areas, the need was for drainage; nearly 85 million acres of agricultural land were reclaimed by CCC workers, many of them Native Americans.

In other areas, the CCC did extraordinary and heroic work during natural disasters, like the Ohio River flood of 1937, the 1938 New England hurricane, floods in Vermont and New York, and blizzards in Utah and Wyoming. The CCC also developed recreational facilities in national, state, county, and metropolitan parks. Here in Texas, 29 parks were created or improved by the CCC. Nationally, by the close of the program in 1942, the CCC had developed more than 3 million acres for park use in 854 state parks, as well as 46 recreational demonstration projects in 62 areas within 24 states. In national parks and wilderness areas, CCC work on park trails, campgrounds, and picnic areas resulted in large increases in recreational use, which in turn improved hundreds of local economies.

The CCC was not without its difficulties, of course. Early efforts to integrate white and black enrollees ran into trouble, both in the camps and in nearby local communities. Logistics—moving men, materials, and equipment through difficult terrain—presented large challenges. As the Depression waned and job opportunities increased, fewer men enrolled in the program, and desertions and disciplinary problems increased. And there was the occasional unfortunate instance of fraud. In 1937, Reno Stitely, chief of the CCC Voucher Unit, was arrested for using fake payroll vouchers to embezzle nearly $85,000. Stitely's trial was a media sensation.

By the summer of 1940, France had fallen to Germany, and while Americans were strongly isolationist, President Roosevelt was looking ahead to the possibility of war. He permitted CCC camps to be established on military bases where enrollees built airfields, military facilities, artillery ranges, and training fields. The CCC expanded its educational program to include engineering, blueprint reading, and other skills that might be of military use, and the young men were spending up to twenty hours a week in military drills. When the first one-year military conscription took place in September 1940, enrollment in the camps sharply declined, and by Pearl Harbor (December 7, 1941), many of the CCC enrollees had already entered military service. Camps that were not directly related to the war effort were ordered to be closed by May 1942. A few months later, Congress appropriated funds to close all of the camps. The program was over.

A note about language. To write about the people of the 1930s rural South requires the use of terms that may be offensive to some readers—especially "colored," "colored folk," and "Negro" when they are used to refer to African Americans. Thank you for understanding that I mean no offense.

Susan Wittig Albert
Bertram, Texas

# Resources

Here are some books I found helpful in creating *The Darling Dahlias and the Eleven O'Clock Lady*. You will also find numerous resources listed in the five earlier books in the series.

Cohen, Stan. *The Tree Army: A Pictorial History of the Civilian Conservation Corps, 1933–1942* (1980).

Davis, Ren and Helen. *Our Mark on This Land: A Guide to the Legacy of the Civilian Conservation Corps in America's Parks* (2011).

Hill, Edwin G. *In the Shadow of the Mountain: The Spirit of the CCC* (1990).

Maher, Neil M. *Nature's New Deal: The Civilian Conservation Corps and the Roots of the American Environmental Movement* (2009).

Pasquill, Robert. *The Civilian Conservation Corps in Alabama, 1933–1942: A Great and Lasting Good* (2008).

# Recipes

*If there were no other reason to live in the South,*
*Southern cookin' would be enough.*
MICHAEL A. GRISSOM, *SOUTHERN BY THE GRACE OF GOD*

## *Fried Apples*

*Served over waffles or with buttermilk biscuits, sausage, and gravy, fried apples are a traditional Southern breakfast dish. But they may appear as a side dish, like a vegetable, for dinner or supper—and in fact are even listed as a vegetable in old cookbooks, where they are sometimes flavored with bacon or sausage drippings. Of course, fried apples aren't fried at all—but simply braised over low heat, in a heavy skillet. Use firm, tart pie apples, such as Granny Smiths or Gravensteins.*

1½ cups apple cider plus ½ cup
5 tart apples, peeled and sliced
2 tablespoons butter
1 tablespoon cornstarch
3 tablespoons sugar
1 teaspoon cinnamon
½ teaspoon nutmeg
¼ teaspoon cloves

Pour 1½ cups of apple cider into a skillet over medium heat. Add apple slices and cook until tender. Add butter and remove from heat. Mix together remaining ½ cup apple cider, cornstarch, sugar, and spices in a small bowl. Pour over apples, return to low heat, and stir gently as the sauce thickens.

## *Jam Thumbprint Cookies*

*This traditional butter-cookie recipe appears in almost every cookbook after the Civil War, sometimes with pecans, sometimes without. (Pecans, of course, are a Southern favorite and are added to just about anything.) Children love to fill the "thumbprints" and drizzle the glaze—fun for grown-up cooks, too. Choose a single jam or several different jams and marmalades.*

1 cup butter or margarine, softened
⅔ cup sugar
½ teaspoon vanilla extract
2 cups all-purpose flour
½ cup finely chopped pecans
½ cup jam

**GLAZE**
1 cup powdered sugar
2 to 3 teaspoons water
1 teaspoons vanilla extract

Combine butter or margarine, sugar, and vanilla extract in bowl. Beat until creamy, scraping the sides of the bowl often. Add flour and chopped pecans. Beat until well mixed. Cover and refrigerate at least 1 hour, or until firm.

Heat oven to 350°F. Shape dough into 1-inch balls. Place 2 inches apart on ungreased cookie sheets. Make thumbprint indentation in center of each cookie, and fill with about ¼ teaspoon jam. Bake 14–18 minutes or until edges are lightly browned. Remove to rack and cool completely. To glaze: Combine all glaze ingredients in bowl and stir until smooth. Drizzle over cookies. Makes about 3 dozen.

## Ophelia's Recipe for Cake Flour

*During the Depression, specialty products like cake flour were expensive and were often not stocked in the smaller stores.*

Measure out the amount of all-purpose flour called for by your recipe. For every 1 cup of flour remove 2 tablespoons of flour and replace with 2 tablespoons of cornstarch. Sift 5–6 times before using. (If you don't have a flour sifter, use a strainer. Fill it with flour, hold or place it over a bowl, and tap a knife against it.) Be sure to measure the flour one more time, after it's been sifted and before you use it in the recipe.

## The Diner's Special Southern Corn Pudding

*Southern corn pudding is the savory, whole-kernel version of the sweeter Indian pudding made with cornmeal and molasses that was a Northeastern colonial staple. Corn pudding, also called Puddin' Corn and Hoppy Glop, is traditionally made with fresh corn, but you can also use canned cream-style corn. Cooks developed their favorite variations, adding onions, garlic, cheese, tomatoes, and other vegetables.*

2 cups fresh corn or 1 can cream-style corn
2 tablespoons flour
1 tablespoon sugar
1 teaspoon salt
Pepper
2 eggs
1 cup milk
3 tablespoons butter, melted

Preheat oven to 350°F. Mix together corn, flour, sugar, salt, and pepper. Beat eggs with milk and melted butter, and add to corn. Pour into a greased baking dish. Bake 30 minutes. Serves 6.

### *Raylene's Lemon Chess Pie*

*Southern cooks were famous for their sweet, egg-rich custard pies, including chess pie (also called chess cake, chess tart, and sugar pie). This recipe (which includes cornmeal for thickening) is for the popular lemon-flavored variation; if lemons weren't available, vinegar was often substituted, or buttermilk. Food history expert Karen Hess tells us how this pie got its odd name: "Since the archaic spellings of cheese often had but one 'e' we have the answer to the riddle of the name of that southern favorite 'Chess Pie'. . . (The tradition of making cheesecake without the cheese goes back to early seventeenth century and beyond . . .)"*—The Virginia House-wife, *by Mary Randolph, with Historical Notes and Commentaries by Karen Hess, p. 289*

4 eggs
1½ cups sugar
½ cup lemon juice
¼ cup butter, melted
1 tablespoon cornmeal
2 teaspoons all-purpose flour
⅛ teaspoon salt
Pastry for 9" pie

In a large bowl, beat eggs for 3 minutes. Gradually add sugar and beat until mixture becomes thick and lemon-colored. Beat in the lemon juice, butter, cornmeal, flour, and salt. Pour into pastry shell. Bake at 350°F for 35–40 minutes or until a knife inserted near the center comes out clean. Cool on a wire rack for 1 hour. Refrigerate for at least 3 hours before serving.

## Charlie Dickens' Favorite Grilled Cheese Sandwich

*The Vidalia onion is a sweet variety of onion that was first grown—by accident—in Toombs County, Georgia, in the early 1930s. The fact that they are unusually sweet is due to the low sulfur content of the soil in which the onions are grown. (Sulfur makes onions pungent.) The Piggly Wiggly food chain, headquartered in nearby Vidalia, Georgia, put the onions in their produce bins, and it wasn't long before visitors were taking these oddly sweet onions back home to their friends. The Vidalia onion is now the official state vegetable of Georgia. This recipe makes one substantial sandwich.*

3 strips bacon
2 tablespoons softened butter mixed with
⅛ teaspoon garlic powder
2 thick slices bread of your choice
2 slices Swiss cheese
2 thin slices tomatoes
Italian seasoning, salt, pepper
2 medium-thick Vidalia onion slices

Fry bacon until crisp in a skillet over medium heat. Remove bacon and drain drippings, saving drippings for another use. Generously spread one side of a slice of bread with butter-garlic mixture. Place bread butter-side-down in skillet and top with 1 slice of cheese. Top with tomato slices and sprinkle with Italian seasoning. Top tomatoes with onion slices, bacon strips, and second slice of cheese. Butter the second slice of bread on one side and place butter-side-up on top of sandwich. Grill until lightly browned and flip; continue grilling until both slices of cheese are melted. (Cover the skillet to help the cheese melt.)

## Fannie's Tomato Soup

2 yellow onions, diced
½ teaspoon minced garlic
5 tablespoons butter
3 tablespoons sugar
1 teaspoon salt
½ teaspoon black pepper
1 (15 ounce) can crushed tomatoes

½ teaspoon dried thyme
¼ teaspoon dried savory
¼ teaspoon marjoram
4 cups water
1 cup half-and-half
4 basil leaves, julienne cut

In a large saucepan over medium heat, sauté the onions and garlic in butter until softened. Add sugar, salt, and pepper. Cook until the sugar is dissolved, stirring. Add the tomatoes and herbs and cook for 5 minutes. Add water. Simmer for 15 minutes.

Set the soup aside to cool. When cooled, puree the soup in a blender. Return the soup to the stove, simmer 5 minutes, and then add the half-and-half. When heated through, sprinkle the basil leaves for garnish.

## Lucy Murphy's Jefferson Davis Pie

*This pie, named in honor of the president of the Confederacy, is a fruit-filled, spiced version of the chess pie (above). Lucy's recipe includes granulated sugar and adds a meringue; other Jeff Davis recipes use brown sugar and omit the meringue. Perhaps it is better not to worry about the "historicity" of these recipes. Anne Carter Zimmer, in her commentary in* The Robert E. Lee Family Cooking and Housekeeping Book *(p. 131), remarks, "I began to realize that receipts {recipes} are a kind of folklore. Like folktales, they are recreated each time they are made or told, and each time they can be—and often are—changed by the taste and times of the maker."*

½ cup softened butter
1½ cups sugar
4 egg yolks
2 tablespoons flour
1 teaspoon cinnamon
1 teaspoon nutmeg
½ teaspoon allspice
¼ teaspoon cloves
1 cup whipping cream
½ cup chopped dates
½ cup raisins
½ cup coarsely chopped pecans
Unbaked 9-inch pie shell

**MERINGUE**
4 egg whites
½ cup sugar

Preheat oven to 300°F. Cream the butter and sugar until light and fluffy. Beat in the egg yolks, then add the flour and spices and mix until combined. Add the cream, dates, raisins, and pecans, mix well, and pour into the pie shell. Bake until set but still slightly soft in the middle, about 40 minutes.

To add the meringue: Remove the pie and increase the oven heat to 350°F. Beat the egg whites until foamy. Gradually add the sugar, and beat until the meringue forms firm peaks. Spread over the baked pie, sealing it to the crimped edges of the shell. Bake until golden brown. Serve at room temperature.

# The Dahlias' Household Magic
## A Baker's Dozen Ways to Do It
### Easier, Faster, Better

1. To keep cake moist, always put a good sound apple in the cake box or tin. And lemons can be kept almost indefinitely if you put them in a glass canning jar with a tight lid.

2. A teaspoon of borax in the last rinse will whiten clothes surprisingly.

3. Keep ants out of the pantry by placing fresh sage leaves on the shelves.

4. Potatoes will bake faster if you put them in hot water for about 15 minutes before they go in the oven.

5. When you buy celery, wash the leaves and dry them until they can be rubbed to a powder. Use to add a nice celery flavor to stews, soups, meat loaf, etc.

6. If you have a worn-out tablecloth that you can't darn any longer, cut it into squares, hem, and—voilà!—you have napkins.

7. To make your cook stove shine more easily, add a little turpentine to your stove polish.

8. To clean copper-bottom pans, rub with a mixture of salt, fine sand, flour, and vinegar.

9. If the electricity hasn't got to your house yet and you're still using kerosene lamps, soak your lamp wicks in vinegar and let them dry before using. They will be less likely to smoke.

10. To trap the flies that invade your kitchen, you'll need a canning jar, a funnel, some bait (fruit, bit of leftover), and 2–3 small blocks of wood. Put the bait in the jar, insert the funnel, and turn the jar and funnel upside down on the wood blocks. The flies will crawl in through the opening beneath the jar and the funnel and be easily trapped.

11. If you're grinding aromatic or strongly flavored spices, run a half cup of rice through the grinder afterward, to remove the flavor and scent.

12. For a nice substitute for crackers, croutons, and breadsticks, roll out a pie crust, slice the pastry into narrow strips, sprinkle with salt, and bake.

13. When you're picking parsley from the garden, pick from the center. Those are flavorful leaves, and you'll help keep the plant from bolting.